P9-AZV-313

DISCARD

FADE to BLACK

Also by HEATHER GRAHAM

A DANGEROUS GAME
WICKED DEEDS
DARK RITES
DYING BREATH
A PERFECT OBSESSION
DARKEST JOURNEY
DEADLY FATE
HAUNTED DESTINY
FLAWLESS
THE HIDDEN
THE FORGOTTEN
THE SILENCED
THE DEAD PLAY ON
THE BETRAYED
THE HEXED
THE CURSED
WAKING THE DEAD
THE NIGHT IS FOREVER
THE NIGHT IS ALIVE
THE NIGHT IS WATCHING
LET THE DEAD SLEEP
THE UNINVITED
THE UNSPOKEN
THE UNHOLY
THE UNSEEN
AN ANGEL FOR CHRISTMAS
THE EVIL INSIDE
SACRED EVIL
HEART OF EVIL
PHANTOM EVIL
NIGHT OF THE VAMPIRES
THE KEEPERS
GHOST MOON
GHOST NIGHT

GHOST SHADOW
THE KILLING EDGE
NIGHT OF THE WOLVES
HOME IN TIME
   FOR CHRISTMAS
UNHALLOWED GROUND
DUST TO DUST
NIGHTWALKER
DEADLY GIFT
DEADLY HARVEST
DEADLY NIGHT
THE DEATH DEALER
THE LAST NOEL
THE SÉANCE
BLOOD RED
THE DEAD ROOM
KISS OF DARKNESS
THE VISION
THE ISLAND
GHOST WALK
KILLING KELLY
THE PRESENCE
DEAD ON THE DANCE FLOOR
PICTURE ME DEAD
HAUNTED
HURRICANE BAY
A SEASON OF MIRACLES
NIGHT OF THE BLACKBIRD
NEVER SLEEP
   WITH STRANGERS
EYES OF FIRE
SLOW BURN
NIGHT HEAT

* * * * *

Look for Heather Graham's next novel
PALE AS DEATH
available soon from MIRA Books.

HEATHER GRAHAM

FADE to BLACK

mira

Recycling programs
for this product may
not exist in your area.

ISBN-13: 978-0-7783-1280-2

Fade to Black

Copyright © 2018 by Heather Graham Pozzessere

All rights reserved. Except for use in any review, the reproduction or utilization of this work in whole or in part in any form by any electronic, mechanical or other means, now known or hereafter invented, including xerography, photocopying and recording, or in any information storage or retrieval system, is forbidden without the written permission of the publisher, MIRA Books, 22 Adelaide Street West, 40th Floor, Toronto, Ontario M5H 4E3, Canada.

This is a work of fiction. Names, characters, places and incidents are either the product of the author's imagination or are used fictitiously, and any resemblance to actual persons, living or dead, business establishments, events or locales is entirely coincidental.

® and TM are trademarks of Harlequin Enterprises Limited or its corporate affiliates. Trademarks indicated with ® are registered in the United States Patent and Trademark Office, the Canadian Intellectual Property Office and in other countries.

For questions and comments about the quality of this book, please contact us at CustomerService@Harlequin.com.

BookClubbish.com

Printed in U.S.A.

R0451895339

For Deborah C. Neff
Incredible bookseller and so much more—
Incredible friend!

CAST OF CHARACTERS

The McFadden brothers—Bryan, Bruce and Brodie, all former military, now registered as private investigators

Maeve and Hamish McFadden—celebrated actors of screen and stage, killed tragically in an accident

The Krewe of Hunters

Adam Harrison—head of the Krewe of Hunters
Jackson Crow—field director, Krewe of Hunters
Angela Hawkins—special agent, married to Jackson Crow

The Cast of *Dark Harbor*

Marnie Davante—most popular character, played Madame Scarlet
Cara Barton—played the matriarch
Jeremy Highsmith—played the patriarch
Roberta Alan—played the sister
Grayson Adair—played the brother
Bridget Davante—Marnie's cousin, a screenwriter
Vince Carlton—television producer/director
Malcolm Dangerfield—popular action actor
David Neal—stage manager

FADE to BLACK

PROLOGUE

Comic Con, Los Angeles

Blood-bone stepped out onto the show floor, his massive black cape sweeping around him, his supercharged sword lighting up the space around him in all colors of the rainbow. The black-masked and black-suited villain was from the new cable show *Wolfson*, which was topping ratings charts across the nation.

The character of Lars Wolfson, the hero of the show, had made several appearances that day as well, some costumes better than others.

But just as they liked to say women love bad boys, people of both sexes and all ages seemed to really love a good villain.

Young men and women, children, old men and old women clapped and all but swooned and rushed over to him. Blood-bone was the most popular new villain to grace the pages of comic books since the beginning of the written-and-drawn comic world.

He suddenly cried out, "Those who oppose me—pay! They pay the ultimate price."

The crowd around the actor—or would-be actor, dressed up

for Comic Con—grew substantially, people everywhere snapping photos.

"We bow to you, Blood-bone!" the crowd called out in turn.

"Jerk," Cara Barton declared beneath her breath.

"He's just playing, creating a good show," Marnie Davante said.

"Lord, who are you? Pollyanna? Mary Poppins?" Cara asked her, letting out a long sigh.

"He's just playing. Let him entertain. Relax. Try to have fun," Marnie said, offering Cara her beautiful and natural smile.

Marnie. She was the type who would make the best of it.

Cara wished that she could. But it was dismal.

No. It was beyond dismal. Continuing to plug a show that had been off the air for ages, just because she had no other options.

And still, sitting at their booth, Cara smiled as graciously as she could. It was a smile that she'd practiced over the years, yet still felt plastered into place.

"How's this?" she asked Marnie.

"Grim, but it will do," her friend said, laughing.

Grim. Yes.

However, Cara kept smiling.

It was amazing; it was an unbelievable thrill. He was able to watch as if he were a fly on the wall, as if he were at a screening, seeing it all unfold. He knew the angles from which the cameras would be rolling; he could just see it all.

And he was the puppeteer. He was the producer, the director...

Everything all rolled into one.

He could already picture the blood.

Cold-blooded Comic Con? He needed a better title...

Act 1, Scene 1...

Cameras rolling.

Action!

★ ★ ★

The damned wannabe actor in the Blood-bone costume was really becoming annoying.

The few people who had been coming toward Cara Barton and the old *Dark Harbor* cast were now rushing off to see Blood-bone.

It was a comic-book convention, Cara reminded herself. And she knew how a comic con went.

Monsters roamed the floor in costumes that rated between the ridiculous and the divine. Superheroes in stretchy, skimpy attire were just as plentiful—some looking quite good, and some who obviously owned no mirrors. Booths sold T-shirts, toy weapons, jewelry, corsets, steampunk clothing and other items, makeup, art and just about anything that might relate to the comic world in any way.

The fans loved connecting with their favorite comics and movies and TV series. Writers' row offered comics, graphic novels and novels of all kinds.

Artists' row offered some fantastic pieces, from those who had long been in the business to those who were just starting out.

And then there was Actors' Row.

The place where used-up B-list stars came to die.

Well, as far as Cara was concerned, it really was a kind of death—it was where one came to pray to sell enough twenty-dollar-a-shot autographed pictures to pay the rent for the month. Maybe that train of thought was a little melodramatic. The show was in syndication, and they all made residual money, but it did not provide for the lifestyle that many a popular actor had become accustomed to, so, in a sense, it was about a particular kind of survival.

But that was all going to hell. They'd been just about to get some fans—and then Blood-bone came out of the woodwork, swinging his great cape and his laser sword. If only he weren't out there—probably paid a fortune by the convention organiz-ers to give the attendees a bit of a thrill for free.

Oh, the bastard! She didn't even know who was behind the mask. Blood-bone wasn't even always portrayed by the same actor. And at this freak show, anyone could dress up. There were actually dozens of Blood-bones roaming the convention room floor; it was by far the most popular costume of the year. Hell, she could put on the damned costume and lift shoes and play Blood-bone. In fact, if they'd let her, she would. That could mean some big bucks again!

But this Blood-bone was evidently committed to pretend-ing to be the real thing. He postured and postulated. Everyone ran up to him, waving autograph books, begging him to pose for selfies with them.

It made her sad.

Yes, sad for herself and for many others.

Just one booth down, the great-great-great—oh, so many *greats*—grandson of a German shepherd of tremendous TV fame was letting out a sad little yelp now and then.

There was a leak in the ceiling. It happened to be right above Actors' Row. The aging star of a long-ago weekly Western TV series was valiantly trying to save his photos from the dirty drop-lets that fell now and then.

It was heartbreaking to see the poor pup and the faded star reduced to this. And now, with that wretched Blood-bone fig-ure running around, for the most part the actors were being left alone.

Ignored.

At least the dog didn't know that he was a has-been.

Only every now and then someone would pause and look and remember them. After all, *Dark Harbor* had been an extremely popular show in its day.

Cara had actually sold a few pictures—mainly thanks to the rest of the cast, especially Marnie Davante. Just a few more and rent for another month in West Hollywood—where she could still hope for the guest spot on a show now and then—was guaranteed.

She looked down the table. There was Jeremy Highsmith. Her TV husband. All those years.

And, now, go figure!

Maybe it was all bearable.

Along with the stupid Blood-bone guy, it didn't help that they'd happened to draw the booth next to Malcolm Dangerfield, the new superhero of cable television.

Malcolm was not dying in any way.

Malcolm was charging a hundred dollars a shot for pictures taken on a cell phone.

People were paying it.

That made Cara's position very hard—well, in her mind. Marnie didn't care; she was chatting with their onetime castmates: Jeremy Highsmith, Roberta Alan and Grayson Adair.

The lines to pay a hundred dollars for a selfie with Malcolm were deep. And now, on top of that, Blood-bone was right in front of them, drawing any possible customers away. Cara didn't think that Blood-bone would be there long, though. She could see that Malcolm Dangerfield was gone, that his publicist was managing his line. He had probably gone to complain to the comic con management about the Blood-bone guy in full costume who was messing with his line.

"Oh, my God!" someone screamed. Cara waited for the screamer to call out Malcolm Dangerfield's name. Or to go running across the floor, amazed that they'd seen the "real" Blood-bone.

But the screaming fan wasn't coming for Malcolm or Blood-bone.

"It's Madam Zeta!"

Cara smiled. A real smile.

She was not Madam Zeta.

Nope!

But she was *with* Madam Zeta.

People might not be coming for her, but at least they were coming toward *her* little group.

Madam Zeta had been played by Marnie Davante.

And Marnie was seated next to Cara—on her right side at the booth.

Marnie smiled, and her smiles were always real. She was ready to greet a fan. She was a good kid.

A really good kid, Cara knew. Marnie hadn't wanted to be here; she hated doing comic cons. She didn't say as much to Cara because she was a nice person. She had agreed to come along because she knew that signing pictures was how her old costars—Cara, Jeremy, Roberta and Grayson—survived.

None of them had gone on to find work on another series.

But Marnie *had* moved on. Marnie had kept acting. Cara had kept waiting for a new TV series or, at the least, a good supporting role in a movie.

Marnie had gone back to theater, which she loved. Theater didn't always pay well in LA, but Marnie had also caught the occasional commercial or modeling gig. Like everyone else, she went to dozens of auditions for roles, but she seemed to accept that easily and kind of kept on ticking—just like the Energizer Bunny.

Marnie hadn't cared if Hollywood was calling—or if she was cast in a road show, just as long as she was working and she fulfilled her professional obligations. She had done okay, maybe not as a multimillion-dollar-earning star, but as a working actress. She was even about to open her own theater, which would be named for her dad—The Peter Davante Theater for Young Artists.

Fancy name for a kids' theater, but hey, to Marnie, it was living the dream. Personally, Cara thought that working with young people—children—was akin to water torture.

But Marnie loved theater and she loved kids, so...go figure. For her, it worked.

But Cara felt that Marnie also thought that the conventions were where washed-up stars came to die. Metaphorically, at least. There were, of course, those few—like Malcolm Dangerfield— who were at the top of the game, making enough in a few hours to pay Cara's rent for the next year.

And then there was Marnie.

She was here—simply smiling through the torture of waiting for fans—out of friendship.

To be fair to herself, Marnie had been young when their show had been canceled—barely twenty-four. And Cara had been...

Well, hell. *Not* twenty-four.

The cancellation of their show—*Dark Harbor*, the story of a town inhabited by vampires and other strange supernatural beings—had been a true death knell for her career.

It was playing out beautifully, as if it had all been rehearsed. Here, Actors' Row, the lineup...a dog, an old dude from some mostly forgotten weekly flick...and then...

Yes, them. The cast from Dark Harbor.

And it was coming closer and closer...

He could feel it.

He didn't know exactly when, and he hadn't known that he would feel this...exhilarated!

But it was alive, kinetic...wired! With anticipation.

Yes, it was coming...

Soon. So soon. He could almost taste it on the air.

For Cara, there hadn't been a lot of great offers to follow the lamented demise of *Dark Harbor*. A few little bits, guest star gigs, here and there. Her agent tried her best.

But when no decent acting offers were forthcoming, there were always conventions. And there had been talk—*just a rumor so far*—that there might be a *Dark Harbor* reunion show. A producer had apparently been a huge fan and now wanted to bring them back.

So far, though, none of the core actors had been approached. Or so they all claimed.

It was still just speculation. And she didn't dare believe the rumor—it was too painful. But then again, she had seen a tall guy with a superhero T-shirt under his blazer walking around, watching them all. Someone had said he was Vince Carlton, a cable show producer and director.

The money from a reboot might not be huge. Still, Cara's agent had mentioned a call that suggested such a thing might be possible—if so, was she willing?

Of course!

Anything would be better than eight-by-ten-picture money.

But it would all be too depressing to believe that it might happen—and then have their hopes dashed on the rocks of Hollywood capriciousness.

For now, fan conventions and picture sales were important.

Thankfully—for Cara and the rest of the cast—there was Marnie. She was like the best kid in the family, the one who looked after and took care of her siblings. She would always make the group complete and show up when needed, helping them all survive the torment of comic cons.

There had been five main players in the series. Cara had been the matriarch of the supernatural family, and still, she'd admit, was the least of the five characters.

But Marnie's role—that of Madam Zeta—had become beloved, and her character was now a classic. Therefore Marnie was the most important person in their group.

And sometimes they weren't invited—or offered any kind of prime slots—unless Marnie agreed she would be with them.

The show had ended five years ago.

Their days in the sun seemed to be over.

Sometimes, Cara wasn't sure if she was more bitter toward the no-name Blood-bones of the world, the Malcolm Dangerfields—with their hundred dollars a pop for a photo—or Marnie, who would always just take her damned lemons and make lemonade.

No! Cara thought. Once again, she wasn't being fair to herself.

Not fair. She loved Marnie. The woman couldn't help being gracious and elegant and kind. She was blessed with a sweeping headful of burnished brown hair and bright blue-green eyes, legs that were certainly what men considered to be wickedly long and a patrician face with perfect features. She was also quick to smile, quick to sympathize and ready to help out. It was her presence here that had allowed them to sell many pictures. Madam Zeta had been the darling of the show. And Cara knew that while she loved Marnie, she was envious, as well. None of Marnie's fault—she was simply still young, and Cara was not.

She realized she was staring at Marnie, who looked back at her curiously.

"I'm not a bad person, am I?" Cara asked her.

"Of course not! You can be a bit Hollywood jaded, but hey, we're in Hollywood. That's to be expected," Marnie assured her with a shrug and a grin.

"Madam Zeta, Madam Zeta, Madam Zeta!" Someone was screaming again, racing up to the *Dark Harbor* booth.

It was a man, tall, gangly and blond and fairly good-looking; when he called out, a few other people turned away from the Blood-bone character on the floor and paid attention to the little group of five in the *Dark Harbor* booth.

"Oh, cool! It's the whole cast!" someone else cried.

And suddenly, Comic Con was good. People had heard. Lots of people were looking at the booth with real interest.

Fans began to come up, and before Cara knew it, they were all signing the best cast picture they had. It featured Marnie as Madam Scarlet Zeta, the family psychic with superhuman strength, who also earned them what they needed to keep up their decaying mansion and most often ferreted out the deadly creatures in Dark Harbor. On each side of Marnie, the rest of the cast was gathered: Roberta Alan as Marnie's older sister, Sonia Zeta, the family member granted the power of cloaking those around her; Grayson Adair playing Nathan Zeta, brother of Scarlet and Sonia, the family member gifted with ability to freeze vampires; Jeremy Highsmith as Theodore, patriarch of the family and the bearer of the legacy that allowed the family to fight off evil and protect the town.

Also, of course, there was Cara herself, as Elizabeth, the dignified and elegant matriarch, caring mother, ever aware that her children met far too much danger, and ever ready to give her life for theirs.

They had that one photo that could be pretty damned hot— that family photo. When it was signed by all of them, it sometimes became a collectible item—sold on internet auction sites to overseas fans for more than they ever got for it. That photo often kept a roof over Cara's head. It was their priciest at fifty dollars, whether they were all in attendance at an event or not. It was up to the buyer to hunt down the rest of the cast if they wanted the complete set of signatures.

And they were all there that day. Now the ball was rolling! They could sell hundreds.

Naturally, it was that one that young, tall and good-looking man wanted, except that he also wanted a few solos of Marnie— though none of the others. She always chatted and tried to get people to buy more, but it didn't even matter that they weren't buying more.

The young man had started an influx of people. They were buying the cast photo.

"Madam Zeta! Mrs. Elizabeth—all of you! Amazing," the young man said.

"Marnie Davante," Marnie said, smiling and taking the young man's hand. "And you're...?"

Who cares? Cara wondered. *Just sell him a picture.*

"David Neal," the young man said. "We actually have an appointment next week."

"Oh?"

"Stage managing position," he replied.

"Oh, wonderful!" she said enthusiastically.

"Marnie does love kids," Cara put in.

Jeremy Highsmith—on Marnie's other side—cleared his throat. "I think we have a bit of a line forming."

"Oh, I'm sorry. Would you like—" Marnie began.

"The cast picture," David Neal said.

So close… So close… He could stand there and smile, anticipate and nearly smell and feel and taste it in the air…

Blood…

Death…

The drama and horror were almost unbearable.

Cara was in heaven. So many people.

They were signing the "family" photo when the Blood-bone character came swinging his way toward their booth, cape flying behind him, mask in place and sword streaking colors through the air.

He wielded the sword well, as if he'd had training in swordplay. Well, many actors had.

He wielded it straight to the booth.

He pushed past some of the fans, and they all laughed, of course. It looked like it was a bit of impromptu theater.

Blood-bone pointed at Marnie. She rose from her chair and pointed at him, playing along.

"Be gone, Blood-bone. You may play your evil games in your show, but you may not come back to threaten ours!"

Blood-bone swaggered toward Marnie, his lighted sword swirling almost hypnotically.

"You won't get past me!" Marnie told him.

He kept coming. So many people were watching!

Cara leaped up by Marnie. She set her arm around the woman's shoulders.

"Don't you dare come for my precious daughter!" she cried.

There was no way that she wasn't getting some attention and play out of this. Who knew who might be out there? Another job could be on the line. That producer could see how dedicated they were.

"I know his every evil thought! He will never get by us!" Marnie cried. She was grinning, and that smile of hers seemed to draw an even larger crowd. Yes, it was all play.

All fun.

And Cara had to get in on it, big-time.

"Indeed, we will smite you. I warn you again—touch my daughter, you evil thing, and we will see that you rot in hell forever!"

The Blood-bone character looked at her. She could have sworn that beneath the black mask, the man smiled.

He raised his sword...

Cara pushed past Marnie.

"Don't you dare!"

But his sword was poised.

And it came down. Again and again.

Cara really didn't know what hit her. At first, there was nothing, and then there was an incredible burst of pain. The kind of pain that brought brilliant stars bursting before her eyes, that brought a sea of darkness, black sweeping away the tiny bursts of light...

She gasped.

She felt something trickling on her.

Felt herself falling...

She heard Marnie scream, felt Marnie's arms go around her.

Theater, it was all theater, all show...

But it wasn't.

Blood-bone was gone, swooping his way back into the crowd.

Cara was bleeding; her grasp on Marnie was weakening.

"No, no, no, stay with me, Cara. I love you, my friend, stay with me," Marnie ordered.

But Cara knew that she could not.

Comic Con. It was a comic convention.

And Cara had just never imagined that—for her, at least—she could be so very right.

That it could be, quite literally, where old stars came to die!

CHAPTER ONE

Bryan McFadden could always *feel* her, of course. As soon as she decided to grace him with her presence.

Yes.

She was there again.

Watching him, his every move.

He pretended that he didn't see her. He also did his best to hide a smile.

She wanted something, of course. Or he was due for a lecture, a long litany on how to live his life.

He'd been splitting logs outside his cabin when he'd first become aware that she was there; he continued to chop firewood. If she was going to haunt him because she wanted something, she was bloody well going to have to do so with more than a bunch of her dramatic sighs.

He paused for a moment; the sun was riding in the sky on a beautiful day. The mountains and valleys of Virginia were, in Bryan's mind, the most beautiful places in the world to be. Here, right at the base of the Shenandoah Mountain, he could enjoy both.

This place had been—as long as he could remember—a haven.

He and his brothers, Bruce and Brodie, had always been able to go a little wild out here. They'd never been bad kids, but they had been full of energy and ready to run, climb, fish, swim and love the rugged beauty of the land.

The family cabin was just a weekend retreat.

Home was DC, near the National Theatre, a half-dozen other theaters and easy access to the casting agents who were closer to their parents—Hamish and Maeve McFadden—than any blood relative might expect to be.

Though he and his brothers had long ago left their boyhoods behind, they had managed to stay in the same basic area. And, mainly because each of them had joined a branch of the service— Bryan, the navy; Bruce, the marines; and Brodie, the army—they had maintained the manor house close to a river in Northern Virginia where they had actually grown up.

He was heading back there in the morning. His time here— used to reflect on his choices regarding the future—was at an end. He wasn't sure he was feeling more certain any one course was right above the others. Bruce and Brodie were coming in the following week; it was time for them to really decide what they were going to do.

As kids, they had quarreled and squabbled. Tumbled on the ground and tussled now and then—and stood ferociously against anyone who insulted one of them or dared to speak ill of their parents.

But life had gotten hard—and made them close.

They were all pretty sure they could work together; they'd talk it out for the final decision in the weeks to come.

Of course, she was still watching him. Still waiting for a response.

She sighed again. Maeve McFadden was certainly an example of the word *diva*. Not so much in a bad way—she had an ego, but not the kind with which to hurt others. She was passionate, she was demonstrative; she didn't just "talk with her hands," she talked with her arms, with her whole body.

But if she wanted something now, she was going to have *to talk* to him.

With words.

Finally, she did. She rather *wafted* over and leaned against the wood rail fence that surrounded the little cabin and the area with the chopping block where he was working.

"Bryan McFadden, you're ignoring me!" She pouted.

"And it's not working, eh?" he asked, but he smiled at her— she was his mom, and he did love her.

She smiled back and then plunged right in.

"Her name is Marnie, and she really needs help. My friend Cara—Cara Barton, I know you must remember her. She was one of the stars of that yummy vampire show, *Dark Harbor*, and before that, we were both way younger and in a Christmas romantic comedy together. That doesn't matter. What does matter is this—Cara was tragically cut down. And now Marnie needs your help. I'm not sure she knows it yet, but Cara has told me. And poor Cara! She's dead. Most horrifically and dreadfully dead."

"Mother—"

"Don't you dare tell me that dead is dead—dreadful or otherwise. She was murdered. Viciously murdered by a sword-wielding villain. Well, someone in a costume. But… Oh, Bryan. It was horrid, quite horrid—you must have heard about it on TV or in the news online!"

"Nope," he told his mother.

"How could you have missed the news?" Maeve demanded. "Oh, I do hate to say it, but Cara is far more famous now in death than she was in life."

"I come out here to enjoy the mountains and scenery, Mom. Not watch TV."

"The news would be on your phone."

"News is on *anywhere*, Mother, if you look for it."

"All right then, I'll tell you about it. Comic Con—West Hollywood."

"I thought the big comic cons were in San Diego. Maybe New York."

"Comic cons are all the rage—they are cropping up everywhere," Maeve informed him. "And this— Oh, son... Horrible, horrible, horrible. Cara was my good friend. Okay, so imagine this. The cast of *Dark Harbor* is lined up at a booth. People are flocking over to them for signed pictures. There's a Blood-bone character whipping his sword around—at first, all to the delight of the crowd. Then he walks up to the *Dark Harbor* cast booth and starts off as if he's performing with them—and then he brought his sword down, slashing poor Cara to death, right across her throat!"

"In the middle of a crowd of people, some costumed character slashes a woman to death and walks away?" Bryan demanded, incredulous.

"Well, that's just it. People thought it was a performance. Cara fell dead, the others began to realize it—people were clapping, thinking it was just an impromptu show done very well. Blood-bone walked off... The cast began to scream. Cops came, but by then, the killer was gone. From what I understand, it was a zoo."

"But no one noticed a masked man in costume?"

"Well, of course, they did. They gathered up at least twenty Blood-bones—you know, conference attendees in Blood-bone costumes—but they don't believe that the killer was any of the men, or the one woman, with whom they spoke. They couldn't find a Blood-bone with actual blood on him or a lighted sword that was really a sword. Don't you understand? Someone is going to get away with this. Bryan, you have to do something."

"Mom, at the moment, I'm not a cop."

"Don't be silly, darling, I know that. And if you had stayed on the force, you'd be a Virginia cop, anyway. However, you did get your PI license."

"Yes, I did."

"So you need to get out to California and help Marnie Davante. Please."

"Mom, you know that I'm supposed to be meeting with your other sons next week. They'll be back by then."

"I know where they are," Maeve said indignantly. "Brodie took a temp job as a bodyguard for that chain store CEO, and he's still in China somewhere. Bruce was helping out a friend who is with the Texas Rangers."

"Right. But we're due to get together and decide if we do want to form an investigation company."

"That would be in the near future. You need to help Marnie now."

"Mom, I have no ins with the West Hollywood Police or even the California State Police. I'm sure they would resent—"

"Please."

"Mom, again, I'm not in Hollywood. I'm sure there are very capable police out there. Your friend isn't being threatened—she's already dead. I'm not sure—"

"It's Marnie! Cara is terribly worried about Marnie."

Bryan stopped pretending that he could continue chopping wood. He leaned on the ax and looked at the ghost of his mother.

"Does Marnie know that she needs my help?"

"How could she?"

"Come on then, what do you want out of me?"

"Someone who is invested in the horrible thing that happened—and in Marnie—believes that a dead woman is out there trying to help solve her own murder. Please, Bryan. It's you—you need to help. You were just working with that FBI friend of yours, helping track down that missing child. And you said that he knows Adam—my friend Adam Harrison? Well, my friend and dad's friend. I think your father knew Adam first."

"Yes, I was working with a friend named Jackson Crow, and we were lucky—we found the missing child." He didn't mention that his old friend was with a special unit of the FBI, or that he'd suggested that Bryan might be just right for that unit.

He could only hope that she didn't know that her old friend Adam Harrison had actually created the unit.

"How is Adam? Such a dear man."

Hopefully, she hadn't seen Adam since she'd...

He could never think the word *died*.

Maybe because she was his mother, and he did love her.

And maybe because she had never really gone anywhere.

"And you—all three of my boys—still at odds and ends, taking on various odd jobs."

"Good jobs, Mom. We help people. You should be a happy camper. All three of us served our time in the military and went through college. And yes, in the last year or so we have taken on some strange jobs, but they've been good ones, jobs that help people."

"And here's someone who needs help. Yes, I hope, eventually, you and your brothers are going to get together. You're looking to form a company. I do like that idea. You want to know what to do with your life? You're doing quite nicely at the helping people thing, and this—this!—would be an important part of that. I mean, you broke my heart when you completely ignored the fact that your father and I were known for our extreme talents and absolute love of live theater. And you didn't even want to head in the direction of film. I must say, I created—I created!—three of the most handsome men one could ever want to imagine, and you've no interest in using that beauty to a good—to a paying—end."

"Mother," Bryan said, "I believe you and Dad did emphasize that in life, looks mean nothing, that the heart and soul of a man or a woman matter most."

Here she was, giving him a pitch about helping someone.

And she was still brokenhearted she hadn't produced a single actor among them.

"Yes, well, of course," Maeve said, sweeping back a long, curling strand of her dark hair. "Looks do not matter. Heart and soul and kindness and compassion. Things like that matter most with everyone you meet. Seriously, of course, decency—it's a total given. But I have these three strapping lads! Strapping, I say—tall, dark and absolutely, stunningly handsome—and not one of you chose to use such wondrous good looks."

"Mother, you don't think you might be a little prejudiced on that?"

He moved past her to fetch another piece of wood.

She waved a hand in the air. "One can only be so prejudiced!" she said. "But that's so far beside the point. I am afraid that I must have done something terribly wrong if not one of you felt the lure of the stage. The military! Well, I do understand. Your father and I were gone and… The military. Noble. What an honorable and lofty ideal—to serve one's country. Yes, that was all quite fine, and thankfully you all came home in one piece. But that was then, and this is now. You went out and got a PI license. You've been working with the FBI and cops. You do realize that if you were to just choose to be an actor, I might not be so determined to haunt you?"

Bryan had the strange feeling that, one way or another, his mother was going to haunt him. And Bruce and Brodie. At least he had two brothers to share the burden. Of course, mothers were known to torment their sons.

Not usually, though, mothers who had passed away.

Bryan was the eldest; he had been twenty-four on the day that Hamish and Maeve had been leads in a DC run of *Murder by Gaslight*; they had both been killed—hand in hand—when *the* famous chandelier had fallen onto them both, killing them instantly.

It might have been fitting—they were known for having

achieved the rarest of the rare, an amazing marriage and a true love affair; they were always together, beautiful people, blessed to have a wonderful family with their love and their three strapping sons.

It had been an incredible tragedy—for their sons more than anyone else.

Bryan had been the first to pull himself together. He'd been the first to see his mother. She had tiptoed behind him at her own funeral, bringing a finger to her lips and whispering, "Shh!"

He'd assumed he was suffering from PTSD—they'd lost both parents in a single blow.

And then he'd heard his father's voice.

"Stop that, Maeve. I believe the boy can hear you. Don't be a tease."

"Don't be silly. We're dead. The living can't hear us. I'm simply being a diva, darling," Maeve had assured Hamish. "I'm making sure that the funeral is appropriately massive and…well, that people are properly *emoting* for us."

"They're emoting all over, including our sons," the ghost of his father had said sternly.

"Oh, dear, yes—our precious boys!"

Then they had been gone. And that night—after an appropriate amount of Jameson whiskey—Bryan had convinced himself that they hadn't really been there. That it was the shocking loss affecting him. Because he'd known it was what they would have wanted: a massive funeral with all kinds of press coverage.

Even if he and his brothers wanted to believe that they were strong and capable of managing the tragedy, they had loved their out-there, talented and ever so slightly crazy parents. It was natural that the grief might be intense.

Then…

They had moved back in.

It had been quite the night when each one of the brothers had tried to pretend that he wasn't seeing the ghosts of his parents. But Maeve had heckled and teased—she was really quite as good at being a ghost as she had been at acting. She had quickly learned how to make the fire snap, how to press a glass just hard enough so that it appeared to move across the table and how to touch them…with a gentle stroke on the cheek, the way she had touched them in life.

Brodie—the youngest—had been the first to snap. Maeve had counted on that; Bryan was certain. Eventually Brodie had leaped out of his seat and screamed, "Can't you see them?"

Bryan had looked at Bruce, and in that moment, they had realized that their parents, while not alive, were still with them.

Hamish was worried; he didn't know why he and his wife were still there, and he was sorry—a father needed to let his sons lead their own lives. But they were young. Maybe he and Maeve were still there because they were needed. The boys might still need help; they could be there to guide them as they grew older and became men.

Maeve informed them all that she knew the very solid reason they had remained on the earthly plane—were they all daft? To guide their sons, yes. But she and Hamish had been taken too soon. They were kind, decent people—and young and beautiful!

They had basically been robbed of life.

Now they'd been granted the chance to help their boys, though, of course, they hadn't really been at all sure that the boys could see them until Brodie—bless him—had cried out the obvious.

Maeve and Hamish were home.

At first it was wonderful. It was still wonderful. Other than still wondering now and then if he was sharing a terrible hallucination with his brothers.

If it weren't for the *other* dead people his mother and father always wanted to help. The dead they brought home, too.

Because his parents' reappearance had opened some kind of

door, and now he could see the dead. And Bruce and Brodie could see them, as well.

"You do remember *Dark Harbor*, right? The run ended...oh, five or six years ago. You three were grown-up, but I remember that even you said they managed to make it pretty darned scary and that the plots were good."

"Kudos to the writers," Bryan said. He slammed down hard on his hunk of a log.

She came up before him, suddenly very serious.

"Bryan, please. A friend of mine was viciously attacked. And I'm worried sick about a young actress who I thought was wonderful—and who was very dear to Cara. My friend was *murdered*, Bryan. Do you understand me? Murdered—cruelly and with malice. And now, she sincerely believes that the other members of her cast are in trouble."

"And why is that?"

"Because of the way the killer came to the table. Cara was always ready to jump up and get out front, and that's what she did, and she was worried that, well, maybe someone else was the intended target."

"Someone else."

"There were five main cast members, Bryan. I know you remember the show. You would have had to have slept through seven years to have missed it. Cara Barton was the matriarch, but Scarlet Zeta was the most popular member of the cast—and she was next to Cara when she was killed."

"Scarlet Zeta?"

"Marnie. The actress's name is Marnie Davante. Her role was that of Scarlet Zeta."

Bryan did actually know. He'd seen the show. He'd actually enjoyed it. He wasn't usually that big on the paranormal—especially now, living a life in which his dead parents haunted him and brought home their dead friends now and then.

But *Dark Harbor* had been good.

And he knew who Cara Barton was—or had been. He grudgingly remembered that she had come to the funeral when his parents had died; she had been kind.

And he knew who the actress Marnie Davante was—true, only someone who had been on Mars for the past decade or so would not. She had been great on the show—sexy and endearing, an American sweetheart who might well have sent a few adolescent boys into their first solo sexual experiences. But on many talk shows she'd also come off as an amazing human being. She loved animals, gave to all kinds of children's charities and appeared to be a really decent human being.

"What is Marnie Davante now, about twenty-seven, twenty-eight?" he asked.

Maeve sighed. "Twenty-nine, but what difference does it make?"

"I'm trying to find out about her. She has a good reputation among coworkers, right?"

"Yes."

"They're all in danger, so you say. Why are you most worried about Marnie Davante?"

"Because," Maeve said, "I told you, the Blood-bone-costumed guy was coming for Marnie first. Cara wanted the extra attention and pushed her way forward. Maybe the killer got mixed-up. Maybe it was supposed to have been Marnie."

"I'm assuming the police are already looking into it."

"Ah, but will they look far enough? Bryan, someone who cares, who is willing to give the murder his full attention, needs to be out there."

Bryan looked up at the sky.

When he'd gone to help in the missing child case, he'd been asked for his assistance.

Getting in on a high-profile murder case where police certainly had to be touchy, and might not want an outsider's help, wasn't a pleasant contemplation.

"Well?" Maeve demanded.

He didn't answer right away.

Then he heard his father's voice.

Yep. The ghost of Hamish McFadden was there as well, standing behind his wife. His father was a dignified man, and someone who might have been a performer, but who had also lived his life always trying to do the right thing.

"Might as well say yes, son. I believe the young lady will need you. Not to mention your mother will haunt the hell out of you, day and night, until you do. You know that what I'm saying is true."

Bryan looked up. His father had been an exceptional actor; he'd won an Emmy and a Tony. He was a tall solid man with ink-dark hair that he'd passed on to all three sons, along with his formidable height and shoulder breadth.

Somehow, his father *and* his mother had kept their careers and been good, loving parents, as well. They'd chosen work to stay as close to their sons as often as they could.

Yeah, they'd been damned decent.

"Please!" Maeve wheedled.

"She'll torment you to tears, son," Hamish reminded him.

"This girl doesn't even know she wants help," Bryan protested. "And there are police out there, and..." He sighed. "Miss Davante has no idea she needs my help."

"Oh, don't worry about that," Maeve said.

"And why not?"

"Cara will let her know."

"Cara is dead."

Maeve smiled. "Yes, she is. But she's still hanging around, too. Because, of course, she is worried about Marnie, so...not to worry! She will let her know."

He paused and looked at his mother curiously, frowning. "And just how do you know all this?"

"Oh, I talked to Cara, of course."

"How?"

"Well, your father and I saw the news, even if you didn't. I was horrified, of course, and then I saw Cara was trying to get through on the computer."

"You can use a computer?" he asked his mother, incredulous—and somewhat disgusted with himself.

"She does—I don't," his father said. "Your mom has always been the family communicator."

"A new ghost managed to contact an old ghost?" he asked.

"It's difficult to explain, but it's like we Skyped," his mother said.

"But how— Never mind. Never mind. I'm not sure I even want to know. So, Cara has shown herself to this young lady, this Marnie Davante?"

"If she hasn't, she will," Maeve said.

"I really hope so. And I hope, Mom, I can even get near her."

"Of course—you're our son. You can go just about anywhere, using the name," Maeve assured him.

"I believe she is right on that," his father said.

Bryan set down his ax and headed for the cabin.

"Where are you going?" Maeve asked him.

He turned to look at her wearily. "I'm going to go check out flights to LA. God knows you haunt me enough that I spend more time with the dead than the living."

He saw the look of relief and pleasure on his mother's face.

And his father's approving nod.

Oh, hell.

Hollywood.

Well, he did have a bit of time on his hands. He'd spent enough time fishing and splitting logs and wondering if he and his brothers should form an agency.

Or if he should go ahead and look into the position that had been offered.

If he should join the FBI.

With the unit known unofficially as the Krewe of Hunters.

But his mother and father had come to him, and he wasn't committed to any path as yet.

He was going to LA.

Marnie had definitely spent too much of her life in Hollywood.

It was impossible to grasp the fact that what happened was reality.

Someone was going to yell, "Cut!" Then the director was going to step forward and tell them what a great job they had all done; they had gotten the scene in one take.

And then Cara Barton would get up. She would straighten her shoulders and look at Marnie and say, "Of course! I'm a pro. I really was great, wasn't I?"

And Marnie would laugh. Cara had been ambitious; she had even been obnoxious at times. But from the get-go, she had been good to Marnie, and they had been true friends.

And now Marnie had held someone she loved as she had died.

Even then, even as reality reared its ugly head, she expected everything would happen as it did in the movies or on television. The detectives would look like Josh Hartnett or maybe Ice T, and within an hour, they'd know who had killed Cara Barton.

That hadn't happened. It had taken them way more than an hour just to sequester Marnie and her fellow surviving cast members, and to begin to round up all the Blood-bones who filled the convention hall.

The day had been a nightmare, endless. Filled with scores of police. With sirens, with medical personnel, with a medical examiner, with crime scene techs.

In the end, though, there were two detectives assigned to the case. One was an older man who, to be honest, in Marnie's mind, would have been perfect for the movies.

For being a homicide detective, his voice was bizarrely soft and gentle. He was tall and thin, clean-shaven, and possessed a full head of silver-gray hair. His eyes were a powdery blue, as soft and gentle as his voice. His name was Grant Vining.

His partner was his total opposite. She was young, and when she spoke, it was apparent that she was not to be taken lightly. She was a tiny blonde with brown eyes and a powerful voice that apparently made up for her size—she had no problem being heard over any amount of chatter or noise. She seemed to do the corralling and instructing while Detective Vining did more of the intimate interviews. Her name was Detective Sophie Manning. She wasn't mean—she was just blunt. She started a bit harshly with Marnie. But then Marnie had been holding Cara Barton as she had died.

Good cop, bad cop? Did cops really play it all out that way? Marnie didn't know.

In the midst of it all, Detective Manning turned to her and said, "We've got your statement. I'm going to take you to the station. We're going to need your clothing. Yes, I know you're thinking this is horrible and the blood on you belonged to your friend. But the killer might have cut himself. His—or her—blood could be on you, too."

"The killer was wearing black gloves," Marnie told the detective.

"Yes, still, we need what you're wearing. It will be returned."

Marnie looked around. A group had gathered by Malcolm Dangerfield's booth; the actor was just beyond the crime scene tape surrounding the *Dark Harbor* booth.

Close and yet oh, so far away! Marnie thought. To his credit, he appeared to be stunned and horrified.

Malcolm Dangerfield wasn't paying attention to any of his fans. He was staring at Marnie and the police as if he were in shock. Someone spoke to him. He didn't seem to notice. His publicist waved the person away.

Detective Grant Vining was speaking to Jeremy Highsmith,

asking him about the numbers on the table. Jeremy shrugged and told him he imagined that it had to do with five of them being there—five chairs. What could the numbers mean other than that? Had they been there all day? Yes, they'd been at the table when they'd arrived, just as their nameplates had been there. It was all set up by the comic con people. Did they change anything around?

Jeremy looked at everyone else. No one seemed to have an answer.

"Who knows?" he replied, his voice sounding broken. "We just...sat. We're all friends. We wouldn't have cared where we sat. When we get together...we talk." He swallowed and then said, "It makes these things bearable. For me, at least."

"I think we more or less sat where our names were," Roberta Alan said. "I have personally never seen numbers before, and we're all friends. We don't care where we sit, and I just honestly don't remember if we sat by number. Oh, maybe Marnie and Cara switched around... I'm not sure. It's honestly like I said— I don't remember. It never mattered to us. We even sometimes play musical chairs. That way, we all got to talk to each other. Oh, yeah, and after these things, at least one of the nights, we'd head out for a meal together."

"She loved those dinners we'd have," Jeremy said. When he spoke, he looked old. He wasn't a spring chicken, but he usually appeared like a very handsome and distinguished older gentleman with his thick iron gray hair and straight and elegant posture.

Now, he just looked old.

"Tonight," Marnie said softly. "We were all supposed to be together tonight."

"We really were her family!" Jeremy said.

There was a little more conversation, none of it really helpful toward finding out why a Blood-bone-costumed killer would have singled them out.

"God knows, maybe it was random!" Sophie Manning murmured to Grant Vining.

"No, no. It wasn't random. Trust me," Vining said.

Finally, Marnie found herself being led out by Detective Manning. She went to the police station, she turned over her clothing and she was given a strange rough outfit to wear—it made her feel as if she had been arrested herself.

Detective Manning wasn't so bad; she asked Marnie if there was someone she should call.

Marnie's parents were going to hear about what happened, but they were off on a dream trip to Australia and New Zealand. She would just text them that she was fine, and she was going to be home and trying to sleep, and she would talk to them in the morning.

She had friends, of course.

But no one that she wanted to talk to at that moment.

Her cousin Bridget lived in the other half of her duplex. She would hear about this soon, but Bridget was down in San Diego for the weekend, visiting one of her friends from college who was there for a writers' retreat. There was no way she could have gotten home yet.

"I just want to go home," she told Manning.

"All right, of course. But you know, I can take you to a hospital if you wish. You might not want to be alone. You might be suffering a form of shock."

"I just want to go home."

"Of course."

The detective didn't call for a patrol officer. She brought Marnie home herself. She checked out the duplex off Barham Boulevard where Marnie lived and declared it safe.

"Do you have an alarm system?" Manning asked.

"No, but I do have a camera that watches my living room, and it's connected to my phone, so in a way...it's kind of an alarm system."

"No, it's not," Manning told her. "It's bizarre. Just your living room?"

"I played with the idea of getting a dog."

"I see. Well, a dog would have been good. When I leave, just make sure that you lock yourself in."

Marnie looked at her, startled. It hadn't occurred to her that she might be in danger.

She'd only known that Cara was dead.

That Cara had stared up at her while the light had gone out of her eyes.

She shook off the notion of fear. Really. She just wanted to be alone. She did have good locks on her windows and on the front and back doors. She had bought the duplex; she shared it with Bridget. She had made sure they had windows and doors that were up to code—thinking more about earthquakes than home invaders—but whatever the thought, her place was solid.

"I'm good. Really. Quality locks on the windows. My doors would need a battering ram if someone wished to break them down, and I have three bolts on each."

"All right, then. We'll be in touch. Oh, my card—" Manning paused, digging around in her suit pocket "—and my partner's card." She shrugged. "People tend to like him more. If he's easier to call and you do need help or you think of anything, call him, or call me."

"You will find out who did this?" Marnie whispered. She winced. Oh, Lord. It sounded like such a Hollywood line.

Manning smiled. "We're good, Miss Davante. My partner and I are good together. We're going to do our best. But…if there's anything, call us. There's one thing that Grant Vining taught me right off the bat—if you can get help from somewhere that will solve a murder—take it. So…"

"I wish I had something to tell you. I wish I had something to say," Marnie assured her.

"Lock up."

Manning left, and Marnie did so. She headed to the bathroom and turned on the hot water.

She must have stayed beneath the showerhead for an hour.

When she came out of the bathroom, she got in bed and turned on the television. She didn't seem able to find a channel that did anything but talk about the murder of Cara Barton that day.

Finally she found the Three Stooges.

And still...

She stared up at the ceiling. So exhausted...

And so unable to sleep. Eventually, she closed her eyes. She could still faintly hear Moe, Larry and Curly as they taunted and teased one another.

Her phone rang; it was her mother. Naturally, her mom was hysterical. Her parents had known Cara Barton. They had visited the set. But not only that, it could have been Marnie who had been killed.

It hadn't been.

The only way to get her mother to calm down was to remind her that sometimes in life, Cara Barton had been a wee bit... obnoxious. She might have offended someone.

It took her twenty minutes to convince her mother *not* to cut short her dream vacation. She was okay. Not hurt at all. She wasn't alone in the city.

So Marnie had a nice long conversation, calming down her mother.

Then she had to talk to her dad.

When she hung up, she found herself talking to the air.

"I'm sorry, Cara, I hope I didn't sound uncaring. I had to get my mom to be okay."

Sleep...

Watch Moe, Larry and Curly, and be grateful for the channels that kept old classics alive.

Yes, sleep.

She drifted. And as she did so, she thought that she felt a gentle touch on her face and heard a soft whisper beneath the canned laughter on the TV.

"Darling, I know you. I know you didn't mean anything evil at all. Not to worry. I'm here. I'm with you. Get some rest, sweet Marnie. You really were a friend."

It was nice; it was kind. As if Cara were trying to help Marnie accept what had happened.

Marnie couldn't forget that day.

I'm not a bad person, am I? Cara had asked her.

And that had made Marnie smile. *Nope. Not bad. Ambitious, trying to get by and just loving it when you did get the limelight!*

"You were never a bad person!" Marnie murmured aloud, half-asleep.

And she could feel those gentle fingers touch her hair in what she assumed were her dreams.

"Such a good friend, Marnie. And now... I'm so afraid for you!"

Marnie frowned, jerked from sleep. She leaped from her bed, running through the duplex, turning on lights.

Maybe not the smartest thing to do if there was a prowler in the house!

But there wasn't.

A check through the window by her front door showed no one at all in the yard.

She looked through the peephole. No one was there.

It was probably about five in the morning.

And she was afraid of darkness and afraid of sleep.

Maybe she'd stay in the living room.

Eventually, she fell asleep on the couch.

As she drifted off, she could almost swear that she smelled the slightly sweet scent of Cara Barton's perfume.

He didn't go in; he looked at the house in the dark, and he marveled at how he had enjoyed the day. Never—in a thousand years—could he have imagined what this would feel like.

Perfect. Everything perfect.

Using Blood-bone—pure genius.

The police were clueless, asking, questioning…and getting nothing.

There was nothing to get. And they just might understand why when the time came.

But for now…

It was delicious. It was the movies, all over again. Marnie was inside her home—the beautiful young heroine—terrified. Waiting…

For the killer to strike.

It was…

Euphoria!

CHAPTER TWO

There had been something about Marnie Davante in her role as Madam Zeta that had been magical. The show had been cast well. It was one of those in which the chemistry between the players was just right on, and because of it, the show was incredibly watchable, and it was still doing very well in syndication.

Bryan had downloaded a number of episodes to watch on his phone during the cross-continental flight. After a few, he felt he knew Scarlet Zeta—except, of course, who he had come to know wasn't a real person—he had come to know a character.

His first stop was with the major crimes detectives who were handling the case. The detective he'd finally managed to speak with over the phone before his arrival—Sophie Manning—was still confused as to why he was coming out from Virginia.

That was all right. In a way, he was still confused himself.

He was asked to wait by the desk sergeant, and soon a small woman with a purposeful gait came toward him. She assessed him quickly, apparently noting that he'd probably hold his own in a fight since she gave him a sort of approving nod. While she was a tiny thing, Bryan figured she'd had some training herself, and while she might not be able to throw much weight around, she'd be damned good throwing around what she did have.

"Mr. McFadden?" she asked, offering him a hand. She had a good grip.

"Bryan McFadden, yes. And you're Detective Manning."

"I am. If you'll come with me, my partner is upstairs in one of our conference rooms."

Upstairs, he met Grant Vining; once again, he was impressed. Vining didn't appear to be at all intimidated, nor did he seem to resent Bryan's presence there. If anything, he was curious— something that he voiced almost immediately.

"You're out here from Virginia?" he said.

"Yes, sir. Virginia is my home. At the moment."

"Military brat?"

"Military myself for a few years—a few years back. My parents, no. They were actors."

"I see," Vining said. Then he scratched his graying head. "No, no, frankly, I don't see at all. You're a private eye?"

"Yes, recently licensed."

"And you've been hired by someone out here? You're acting for someone? I can assure you, we really are a competent operation. Hollywood is our jurisdiction, which might seem cushy. But in many ways, that makes our work harder—under a spotlight, we have to be better."

Manning—the respectful junior in the duo—stood quietly, watching the exchange.

"I have absolutely no doubt that you're exceptionally fine detectives and that this is a crack unit," Bryan said.

"But then—"

"I'm acting for the deceased," he said quietly.

"For—for Cara Barton?" Vining asked.

Bryan nodded. "I was actually born out here. My parents were Hamish and Maeve McFadden. If you're a fan of AMC or any of the TV channels that keep old movies afloat, you might have seen them. They were, however, working in theater the last decade or so of their lives."

"And?"

"Cara Barton is—was—a dear friend of my mother's," Bryan explained.

"The chandelier!" Manning suddenly exclaimed.

Vining and Bryan both looked at her. She flushed but went on enthusiastically. "I know who your parents were now! Your mother—wow! She was stunning. And your dad, too. I actually told my mom when I was little that I was going to grow up and marry him, and, of course, she told me that he was already married, and then later, she told me that he was…"

"Dead," Bryan finished for her.

She flushed again. "Yes. I'm so sorry."

"So…this is in your mom's memory then, kind of. Or do you have a client?" Vining asked.

"That would be me. I am my own client on this."

Vining studied him for a long moment and then nodded. "All right, fine. Let us bring you up to speed—and remind you that we are the police here. If you make any pertinent discoveries— that is to say, any discoveries at all—they will be shared with us immediately."

"Absolutely," Bryan promised.

"We have had all kinds of meetings, bringing in every precinct in the county and sending information out far beyond. We've shared what we have with the FBI, the state police and the US Marshals Service. What we have is very little, but I will see that you receive copies of the files. On the one hand, it is an extremely bizarre case—a woman was killed by a person wearing a comic costume and wielding a sword. Apparently, such light-up swords have become extremely popular toys and costume items, making it a daunting task for police and security on hand at the convention at the time of the murder. Such a sword—a real one, with a killing blade—was not found. And while precisely thirty-six persons wearing a Blood-bone costume were stopped and questioned by the same officers, not one was found with a speck of blood upon them or their weapon. In other words, someone wore this costume with a sword that appeared as harmless as the hundreds—perhaps *thousands*—on sale at the convention. No blood other than the victim's was found anywhere near the victim or on those around her. No fingerprints were found other than those belonging to the cast and crew. We are, at this moment, relying on good old investigative work, searching through the victim's past acquaintances and anyone who might have had a grudge against her. Oh, on that—well, people don't like to speak ill of the dead, do they? Getting the truth out of cast and crew isn't easy. Also, remember, anyone pertinent to the investigation has already been grilled by police. They will not look upon you kindly."

"I don't intend to grill anyone," Bryan said.

"Ah, well, then..." Vining just stared at him.

"My most sincere thanks," Bryan said. "I appreciate you allowing me to work in your jurisdiction, and I'm grateful that you're willing to share information."

"We did investigate you, of course," Vining told him.

"I'd expect no less. I will be in touch." He hesitated. "As far as the comic con goes, are there markers at the table that suggest who sits where?"

"Yes, there were numbers on the table. Along with their nameplates," Vining said.

"Were they in order?" Bryan asked.

"In order?" Vining frowned. "What order would that be? We believed the numbers to have been set out by the organizers. Along with the nameplates."

"Were such numbers available on other tables?" Bryan asked.

"They were between a descendant of a famous German shepherd and Malcolm Dangerfield," Vining said. "Just one dog. And in Malcolm's case—just one man. Oh, yes, and his publicity manager and reporters and God alone might know who else during the day. Dangerfield is what might be a called an 'It boy' this year. You think that the numbers mean something?" he asked.

Bryan shook his head. "I've seen the news. That's about it. I don't think anything as of yet. And even if someone had been offended by Miss Barton, this was one drastic method of showing displeasure."

"Yes," Vining said. "You have contact info for the comic con organizer and his secretary for operations there. I can't tell you how many people are involved. There are some closed-circuit cameras around the convention floor. But not enough to cover the entire area. I'm willing to bet, however, that there are tons of cell phone videos of the event out there, videos we have yet to see here, though we did pick up many. If you find any..."

"If I find more video, I'll let you know."

"Precisely," Vining said.

Sophie Manning cleared her throat.

"The funeral is tomorrow afternoon. The medical examiner released the body, and... I guess everyone wanted it to happen. She was just killed on Friday. We're frankly surprised that the ME did release the body so quickly, but he has extensive notes—"

"I know," Bryan said.

"You've been to see Dr. Collier already?" Vining asked a little sharply.

"No. I just know of him," Bryan said. "And he is top-notch."

"There will be a reception following, but I can't help you get access."

"That's fine. I'll manage," Bryan assured him. "And thank you again."

"You just keep in touch," Vining said firmly.

"It's a promise," Bryan assured him.

Before he'd actually reached the street, Bryan had received a digital folder. Vining clearly meant to keep his word.

A glance at his email showed him that he'd received the autopsy notes, as well. He could have told Vining that Dr. Edward Collier had been a medic on Bryan's ship during his first two years in the United States Navy. Maybe he should have done so, but that wasn't pertinent to the case.

He headed on out for his third stop that day.

He wanted to see where Marnie Davante lived.

Just to observe. It was a day for gathering information.

Tomorrow would be time enough to put some of it to use.

Marnie Davante stood quietly by the graveside and listened while the priest spoke about life and death, and his certainty that while they buried the *mortal* remains of Cara Barton, her soul went on to a better place, one where there was no pain and no fear, and where love reigned.

Marnie hoped it was true.

For a moment, she thought she saw Cara there, dressed beautifully in the red-and-black tailored suit she'd been dressed in for her viewing, enjoying the attention her funeral was receiving.

Marnie had truly loved Cara, but she knew as well that years of fighting to maintain a career had left Cara jaded and weary. She had dated many a heartthrob, but she had never married. Her parents had long ago departed their mortal coil, and she'd had no siblings. So she left behind no one with very close ties to her. But in Marnie's mind, there had been many wonderful things about her friend. Cara had cared deeply about animals— she had raised money and awareness for humane societies and no-kill shelters. She had given what she could to children's charities.

And Marnie had had a chance to talk about all the good in Cara lately—she'd been interviewed right and left, almost to a point of embarrassment.

Cara would have been happy.

In death, she was incredibly famous.

So much was being written about her. Every celebrity and pop culture magazine out there was doing an article on her.

Marnie was somehow the golden girl in most interviews, and it was very uncomfortable. She had remained friends with her fellow castmates from *Dark Harbor,* and she hoped to God that they knew she had never mentioned herself as the "success" story from the show while the others had gone on to face less-than-stellar careers.

She wasn't sure how exactly anyone measured success. It wasn't as if she'd suddenly been besieged with scripts for blockbusters. She'd just managed to keep working, and a lot of that had been theatrical work.

The priest was going on. He was a good man, Marnie knew. He and Cara had been friends. That was one thing people hadn't known about her. Cara had been a regular churchgoer.

A cloud shifted in the sky.

Marnie thought that the late-afternoon sun must be playing tricks on her; she could have sworn that Cara—or someone dressed similarly, wearing one of the ridiculous giant black hats Cara had worn—had just slipped behind the priest.

Someone was sobbing; it was Roberta Alan, Marnie's sister from the show. Well, of course. Roberta and Cara had often bickered, but they had been very close. Since Cara had lacked real family, her *Dark Harbor* fellows were being seen as her closest relations. To be fair, they had been something of a family for a time. Marnie had been so young herself when she'd started—just turned sixteen—she had leaned on the others. While Cara had been huge at emoting—larger than life, more than a bit of a diva—she'd always been kind and something like a very whacky but caring aunt for Marnie.

For a moment, she closed her eyes, wondering if she was still in shock. Marnie had done enough crying herself, the night at the hospital when she realized there had never been a chance for Cara, that doctors had gone through the motions, but there had been nothing they could do.

Since then, she had just been going through the motions. Moving by rote, speaking by rote...

Getting herself here today...she didn't even recall how.

As Roberta softly sobbed, a spate of flashbulbs went off. Marnie could see them even through her closed eyelids. There was press everywhere. There had been ever since Cara died.

The priest, deep in his reflection, didn't miss a beat.

Marnie opened her eyes again.

That was when she saw her fully. The woman dressed like Cara.

She was on the other side of the coffin, standing beside one of Hollywood's hot young leading men and an older, well-respected actor. They didn't seem to notice the woman.

How the hell they didn't, Marnie didn't begin to understand.

She looked just like Cara.

As if completely aware she was being watched, the woman turned to stare at Marnie. She winked, waved and smiled deeply—as if it were a terrific joke, as if she were hiding, as if it were normal that no one else seemed to see her.

It was Cara.

Cara Barton.

It couldn't be. Of course, it couldn't be. Marnie had seen her die.

She had seen the sudden surge of blood that had erupted from her friend's throat.

She could remember staring, frowning, in absolute disbelief and confusion. Because what had happened—Cara being sliced apart by the lighted sword as if it were a real blade—was impossible. It was just a comic con, for God's sake...

But it had been real. The blade had been real.

And she had screamed and screamed, and hunkered down by her fallen friend, trying desperately to staunch the flow of blood. Everyone had been screaming, people had been running. Some—even more confused than she had been—had applauded!

Not at death, no, not the horror of death.

They had thought themselves privy to a very special show. But then the EMTs had arrived and the police and the crime scene investigators. And she had been inspected and questioned, and then inspected and questioned some more. And she had tried to remember everything there had been to remember about that day: the beautiful German shepherd by them, whining every time his nose got hit with a drip of water from the leaky ceiling. She had spoken to Zane—the old Western star—and been impressed with his charm and humility. They hadn't met before. She'd had her picture taken with at least two dozen guys dressed up as Marvel superheroes, another dozen or so zombies and, of course, because of *Dark Harbor*, tons of vampires, werewolves and shape-shifters.

And, before *that* particular Blood-bone had appeared, she'd had her picture taken with a few other people dressed up as the character, as well.

It was highly possible, the police had told her, that one of them had been the killer.

Cara Barton was dead. She had died in Marnie's arms.

And yet there she was, watching the proceedings, nodding with approval as the priest went on emotionally, as Roberta cried softly, as others followed suit.

The priest's words came to an end. Marnie remembered that she'd been holding a rose; a number of people, those who had been closest to Cara in life, were stepping forward, dropping their roses onto the coffin. It was almost time to leave. Cara's coffin would be lowered into the ground.

Dust to dust. Ashes to ashes.

Cara had always known that she would be buried here, in Hollywood's oldest cemetery, close to so many actors, directors, writers, producers and musicians she had known and loved.

She'd adored the place. Marnie had come with her once to see a showing of a black-and-white silent classic on one of the large mausoleum walls; Cara had giggled and said it was like a living cemetery. They could catch a flick—and leave roses on the graves of Rudolph Valentino, Cecille B. DeMille and so many, many more. Sometimes there were concerts in the cemetery. Johnny Ramone would surely love it.

Cara Barton was dead. Cara Barton would soon be lowered into the ground in the cemetery she had always loved so much—where she had always known she wanted to be.

Someday.

It shouldn't have been so soon...

Marnie blinked. She could still see her.

The woman looked just like Cara. She was grave; she was sad, and then she clapped her hands and wiped her tears, delighted as the hot star of the day stepped forward, casting down a rose and saying, "She was truly an enormous talent! Such a devastating loss!"

Marnie followed Roberta Alan, Jeremy Highsmith and Grayson Adair, all casting their roses over the coffin.

She stopped dead, staring across the coffin.

Cara was there. Cara. Not someone who looked like Cara.

She looked at Marnie and smiled sadly. "Did you see? Oh, Marnie. Everyone is here. Oh, my Lord. I mean everyone who is anyone. This is so wonderful. If only..."

Marnie froze. Obviously, it had all just been too much.

Cara dying in her arms.

The blood.

The EMTs taking Cara's body from her. She had just sat there. She could still see the blood, feel the blood, smell the blood.

And see the character—Blood-bone.

For what had seemed like an eternity, he had just stood there, staring at them all while those in the crowd went crazy clapping.

Then he had turned and disappeared into the crowd. It had

taken forever, so it had seemed, for people to realize that her screams were real, that something terrible had really happened. It had been no performance.

Crazy. So damned crazy.

And every night now, Marnie had nightmares that featured Blood-bone dancing before her, wielding that sword with its array of colors...

Not just a light-up sword. A real sword.

She had made it through the day. Through the comic con being closed down. Through the questioning by the police. Through the hours of smelling her friend's blood...until she could finally change into the police-issued scrubs.

And she was still moving. She didn't know if she was or wasn't in shock. She just kept going through all the right motions.

She had to be in shock. Or *the events* being so crazy had turned into *her* being crazy.

"Marnie?" Grayson Adair had turned back to her. He looked at her with sorrowful affection, like a real big brother.

She blinked. She cast down her rose, looking across the coffin to the other side of the grave.

Cara was still standing there. She gave Marnie a thumbs-up.

It was impossible. Apparently, Grayson Adair did not see Cara.

Surely that meant that Cara was not really there. But Grayson not seeing Cara was not the only reason she could not be there. Cara could not be there because Cara was dead. Her poor murdered body lay in the coffin.

Cara wasn't there—not really. She was just there in Marnie's worn and tormented mind. Marnie took a deep breath and pretended she wasn't hallucinating.

It wasn't going to be easy.

"Marnie?"

Grayson was speaking again, looking back at her and offering her an arm.

Marnie took it. But as they started out, she felt something.

Something extremely strange, as if a cool fog had formed into some kind of substance on her other side.

She looked to her left. To her free arm.

It wasn't free; Cara had come up beside her. She had slipped her arm through Marnie's and was walking at her side.

"At least it was a sensational funeral," Cara said. "I'm so grateful. Oh, not for being murdered, though, of course, that does mean that I'll be famous forever. I've seen the headlines— Famous TV Matriarch Brutally Taken by Blood-Bone Character. And they said that I was beautiful and aging gracefully. I've seen everything you've said, too. You are just such a little doll. Frankly, you're a little too good and innocent, and you really don't belong in Hollywood. Where was it you came from originally? Atlanta, right? How rude of me not to really remember, but then again, I was meant to live in the dog-eat-dog and plastic part of Hollywood—I do believe that it is all about me!"

It sounded like Cara Barton; the voice was just a little bit raspy, as if it had been created from the wind or the air. The cadence was all Cara, as was the admission that yes, the world was all about her.

Even when she was dead.

Or *especially because* she was dead.

Someone called out and Grayson paused, turning to talk to the man. It was another reporter.

"Really. Lovely funeral. I'm sure you had a part in planning it? And if I know you, you made sure that it was more than public notice—that everyone who is anyone would be here," Cara said approvingly.

"You're not really here, and I can't hear you," Marnie whispered, and she knew that her tone was low, that her words were breathy.

For a moment, she felt that she was going to keel over. No,

she couldn't pass out. That would bring attention to her, away from Cara. And Cara wouldn't be happy.

Cara was dead.

Yep. Dead.

And yet Cara was still standing next to her.

"Marnie?" It was Grayson speaking again. He was looking at her with dark, concerned eyes.

Grayson had always been known for his good looks. He was tall, and his hair was as dark as his eyes. He was truly concerned for her, Marnie thought.

But he was also extremely aware of the cameras going off all around them. Yes, he was aware of the press and of the possible headlines: Marnie Davante Stumbles from Cemetery in Shock, Held Up by Manly Hands of Former Costar Grayson Adair.

"I'm fine," she said softly.

"Oh, please, you're not supposed to be fine!" Cara's ghost protested. "I'm dead! I was murdered. You're not fine."

"No, I'm stone-cold crazy!" Marnie said.

"What?" Grayson asked, twisting around to look at her, a frown creasing his handsome features. "There's that hot gossip blogger coming toward us. Are you all right? Really?"

"Yes, you're fine now," Cara said. "Be sure to tell them how wonderful I was, how much you loved me. I do bask in all this!"

The blogger came forward and brashly shook hands with them both. He apologized for disturbing them then; he was afraid he wouldn't get near them once they had reached Rodeo, the trendy new restaurant where they'd be having the reception.

Marnie told him how much she had loved Cara; she told him what a wonderful actress she had been in a scene, in an ensemble. She vowed they would hound the police until the killer was found. They would never stop.

"Wonderful," Cara said.

"Excuse me," Marnie said, escaping from Grayson's hold and turning to head back to the grave site. The funeral workers—

who had been about to lower the finely carved coffin into the ground—stepped back, obviously surprised and a little annoyed that their time was being taken. They did, however, respectfully move away, allowing her personal and intimate time with her dearly departed loved one.

Marnie stood there for a moment, breathing. And then she spoke softly and firmly. "You are dead, Cara. I cannot see you, I cannot hear you. God help me, I am so, so sorry. I will miss you. Honestly. But you are dead!"

"That isn't going to help."

Marnie was so startled by the sound of the deep, masculine voice—so near to her—that she nearly fell over the coffin.

Luckily, she caught herself and looked over it instead.

He was tall—taller even than Grayson Adair. And, if possible, his hair was darker. His eyes, however, weren't dark, they were green or gold or a startling combination of both, and they sat in a ruggedly masculine face that could well have been the next to grace every pop culture magazine out there. He was well built—he was quite simply both rugged and Hollywood drop-dead gorgeous.

And she was just staring at him.

"Wow," the specter of Cara murmured, standing close behind Marnie once again. "Did he grow up fine. That's one of the McFadden boys. Of course, you must understand, the parents were to die for—what an expression. Terrible."

"You're not there," Marnie whispered desperately.

"It's not going to help," the man said gently.

Stunned, Marnie realized the truth. Whoever he was—McFadden boy, whatever—he was aware of what was going on.

"You—you—you see her. You hear her, too?" Marnie said.

He nodded. "Sorry, I didn't mean to startle you. My name is Bryan McFadden. I'm... I'm here to help you."

McFadden.

"No." Marnie shook her head vehemently. "You've got to

be kidding me. I'm having hallucinations and you're…having the same hallucinations. And you know it… Oh! It's a sham. You're from a paper. You're trying to make me look crazy… I have to go."

Marnie turned, ready to hurry back to Grayson Adair and the rest of her old cast and crew.

"Miss Davante," he said.

She bit her lower lip and paused, not turning back but listening. On the one hand, she wanted to run.

Then again…

It was too…too…

Real.

And if he *could* help her?

She stayed there, wanting to run, afraid that if she did so she'd lose any chance of fighting off whatever was happening.

He didn't speak again right away. They were too close to the cemetery workers.

He came up behind her. Not too close. He didn't touch her. But close enough. She was aware of him in a way that she seldom felt, as if he were almost inside her skin, as if his fingers did touch her just as the warmth of his words reached her. He whispered softly, his tone still deep and rich and strangely ringing with truth, "She's here, Marnie. You are not going crazy. She is right next to you. Trust me, I've been through this—too many times now. And here is the thing—she won't go away. Not until we discover exactly why she's still with us. Maybe it's to see that her murder is solved. And maybe it's to prevent something terrible."

"She's already dead. So, prevent something such as?" Marnie demanded harshly, giving herself a fierce mental shake. She stared at him. He might be incredibly gorgeous, but he had to be stone-cold crazy, as well. "Such as?"

"Such as another murder," he said bluntly. "As in—possibly—yours!"

CHAPTER THREE

Maybe it wasn't fair for Bryan to judge the funeral as a carnival with all kinds of acts being performed beneath a big tent. His mother had always assured him that there were many people living in Los Angeles—even those who were deeply enmeshed in the film industry, and despite its reputation for shallowness and ruthless ambition—who were decent and wonderful people. It was true. To be honest, he knew many people who were "Hollywood" all the way and who were fine, decent, caring and more.

Still, the worst of the business seemed to come out when news cameras were rolling.

And everyone, to paraphrase the artist Andy Warhol, wanted their fifteen minutes of fame.

There was no way out of it; in this city, most bartenders, servers and so on were also actors and actresses. Bankers and lawyers handled accounts for directors, producers, screenwriters, actors and costumers, puppeteers—and more.

It seemed as though everyone wound up being involved. But Greater Los Angeles was huge; its population had soared to over ten million people. Many were teachers, electricians, nurses, all the usual—you name it. And yet it all boiled down to the movies in the end. Teachers had actors' children in their classes. Doctors patched up production assistants and prop managers and all manner of crew amid their other patients.

And while Hollywood might offer up a world of make-believe, it could also be—as his mom had always claimed—a nice place where many people wanted what everyone wanted: a family filled with love and happiness.

Before returning to the theater, Maeve and Hamish McFadden had been part of the Hollywood crowd.

In retrospect, since they had died together onstage, coming back to the theater in the DC area had perhaps not been a good decision. And yet, in those years before the accident, life for the McFadden family had been great.

Bryan had learned that death shouldn't put a person on a pedestal. Still, when he looked back, they had been really good parents. They had put the needs of their sons above their own. They had left Hollywood.

But they had been a big part of it at one time, which made it possible for Bryan to be where he was now—rubbing shoulders with A-listers at a funeral reception that had become the hottest ticket in town.

It was obvious that Marnie Davante had thought she'd shake him when they reached the reception; there had been all kinds of gawkers and strangers who had managed to get close to the funeral. After all, Cara Barton had been buried at a cemetery often crawling with tourists. But the reception required an ID, to confirm the name on the guest list. Otherwise the masses would have readily joined in the reception that followed such a high-profile funeral.

However, as a McFadden, he'd managed to charm his way onto the list.

He saw Marnie standing with a group of people, Malcolm Dangerfield among them. Hollywood was often fickle—the hottest new star one year could be yesterday's has-been by the next.

At the moment, Malcolm Dangerfield was on the hot list. He would be, Bryan knew, considered to be more of a personality than an actor. He was basically always himself on-screen. But as himself, he was charismatic and it worked. On the other hand, while Jeremy Highsmith had only been cast in supporting roles since *Dark Harbor* had been canceled, each of those roles had been entirely different. Jeremy Highsmith was—Bryan knew his parents would judge—a true actor. A fine actor. Not a personality.

In their own way, his parents had been snobs. But to be fair, they had both loved their craft. They didn't have to be performing themselves—they loved a good performance by another actor, singer, musician or even stand-up comic.

Marnie was barely holding it together, Bryan was pretty sure. But she managed to nod and speak now and then as she stood in the group with Malcolm Dangerfield, a producer, some young director and the rest of her castmates: Roberta Alan, Jeremy Highsmith and Grayson Adair. She was five foot nine in stocking feet, and taller here in low heels. She was regal. Despite the way she looked at him, with suspicion and irritation, Bryan couldn't help but feel a tug of sympathy. She had an aura about her he couldn't quite place. She was regal, and yet she appeared quick to smile at something said by a friend. Then the sadness would descend over her eyes again.

There was definitely something about her. He couldn't help but feel the attraction that certainly drew many, many people to her. She was fascinating, charismatic and sensual with each sleek movement.

The perfect actress.

Photographers—authorized ones who were on the guest list— were seizing pictures constantly. It was hard to imagine how anyone could actually mourn in all the hubbub, and yet he remembered his parents' funeral.

Much like this.

And it had been hard to mourn. Hard to be the eldest of their children; hard to hold it all together and grieve with the carnival atmosphere going on.

"Bringing back memories, eh?"

He didn't turn; he knew that Cara Barton was standing next to him.

He lowered his head. She knew that he acknowledged her—saw her and heard her.

"So lovely. I mean, it may be terrible, but I am truly grateful to see I did have this many fans—okay, even if some are people using such an occasion for a publicity advantage. A grand funeral, I do say. I do *so* wish that I could have a sip of that champagne…" She paused, and Bryan knew that she was waiting for his response. While he stood a bit off in the corner of the restaurant, he wasn't going to allow himself to appear to be speaking to the air.

Cara Barton apparently realized that he wasn't going to answer her right then. He'd been at the cemetery early, and he had spoken to her. She might have figured out a ghostly way to contact his mother, but maybe she hadn't really believed that she could get through to the living. She had been thrilled he could see her. She had been trying to torment the cemetery workers and the funeral director, and all she'd managed to do was to get one man to say that the cemetery, even in broad daylight, was incredibly creepy. She'd been ecstatic that Bryan could see her, hear her, because she had something important to say: she'd been murdered. She was afraid for the others.

She wanted the truth.

So right now, she didn't really expect Bryan to reply.

But she kept talking.

"I remember sitting there that day…the day that I was killed," she said. "I guess it's good I don't remember the pain. I do remember bits and pieces of my life shooting before my eyes…out of order, things when I was a child, things when I was older. And I remember thinking it was horrible, so unfair—that comic con really was, for me, where I'd come to die. And I remember Marnie, of course, holding me, shocked, horrified...such a sweet girl. Better than this world we're in," she added softly. "But I just don't understand. Why in God's name would anyone want to kill me? I mean, he probably was after Marnie. She was the one who had the most obsessed fans. You know she didn't really want to have a reboot of *Dark Harbor*? A comeback, you know. She just loves the theater. She wants to direct. Children. Horrible little snot-nosed beasts, in my opinion, but...the thing is, there was no reason for anyone to kill me!"

He turned briefly, making a pretense of studying a painting above the bar.

"We'll talk later," he said.

Right now, he was trying to watch anyone who spent too much time with the four remaining actors from *Dark Harbor*.

Golden boy Malcolm Dangerfield seemed very interested in Marnie and her friends. But then again, the photographers where milling around them that day. It was the center of the action.

He also noted another man.

"That's Vince Carlton," Cara said. "He's the one who wants to revamp *Dark Harbor*. I was so thrilled. I mean, that would have been a whole new life for all of us! On the top again. Okay, so not all shows make it. But we would have had a pilot and at least a season, I'm sure of it. Vince is a nice guy. But, of course, I'm dead now. So..."

Vince Carlton appeared to be in his early forties. He was known for having produced a number of successful fantasy and sci-fi projects. He appeared sympathetic and respectful as he spoke with the group.

And Malcolm Dangerfield, who had determinedly remained with them throughout the afternoon. Maybe that was natural; he had been standing close to Cara when she was killed.

He had watched her be cut down in cold blood.

"What does a comic creature like Blood-bone have to do with a show like *Dark Harbor*?" Bryan wondered softly aloud.

"Nothing—nothing that I know of, anyway. And the thing is, Blood-bone is like Darth Vader—that kind of a costume. Just about anyone could be in it. Well, it works best with a certain height and size, but…it could be anyone."

There had to be some kind of a relationship. Either that or the killer had chosen the costume because there would be so many people dressed up the same, making a getaway easy.

Which it had apparently been, according to Detective Vining. Dozens of Blood-bones had been stopped and searched and questioned. And each had been the wrong Blood-bone.

"Anonymous," he murmured.

"What?" Cara asked.

Bryan pulled a set of earbuds out of his pocket and inserted them into his ears. While he found it incredibly rude that people seemed to be talking on the phone everywhere and through any occasion these days, the cell-phone-earbuds craze was a good thing—for a man who talked to the dead.

"Anonymous," he repeated softly. "Such a costume means that it could be anyone inside. Do you remember anything about the killer, a scent, the way he moved, the size of his hands…anything that felt familiar?"

"I've racked my brain," Cara replied, "but I can't imagine who it was in that costume."

"So not necessarily someone you knew. If there was a specific target, the murder could have been perpetrated by the person who wanted them dead, or because of the costume, a killer could have even been hired."

Cara gasped. "You mean the bastard who did this to me might not have even had the balls to do it him—or her—self?"

"I'm thinking aloud, Cara. Give me a break. I just got out here."

"You got out here yesterday."

"Doing my best," he said.

She harrumphed.

Loudly.

Bryan noted that Marnie had heard the sound. And she turned. At her side, Roberta Alan turned to see what Marnie was looking at, and both of them stared at him.

Maybe it was time.

He pocketed his earbuds and walked up to the group, extending a hand to introduce himself.

Marnie looked at his hand as if he had offered up a snake.

But Roberta Alan took it, staring at him curiously, a smile on her lips. "Well, hello, gorgeous!" she said, her voice and tone an excellent mimic of that used by Barbra Streisand as Fanny Brice in *Funny Girl*.

He grinned. He could play the game.

"Hello, gorgeous, yourself," he told her. "My name is Bryan McFadden. My parents—"

"Oh!" Roberta exclaimed. "I know—yes, you're so like your father. And your mother, really, and they both were truly gorgeous. Well, your dad, of course, was very manly. You're manly, too, naturally, and I... I'm just making a fool out of myself here. Mr. McFadden, may I introduce you to my costars? Grayson Adair, our brother. Jeremy Highsmith, good old dad. And Marnie Davante—"

"Scarlet Zeta, Madam Zeta," he said.

Marnie forced a stiff smile. "How do you do, Mr. McFadden?"

"Nice to meet you, son. I knew your parents. I was so sorry when they...died," Jeremy Highsmith told him, wincing a little.

"Thank you, sir."

"And they say that Hollywood is murder. Well, in this case... Oh, hell, I can't get out of this one."

Malcolm Dangerfield suddenly cut between Jeremy and Marnie, offering his hand. "Malcolm Dangerfield," he said. "Are you looking for work out here? Acting?"

"No. I'm not an actor. I'm actually a private investigator," Bryan replied curtly.

"Hey, let me tell you—bodyguards are in high demand right now. You know, after what I witnessed, I'd take on another. Call me if you're interested in anything like that."

"Actually, I'm out here to work the case of Cara Barton's murder," Bryan said.

Marnie stared at him, startled.

And wary.

Very wary. She obviously didn't trust him. At the moment, he was sure, she didn't trust herself. Why should she trust a man claiming that he could see a dead woman, too?

"Well, nice to meet you," Malcolm said.

"You sure you're not trying to get into the movies?" Jeremy asked him. "Names and nepotism have been known to open doors. Are you...looking for a role?"

"I assure you—I'm not looking for a role," Bryan told him.

They all continued to stare at him suspiciously. Except for Roberta. She remained curious and intrigued. "You're here because your family knew Cara, I imagine. But...the cops are trying everything. They're looking at every angle," Roberta told him.

Jeremy Highsmith cleared his throat. "Every angle. They've told all of us to keep special care, to keep our doors locked and to watch out for strangers. Oh, yeah. They've suggested we all avoid comic cons for the time being, and any place that a man or woman could dress up in a costume that would make them totally anonymous. Just in case Cara isn't the only target."

"They do say that it could have just been random," Malcolm said. "That the guy—or woman, but the dude was pretty big, so I think it was a man—was just out to kill. Someone, anyone, a guest or a celebrity."

"You know, like it might have been some kind of an exhibitionist," Roberta supplied.

"Marnie was going along with the show," Jeremy said. "And

Cara—Cara was never to be outdone. She hopped up and got right into it."

"Miss Davante," a male voice said softly, interrupting them.

They all swiveled around to see who had spoken.

Bryan had seen the man before—in the cell phone footage of the killing that had gone viral around the world. Most of the news stations had shown the footage with some respect. Many social media sites had posted it in all its graphic detail—until the pure horror of it had been caught and taken down by whatever powers that be, those with some common decency.

The man had been standing at the booth when it had happened. He'd been speaking with Marnie, or so it appeared. A fan?

"Miss Davante, David Neal. I was there… I just wanted to say I'm so sorry. I… We…we have an appointment tomorrow. I wasn't sure… Anyway, I wish you luck with your future," he said. He backed away awkwardly, looking at all of them. "I'm truly sorry—all of you. She was a great talent. She was…a talent. Yes. I'm sorry. Miss Davante, I hope that… I hope that you won't hold this against me when…when you're looking to hire again."

He nodded uncomfortably to all of them and then moved on.

"Rude," Malcolm said. "We're at a funeral, and he's worried about a job."

"He was just apologizing," Marnie said in the man's defense.

"As he should have been," Roberta murmured.

"We're here for you," Jeremy said. "We're all here for each other. Oh, look, there's Vince Carlton. I'm sure he's hurting, too. He'd been in talks with Cara for a while," he said to Bryan. "I'm going to say hello again. Excuse me."

"And excuse me," Marnie said. She stared straight at Bryan, and he knew that he was the reason she wanted to be excused.

But he couldn't stop her. And he wasn't sure that he should, not at that moment.

"Miss Davante," he said, lowering his head as she stepped by.

"So," Roberta said as Marnie walked away, "may I get you a drink? I suppose you used your family connection to get in here today. Because though we had help from a few others, we were Cara's family, and we pretty much put the guest list together. Naughty, naughty, Mr. McFadden—you weren't on it! Then again, neither was that young man, David Neal. You have a connection. How did he manage it, do you think?"

"I don't know," Bryan told her. "But it would be interesting to find out."

There was someone in her house. But that wasn't unexpected.

Marnie had driven herself to the service, though she could have gone to the funeral and the reception in the cast limo.

She had chosen not to, explaining that she might not want to stay long at the reception, and she'd really like to have her own car available.

She pulled up to her duplex. Her home was in a perfect location—close to Universal Studios, a hop on the I-5 to either Hollywood or to places up north. She wasn't far from Burbank and the airport there.

Also, she had just loved the home when she had first seen it. The yard was surrounded by a white picket fence. There were three gates—one at the walkway from the sidewalk, and one on each side for her and Bridget to bring their cars into their parking spaces. Really, for the location, her duplex had been an amazing deal.

The charm of the duplex was, in a way, odd. There were dozens of skyscrapers nearby, but her place looked like it might have come out of *Home and Garden* for the rural crowd. But it was that kind of a neighborhood—houses for the median-income crowd along with businesses and skyscrapers. She'd loved where she lived since she'd bought it, at the height of *Dark Harbor*'s popularity.

She kept the place whitewashed with green trim. It had been

built right when Art Nouveau had been giving way to Art Deco. There were window boxes and arches and all kinds of charming little details in the architecture.

Using her remote control, she opened her driveway gate and pulled her little Honda into place.

As she exited the car, Bridget came flying out from her front door.

"Marnie! You're back so early. Are you all right? I knew I should have gone with you. Oh, they weren't rude or mean or anything, were they?"

"No, I'm fine, really," Marnie said, and she really hoped that she was a good actress, good enough to pull off that kind of a lie to her cousin. "I just... I just needed to leave. To come home."

"I'll make tea. My side? Your side?"

"My side. I know it's just getting toward evening, but I'm thinking about to going to bed really early."

"Right after tea," Bridget said. "Oh, and food. You'll need food."

"I just left a reception," Marnie argued. "There was food."

"And I know you. You didn't eat any of it."

Marnie hadn't eaten. Neither had she had anything to drink.

Nope, not a drop of alcohol, and still she had seen and heard a dead woman.

"It's okay. Don't worry. I'm really not hungry," Marnie said. "Honestly."

"Yeah, but you have to eat something. This is terrible, tragic— but you have to go on living. If you're going to get that children's theater up and running on schedule, you're going to have to start functioning again. That real estate agent, Seth Smith, called. I told him that you were a bit preoccupied right now, and he's being understanding, but doing up a budget and taking care of all the details will take time—you have to start moving. He told me he has other offers. Of course, that could be a come-on, but..."

"I'll go see the accountant tomorrow," Marnie promised. She smiled at Bridget. Neither of them had siblings, but their dads were brothers and had become the proud parents of baby girls the same year. Marnie and Bridget were as close as siblings—maybe closer. They had never had to fight over anything since they'd grown up in different homes.

They weren't, however, much alike in appearance. Bridget had very wild red hair and soft amber eyes in contrast to Marnie's blue-green eyes and dark chestnut hair color.

At the moment, however, Bridget was sporting some swatches in aqua and pink—very in the now. So far, Marnie had chosen to retain her own hair color. Her future was still uncertain; she made a lot of her current income from commercials she'd garnered here or there, and she was afraid of doing anything a bit off—even if hair did fix easily—when needing that money was still a major part of life.

For Bridget, of course, it was different. She didn't act—in fact, she hated acting. She also hated crowds, which was one of the reasons Marnie had talked her out of attending the funeral. Bridget was a writer; she had a great job as full-time writer for several shows on the new Sci-tastic cable channel, an outlet that specialized in sci-fi and fantasy themes.

Bridget followed her cousin into her side of the duplex and headed straight for the kitchen. Marnie loved her kitchen. It was painted yellow, with herbs and flowers growing in the huge tiled bay window that overlooked the yard.

Marnie walked into the living room and crashed onto one of her rich chocolate leather sofas.

"How was the reception?" Bridget asked. "I can imagine it was a zoo. Everyone who hadn't had a second for Cara Barton in life probably was there—I mean, what self-respecting actor would miss out on an opportunity for exposure like that? There was a ton of press there, right?"

"Yep."

"A zoo, I'm sure. Hey, did the police get anywhere yet?"

"No. I think they were at the funeral, but they all kept their distance. They were watching, I'm certain. I actually saw Detective Manning and her partner, Detective Vining, at the wake yesterday. They were..."

"Watching?"

"Yes, I guess so."

"Well, someone killed Cara."

"Yes, but those closest to her obviously didn't do it. I mean, we were all there."

"Water is on. Look, you have some little meat pies in the freezer. I'll pop a few of those into the microwave. It's not gourmet and maybe not even really too healthful, but it's something."

"Sure," Marnie said, picking up one of the pillows on the sofa and holding it. She closed her eyes. Life was a nightmare. It was good to have Bridget in here, chattering away.

Someone had killed Cara. Why?

And why was she imagining that she saw Cara?

"Hey! Someone is here," Bridget called from the kitchen. "And... Whoa. Be still, my heart! This guy gives new meaning to tall, dark and handsome. Are you hiring a hero type for the theater? Or did you get some kind of an offer? Did your agent send this guy? I mean... Wow. Wicked-wow!"

Marnie didn't have to look out the window to see to know that Bryan McFadden had come to her house.

She groaned out loud, looking around her living room.

No. There was no dead woman there. Maybe it was him. Maybe he was somehow causing her to have some kind of a delusion.

"Don't let him in!" Marnie said.

"Don't let him in? Are you kidding? Who is he?"

"Bryan McFadden."

"And who is Bryan McFadden?"

"He's no one. His parents were actors. He thinks he's some kind of a cop or something. Just make him go away."

"Oh, Lord, I have done some things for you in my life, but make him go away? I'm not married, you know. I'm not engaged. I'm not even dating. And you want me to make this guy *go away*?"

"Yes. Do it, please."

"McFadden, McFadden… Oh, he looks like that old matinee star Hamish McFadden. Is he—"

"Yes. Make him go away. Please… Oh. Never mind!"

She'd make him go away herself.

Marnie leaped to her feet and flew to the front door, opening it.

He was a solid six foot four, and in the dark suit he'd chosen for the funeral, he was definitely impressive in his size and stature. He had a way of looking at her so directly that it was unnerving.

He was attractive; that was certain. Very. In a land of attractive people, he had something else, as well. Maybe it was that very steady way he had of looking at a person. Rock-solid. More. She felt as if Bridget could create one of her sci-fi ray guns based on his gaze: a green ray of light that drew her to him while she wanted to run away—or at least slam the door on him.

Yes, his very stature was imposing.

He probably knew it. Maybe he even used it to bully people.

She didn't let him speak.

"Mr. McFadden, I left the funeral reception to avoid you. I don't appreciate you coming to my house to hound me. You may be working with the police, but if you harass me, I will get a restraining order against you."

"You're going to need me, Miss Davante," he told her. He produced a card. "My cell number is there. Call me when you've figured out the fact that you can't do this alone."

"Oh, hello there!"

Bridget had come to stand behind her and was looking at him over Marnie's shoulder.

"Hello," he said pleasantly, lowering his head slightly to see her. "Bridget Davante, I presume. A pleasure to meet you. I watched *Deadly Venom and Bloody Claws* the other night. Very tongue-in-cheek. Absolutely ridiculous, but the writing was wonderful."

"Thanks! I was head on that project," Bridget said. "Would you like some tea?"

"Mr. McFadden was just leaving," Marnie snapped.

"Apparently, I'm leaving. But thank you," McFadden said. He turned his intent gaze back to Marnie. He spoke lightly, but there was something very serious about him. "Call me when you need me."

Not *if* you need me. But *when* you need me.

He had some ego.

"Sure," she said.

And she closed the door, leaving him standing there with the card in his hand.

She turned around and leaned against the door. Bridget stared at her.

"Are you crazy? If that man came to my door…"

"Don't you dare let him in if he comes to your side!" Marnie told her.

"Why?"

"He's—he's annoying!"

Bridget sighed softly, her hands on her hips. "Poor Marnie. I am so sorry for all you've been through. You need rest. I'm going to finish with the tea, get you to eat something and then leave you to get some sleep."

Bridget was wonderful. Marnie told herself just how lucky she was. Adoring parents, a cousin like Bridget and friends in film and theater who were truly wonderful, too.

Even the dead ones!

The thought came to her unbidden. She pushed it aside.

Damn McFadden!

If he hadn't fed into her fantasy, she'd be fine now. If he hadn't shown up at the funeral reception, she would have stayed. She would have talked about Cara with others. She'd be on her way to feeling normal.

Maybe...

Bridget was back in the kitchen.

Marnie walked through the living room, past the dining room and down the hall that led to the two bedrooms: hers and the one she kept for guests—mostly her mom and dad when they came to visit.

The guest room was quiet—with no attendant ghost.

Her room was equally empty.

She drew the curtains across the windows out to the back, overlooking the small kidney-shaped pool that was shared by the duplex.

The yard was empty.

She checked the back door while she was making her search; it was locked and bolted.

"Did you want to eat in the dining room?" Bridget called to her.

"No, the living room is fine, thanks!" she called back and hurried to join her cousin in the kitchen.

Bridget was taking the meat pies from the microwave.

"I'll pour tea," Marnie said.

When they were set, she carried out a tray while Bridget set up two little card tables for them. "Did you want to watch TV? Probably not the news..."

"It's okay. You can turn on the news. It happened, and it's all over. Cara is dead and buried now, and I have to get accustomed to the facts. Here, I'll turn it on."

A cable news show flashed onto the screen; the coverage was on the funeral.

Marnie saw herself and her fellow castmates.

She saw Malcom Dangerfield and Vince Carlton and David Neal and many others.

She saw Bryan McFadden in the background: tall, stoic, reserved...

She saw no sign of Cara Barton.

It must have all been her imagination; she had been under way too much pressure.

And at the funeral, that wretched man had fed into her guilt and fear and misery.

"I don't quite understand what you've got against the man," Bridget murmured. "I mean...tall, dark...gorgeous. Strong. Polite and courteous."

He is trying to convince me I'm seeing a walking corpse.

Marnie told her, "He's after something. That's all. Leave it be, Bridget, please?"

"Of course," her cousin said.

They watched more of the spectacle. The channel went on to show dozens of clips from Cara Barton's many performances.

Marnie was in many of the clips. Naturally, as Cara had been her TV mother.

Marnie realized that they had both finished eating long ago. She stood, picking up the paper plates their microwave meals had been on.

"I'm going to get some rest," she told her cousin. "I'm okay. Really."

Bridget stood up and stared at her, nodding. "You're not okay. But I will leave. Anyone who won't even talk to someone who wants to get to the bottom of this...and frankly, anyone who won't talk to *him*... You're just not really doing well at all. But try to rest. And make an appointment with a therapist. That is not just a Hollywood thing—people all over the country are living better lives because they see someone they can talk to."

"I promise I'll look into seeing someone. Even though I'm

not the one who writes scripts about alien vampires battling genetically altered South American lizard people, but hey—yep, I will seek help."

"Hey! *Dawn of the Lizard People* had a huge audience when it aired, not to mention that it did incredibly well in syndication."

"Personally, I loved it. Bridget, I'll be fine. I just need to… sleep." Marnie couldn't tell her that she needed to be alone— without seeing the dead woman who had been buried that day.

Bridget walked to her and gave her hug. "I'm only a phone call or a wall-knock away."

"Thank you. Really. Love you—but you can go," Marnie said.

Bridget left. Marnie followed her to the door, locked it and slid the bolts.

She turned and looked around the living room, and then let out a sigh of relief. There was no one there.

The news anchor had actually gone on to talk about the weather—LA would enjoy exceptional late spring–early summer weather: sunshine and balmy breezes, a beautiful temperature of 80°F during the daytime hours, dropping just down to 70°F by nightfall.

"Bed," she murmured aloud.

She would leave the TV on. The ambient noise would be good for her nerves.

She walked tall and straight, as if there were someone there to see her courage.

All the way back to her room. Once there, she shed her clothing, letting it lie in a heap, something she didn't do often. She found her favorite soft cotton Disney sleep T-shirt and slid into it, and went to brush her teeth. Moments later, she crawled into her bed.

The lights remained on in the living room, and while she had the drapes closed, there were floodlights over the backyard and pool area. It was enough so that she didn't feel plunged into darkness. She hated the dark—the true dark. She always had. There hadn't been any childhood trauma to bring on such a feeling. She simply hated the dark—the unknown, or so she had heard.

She lay down, aware that she was truly exhausted. She hadn't thought of anything but Cara since her friend had been murdered before her eyes. But she had been busy. That day, there had been the police, the shock, the grilling. Then there had been the arrangements—she and Roberta, Jeremy and Grayson getting together to do their best to do right by their friend. There had been the wake. And today, there had been the funeral and the reception. And now...

Now it was over. It was time to get on with life.

Something clinked on the ground out by the pool.

Marnie shot out of bed and stood there, shivering and listening.

Nothing.

She forced herself to walk to the drapes, to pull them back and to look out.

She waited, watching, not aware that she wasn't breathing until she suddenly and instinctively sucked in a lungful of air.

Run. Wait, don't run—where to run to? Just go pound on the wall, head over to Bridget's side of the duplex...

No. She gave herself a shake—mentally and physically. The police were working on the case. She was home, safe.

If she ran now—out of the house, even over to Bridget's—she would never have the courage again to just live, to be herself, to chart her own course in the world without fear.

There was nothing in the yard. She was still grappling with the idea that she had seen the specter of Cara Barton at the funeral, but her house and yard were ghost-free right now.

She let the drapes drop and lay back down. She stared over at the window.

And then she saw a shadow; it was definitely the silhouette of a person, someone walking across her yard.

She leaped out of bed. Her phone was in the front of the house, in her purse. She had to fly to it, call 9-1-1, get help...

She raced toward the living room.

As she fled her room, she heard the crash of glass as something slammed hard against the window.

CHAPTER FOUR

The man saw him. He was agile and quick, and was back over the little picket fence that surrounded the duplex property even as Bryan made a leap to reach him.

Bryan had noticed the man walking down the street, hands stuffed into the pockets of a dark hoodie—it was actually brown, not black. But that didn't matter. He'd held his head low—no way to recognize him.

He stood about six foot even and weighed maybe 180 pounds. Bryan took note and had watched him. Then he gave chase as soon as he'd seen the man slip over the fence into Marnie's backyard, breaking into a sprint when he heard the crash of shattering glass.

The guy was extremely nimble.

Stuntman, maybe?

Didn't matter during the chase. Bryan hopped back over the fence, tearing down the side street off Barham, heading up the hill where some of the houses were mansions and some of the yards offered too-good places to hide.

Yes, but there were alarms up that way, too.

Bryan could run—he'd kept at it since he'd left the military. Running was a good thing to be able to do well, especially when you knew that you wanted to be in the investigative or law enforcement fields.

This guy had to be Olympic quality. He was gaining distance.

Bryan's feet struck hard on the pavement; they were moving farther uphill.

He began to gain a little ground. And then, as he swung around a corner, he dropped just in the nick of time. A whoosh of air too close to Bryan followed a loud crack.

The man had fired at him.

He rose, drawing his own weapon, but in those few short seconds, he knew that he'd lost his quarry. Panting, he paused, hands on his knees, looking up at the street and the way it divided. No clue as to which way the man had gone. He slid his Glock back into the small holster at the back of his waistband. As a precaution, he'd applied for a special carry permit as a security contractor working temporarily in California. He hadn't been sure he'd need it, but now he was glad.

A car whizzed by him. He hadn't noticed vehicles at all until now, and Barham was a busy street. Down below, there were multistory apartment buildings, with restaurants and businesses scattered here and there. Farther up the hill, the houses became bigger. And more lavish.

Marnie Davante's house was right between. It was a charming little duplex, not a mansion—nor a multistoried dwelling where the rent was high for little more than broom closets.

He wondered where the hell the bullet fired at him had gone, and if, in the dark, he had a prayer of finding the bullet itself or the casing.

He paused, judging the distance from where the man had fired. He turned on the flashlight feature on his phone and searched the ground. The light glinted off the silver foil wrapper from a stick of gum first, but then it shimmered on something metal: the casing.

He wasn't walking around with evidence bags, but he pulled off his tie to secure the casing without touching it.

Fifteen minutes later, he still hadn't found the bullet.

He'd try again in daylight.

At last he headed back toward Marnie Davante's house and his car. He'd been sitting in it, parked just down the street ever since she'd told him to go away.

He hadn't been expecting a home invasion.

Rather, he'd hung around because he'd been certain that the ghost of Cara Barton was going to show up again, and whether she admitted it or not, Marnie was going to need his help coping with that.

Bryan was angry with himself.

He should have parked closer to the duplex.

He should have been on the guy sooner.

He pulled out his phone and dialed Grant Vining's cell phone.

Vining answered almost instantly and told him that a 9-1-1 call had come in. The uniformed cops who had been closest on call had in turn called and informed him about the near break-in at Marnie Davante's house. He was already on his way.

"You scared the guy off, huh—but didn't catch him."

"He took a shot at me. I lost him when he did."

"Pity. We could have maybe learned something. What do you think the chances are that it was just a run-of-the-mill home invasion and had nothing to do with Cara Barton's murder? Damn. It's really too bad you didn't get him."

Bryan heard Sophie Manning speak up next to her partner.

"Probably a nice thing he dodged the bullet, too," she said drily.

Bryan smiled and started jogging down the street.

"I didn't think he was armed. He didn't shoot until I started gaining on him. I don't know if the guy is the murderer, but he is armed and dangerous. After this, I think that Miss Davante is going to need some kind of protection."

"Miss Davante, Miss Alan… Highsmith and Adair. You know

that the city is struggling under budget cuts. I can have patrol cars doing drive-bys, but…they're celluloid people. They can hire on some private security. I take it you're on your way back? We'll see you at Miss Davante's house."

"Yep. I'm on my way."

Empty-handed.

But alive.

And now they knew for sure that a killer was out there, targeting Marnie. Whether she admitted it or not, she needed help.

And the ghost of a dead actress wasn't going to be enough.

"There's no reason, is there, to suspect that this was anything other than an attempted burglary, right? An attempt that wasn't very well-thought-out, at that," Marnie said. "Breaking glass means a ton of noise. Cell phones mean police can be somewhere within minutes."

Bridget, wrapped in a robe covered with cartoon superheroes, was at Marnie's side. They stood on the porch, the little expanse of tile and pillars that ran the width of the duplex and led to both front doors.

Detectives Vining and Manning were with them while three crime scene technicians worked in the backyard, and one scanned Marnie's bedroom amid the broken glass.

Vining stared at Marnie, thinking out his answer.

Manning gave her no such courtesy. "How the hell long do you think it takes to shoot someone, Miss Davante? Perp gets in here, *pop-pop*, and then he's gone. Before you can do so much as dial 9-1-1."

A shiver snaked down her spine.

"Oh, God," Bridget cried softly. "So what do we do?"

"Detective Manning," Vining said firmly. "There is no reason to assume that the only reason someone was here was specifically to harm Miss Davante. Sadly, this city is not without crime—ordinary crime, if such a description can be made of crime, period. Break-ins do happen."

Marnie couldn't help it. She looked at Sophie Manning. "You've drawn a possible scenario, Detective. But as Detective Vining just said, the man might have been a burglar."

"One with a gun," Vining qualified.

"You know he had a gun?" Bridget demanded.

Just as Bridget spoke, Marnie saw that a man was running down Barham, coming their way.

McFadden. He managed to run in a suit without looking ridiculous. For some reason that made Marnie resent him just a little bit more.

Apparently he had been there. Somewhere near, watching over her. He had gone after the man trying to break in—and *he* knew the man had been carrying a gun.

She looked away from him and stared at Sophie Manning. "So what do you suggest? What do you propose I do? What are you planning to do for my safety? Can you leave a patrol car here—or a cop, one who is more than welcome inside. I love coffee and I have tons and tons of it."

"And tea," Bridget offered. "She loves tea, too. But, Marnie, your bedroom is all…glass. You'll have to stay at my place."

The detectives weren't giving her their full attention anymore. They were watching as Bryan McFadden came jogging up—leaping over the little white picket fence—to join them.

He had something wrapped up in his hand, which he offered to Detective Vining.

"Bullet casing—haven't found where the bullet itself lodged. I'll get on it in the morning," McFadden told the cop.

"Oh." Bridget clutched tightly to Marnie, looking as if she was about to have the vapors or pass out or do something very melodramatic—but real.

"Hey!" Marnie caught her cousin, but Bryan McFadden had already reached out. Bridget looked at him with adoring eyes.

"I'm—I'm all right!" she said. She found her feet and her own strength.

"I'll stay here tonight," Manning said. "In the living room."

"Detective," Vining began sternly.

"Just for tonight. Maybe Miss Davante will need to stay somewhere else for a while, as we search for Cara Barton's killer. Maybe…"

"Sophie," Vining said firmly. "You can't."

He stopped speaking, looking at Marnie. "We can keep a patrol car out here for a few days. We'll investigate the situation fully."

"Yes," Manning said. "We'll investigate, but what if Mr. McFadden hadn't taken it on himself to look after Miss Davante? He was on the would-be home invader in a matter of moments."

"Sophie," Vining said, and his tone was a little sharp. And Marnie understood, of course.

Police funds were limited. She couldn't expect full-time protection services from them.

"It's fine. I'll stay out in the car," McFadden said. He shrugged. "I won't cost the taxpayers a thing."

"You are not staying outside!" Bridget insisted. "Marnie is moving over into my side of the property, and you may have the couch, Bryan. Is it all right if I call you Bryan?"

"Of course," McFadden said.

Manning was looking at him. "I can and will stay tonight. I'm off duty, and I don't intend to put in overtime. After tonight, you can do whatever you need so that you can come on guard duty full-time."

"Yes," Marnie said. "I mean, no… I mean, I don't think I need anyone twenty-four hours a day. I have things to do, people with whom I must meet…"

"That would make staying alive a good thing, wouldn't it?" McFadden asked her. He turned to Manning. "Thank you for helping out," he said.

"I'll get crime scene people working on locating that bullet," Vining told McFadden. "You'll have to let the techs know where you were. If you'd like to see the crime scene at the convention hall, meet me tomorrow morning?"

McFadden nodded.

He looked at Marnie, his eyes seeming to catch hers as strange beats of time went by.

"Good night, Miss Davante. And, Miss Davante," he said, smiling as he looked at Bridget, "I'll see you in the morning."

Then McFadden turned and walked back toward his car.

"Well, it wasn't late, but now it is. We probably should try to get some sleep," Bridget said.

Marnie knew that she needed sleep. She had an appointment in the afternoon with a Mr. Seth Smith of the Wexler Realty Group to find out if she was going to be able to rent the old Abernathy Theater in Burbank. It was old, it was beautiful and it was right off I-5. That made it easy to reach. It also had parking; if she could offer free parking, that would be an incredible boon. And, personally—even though on the old *Tonight Show* Johnny Carson had made fun of it—she loved Burbank. It had families and homes and still had some shops and boutiques that were family or individually owned. It had Dark Delicacies, one of the best bookshops ever.

Yes, sleep would be good. And he was gone—Bryan McFadden, who had somehow managed to tip her whole world, entered her bloodstream, encourage delusion and...*possibly saved her life!*

It suddenly hit her that she was so very vulnerable. It felt wrong.

"Okay," she said, squaring her shoulders. "Detective Manning, thank you so much. I admit to being very frightened this evening. We don't know if we did just have a run-of-the-mill home invasion, but run-of-the-mill or not—he might have killed me. I am alive. We can move over to Bridget's for tonight, and in the morning get the glass fixed and an alarm system installed. So..."

"Let's head on in," the detective said.

It felt a bit ludicrous that Sophie was the brave cop and Marnie was the frightened victim; Sophie was about five foot four and Marnie towered over her by almost six inches. But one look at Sophie Manning, and—while she was extremely attractive—it was evident that she was confident, fit and ready to face whatever came her way.

Detective Vining waved them off. "I'll be here until the crime scene people finish up. You've signed the incident report... Go get some sleep. Manning, I don't want to see you until at least noon tomorrow, do you understand?"

"Yes, sir," Manning said.

When they were inside, Bridget said, "Tea? Yes, tea. It's always good. Maybe wine would be better. Or, what the hell, a shot of whiskey!"

Sophie laughed. "I'll stick with tea. In fact, coffee might be best for me."

Bridget's half of the duplex was the same as Marnie's, except that it was reversed. As Bridget brewed a pot of tea, Sophie and Marnie sat at the barstools. The detective told them she'd always wanted to be a cop—her dad had been on the force. She'd lost him recently to cancer, but he had seen her go through the police academy and he'd seen her rise to rank of detective.

Marnie and Bridget explained how they had both been only children, cousins just about the exact same age.

While Bridget talked away about how she'd always created stories and then asked Marnie to act them out with invisible costars, Marnie found herself zoning out a bit and looking around.

She should have been terrified an armed assailant was going to try to break in again.

But she was more afraid, she realized, that she'd see the ghost of Cara Barton.

She did not.

Sophie asked her curiously about her plans for the future.

Marnie returned her attention to Sophie and Bridget and smiled. "Well, I'd been feeling pressured to do a revamp of *Dark Harbor*. Vince Carlton really seemed to want to make it happen, and he had the right people in place, but...well, I would only have done it because it meant so much to the rest of the cast. I've been saving for years to open my own theater for kids. I mean, some kids, the ones with aggressive stage moms, have a chance at getting into the movies. I want a venue for the kids who need a different kind of opportunity—right here, in Hollywood. Don't get me wrong. There's nothing wrong with film— but my dream is for kids like Bridget and me. Those who want to grow up to do things other than be movie stars. To write, to design, to become fabricators and create fairies and monsters..."

She broke off, shrugging.

"Anyway, that's my plan. I'm seeing a man tomorrow about renting the space I want. And from there..."

"No more *Dark Harbor*," Sophie said, sighing. "Have to admit— I loved the show!"

"Thanks. Hopefully, it will remain a classic. And, hopefully, we will all—the remaining cast members—continue to survive on syndication!"

She rose from her barstool. "Okay, I'm really going to try to sleep."

"I'll be here on the sofa. One scream will bring me running. And I am a crack shot," Sophie promised her.

Marnie went to the guest room and crawled beneath the covers.

Two hours later, she realized she wasn't going to sleep.

She lay there through the night, staring at the ceiling.

Waiting for the sound of breaking glass...

Waiting...

For a dead woman to appear before her.

Bryan had checked into a boutique hotel just down the hill from Marnie Davante's duplex.

If he was going to manage to find a killer and keep Marnie alive, he was going to have to stay at the top of his game. That meant sleep. But he knew, as he returned to his room and pulled out his computer, it also meant he'd need some help.

For a moment, he drummed his fingers on the laptop. He was pretty good at research, but as far as trying to determine who—in a Hollywood sea of fans, directors, writers, actors, producers and others—might have wanted Cara Barton dead, or if Cara had even been the intended victim, he wasn't even sure where to begin.

He sat for a minute, mentally recalling all the videos he had seen of the crime actually taking place in real time. The whole thing had appeared to be an on-the-spot and accidental performance, but unlike any other spontaneous shows that popped up here and there at a comic con. Especially in Hollywood, where you had not just fans cosplaying, but professional actors and hopeful actors in costume everywhere.

The police had interviewed dozens of people who had been wearing a Blood-bone costume.

Even though it had been possible to rule some out based on observations and enhancement of some of the videos gathered at the scene, including determining which costume manufacturer had sold the one worn by the killer, they were still left with twenty-six Blood-bones who had been questioned more thoroughly.

Not one had had a drop of blood on them. Not one had appeared to have been sweaty or shown signs of recent physical exertion. Most likely, the Blood-bone who had committed the deed had been long gone while confusion reigned—before anyone realized that a murder had actually been committed.

"This isn't just finding a needle in a haystack," he murmured to himself. "It's like finding a needle in a stack of needles."

There was a light tap at his door. He frowned, wondering if one of the detectives wanted to speak with him that night. He rose, one hand drifting almost subconsciously to the holster at his back, and carefully looked out the peephole.

He felt his tension ease and opened the door.

It was Cara Barton.

"You didn't just come in?" he asked her.

"I'd never be so rude, darling! You're a handsome, able-bodied man in his prime and...well, who knows what you might be doing," she said with a wink.

"I'm here to solve your murder."

"You're still a young and virile man and... Oh, I could say more, but you are the child of my dear, dear friends, so I won't. Suffice it to say that I was—whatever my other faults—courteous in life, and therefore, my darling boy, I shall continue to be so in death."

"How nice. Do come all the way in."

Cara glided past him. She didn't actually walk—but then, she never had. She was a diva in the old Hollywood sense of the word. Not mean in any way—simply above it all, and everyone else she encountered, as well. "So, what can you tell me?" he asked her. She perched elegantly at the end of the bureau that held the wide-screen TV.

She sighed dramatically. "I don't know... I just keep thinking he might have been after Marnie. She was laughing and plunged right into an improv." She was silent for a minute. "You know, I love that girl. When others were not so kind, Marnie always was. It's so odd, because, in a way, I must admit I was jealous, as well." She waved a hand in the air. "Not because she was young and I was...older. But everything about her is so natural. And most of us want to be the ones with our names in giant lights. Marnie just loves literature and theater and the art behind it all. I mean, it's almost nauseating!"

He lowered his head. He agreed that Marnie had a charming authenticity to her, but he didn't find it nauseating. Every time he came close to Marnie Davante, he felt more determined to save her life.

Whether she wanted saving by him or not.

"So, one theory. The killer was actually after Marnie."

"One theory..." Cara murmured. "What could be another? Oh, that people hate me. Yes, I'm afraid that's possible. But...they don't hate me in the way you'd hate someone and then want to kill them. I mean, honestly—good God, I hate to say it—I don't think killing me, to anyone, would be worth the prospect of a life sentence. But... I am dead. You start with theories, right? More or less. So...why? Why am I dead?" she whispered miserably.

"I'm so sorry," Bryan said softly, and he was. Seeing her sitting forlornly in his room, her grand diva presence dropped for the moment, he was truly sorry.

"Another possible theory—a random killing," Bryan continued. "Maybe whoever this was just wanted to kill someone and make a massive statement. Perhaps an unhappy actor, one of those people who do need to see their names up in bright lights."

"They wanted me dead, they wanted Marnie dead, or it was random," Cara murmured. "It wasn't a sudden murder—not a killing out of passion or anger. Whoever did this—for whatever reason they did it—they thought it out. Blood-bone is one of the hottest comic characters at the moment, even if he is a villain. Bad guys can be very popular, though, the best, I think, is a character like Marvel's Deadpool—a good guy who can act badly when he needs to! Oh, I'm digressing... It has to be Marnie. Someone tried to break into her house tonight, and on her side of the duplex. I mean, who would want to kill the writer? Wait—let me go back on that. There have been dozens of times when I thought the writer ought to be smacked in the head if not shot! But once again..."

"The break-in could have been random," Bryan said.

"But you don't believe that for a minute, do you?"

"No."

"But you've left her there alone."

"I've left her alone with a very capable police officer."

"You don't even know her."

"She's capable and trustworthy."

"How do you know?"

"I just know! Damn it, Cara—"

"Oh, dear!" she exclaimed suddenly, and he realized she was fading. He sank down at the foot of his bed and watched her; he'd seen the phenomenon before—it wasn't always easy for spirits, especially new ones, to stay in the world.

In all, he'd had a fair amount of exposure to the souls of the departed. However they did it—be it through the power of the mind and the vast portion of the human brain never normally used, or by some other method, scientific or spiritual, yet to be discovered—learning to maintain a physical image was not something that just came with the territory of being dead; making themselves known to the living took practice.

As to his parents, Bryan figured they felt they needed to stick around and look after their boys.

Once Maeve and Hamish had realized the determination in their sons, and it became clear the boys all had the bizarre talent of seeing the dead, they hadn't hesitated to use those talents to help their friends.

There was usually a strong reason for a soul to stick around. Often, there was some little thing, and then the dead moved on. Sometimes it was just confusion.

One time, it had been an elderly friend who had been helped to death by a nephew. Bryan, with Bruce as backup, had convinced the nephew to confess.

"But I'm really good at this!" Cara protested as she faded. "I can knock on doors!"

With that protest, she was gone.

Bryan got ready for bed and lay down to sleep. The next days would be long ones.

But he couldn't stop thinking about the theories. Yes, you had to look for motive, or even lack of a particular motive, such as in a random killing, to find a killer.

Everyone apparently loved Marnie Davante.

Everyone apparently did not love Marnie Davante.

The comic con had offered an amazing stage for a dramatic murder.

Facts and images filtered through Bryan's mind. He didn't fight it; sleeping on a problem often helped.

In the realm of sleep somewhere, something else in his mind kicked in.

He was walking through a graveyard. With Marnie. It was Hollywood Forever, where so many of the beloved stars lay. The owners tried to make the beautiful cemetery relevant to the living as well, showing movies on the mausoleum walls, hosting music events and more.

There was a band playing in the cemetery in his dream. As he looked at Marnie, he felt a sharp stab in his heart as he feared she might be dead.

But she wasn't. She was flesh and blood, alive, beautiful, looking up at him with amazing trust in her eyes.

"I'm so sorry—fear does it, you know."

"Fear of the dead?" he asked her softly. "They will not hurt you."

She smiled ruefully. "Fear of you."

"Of me?"

She didn't answer him; she looked ahead and told him, "There. One of my favorite graves here. The statuary really means something—it's Johnny Ramone and his guitar." Then she paused and looked at him. "But we're really here for Cara!" she said.

"Cara," he agreed.

"It was supposed to be me," she whispered.

He woke up; his alarm was going off, and a brilliant sun was shining through a slit in the drapes.

It was time to find the truth behind the theory.

CHAPTER FIVE

Marnie was not sure if she had drifted off for a while or if she had actually slept. She must have done so; she had a dull, throbbing headache, but the night had been all but torture.

She threw off the covers of the guest room bed and slid her legs out, yawning as she came to a sitting position, her feet on the floor.

It was good that her feet were on the ground.

Cara was back.

She was seated in a wingback chair beside the dresser.

"I thought you were going to sleep all day," Cara told her.

Marnie covered her face with her hands.

She almost screamed aloud. She held it in.

It wouldn't help, she knew.

Instead, she spoke softly. "You're not here. Oh, dear God. You are not here. You are not here!"

"Marnie. Please, I'm so sorry. I am here, but you mustn't be upset. I don't want to hurt you. You are probably the best person I ever knew. I mean, actually, really kind. Some people are fair-weather friends. Not you. Some people only want to use you—and they're terrified of being used by you. But, Marnie, you're just the best. I don't want to torture you. Though, in truth, this ghost business is not so bad. I do intend to become very, very good at it. It's not so easy. If you can just accept that this is really a cool thing, all will be well."

Marnie swallowed. She could hear Cara as clearly as if she were there—in the flesh. Her voice was just a little bit raspy; a little bit like the wind.

"I need a therapist," she murmured.

"You don't already see a therapist? This is Hollywood—everyone in Hollywood sees a therapist."

"Technically, this is just Los Angeles," Marnie said.

What an idiotic argument. Almost everyone out here did see a therapist, that was true. And she clearly needed to talk to someone about what was happening to her. What would she tell them? That she spoke with a dead friend?

"The thing is, Marnie, you are in danger!" Cara said.

There was a knock at the door. Bridget's concerned voice came through. "Are you all right?"

"Fine, thank you."

Marnie stood and walked over to the bedroom door. Her cousin stood there looking at her, anxiety clear in her eyes. Detective Manning stood just behind Bridget.

True to her word, she had stood guard through the night.

"Hey, I really didn't want to disturb you, but it is getting late. And there's a guy here. He said that you had an appointment. Don't worry—I didn't go talk to him, Sophie did. I'm still a wee bit shaky after last night."

"It's David Neal," Sophie said. "I know him because Detective Vining interviewed him the day of Cara's murder at the comic con. He said he was coming to see you about a stage manager's job. I told him it had turned out to be a very tough set of days for you, and he was immediately apologetic. But none of us know your schedule, if you do need to see him."

Marnie had to lock down her rental space before she could

make any promises, but getting a good stage manager had been at the top of her list.

"Oh, see the poor boy," Cara said.

"When I'm ready!" she snapped.

Both Bridget and Detective Manning looked shocked by her sudden rudeness.

She pursed her lips, looking downward.

"I'm so sorry," she said. "Tell him two minutes for me, if you will please. Again, forgive me. I'll just shower quickly—I can do that, you know I can, Bridget—and I'll be right out."

"I'll let him in and chat with him in the living room. He was there, after all—almost within touching distance—when Cara was killed," Sophie said. "That's what he said, and what I learned from other eyewitnesses."

Marnie frowned. "Which means he couldn't have killed her."

"Physically, no," Sophie said, turning away.

"There's coffee on, when you're ready," Bridget told her.

The door closed. Marnie turned to stare at Cara.

"Oh, dear!" Cara said before Marnie could berate her.

And then she was gone.

Marnie sank back to the bed, shaking. She inhaled deeply. Had she just imagined Cara Barton?

But Bryan McFadden had seen her, too. He had taken it in stride that Cara Barton had attended her own funeral.

Here was the thing: it was traumatic, but her friend was dead. Gone. And she did have to move on. Before the comic con, she'd been so excited that she'd actually saved up the money to open her own theater, to become a producer of children's theater.

So she would do the Hollywood thing.

She would get a therapist and deal with whatever was happening to her.

With that in mind, she marched into the shower. She made the water hot, washed quickly, emerged and vigorously dried off.

And then she remembered that she wasn't really in her own

home—her property, but Bridget's half of the duplex—and she was standing there in a towel.

But she needn't have worried. Bridget had apparently run over to Marnie's side of the duplex, grabbed some clothes and had laid out jeans and a tailored cotton shirt along with clean underthings and socks—though, she realized, they had both forgotten about shoes.

That was fine.

She dressed hurriedly and headed out to the living room. Bridget, Sophie and David Neal were sipping coffee and, to her surprise, talking about local plays rather than the murder.

Seeing her enter the living room, David Neal leaped to his feet. He smiled at her uncertainly. She liked his manner. He was here—that meant he was determined. He was uncomfortable, which meant he had feelings for the fact that she had just buried a friend.

"Miss Davante," he said. "Forgive me. I didn't know if you remembered you were going to meet with me."

"To be honest, and forgive me, I knew we were meeting, but I had forgotten when. I still have to find out about my venue, so all is really moot until that is sorted, but…assuming all goes well, I'm glad to meet with you face-to-face."

He was a good-looking young man, somewhat thin—or maybe just not old enough yet to be really filled out. Dirty blond hair a little long but neatly brushed off his forehead. He might be just what she was looking for—someone with enough experience to corral children, but not so much that he wanted to tell her what to do in her own theater.

"I sent in my résumé—"

"Of course. I have it. I've read it. Please, sit down again," she said.

"Thank you," David Neal said and sat.

Bridget leaped up. "I'll get you coffee," she told Marnie.

"I'll just sit here and listen," Sophie Manning said. "If that's all right."

"Of course," Marnie assured her, casting her what she hoped was a grateful glance.

She forced herself to remember the résumé David Neal had sent her. It wasn't that hard; she hadn't received many applications from people who had much more experience than from a theater magnet school or university of the arts. That was fine. She wanted to give young people a break—and she would eventually hire an assistant for her head stage manager.

Bridget brought coffee.

She listened as David described some of his work; he was most effusive when talking about the work he'd done with the Gallaudet Theatre for the deaf. She glanced at Bridget and Sophie as he spoke; they both seemed to like him. She thought she did, too.

She was sipping her coffee when Cara suddenly made an appearance again—or at least spoke up again.

Her voice came from right behind Marnie, almost at her ear, causing her to jump, dribble coffee and nearly pitch her mug.

"Oh, please. Ad nauseam!" Cara said. "Gag, gag. Too good to be true."

Marnie couldn't help but look around at the others in the room—surely they saw Cara or heard her.

They did not.

Marnie stood, smiling stiffly, trying not to show the way her coffee was swishing about in her cup as her hand shook.

"David, it's been a pleasure. I have a ways to go, as you're aware. I have an appointment about the space this afternoon, and after that... Well, give me a few weeks."

"Of course, of course, and I'm sorry for... I'm so sorry. And thank you," he said, standing, as well. He thanked Bridget for the coffee and Sophie for her help, and then he thanked Marnie again and left, heading out of the duplex. Bridget was on his tail to see him out and lock the door once he was gone.

Sophie looked at Marnie curiously. "Is something wrong?" she asked.

Marnie gave her a weak smile. "No, nothing."

"A patrol car went by as I saw David out," Bridget said, joining them again. "The officer waved at me. They're watching over us."

"We're true to our word," Sophie said. She glanced at her watch. "I have several hours left. It's just nine, and Grant doesn't want to see me until noon. They are investigating what happened last night. But...frankly, you need an alarm. Or a dog, at the least. A big one."

"An alarm, cool," Bridget said. "A big dog—cooler! What do you say? A big, big dog?" she asked Marnie hopefully. "The property is really Marnie's. Writers do okay—Marnie does better, even after all these years with *Dark Harbor* just in syndication."

Marnie flushed. She was grateful to *Dark Harbor*. She just hoped that the role wasn't going to prove to be the entire essence of her existence.

"I always thought it would be cruel of me to have a dog," she said. "I'm gone too often."

"But I'm not! A dog—we'll get a dog! I will hug it and pet it and squeeze it!" Bridget said, grinning.

"And walk it and feed it?" Marnie asked her.

"Yes, duh, of course. But mainly pet and hug. A dog—perfect!" she said.

"Really?" Sophie asked, looking over at Marnie.

"We both love dogs. I just know I travel too much to be a good pet parent," she said.

Sophie produced a card. "This is my friend Jack. He works with police dogs who were injured or retired. He's got some great guys you might want to take a look at."

"Awesome," Bridget said, taking the card. "You go get a theater today. I'll go get a dog!"

"Okay," Marnie said. "We need to get someone in here, too. The glass in the back, in my room, is shattered all over the place."

"I'm on it," Bridget told her. "I've already called a window installer. They'll be here before Sophie has to leave."

"Sophie has a life, you know," Marnie said to Bridget.

"Not much of one, I'm afraid," Sophie said. "I'm happy to be here this morning. But you're right. My gun and I can't be here at all times. Get the glass fixed. Get the dog. And find out about an alarm system. You need the works. It might even be a good idea—if you can—to stay somewhere else for a while."

"But we'll have a dog," Bridget said happily.

"We can't run forever, and we can't be afraid forever," Marnie said.

"You need to be afraid right now!" Cara's ghost snapped suddenly.

She startled Marnie, who swung around at the sound of her voice.

Cara was now seated in the chair David Neal had recently vacated.

"Marnie, are you sure you're okay?" Bridget asked her anxiously.

"I'm fine, just fine," Marnie said. "A dog will be great. I can't wait!"

Bryan looked at the blood on the convention hall floor.

He had seen the recordings. He'd seen everything that the police had managed to get from a public that went a little crazy over cell phone videos and photos.

The problem was it was impossible to tell where the Bloodbone character had come from. Had the killer walked the floor all day long? And how the hell had he—or she—gotten out with a sword that was dripping blood? As of yet, they hadn't found the murder weapon.

The crime scene tape was going to be coming down soon; the techs had been over the place. The management of the convention hall had been completely helpful, according to Detective Grant Vining, but it was time for life to move on. They could only put things on hold for so long when money was involved.

Setup for the next convention wouldn't be until the end of the week, so it was easy enough for Vining to take Bryan to the hall and show him exactly where the murder had taken place.

"It's just about impossible to place the killer," Vining told him. "You can see the size of the hall. It was brimming with people. And these shows…they're bigger than some of the events that offer A-list actors. People love to dress up and cosplay comic and graphic characters. The Blood-bone character is relatively new. He was created first, as you can imagine, as a comic character. Now there's a TV series with him in it. Go figure. *Wolfson.* It's always hard to figure what will become the rage. Blood-bone is the villain. A character named Lars Wolfson is the hero—yeah, you got it, something genetic turns him into a superhero wolf. Kids love Lars Wolfson, too—he wears a really great costume when he's a wolf. Anyway, it's all set in a futuristic world—supposedly a realistic future world, just one that suggests what we might become in another few hundred years. Genetic splicing and all that. Thing is, the villains become just as big as the heroes in these things—just as popular, and sometimes more popular."

"You a fan of the comics?" Bryan asked him.

Vining winced. "I have sons and grandsons," he said.

"That's okay—I love a lot of comics myself."

"Your folks ever play comic characters?" Vining asked him.

Bryan grinned. "Yep. My mom played an Egyptian goddess, thousands of years old, who could come back to defend her descendants. It wasn't bad—but honestly, my mother and father were theater hounds, more than film."

The detective studied him. "And they died onstage—together."

"Ironic, huh? Anyway…"

"Anyway, the cleanup crew hasn't been in yet," Vining said. "The crime scene folks spent about thirty hours here, things have been shifted around… But the *Dark Harbor* cast was right there—right at that table—and Cara's blood is still visible. You're just in time. Funeral yesterday, and the cleanup—specialty, hazardous material, blood and bio matter, you know—due in later this morning."

Bryan nodded. He knew the detective was studying him.

Determining if Bryan was really worthy of working the case along with him and Manning. Bryan liked the man; he was more than willing to accept help. He just wanted to check out that help.

Bryan reimagined the killing. In his mind's eye, he saw the various tables. He could hear the German shepherd whining and picture the aging Western star.

And Blood-bone.

Performing, drawing a crowd. Delighting all those around him with the impromptu—and free—performance.

And then… Cara playing into it. Marnie there. The others…

And the sword, appearing to be nothing more than plastic and light, but oh, so much more!

The attack had been brutal and vicious; slash after slash had ripped the actress to shreds, tearing through her shoulder, slicing into her throat.

The blood remained, dried and caked now.

"What did the medical examiner say about the blade?" Bryan asked.

"Steel—fine steel, extremely sharp, a blade well honed," Vining said.

"And the weapon was never found?"

"Despite many, many Blood-bones gathered up. And, of course, that's just it."

"What's just it?" Bryan asked.

"If we had found the right Blood-bone… Well, you can just imagine. See the scene before you? The killer should have been covered in blood. We interviewed no such Blood-bone."

"And nowhere here, in the convention hall, did anyone find discarded clothing…drips of blood, anything?"

"It's as if he vanished into thin air," Vining said, shaking his head. "Now, consider that it was a sword and held from the body at a distance…" He paused, reflective. "Nope. Killer must have had blood on him. But in the midst of the melee, the screaming, the crowd… Other than Marnie and the rest of the *Dark Harbor* cast realizing that it wasn't any kind of a performance, the killer walked out. He just walked out. People didn't know. They didn't get it. In fact, from what I understand…"

"What?"

Vining shrugged. "They applauded," he said softly. "They applauded—and marveled at the incredible special effects."

Sophie Manning was going to have to go to work. Still, she didn't seem pleased about it.

"The thing is… I think it's dangerous for you to go out today. Until we know more about what's going on. I mean, you do want to live, right?" she asked Marnie.

"Of course," Marnie said. *Preferably without being tormented by a ghost!* "Yes, of course. But I'm also afraid of becoming paranoid. I don't want to be afraid to walk the streets. I mean, what if you never discover what happened, who killed Cara and who tried to break in here? We could wind up being…two agoraphobic old ladies!"

Sophie smiled.

"Hmph. Speak for yourself," Bridget said.

"I just don't want to give in to all this—give in to fear and paranoia when I might not even be in any danger."

"Then again," Sophie said, "think about the way Cara Barton died."

That was sobering.

But Marnie didn't have to reply. There was a knock on the door.

Even Sophie jumped, reaching for her gun.

They were on Bridget's side of the duplex. Was someone, just maybe, after Bridget? Who knew Marnie was on this side of the duplex? Other than the cops and…the killer. Or would-be home invader.

"Hello! It's all right, it's me!"

A voice, deep, rich and masculine cut through the sudden fear that instilled itself in Marnie.

"Sorry—me, as in Bryan McFadden."

"I don't really think that a killer-slash-home-invader is going to knock," Marnie said. She tried to smile. "And, obviously not, since it's McFadden."

She walked to the door, looking back at Bridget and Sophie wryly, and opened the door.

At the moment she was even glad to see Bryan McFadden.

The man who also saw ghosts.

The man was dressed in a suit again. It fitted him perfectly, but then he did have the kind of physique that allowed for a suit to fit perfectly. His shirt was simply blue, the tie a darker shade. But the cut of his clothing really was exceptional. Subdued but tailor-made, Marnie thought.

Did that make her like him more or less?

Neither, she realized—it was totally neither here nor there. But she wondered if she was wary of him because of his very… being. It wasn't that he was so good-looking. Her world and realm of work offered an endless stream of good-looking men.

It was that he was solid. Real. Even the low-key scent of his soap or aftershave seemed rugged, clean and masculine.

"Good morning. Do come in."

He obviously heard the sarcasm in her voice. She thought that the look he gave her was rather a superior one, as if he were dealing with a spoiled child.

She winced. Maybe she was acting like one.

But her friend had been murdered and was now walking around and talking to her and then disappearing and then reappearing...

And no one else saw or heard. Except for this man.

"I came by to check on everyone. Detective Manning, is—"

"Everything is fine," Sophie said, "But I do have to leave. I'm trying to talk some sense into Marnie. She shouldn't go out. Not now. She might well be a target."

McFadden looked at Marnie. "Your life is worth whatever it is you think you need to do?" he asked. He made it sound as if he thought she was truly foolish.

"You don't understand. And while Sophie has been great, she doesn't understand either. This could go on forever. We won't be able to exist if you don't find anything, and days and then weeks go by. We—we've established the fact we're going to buy a dog."

"A dog?"

"A big one!"

He lowered his face, and Marnie actually thought he was grinning.

"I think a dog is good idea," Sophie offered.

"I love the idea!" Bridget said.

"There's nothing wrong with a dog. But you can't count on it to protect you. And that doesn't really solve the problem of you going out today." He paused and turned to the door to look out. Marnie hadn't heard a thing.

"It's a...glass company," he said.

"Oh, wonderful," Bridget said. "They're here to fix the back window. I'll handle it."

"You need to wait just a moment," McFadden said.

He went out. The three women walked to the windows.

He was demanding ID from every one of the three workers who had arrived.

Then he made a quick phone call and then finally hung up and nodded to the men. He returned to the house, telling Bridget that the men could come in and work.

There were a few minutes of craziness as Bridget went out and the workers unloaded their stuff, and then Marnie went out—followed closely by McFadden.

"What the hell are you doing?" he demanded.

"It's my bedroom—and I own the place!" Marnie said.

Bridget was already talking to the workers; she'd just come out to listen. An older man, the head of the crew, told her that they'd replace broken glass, but the cleanup was their responsibility. Bridget assured him that was fine—they just needed the glass replaced.

The workers headed into Marnie's side of the duplex.

Marnie, McFadden and Bridget all returned to Bridget's living room.

"Everything all right?" Sophie asked. She smiled ruefully. "I almost followed you all out. Like a comedy of errors. Thought that might be overkill."

"Everything is fine," McFadden said.

Sophie told him, "Good. I need to report to work."

"Yes, I know. You were great, really kind, staying with these ladies. I'm very grateful," he said.

He was grateful? And very, very annoying. It was her place to talk! Marnie thought.

Stiffly, she voiced her own appreciation to Sophie, with Bridget chiming in.

"It's fine. Felt good to help," Sophie assured them.

"Here," McFadden said, offering her a bundled handkerchief. "I found the bullet that was fired at me last night. It had lodged in a tree branch. Maybe ballistics can figure out something."

"I'll get it where it needs to be right away," Sophie said. She looked back at Marnie and smiled grimly. "I know this is hard to fathom and very hard to accept."

"But someone may want to kill you," McFadden said quietly.

Marnie nodded. "I understand. However, in broad daylight? The streets of the city are not part of a comic con. I have an important meeting. It's about the entire rest of my life, which—don't say it—I know! May not exist if I'm not careful. Still..."

"I'll take you," McFadden said.

"Perfect," Sophie said. "I can go to work. You can take Bridget by my friend's place to pick up a dog and then take Marnie to her meeting."

"I, uh, imagine you have other things to do," Marnie said, looking at McFadden.

He shook his head. "No, not at this moment. I'll be happy to oblige."

"But we'll be picking Bridget up with a dog. I mean, this is complex. We can't just leave with workers here, and, at the same time, we can't go and come back for Bridget and then go get the dog—"

"Why not?" Bridget asked. "I hardly think anyone is after me."

"Frankly, we don't know that," Marnie argued. "And McFadden may not want a dog in his car—"

"The car is a rental," he said.

"Perfect," Sophie repeated. "It's a plan. Good afternoon, all. I will be in touch, and if anything happens, please call on me or Detective Vining at any time."

She slipped out the front door.

Marnie stared at Bryan. She wanted to know if he saw Cara all the time—or just sometimes.

She wanted to know why he seemed to so easily accept the fact that he was talking to a dead woman.

She wanted him...out and away, taking the ghost of Cara Barton with him.

But at the moment, she needed him.

"You really don't mind?"

"Miss Davante, at this time, I am entirely at your disposal. I will look after you to the very best of my ability, up to and including the act of jumping in front of a bullet—unless you behave so stupidly that I have no choice but to let you go."

She'd just begun to almost like him or, at the least, be grateful.

"I do not behave stupidly—" she began.

"Oh, that's wonderful! Too wonderful for words. Thank you, thank you, Mr. McFadden!" Bridget said.

"Excuse me," he said. "Let me check with the repairmen and find out how long the replacement will take and just how long they'll be."

He left Bridget's living room; her front door closed in his wake.

Bridget spun on Marnie.

"What the hell is the matter with you?"

"What? What are you talking about?"

"He's tall, he's dark, he's handsome—he's to die for! And you're being incredibly rude."

"I'm not being rude."

"You should be saying, 'Lord Almighty, bless me and this bizarre spark of luck. He wants to look out for me. Some manifest of Heaven has sent this guy—'"

"Oh, Bridget, please. Come on. Manifest of Heaven? I don't... I don't trust him. I mean, I don't get it. He's not even from California."

"His mother knew Cara. I understand that. And he's looking out for us—for you."

"Bridget—"

"Seriously. As usual, you're going to get tall, dark and handsome, and I'm getting a dog! At least this time, it's going to be a literal dog. Please, Marnie—for me, be nice to this guy. Let him make sure you don't get killed—that I don't get killed—that *we* don't get killed. Please, Marnie, if you can't be nice, at least be decent to him."

"I am being decent!"

"Be decent-er!"

"All right, all right!"

There was a tap at the door; McFadden came back in.

"They're just about done, I'll help with the glass when we get back here this afternoon," he said, looking at Bridget.

"I'll be helping with the glass, too," Marnie said. Did he think that she was some kind of a diva? That she didn't do any kind of physical labor, and just had Bridget do it all?

"Well, with three of us, we should get it done quickly," he said. "So, as soon as they're out of here, we'll get in the car and go."

Bridget grinned and offered him the card that Sophie had given him. "I do believe you can leave me there to choose the right dog. I can't imagine anyone would try anything when I'm surrounded by a truckload of retired police dogs!"

"Right," McFadden agreed.

"Marnie won't have a dozen dogs around her," Bridget said. She grinned as she stared at Marnie. "But I think she'll be okay. She'll have you!"

"Yes," McFadden said, his eyes flashing and his tone light as he added, "She'll have me. It will be...just the two of us."

Just the two of us! Marnie thought.

And she wondered if that wasn't a bit more distressing than the truth: it would be just the two of them...

And a dead woman they could both somehow inexplicably see.

CHAPTER SIX

Seth Smith of the Wexler Realty Group was a small man in a designer suit. He was about fifty-five, and projected an image of confidence and assurance—an image Marnie was sure helped a great deal in the sale and rental of prime LA property. She was sure he'd negotiate with her, and she wondered if she could pull off a determined look that would equal his professional aplomb when she reached her meeting with him.

Even with the residuals she received from *Dark Harbor*—and the income here and there from advertising appearances—she hadn't saved enough to *buy* the Abernathy Theater. She was hoping to put forth her business plan, and have Mr. Smith advise her on the financing.

"Feels odd," she murmured.

Indeed, it all felt odd. McFadden was driving her to the meeting at a restaurant on Sunset Drive in his rental car.

She had a perfectly good car, but he explained that he could probably still drive if bullets suddenly flew from somewhere while she'd have to duck. Unless, of course, the shooter took dead and unexpected aim at him.

He'd said it all without batting an eye, and she'd realized that he had meant it. If someone was out to see her dead, taking aim at her in a car wasn't half as far-fetched as a Blood-bone character slashing down a victim at a comic con.

"What feels odd?" he asked, glancing her way.

"That I'm still taking this meeting. When Cara has been gone less than a week." She hesitated. "Having you drive me—being afraid I'm a target. It all feels odd. What else? Oh, the fact that a dead woman talks to me."

He glanced her way but quickly gave his attention back to the road. The way he watched the mirrors, she was certain that he was also watching for unusual traffic around them.

"You'll get used to it," he said.

"A dead woman, popping in and out—I'll get used to that? And…you do see her, too, right?"

"I do."

"That's it? That's all you have to say? Yes, you see her? And it's just…part of a usual day?"

"More or less."

Marnie hesitated, frowning as she watched him drive. His attention was on the road. He was listening to her, she knew. He didn't seem concerned in the least it really wasn't considered at all normal to walk around talking to the dead.

"So, you see Cara Barton frequently."

"Frequently? No, I've just begun to see her. And she doesn't stick around long because she doesn't have a lot of stamina yet."

"Yet?" Marnie asked weakly. Oh, Lord! Did that mean that Cara might suddenly decide to be with her …all the time?

He flashed her a quick smile. "I don't have all the answers. In fact, I barely have any answers. I do know it's not common to see and speak to the dead, and yet, it's not quite as uncommon as you might think. The thing is, those who speak to the dead—who really speak with the dead—don't advertise the fact. Because not many people would believe us."

"You know other people who see and speak to ghosts?" Marnie asked.

He nodded solemnly, not looking her way.

"My brothers," he told her. "There are three of us. Our parents visit us."

"Your parents are ghosts?" she asked.

He cast her another one of his quick smiles—quite charming and seductive, really—and said, "They weren't always ghosts."

"Ah, yes, but they died together, so tragically. When the chandelier fell."

"Yes. Doing a show they loved and loving the fact that they were working together." He hesitated then. "They were theater people. They truly loved a live audience."

"I know. I think that's why I always loved hearing about them," Marnie said. "I mean, film is great. But it's different. I guess I'm kind of like your parents. I love theater—and I love children's theater. Kids are still so full of wonder, you know. They love to suspend belief, and... Wait! I'm getting off course here. So, your parents were killed tragically. And then...they came back. And you saw them. Dead. Or did you see dead people before they died?"

"No, I never saw or spoke to a ghost until my mom and dad came back. And then my brothers—Bruce and Brodie—and I all tried to pretend that we didn't see them. I know we all felt the way you did—that it couldn't be possible. Then Brodie—the youngest—just hopped up and demanded to know if Bruce and I could see them, too, and we all had to admit that we did. Thankfully, there are three of us. Because, frankly, I think I would lose my mind if my mother had no one else to torment—er, haunt! She was quite the diva."

"I would have loved to have known her."

"Be careful what you say," he warned.

"Is she...here? Are your parents around? Do only certain people see certain ghosts?" Marnie asked.

"No. At least, I don't think so. Like I said, there's a lot we don't know. My mother and father believe they stayed behind to help their sons—we're unfinished business to them, I guess. Except they seem to have gone on a mission, as well. They bring their friends to see us."

"They bring their friends?"

He nodded. "Here's what I think. Whether it's right or not, I don't know. The ability to see and speak with ghosts is something similar to an inherited ability to sing well, perhaps to paint or draw—to love math and science or excel in some kind of learning. Maybe even something like the way we inherit eye color. Like other traits, it may skip generations. So there's our ability to see them, but there's also the ghost's ability to be seen. They can be shy. Or outgoing. If you go by the concept that we are souls and energy, it's easy to imagine a ghost is the same person they were when they were alive. New ghosts have to learn to maintain their visual presence for those of us who sense it. Older ghosts often learn how to appear and disappear at the blink of an eye." He looked her way quickly again and grimaced. "My parents now have that ability."

"You still see them regularly, your folks?"

"Yes."

"So Cara Barton could haunt me...forever?"

He laughed softly. "Maybe. But most of the time, ghosts stick around to right a wrong or help someone. Cara is trying to help you. Perhaps you might want to be a bit grateful."

Just when she was starting to—if not actually like him—appreciate him a bit.

"You're a jerk," she said very quietly.

He didn't reply, and she was furious with herself, yet she couldn't help but be defensive.

"I am really a decent, nice person," she told him.

"And you might be alive simply by good fortune and accident," he reminded her. "That Blood-bone character could have been coming for you—not Cara."

"Cara did make some enemies. Or it could have been a madman."

He was thoughtful. He shook his head. "Not a madman. That murder was well-thought-out. Blood-bone performed. He knew his positioning. He came to the booth, knowing you all would be game to play along with an impromptu show. He knew his target."

"Cara."

"No, his target as in *someone* among the cast of *Dark Harbor*. Anyway, sorry for being an ass. But for such a sweetie, one of America's own princesses, you're kind of an...ungrateful little witch."

He said it so pleasantly. She winced, really wishing she could escape him, not knowing why she wanted to get away—she didn't want to get killed—and completely confused as to why she couldn't just say thank you.

She drew in a deep breath. He didn't like her.

She didn't blame him.

She wasn't so fond of herself at the moment.

"You know, I'm okay with being on my own. I know how to be careful and avoid people. You are not obliged to me in any way."

"Yes, actually, I am."

"Why is that?"

"My mother was friends with Cara."

"Oh, yeah, right."

"And Cara is worried about you. And as long as she's worried about you, I'll be worried about you. I sure as hell can't take being even more haunted by my mother."

Marnie didn't realize that he had found street parking just off Sunset and that he'd turned off the engine—and was now looking straight at her.

"Your meeting is there, right? The Asian restaurant?"

"So it is," she murmured.

"Let's go then, shall we?" He stepped out of the driver's seat. She could exit a car perfectly fine on her own, but before she could do so, he had come around to her side.

"You always wait for me," he told her softly.

"But—"

"Safety 101. You always wait for me. Agreed?" he demanded.

"Agreed," she said, getting out of the car. "Okay, so, are you waiting for me in the restaurant?"

"You bet. I'll be waiting right at your table," he told her.

She had to admit she wasn't surprised.

And yet, neither was she dismayed, which was, actually, the surprising thing in the situation.

It was ludicrous that anyone would want to kill her. That a comic-book character had killed Cara.

That this man's dead diva mother was telling him to watch out for her...

But she wanted to live. She had seen Cara slashed apart, felt her die in her arms.

She was afraid. Very.

And she wanted to be grateful.

It was just so hard to be grateful to...ghosts.

Marnie Davante had a reputation for being one of the nicest people in the business.

To Bryan, as they walked into the restaurant on Sunset, he was finding it hard to believe. So far, she wasn't being particularly nice or grateful to him. Hired security—God only knew how good—cost an arm and a leg, especially in Hollywood where many stars were convinced that they needed protection from deranged fans.

Some did, as history had shown.

But supply and demand made bodyguards an expensive acquisition.

Especially those who would really take a bullet for you.

Of course, Marnie had to be completely off her usual mode. Her friend was dead, and that same dead friend was talking to her.

Not many people would do well with that scenario, he imagined.

The only friends—other than his brothers—he had who spoke with the dead were long accustomed to them walking about and talking now and then. But those friends had made their talents pay.

He'd just been working with Jackson Crow to find a kidnapped child, and they'd been helped along on that quest by the ghost of a Revolutionary soldier who had led them to the buried shack in the woods where the little boy had been taken.

Jackson headed a special unit of the FBI. His direct boss was Adam Harrison, a theatergoer who had once been very good friends with Maeve and Hamish McFadden; he was also a philanthropist who had lost his beloved son, Josh, when the boy had been a teenager. He had always had some kind of a special ability, and when he had died, he had passed it on to his best friend, Darcy Tremayne. Darcy had then helped out a sheriff because she'd gained Josh's abilities of the paranormal or "special" sight.

Adam Harrison, in his quest to see his son as that young lady had seen him, had become obsessed with those who could see and speak to spirits. He then went on to become equally obsessed with having those people help out law enforcement, since it seemed so many of the dead came back because they sought justice or because they were worried about someone left behind.

Jackson Crow had been Adam Harrison's first recruit when he'd determined to turn his prowess for finding the right man—and/or woman—for any particular *unusual* case into something more official. With Jackson Crow, Adam had relied upon his years of association with lawmakers and law enforcement in

Washington and taken it up a notch, creating the FBI unit that had become unofficially known as the Krewe of Hunters.

Bryan's last case had a happy ending. Kidnapper arrested; child safe in his mother's arms.

It didn't always happen that way. But Jackson had known how well Bryan knew the area and had called on him.

That morning, Bryan had put through a call to Jackson, explaining all the details of this case as he knew them. He knew help would arrive—important, since he couldn't offer his body as a shield for Marnie Davante and explore all options of investigation at the same time.

In spite of the incredible way they were getting along—*jerk*, *witch*—he was discovering he was fascinated by Marnie Davante. She wanted to be independent, and she certainly wanted to go through life being a decent human being. She was a mess over the situation—who wouldn't be? She was also capable of looking at him with very steady—and beautiful—eyes, and giving him her real attention.

Of course, he didn't have it at this moment.

He was leaned back in a wooden chair at their table in the corner of the restaurant near the back exit—his choice of seating. Seth Smith and Marnie were involved in a passionate discussion. She wanted to work out a situation where she could rent to buy. Seth Smith was skeptical she could pull off her business plan.

"Thing is, with programs for children," Smith was saying, "there's usually some kind of a benefactor—a large nonprofit corporation financing some of it. You know—for the betterment of humanity or whatever. Kids don't pay to go to plays. Kids don't even like plays. They like video games. Like that new one that's out, with that Blood-bone— Oh, man, sorry! I am so sorry. I know you were close with Cara Barton. Naturally."

"It's all right," Marnie said, her voice flat, something in her eyes turning a bit cold for a moment. But she swallowed and went on. "I believe you're wrong. Kids love interaction. And children's theater can be wonderfully interactive. I also have a plan that will bring the adults in while the children are working. See…"

Marnie produced her cell phone. She had drawn up a decent floor plan of the Abernathy Theater, showing the different areas that might be utilized. "This area, a coffee shop for the parents. We'll show old movies here, offer readings by authors and maybe have small or solo music artists appearing now and then. It can be open to many things. Here, the black box or smaller theater—classes and experimental plays. The main stage we'll keep for the plays that will bring in the largest audiences. I've already started networking with LA schools."

She was earnest; she was sincere. In Bryan's mind, she put forth an excellent argument proving she'd manage to create not just a wonderful experience, but a sound business enterprise.

"They don't even teach history anymore," Smith said, shaking his head, "and you think the schools will help you get kids out in an arts program?"

"Yes. Teachers still know and value the arts. They will help," Marnie said without hesitation. "I can make it happen. I know that I can. I have every friend known to man in the business. Actors, set designers, lighting designers… I have the right people behind me."

"Along with a bodyguard," Smith said, glancing Bryan's way. "How many people are going to send their kids to a place where bodyguards are needed?"

Smith just might have caught her by surprise there; she had obviously expected to get hit with the fact Cara Barton was dead somewhere in the conversation, but Smith's last comment threw her.

"Ah, well, Mr. Smith," Bryan said. "You have to realize this is just for a few days." He slipped an arm around Marnie's shoulders, pulling her closer to him. "I'm really an old family friend, and you know family—I'm hanging around so the rest of the family doesn't drive us all crazy!"

That was about as true as it could get.

"But they haven't found Cara Barton's killer yet," Smith said. He frowned. "Mr. McFadden, are you a part of the police or another law enforcement agency?"

"Private investigator, Mr. Smith," Bryan said, forcing a smile. "PI and family friend. And I can absolutely assure you, the killer will be found."

Smith studied him and then looked back at Marnie.

"I like you," he told her. "It's a massive commitment you're asking us to make, renting to you with the option and perhaps rent-to-buy steps being taken. You are aware of the pitfalls that might come your way. You're a bright young woman with a steady vision and not just a dream." He hesitated.

"So...?" Marnie said. Her shoulders seemed as cold and frozen as an ice block beneath Bryan's arm.

Smith looked at Bryan. "How do I say this... I feel we must wait."

"Wait for what?" Marnie asked.

Smith cleared his throat. "There are all kinds of rumors swirling around out there. Some say the cast of *Dark Harbor* is cursed. That the creatures of the current time are forming together to kill off the rest of the cast."

"What?" Marnie said incredulously.

"Creatures aren't real," Bryan said, leaning forward. "Bloodbone is a creation. He can be played by anyone. By a killer."

"Hollywood can be a superstitious place," Smith said. He sighed deeply. "I won't rent to anyone else. But let me meet with some of my peers and, of course, Mr. Wexler. I'd like this to happen for you. Frankly..."

His voice trailed again. Bryan could feel Marnie growing frustrated—and angry.

"Frankly?" he asked quickly.

"You're a bit of a business risk right now. We just want to make sure you're...alive," Smith said.

"I am alive. I'm in front of you. Flesh and blood!" Marnie said.

"We need you to stay that way," Smith said. He glanced at Bryan and then at Marnie and grimaced. "Let me talk to Mr. Wexler. Let's see how the police do. If all is well in a few weeks, we'll look at making this a go. How's that?"

"I guess it's a win for the moment," Marnie said. "And thank you. Thank you so much for your time."

"I'd like to see it work, young lady," Smith said. He rose. Bryan quickly rose as well, as did Marnie.

Bryan realized he dwarfed Smith; Marnie was a few inches taller, as well.

But at least Smith didn't seem to have a Napoleon complex. He hadn't tried to make anyone miserable to make himself taller in his own mind.

He had just been honest.

"I'll see the waitress on my way out," Smith said.

"It's all right. I've taken care of it," Bryan said.

Smith surveyed him. "A bodyguard who pays. Now, that's new in Hollywood. We may just work this all out, Miss Davante!"

Bryan wondered if Smith was aware Bryan had been studying him all the while as well, making his own observations and decisions. And one thing was in Smith's favor—the man might be playing the game, hedging his bets.

At least it didn't seem that he was out to hurt Marnie Davante in any way.

But who the hell was?

Someone from Marnie's life?

From the cast of *Dark Harbor*? Maybe. He'd start with them tomorrow, and with the producer who wanted to get the show going again—and then with anyone close to or invested in the revamping of the series. Possibly someone who didn't want it to happen?

When he had called the Krewe offices and talked to Jackson, asking for help, he knew the man would get his team working on bios of everyone involved, down to the nitty-gritty—things that couldn't be learned from the star magazines that proliferated the grocery store racks.

They watched Smith leave, and then Bryan turned to Marnie. "That didn't go so badly, right?" he asked her, his voice soft.

She looked up at him and gave him a real smile. It was weak, but it was real.

"Thank you," she told him.

"I didn't do anything, really."

"Yes, you did, and you know it. You stepped in at the right moment." Her gaze at him then was slightly amused and slightly sardonic. "I hadn't thought of humility as being one of your virtues—or faults," she told him.

"Don't worry, it's not," he assured her. "So...what now?"

"Bridget, and our new dog, of course," she said.

"Ah, yes, how could I forget?"

He had given their waitress his credit card on their entry to the restaurant; she saw them standing and came quickly for his signature and to return the card.

Bryan took Marnie by the arm, keeping her close as they left the restaurant and headed for his car.

"You didn't have to pick up the bill," she told him.

"If it will make you happier, I can total up expenses," he said.

"Oh, no. You can pay the bill. I'm just saying you didn't have to."

They'd reached the car. He shielded her as she slid into the passenger's seat. He walked around to the driver's side, stepped in and revved the engine.

They moved onto Sunset with no incident.

It had all seemed so simple at first.

He'd really believed that he was just making the only move possible for the future to fall in as it should. For his future to fall in as it should, really.

He'd never imagined how much he would like it.

The planning. Seeing such a plan executed. It was exhilarating. It was beyond exhilarating.

He began to wonder how it would feel to wield the weapon of death himself. Would he love it? Seeing the light go out of someone's eyes, watching the person cling to the hope of life…and know that no matter how one begged or prayed, it was too late.

Life was over.

And yet, being the orchestrator of it all—without a speck of blood on his hands—was an amazing feeling, as well. Such a high. And for now…

He'd been so close. She might have seen him. Marnie might have noticed him. But what if she had? There was nothing odd in the least about him meeting a friend for lunch on Sunset. She'd never suspect that the "friend" he was meeting for lunch was the very Blood-bone who had killed Cara Barton.

It was rich. So rich.

He wished that she had seen him. "You know," the Blood-bone killer told him, "it was one thing pulling it all off at the comic con. Risky, yes, and daring. But the difference was no one was expecting something like that. It was easy for me just to disappear through the crowd. No one expected a Blood-bone to be escaping. No one thought it was real until I was pretty much gone. But now it's all changed. Last night… Well, that was a little hairy for me. I could have been caught. Her macho friend was watching the house. That guy she's with… I've heard about him. I mean, half of Hollywood knows who the guy is because he had famous actor parents. He's been in the service—he was deployed three times. He's a crack shot. He's taken just about every kind of martial arts training there is. He was a SEAL, for God's sake. The stakes have changed."

"You're telling me that you're out? You…coward!"

"I'm not a coward. I'm smart. I can't kill her. I tried. I was nearly caught. You need to get someone else on this."

He felt fury boiling up inside him. Horrible fury, like the rush of volcanic lava racing through his veins, tearing him up.

He was the orchestrator.

The great orchestrator.

And now this pawn…this stinking wretched pawn…

"Be happy with what you've got," the Blood-bone killer said.

He leaned against the table, pointing a finger at his "friend."

"You fucked up," he said flatly.

"Doesn't matter. Whatever. I'm out. Find someone else. You'll get your money back. I am a professional, and while I'm pretty sure I did damned amazingly well, if—in your mind—I fucked up, you get your money back."

"Not in my mind. In fact."

"Fine. But I'm out."

The lava racing through him threatened to cause him to melt, to drip in a pile of molten fire to the floor, to explode, implode…

His orchestration was going to hell.

Then again, he had wondered…

Yes, he'd wondered what it would feel like. To wield a weapon himself. Not just to order the taking of life, but to take it himself.

He'd never imagined the rush of orchestration.

Maybe it was better—seeing the light go out of living eyes. Seeing the panic and the fear. The denial. And then, inevitably, the death.

He forced himself to lean back. To nod. He didn't want to look at all happy with the situation; in fact, he had a right to be pissed.

"Yeah," he said coldly. "I'll need the money back. I'll need it to get the job done. Right, this time."

They'd left Bridget at a beautiful place in Toluca Lake. It was the home and training-and-care facility of Sophie's friend, retired police lieutenant Jack Snell.

He had almost two acres of land; it was hard to imagine the value of his property. Snell was a tall, bald, sixtyish man composed of lean muscle. Bridget and he had obviously gotten on famously. They were chatting and laughing when Bryan and Marnie arrived, seated on a handsomely tiled front porch with a hundred-pound shepherd mix seated between them in front of a bag of dog paraphernalia.

"Come meet George! We're going to adopt him, okay?" Bridget called out.

"George!" Marnie echoed.

Bryan thought he'd never quite figure out how amazing dogs were; as soon as Marnie said the name, "George" stood, barked once in greeting and ran to her, wagging his tail.

Marnie set her hand on the animal's head as they walked on up the path to the porch, joining the two seated there.

"He's a good boy, Miss Davante. He has a little limp—he took a bullet in a drug bust. But he's as loyal and good as they come. And he's already taken to your Miss Bridget here and, obviously, you."

Jack Snell was on his feet, shaking hands with Bryan. "Heard all about you and everything that's going on, of course," he said. "From Sophie. Love her. Amazing little woman, super cop. Anyway, George is yours."

"Oh, George can't just be ours, sir," Marnie said. "Let us contribute something to help look after the other dogs, this place…"

Her voice trailed. They all knew what property in Toluca Lake cost.

"Sophie told me the story. He's a gift. And as for this place, well… Once upon a time, I arrested a girl. She was high, and I brought her in for possession of cocaine. She kind of haunted me, though. And I checked up on her and got her into a rehab and… Sorry, I was trying to make a long story short. Anyway, that girl is my wife of forty years now, and she just happened to be a peanut heiress. So go figure. Here I live, and here we work with our injured service dogs. So, there you go."

"What a beautiful story," Marnie told him.

"Yeah, go figure," Snell said with a grin. "So, take George, love him, squeeze him—all that. He'll watch out for you!"

They thanked him.

Bryan still kept Marnie by his side as they headed to the car. There didn't seem to be anyone near them, but he wasn't taking chances.

A big shepherd mix—a guard dog—was great.

But a dog couldn't anticipate a sniper's bullet.

Bridget slid into the back of the car and patted the seat. George looked from her to Marnie and whined.

Marnie laughed. "Aw, he is a good dog! He doesn't know which of us to watch. We'll make it easy—I'll hop in the back. It will be a bit crowded, but that's okay." She looked over at Bryan as he placed the bag of pet supplies in the trunk. "If that's all right?"

He nodded. "We'll all just keep our eyes open," he said.

"Keep our eyes open," Bridget said. "That's so cool. You know, I rode with a patrolman friend one day. He told me about keeping my eyes open. To look for what was strange. Like cars following other cars too closely—or relentlessly. If you're driving, you have to watch out for someone trying to be neck and neck, as well. That's how gangsters shoot other gangsters."

"If you're trying to take dead aim at someone, yes, you definitely have to watch out for someone trying to line up to take aim. And you're watching for cars that stick to you like glue. I don't, however, think that someone is going to take a potshot at us. Thing is, you just never know."

"Right. This killer was hands-on. Blood everywhere," Bridget said.

"Bridget," Marnie moaned.

"But the guy in the yard had a gun. And he shot at you,

Bryan," Bridget said. "And he threw the lawn chair, breaking the window."

"Yes," he agreed. "So, you never know. This guy doesn't want to get caught, though. Last night…it was dark. The streets were quiet. And he was taken by surprise. He had no idea someone was watching the house. He didn't expect a chase. I don't think—"

"He didn't intend to shoot Marnie. He wanted to kill her much more brutally!"

"Bridget!" Marnie exploded.

"Sorry," her cousin said. "Really, sorry. I'm trying very hard to face the facts here. I don't want you to die. I don't want to die!"

Bryan pulled in front of Marnie and Bridget's duplex.

"George, this is it. We're home, your new home," Bridget said.

The dog barked, as if he completely understood. He bounded out of the car. He waited while they opened the gate, then rushed in and began sniffing around the yard. Then George started to act funny. He began barking excitedly, running back and forth through the yard to the rear gate—as if he would jump it or ram it.

"Watch it," Bryan said. "Get behind me!"

They fell in place, Marnie thrusting Bridget between herself and Bryan, but both of them staying close as they followed the baying George around back.

When they reached the backyard, George was standing by the swimming pool.

Barking.

There was someone in the water, floating facedown.

The body was surrounded by a fading cloud of red.

CHAPTER SEVEN

Marnie realized that, in her head, she was trying to live in a world where it would all just go away.

No more dead people talking to her. No friends murdered in front of her.

No dead man in her pool.

She sat on a chair in her living room, trying to stay with it, trying very hard to not just slip into a place of absolute oblivion.

George was at her feet, ever vigilant. Bridget was in a chair near her, but the dog had apparently decided that Marnie needed watching more than Bridget. He'd also taken easily to Bryan McFadden—almost as if he recognized the man as being a part of the household. The very thought made her shake, and she wasn't sure if it was with anger—or with something else she didn't even want to recognize.

The police had come; Sophie Manning was back and Detective Vining was there, as well. A half-dozen officers in uniform moved about, inside and out, and Marnie wasn't even sure what they were all doing.

The house was swarming with crime scene people, and she'd met a woman she might have hoped never to meet—one of LA

County's finest medical examiners. Her name was Dr. Priscilla Escobar; Sophie called her Doc Priss, which allowed Marnie to realize she and Detective Vining had worked with her many times.

It was just the same way it had been at the convention center when Cara had been killed. Except, of course, the woman had died in her arms.

She'd been drenched in Cara's blood.

And Cara had been her friend.

And, of course, it had been a convention center.

This was her home. The dead man was a total stranger. All this was going on *in her home*.

She'd had to look at the dead man; of course, she'd had to look at him. Bridget, naturally, had been asked to look at the dead man, too. Did either of them know him? No. Marnie was certain she'd never seen him before in her life.

And he was recognizable. Not too bloated, as one cop muttered to another. "Floaters" could be extremely bad. But this guy looked…not bad but still *dead*. That was because, according to Doc Priss—a slender, dark woman with deep flashing eyes and a rich and compelling voice—he hadn't been in the water that long. He'd been in the pool no more than a few hours. He had not drowned. He had been shot and had died, she was pretty sure, before he'd hit the water.

She could verify those findings at autopsy.

For the time being, he appeared to be a healthy Caucasian male, thirty-five to forty years of age. Well, healthy, other than being dead. He had been healthy—before he'd been shot. He'd stood at six-one and weighed in at just under two hundred pounds.

There was no ID whatsoever to be found on him. No wallet.

Detective Vining had pressed: Were they sure they'd never seen him before? Had he ever come to clean the pool, do lawn work—maybe he'd come as a representative from the cable or electric company?

Marnie was absolutely certain that she'd never seen him before.

So was Bridget.

It appeared that no one had entered the house; there had been no break-in. The man had simply been in the backyard. He'd been shot, and then he'd fallen or been pushed into the pool. The body wasn't brought through the house. Marnie was grateful for that small fact, at least. He was brought around the side and into a waiting conveyance.

Doc Priss was nice. She was pleased to meet Bryan and assured him that he was welcome to observe the autopsy; she was very kind to Marnie, sympathetic. She complimented her on the work she'd seen her do on *Dark Harbor*, and she spoke to Bridget very nicely, too—complimenting a number of the sci-fi shows that Bridget had written or for which she'd been part of a writing team.

A very nice woman, really. Marnie was somewhat surprised, although she didn't know why she should think a medical examiner wouldn't be the same as any other human being.

Maybe because she just didn't normally have any interaction with people who dealt with dead bodies regularly. And as she was discovering, speaking with the dead wasn't easy, so working on them had to be very difficult, as well.

"I don't think we should stay here anymore, even with George," Bridget murmured suddenly. She was looking at Bryan McFadden, Sophie Manning and Grant Vining. The three were standing together by the door; they had just seen the medical examiner out.

Marnie was suddenly angry. This was her home. It was simply a nice home. A despicable human being had sullied it with murder, yes. But it was still her home. She kept it painted, she designed her own little space—she loved her bed and her pillows and so many things. Of course, they could be moved, but that wasn't the point.

"I'm staying here," she said firmly.

As if in agreement, George woofed.

"But," she added quickly, "Bridget, you have to do as you feel is right. I mean, I won't be offended or mind at all if you choose to stay in a hotel until…until they catch this killer. Or rent a different place for a month or something—whatever will make you feel safe."

"Oh, no—I won't leave you, Marnie. I wouldn't do that."

"But you should," Marnie said emphatically. "I would seriously want to die myself if anything happened to you."

Bridget made a face and shook her head. "If something happened to me here, it would probably happen to you, too, so that point would be moot. But you're right. This sicko isn't going to put us out of our home. We do have George. And tomorrow we'll have an alarm system. I swear it. I have a meeting tomorrow morning with the writing staff for *Aliens vs Super Crocodilian*, but when it's over, I can just wait right here until the alarm company arrives."

Marnie didn't get to answer.

Bryan McFadden walked over to them.

"Do you want to stay somewhere else until…this is sorted out?"

"No," Marnie said determinedly. Then she wondered if she was an idiot. She didn't want to die. She should be throwing herself at the feet of the police, begging them for twenty-four-hour protection.

"I thought you might say that," he told her. He hunkered down by her, petting George.

"I'm going to call an alarm company right away," Bridget said. "Or," she added, "first thing in the morning. As to tonight…"

McFadden smiled. He obviously liked Bridget. What wasn't to like? Her cousin was bubbly and sweet at all times. It often seemed quite odd that she worked on scripts about weird creatures battling other weird creatures—and munching on human flesh. Bridget had a great smile; she was sincere. She wanted to like people and always looked for the best in them.

"All right, then, what about tonight?"

Marnie realized it had turned into night.

"I don't want to be an idiot," she murmured. "But…we have no idea who the dead man in our pool might be. Bizarre, maybe, but it's possible someone just decided to murder someone in our backyard. We seriously don't know the guy."

"I believe you. We all believe you. That's not the problem," McFadden said. He gave Marnie something of an understanding smile. "These things really can't be random. Cara butchered. A man breaking the window in your bedroom. Now a man being killed and left in your pool."

"He's right. It is getting late, and we can't get the alarm system yet. We do have George now. And he's already proved himself to be a great guard dog. George would die for us, I'm quite certain," Bridget said valiantly.

He smiled. It was a damned good smile, Marnie had to admit.

"What's sad is that George might die for you, and you might still die, too. Don't get me wrong—George is great."

As he spoke, Sophie Manning came over to join them. She hunkered down, too, her smile a little grim as she reached out a hand carefully for George to sniff and then patted him, as well.

"I'm so glad you have the pup," she said, scratching his ears. She looked at Marnie. "I'd stay if I could, but…" She hesitated and then shrugged. "A friend of mine…is ill. I try to spend time with him, too, and…long story, but…"

"I can stay," McFadden said. He looked at Marnie, waiting for her to protest.

She didn't protest. She didn't understand why—certainly not under her circumstances—she was watching both McFadden and Sophie Manning. The young detective was really attractive. The petite bundle of lean energy and determination would probably be perfect for such a man. McFadden was so…alpha. Ah, but maybe two alphas didn't mix so well.

They were both so…*desirable*.

Such crazy thoughts.

Like speaking with the dead.

Where was Cara Barton? Had the ghost of her friend been hanging around her house? Had she possibly seen what had happened?

Why was she feeling jealous regarding Sophie Manning and Bryan McFadden?

"Marnie?" Bridget said.

She was about to answer.

"I don't want to put anyone in an uncomfortable position," McFadden said. "If you're really disturbed by the idea of me in here, or…if there is someone in your life who could be upset, we'll have to start looking at other options. But I really suggest you two not stay here alone tonight—even with George."

"Oh, there's no one in our lives, not at the moment," Bridget told him. "I was seeing Chip Denson—he's an actor. Or he claims to be an actor. I swear, no one knew that he'd starred in that porno when he was hired for *Revenge of the Venus Flytrap*. Oh, he is good-looking, I'll give you that. And…in good shape. But…trustworthy? And an actor? *Revenge of the Venus Flytrap* might have been a bit believable without him!"

"I'm, uh, sure," McFadden murmured.

"Anyway, we are long over, and I'm feeling very, very punch-drunk when it comes to men, thanks to him. And Marnie was dating Ethan Hook—the host on that adventure series—but that just kind of went away with a whimper, you know? He's a little hung up on himself. I think it was when he was so rude to the waiter at the Beverly Hills Hotel and Marnie decided that was it."

Marnie felt her face flaming. She did not need her personal life exposed so…pathetically.

"We're fine with it. We don't want to put anyone out," she said, her tone cold and flat.

"As you know " McFadden said.

"Yes. You're here—because of me. And Mom," she added sweetly.

"Oh, did you know Maeve McFadden?" Sophie asked.

Marnie looked at Bryan McFadden. "No," she said softly. "But Cara did."

"They were friends. Well, that's it then," McFadden said. "When the cops clear out, I'll stay. Pick a side of the duplex. One takes her own room, the other the guest room and I'll take the sofa."

"Lovely," Marnie murmured.

"We were at my place last night. We'll do your place tonight," Bridget said.

"As you wish," Marnie said. "It doesn't matter to me."

George woofed, as if approving the arrangements.

"Excuse me, then. I'll let Detective Vining know what I'm doing," McFadden said.

When he was gone, Sophie looked apologetically at Marnie. "I really like you both so much, and I'm so sorry this is happening to you. I would really love to just stay until… I just…"

Marnie told her, "You've been great—above and beyond. And it's all right. You don't owe us anything, certainly not an explanation. Not many off duty detectives would have stayed with us last night."

Sophie blushed, giving her attention to George. "I know I don't… It's just…my friend Andrew doesn't have much time left, and he needs a great deal of help. There are organizations, of course, but…we were a thing, all through high school. Then college. And we drifted and came back together and then drifted and… I still love him very much."

"Oh, my Lord, I am so sorry!" Marnie said.

"Oh, Sophie," Bridget said, and being Bridget, she slid down by Sophie and hugged her. "And you go to work each day, working so hard. And you still worry about us."

"Hey, it's...life," Sophie said. "But thank you both." She let out a breath, glancing at Marnie. "I have to say, I can't imagine I'm causing you a hardship—having McFadden stay with you. The man is...the man is!"

"Funny, I was thinking you two would be perfect for each other," Marnie said.

Sophie laughed softly. "You think? How bizarre. You haven't noticed the sparks between the two of you, huh? I do believe my chemistry radar must be much finer than yours." She rose, helping Bridget back to her feet.

"I'm taking off for now. We'll be waiting for what information Doc Priss and the crime scene people can give us. Take care—with every move you make," she added softly.

"I'll make sure she does," Bridget said. "I'm going to run next door and get a few things," she told them, looking at Sophie.

Bridget hugged the detective one more time.

"You're amazing," she said.

Sophie looked uncomfortable. "Just getting by—like most of us—the best way we can. Andrew is such a great guy. Did so much for so many people, and now... Anyway! Bridget, I'll step over to your place with you while you get what you need."

"Do you really think anything could happen now?" Marnie asked. "This place is crawling with cops and techs and—guns!"

"I imagine at this moment, this is certainly one of the safest places anyone could possibly be," Sophie said. "But just be careful—in the days to come. We will find out what's happening. Cara's killer will be brought to justice."

"I believe you," Marnie said. "And I will be careful, I promise."

In another hour, her house had cleared out.

There was still crime scene tape all over her backyard.

She wondered if she'd ever be able to get back into her own pool, if she'd ever feel that the dead man's blood was entirely washed away.

She wouldn't think about it now.

It was nearly midnight when she, Bridget, McFadden and George were finally alone. Bridget bid her a good-night, telling her she was going to try to be bright and perky and brilliant for the writers' meeting.

George asked to go out; McFadden insisted on taking him, just out in the front yard.

When he returned, Marnie found she was still restless. She needed to go to her own room—with its nice new glass, all the broken stuff cleaned out now.

She needed to sleep.

But she had no meetings the next day. If anything, she needed to call her agent and find out if there were any offerings out there that might earn her a bit more money while she waited anxiously on her children's theater.

But that was it.

She perched again on the wingback chair in the living room as McFadden walked back in with the dog.

The house seemed incredibly quiet.

They seemed very much alone.

She reminded herself Bridget was sleeping in the guest room.

And she told herself McFadden wasn't that attractive. His scent—his aftershave or whatever—was not at all compelling. He wasn't striking, rugged, just really, really masculine and all the things she might find sensual and hypnotic and...

He hunkered down before her, petting George, who had already taken his position at her feet again. Maybe it wasn't such a good thing the dog had already determined his complete loyalty was to her. People kept getting very, very close to her, just to pet George.

McFadden was very, very close to her.

Sparks, Sophie had said there were sparks, chemistry…

But did she just give in to chemistry? And what if he didn't think there was any chemistry at all?

He smiled a little grimly looking up at her. "Sophie had a great idea here. This guy is perfectly trained, and he adores you already."

"He's amazing," Marnie agreed. "I always wanted a dog, but I've traveled a lot, too. Filming on location, seeing my folks. I'd never know when I was going to be here. Of course, Bridget's work is really close to home. So I don't know why—between us—we've never gotten a pet before."

"Maybe you were just waiting for this guy," he said, and again there was that light in his eyes, the smile curving his face making something in her veins leap just a little bit.

"Maybe," she murmured. She would have backed away then—if she could have. But she was sitting in a chair, and he was so close to her she could almost feel the heat of his flesh…muscle, bone, heartbeat…

"How long do you think this will go on?" she asked. She meant to speak clearly and in a moderate volume. Her voice came out in a breath.

He let out a long sigh, the whole of his body seeming to shrug. "I don't know. I'm so sorry. We never know on something like this. But I do have a theory."

"You do?"

He nodded grimly.

"The man we found in your pool tonight is the man who killed Cara."

"What?"

"Here's my theory. Whoever killed Cara was hired to kill her. Or to kill you, and he missed and killed Cara. Or maybe he was just supposed to murder someone from the *Dark Harbor* cast. At any rate, the person who hired him to kill either killed him in return or possibly hired another killer to kill the killer."

"That's... I mean... How could that be possible? How do you just find hired killers so easily? I mean, what do you do? Advertise on Craigslist?"

He smiled grimly again. "Here's what is very sad indeed—hired killers aren't all that difficult to find if you really want one. But I could be wrong. Hopefully, we'll find out who the dead man is by tomorrow. Whoever killed him left his fingers intact, so it won't be hard getting his prints. With any luck, he'll be in the system."

"If he's a killer—and he's in the system—why would he be out on the streets?"

"He might never have been brought in for murder, but maybe he was apprehended on another charge. Most killers for hire don't just decide in high school that's what they're going to do for a living. They start out with something petty, maybe fall into drugs and drug deals, maybe even human trafficking. Then... well, there's money in killing. Horrible as it sounds."

"I see. But then, if someone wants you dead—really wants you dead—aren't you dead?" she whispered.

"No," he told her. And his smile was suddenly real. "Not when I'm here. You won't wind up dead. I swear it," he vowed.

She didn't know what seized her then, what insanity. She suddenly leaned forward, threw her arms around him and kissed him. She was kissing him hard and passionately, finding the kiss was openmouthed and very wet and very hot and sensual to the core.

Then sanity gripped her with the same ferocious force that had precipitated the kiss.

She drew away. She stumbled up, leaning on him to escape him, almost knocking him over from his hunkered-down position and definitely dislodging George, who whined in terrible confusion.

"I'm sorry. I'm so sorry. Truly sorry. I like living. I don't want to die. I am very grateful. I acted very badly. Excuse me. We need to go to bed. I mean, we need sleep. Separately. I need sleep. I'm so sorry. Excuse me! Good night!"

The ridiculous thing was she had to steady herself on him. Feel his arms. Feel his hands as he maintained balance and helped her. She felt the muscles in his arms. As she had imagined, she felt the heat. And she really needed to flee.

She did.

But he called her back by name just as she reached her door.

She turned, looking at him down the length of the hall.

He was smiling—really smiling. His hair was askew over his forehead. He was rakishly macho and amused and so compelling.

"That was—terrific. Please, don't be sorry for a kiss like that. Lord above us, please don't ever be sorry!"

She swallowed and nodded.

She hurried into her room and closed the door with what she hoped was dignity and finality.

But she'd shut George out.

She had to open the door again, look weakly at the man still watching her, urge the dog in and, once again, close the door.

Bed, yes.

Alone.

Except for George.

And George, amazing creature that he was, immediately curled into a ball at the foot of her bed.

The dog could sleep.

She could not.

She just lay awake. She imagined throwing her door open, rushing out of the room and hurrying across the bit of distance between her and McFadden. She would throw her arms around him… No, she would stop, she would be sultry and subtle. She would stop right before him and she would say, "Never be sorry, huh? Dear sir, I will not be!" And then she would cast her clothing off and stand naked before him, and he would pull her into his arms and...

She'd been working with scripts way too long. If it were scripted, of course, she'd be wearing a silk caftan or robe, and it would flutter beautifully to her feet, and he would be overwhelmed with desire and...

Reality.

She would never do it. Bridget was asleep in the guest room.

And what if he had just been polite? What if he picked up the imaginary silk caftan and drew it back around her shoulders and said, "I'm sorry, Marnie. There's a girl back home." Or worse: "I'm sorry, Marnie, you're just not appealing to me."

No, it would never happen.

But it didn't stop her daydreaming, not until she finally fell into a fitful sleep, and in that sleep, it wasn't dreams of an amazing sexual encounter that plagued her, it was a vision of a black-clad and masked man, Blood-bone, chasing her down with a light-up sword, ready to slash her into ribbons of flesh and blood.

It was never good to become involved with someone you were protecting.

Nope. Not good at all.

They weren't involved. She'd kissed him out of gratitude. She was a smart woman. She was still grieving a friend and worrying about her own life. It had been a moment, nothing more.

Like hell.

There was something there. And he couldn't act on it. He couldn't.

He shouldn't.

He could still taste her on his lips.

His phone rang. He glanced at the caller ID and quickly answered. It was Jackson Crow. For Jackson, it had to be about four in the morning.

"Have you seen the news?" Jackson asked when Bryan answered.

"Uh, not tonight. But there has been another incident."

"I know. Angela was watching for another case we're working on, and she saw what had happened in LA. You might want to take a look."

As it stood, there was no real reason for the Krewe to be involved. Everything that had happened had happened in LA. That meant the local police handled it, and he sure as hell couldn't find fault in Vining and Manning and the other officers—or MEs or crime scene techs—in any way.

The FBI needed to be invited in on a case like this. But now...

"Did anyone give out Marnie Davante's home information?"

"No. They just said a dead man was found in the pool of a Hollywood star. But there was some footage of the outside of her house, so I'm imagining it wouldn't be too hard for anyone to figure out."

He hadn't even noticed the media that night. They hadn't been allowed close, he was certain, and he'd been too concerned with what was going on.

He should have seen someone take a photo, though. He should have expected the media.

"Well, that's just great. I don't suppose it will put her in greater danger. If someone wants her dead already, that won't change. But it may have an impact on her life."

"Assuming she gets to keep a life," Jackson said. "What's the local scene like there?"

He knew what Jackson meant.

Were the cops asses, or were they just seeking to arrest a killer?

"Good. Some of the best I've come across," Bryan said.

"Do you want support from this front? Other than information? Speaking of which, Angela does have info for you—nothing that leaps out, just a few bios."

"Thank you on the info. As to physical help—more people in the flesh from the Krewe? Is that possible?"

Jackson laughed softly. "Adam Harrison is our great overlord," he said. "He has the ability to make anything possible. He's also provided our unit with a private jet. Say the word. We'll get you some support."

Hell, yes.

He had sworn he'd keep Marnie alive. And there was nothing like support once you'd made a promise like that.

"Is this kind of a come-on to get me to join the Krewe?"

"Only if you're willing to go through the academy. It's a requirement, even for our unit. Which, for you, after the service and some of your other stints, might be like child's play. But this isn't a negotiation or a bribe. You make your own decisions. We can send out help because it's what we do. We've even gone in now and then where we weren't really wanted, but, hey, we all want to be wanted. I can send some people in an unofficial way, too. Maybe that would be best for now. I'd tell you I was going to send you my sharpest agents, but all my agents are the sharpest. At the moment, I think I can get out there myself. And I'll see about a few agents who know LA. That would be the best scenario, I think."

"Great. Thank you."

"It's what we do," Jackson repeated.

"And I'm damned glad," Bryan said.

"Hang on. I'll give you Angela."

A moment later, Jackson's wife, Special Agent Angela Hawkins, was on the phone. He knew that she studied all the curious cases they received. Apparently the Krewe—despite the fact the specialized unit grew continually—received far more requests than they could handle. Angela had a knack for reading everything possible about a situation and determining whether the "special" talents of the Krewe would be useful in any given case.

"Hey, Angela," he said.

She greeted him quickly and then went straight to business. "You watched the show, so you know the main characters. Cara Barton, the mom, is dead. Roberta Alan—who played sister Sonia—hasn't met the same kind of fame, but she seems to be doing all right. She has a makeup line and does a ton of infomercials. Apparently when it comes to the old B-list opportunities at comic cons, she doesn't mind. She has nephews who are enamored of the fact that she's at them. I've checked out her finances. She spends a lot of money, but I can't find any major debts or deductions. She takes money out over time and has a reputation for being a major shopper. Jeremy Highsmith—dad to Cara Barton's mom—seems to just be a nice old grandpa. No major expenses, guest performances here and there. He has a pack of grandkids—from a pack of children due to a number of wives—and all of them love him to death. Even the ex-wives speak highly of him. Down to Grayson Adair. Still very good-looking, young enough, and he's had a few failed pilots. But he's also received some decent movie roles, if not in starring positions, with sound speaking roles. He's ambitious like most guys in Hollywood. Oh, family money comes his way, so he's not desperate at all. We're working on finding out more about Vince Carlton, as you asked, as well as Malcolm Dangerfield, the currently hot heartthrob who was nearby when the murder was committed. I've looked into a few other people in the area at the time. The old Western star—oh, yes, and the descendant of the dog star—seems to come out squeaky clean with absolutely no motive. Oh, but one more thing on Malcolm Dangerfield. He was approached by Vince Carlton. Love interest for Marnie, or her character, if the show was revived."

"Interesting. Thank you, Angela."

"We'll keep our people on all the financials. Usually hired killers aren't cheap. Then again, maybe this one was killed rather than paid. Hard to figure and find, sometimes."

"Did you get anything on David Neal? He was here the other

day applying for a job of stage manager for Marnie's theater. I wasn't here when he stopped by the house. Sophie Manning—fine young detective, from what I can see—was with Marnie and Bridget when he visited. I did see him in all the videos that surfaced from cell phone cameras after Cara was killed."

"Ah, yes! Young David Neal. He seems to be good at his craft. He worked with one of the major companies for their ice show when it traveled Europe."

"So why would he want to work for a fledgling theater here?" Bryan wondered.

"He has partial custody of a young son. He wasn't able to see him. He and his wife parted amicably. She discovered that she was simply with the wrong sex. She's married now to a makeup artist, and all three of them seem to get along fine. From everything I've been able to gather, he just wants to be near his son. Anyway, I hear I may see you soon. If Jackson comes out on this one, I think I'm clear at the moment to do so, too."

"Great, I'd love to see you."

"Field Director Crow is reaching for the phone. Take care."

Angela was gone. Jackson was back.

"Turn on your TV."

"Yep. I will do so. And thanks. Yeah, help would be great." They rang off.

Bryan found the remote and turned on the living room television. A reporter, standing in the night with the flood of a streetlight above him, was reporting on a dead man having been found in the pool of one of Hollywood's most beloved celebrities. As yet, the police weren't giving out any information. It was, though, the reporter was sure, a Hollywood homicide.

Even if this is actually LA, Bryan thought.

"Knock, knock!"

He spun around.

Cara Barton was back. She looked at him with huge eyes filled with concern.

"I've told you—I've been telling you! Marnie is in terrible danger," she said.

"Cara, right now I'd say that it was the man in the pool who had been in the most danger. Were you here? Did you see what happened? Did you see who killed him?"

She nodded gravely.

"Who?"

"Blood-bone!" she said. "It was Blood-bone again, only this time, he had a gun!"

CHAPTER EIGHT

Marnie was awakened by something unfamiliar.

A soft whining sound and a wet nose nudging her.

"Good morning, George," she murmured.

Poor boy! When she'd finally slept, she'd slept like a rock, forgetting the pup.

She quickly opened the door to her room, letting him out and hoping that Bridget or McFadden were awake and would let him into the yard.

"George!"

She heard her cousin's effusive greeting; all was well.

"Bridget? Let him out? I'm going to shower and dress."

"You got it!" Bridget called back.

Twenty minutes later, Marnie headed out to the living room. No one was there, but she could smell freshly brewed coffee, and she quickly headed to the kitchen.

Both Bridget and McFadden were seated in the little niche at her hardwood breakfast-nook table, coffee cups before them.

She wondered why things had changed since last night. Now, when she looked at him, it seemed that she heard her pulse racing in her ears, and she was instantly flushed.

How had he switched from being such an annoying ass to being so incredibly appealing?

Okay, to be fair, he'd never really been an ass. He'd come to her when her world had gone to hell, when she'd lost a friend—and gained the ghost of that friend.

"Hey, good morning," she murmured, heading for the cupboard to find herself a mug.

George, who had been at Bridget's feet, uncurled himself, stood, barked and wagged his tail.

"Yes, yes, that's you, too, George, and I'm sorry I overslept and took so long to let you out," Marnie told him, pausing to scratch his ears.

"I didn't hear him. He wasn't making a sound. If I'd thought of it, I could have let him out," Bridget said. "You don't sleep much lately."

"No one seems to sleep much lately," Marnie said.

Her fingers were trembling as she poured her coffee. He hadn't spoken yet, but she felt McFadden watching her. How was she going to deal with this?

Act! she told herself. She had been nominated several times and received an Emmy. Surely, she could manage this.

She took a seat at the table.

"Good morning," he said.

It seemed like there was so much implication in those two words. Good morning, yes, morning, when she'd thrown herself at him last night and now felt…embarrassed, maybe beyond, such as a little humiliated, and still…alive, awake and madly attracted.

She reminded herself that he was here because someone might well be trying to kill her.

And because he couldn't take any more torment from his dead mother.

"Are you okay?" he asked her.

She nodded. "Of course, and thank you so much. I had George at the foot of my bed all night."

"You made him sleep on the floor?" Bridget asked, horrified. "I'd have kept him up in bed with me and squeezed him and hugged and…"

"Called him George!" Marnie said, laughing. "I didn't make him sleep on the floor. He just kind of immediately curled up there."

"He was probably used to sleeping that way with his old master," McFadden said. "He is a guard dog. We acquired a phenomenal dog when I was in Afghanistan. He was a street mutt who attached himself to my unit. He saved a buddy from a sniper attack."

"Wow. What was his name?" Bridget asked. "And then when you left what happened to him?"

"Friends pulled some strings. I brought him home with me. His name was Dog."

"Clever, full of imagination," Marnie said, sipping her coffee.

"Yes, right. He was hanging around a long time before we actually took him in, and I knew I was going to fight to bring him home," McFadden said. "We'd been calling him Dog—I just kept calling him Dog."

"Just like Mad Max!" Bridget said.

"I guess," McFadden said, looking at Marnie.

"Please! You've seen *The Road Warrior*, right?" Bridget asked.

He turned to her, smiling. "I've seen it. And I've heard that blue heeler in the movie was a rescue dog and was so loved by the cast and crew that he was adopted by the stunt coordinator."

"I think that's true," Marnie said. "What did happen to your guy, Dog?"

"He died."

"Oh, no," Bridget cried.

"Natural causes and old age. My vet estimated that he was somewhere between fifteen and seventeen years old when I lost him."

"Oh, that's a beautiful story!" Bridget said.

"Careful—she'll have your story threaded through *Zombie Flesh Eaters from Outer Space* or some other such flick if you let her."

"Hey," Bridget said, "that's not a bad title. Not a bad title at all. When I have the full story for it and run it past the execs, I'll let you know. It will definitely feature a hero who has rescued a great dog."

"That's no idle threat," Marnie told McFadden.

"That's not a threat!" Bridget protested.

"That's no idle promise," Marnie corrected, and for a moment the three of them laughed.

"I'm going to need to go," Bridget said. "We can't survive if we don't work. And I'm one of those lucky people who actually loves to go to work. What I do is fun, and the people I work with are great. And I don't think it's me that anyone is after..." Her voice trailed off. All sense of laughter was gone. She looked at Marnie with misery in her eyes.

"Your wheels will be here in just a minute," McFadden said.

"Her wheels?" Marnie asked.

"I have friends coming. That way we can investigate and keep you both safe," he said.

"And who are your friends?" Marnie asked, her tone a bit skeptical.

Living or dead? she was tempted to ask.

McFadden smiled, as if reading her thoughts. "Actually, my friends are with the FBI, a special unit. You're going to like them."

As if aware that this was Hollywood and they were supposed to appear on cue, there was a short horn blast outside, followed by the sound of footsteps up the walk.

George's ears perked up, then he barked.

There was a knock at the door.

"It's all right, boy. Friends are arriving," McFadden said.

The two women followed McFadden as he went to let the expected callers in. Marnie stood just behind him, curious.

They could have been actors, they were such startlingly beautiful people.

She was a blonde, slim and yet shapely, wearing a pin-striped pantsuit very well. He was dark-haired and tall, his American Indian heritage apparent in the handsome structure of his cheeks.

"Jackson Crow and Angela Hawkins, meet Marnie Davante and Bridget Davante—cousins. This side of the duplex is Marnie's. Bridget lives right next door. Marnie, you might know from her appearances on the screen. Bridget, you might not know so easily, but I understand she is responsible for many a hit on the newest sci-fi channel. Oh, and the furry pile of slobber and integrity at my feet is George. He's the new guard dog."

"Handsome brute," Jackson noted.

Angela and Jackson entered, and then handshakes went around, along with compliments on Marnie's performances. And the FBI agents had done their homework. They even knew which shows Bridget had worked on, and they were quick to praise her, as well.

Then it all simmered down.

"You did it—you really got here in time to go with Bridget to work," McFadden said.

"It's nice when the head of your specialized unit happens to be extremely wealthy and gives you access to his private jet," Jackson said.

"It's pretty cool. We can be just about anywhere quickly," Angela agreed.

"You're FBI?" Marnie asked.

"We are."

"And…you're from…?"

"Northern Virginia. We're part of a specialized unit with our offices in Alexandria now. We've moved around a few times.

We've grown considerably over the years." She glanced over at her husband. "Jackson is our field director."

"I handle queries that come in and determine what is appropriate for us and what is not, and look over the cases we've been asked to come in on. The federal mandate has changed greatly over the past decade or so, and we actually have more leeway around the country, but...at the moment, Angela and I are here as tourists."

"But not to worry," Angela said. "We have our director working on it, so we should have an invite to investigate very soon."

"Um, okay," Marnie said. "Anyway, welcome. Would you like some coffee? Breakfast?"

"Not for me. Bridget, I believe you need to get to work. I'm your companion for the day," Angela said. "We're all set to go. I'll drive and you can navigate. I'm not really familiar with the area."

"I can drive," Bridget said.

"No," Marnie told her. Her cousin gave her a curious glance. "It has to do with ducking," she added sagely.

"Oh," Bridget said, but looked like she had no idea what Marnie meant. She would probably ask Angela once they were out on the road.

"I'll be home early. The alarm company is coming," Bridget said, twisting to speak as she followed Angela back out the door.

"Well, I would have some coffee," Jackson said.

"Of course," Marnie told him, heading back to the kitchen. The men followed—after McFadden checked that the front door was once again securely locked.

George barked an approval.

Marnie noticed that even the dog seemed willing to follow McFadden around and take his every cue from him. Maybe that was a good sign—dogs tended to be much better at judging people than other people were.

"I like your place," Jackson said.

"Thank you," Marnie told him. "It's home. And it is mine—and I'm lucky. My tenant is my cousin. We're both only children, so Bridget is the closest thing I have to a sister. Anyway, between us both having guest rooms, we can accommodate family when they want to visit."

"And guests," Jackson said. "You're comfortable with us being here? We'll take up all the room, you know."

Marnie poured coffee as the two men settled into the breakfast nook.

Jackson Crow was an impressive man, with his height and the breadth of his shoulders. He was obviously friends with McFadden and seemed to regard him highly, as well.

"So," she said, setting the coffee before him. "FBI. And how do you know McFadden—um, Bryan?" she said, realizing that she'd referred to him by his surname.

Was it somehow ridiculously too personal to call him by his given name?

"The head of our unit, Adam Harrison is—among other things—a philanthropist. He was dedicated to public theater."

"Which means he was good friends with my parents," McFadden said.

"So Bryan and I have known one another for several years. We recently worked a case together—kidnapped child, hidden in a bunker in the woods by one very frightening individual. Bryan found the hideout. Underground."

Bryan said quietly, "Amazing outcome. We were all grateful. Sadly, we couldn't explain to the parents that it was all thanks to an old fur trapper who was killed during the American Revolution."

Marnie was glad she had set down the mug of coffee she'd poured for Jackson. Otherwise, she'd have surely dropped it.

She froze, looking from one man to the other.

"Has the ghost of Cara Barton been around this morning?" Jackson asked.

"What?" she whispered.

"Has Cara been around? You see her. Bryan told me you do."

Marnie sat. She almost sat right on top of Bryan, and she barely noticed. She was staring at Jackson Crow.

"You're with the FBI?"

"I am."

"And you see—ghosts?"

"So does every member of my special unit."

She looked at Bryan. "But you don't belong to this unit?"

"He's been asked," Jackson said.

Bryan shrugged. "My brothers and I have been considering our options, one being to open a more or less 'special' private investigation firm. Then again, I am considering the Krewe of Hunters."

"Our unofficial name," Jackson said. "There are many opportunities with the unit, and each member is invited to bring forth any situation they consider to be important."

"That's pretty cool, really," McFadden said.

Marnie nodded, looking a little blankly at both of them. She couldn't find her voice for a minute. It really didn't feel normal to discuss ghosts with one person, much less two—not when everyone seemed so casual about the fact that ghosts existed.

"I—I haven't seen Cara this morning," she managed at last.

"I saw her last night," McFadden said.

"Did she see what happened?" Marnie asked.

"Yes."

"What!" she exclaimed. "Then why are you sitting here? Why haven't you arrested someone?"

"The man in your pool was killed by Blood-bone."

"Blood-bone?" Marnie said.

"A man in costume, I'm assuming," McFadden said drily.

"A man in a Blood-bone costume found this guy in my backyard, shot and killed him and walked away, and no one reported seeing anything odd in the least?" Marnie said incredulously.

burial grounds or cemeteries. They weren't happy places, though many did feel compelled to attend their own funerals. Some tried to comfort those they'd left behind—some determined to know if they would at the very least attract a good crowd of those who then wished they'd been better friends in life.

No essence of a soul lingered in the refrigerated room of corpses.

"Yes, I can see they have a few people who need an ME's tender care," Bryan said.

"Crazy cities here, crazy county," Vining said. "Thankfully, on this, we have some real help. Doc Priss is the best. She came in last night and made sure we had fingerprints from the deceased put through the system. We can hope for something, at least in the way of an ID. We've taken pictures we could release, but I'd rather not go that route. I'd prefer we find out on our own, if possible. But if we don't get something by tonight, I will get his image on the news."

Doc Priss called to them from where she was waiting at the end of the hall.

"Initial cuts in place, my friends. My dernier—assistant—is waiting. If you will? You don't have to be here, but if it is your desire, it is time to get moving."

They hurried down to join her. While the room where the autopsy was taking place was sterile, it wasn't private. Two other autopsies were taking place at the same time; LA County certainly was busy with the care of the dead.

"Sophie told you I did the prints last night?" Doc Priss asked. When Vining and Bryan nodded, she swept a hand through the air over the body and continued, "We are looking at a man who had been in his prime. Fine muscle tone, every organ in his body in great shape. Except, of course, for where the bullet ripped through his gut, where it tore out chunks of liver and lung."

She clicked a little button on a wire around her neck; the rest of what she had to say would be recorded. "Ripped through his gut" not being a medical term, she had apparently chosen not to record until after she had said the words.

She went on in detail that was fit for the recording, noting colors and temperatures and the weight of the heart and what she believed to be the remnants of a hamburger and fries in his stomach. The contents would be tested later.

"Hamburger," Vining said, shaking his head.

"Hey," Manning protested. "This is LA—that could have been one expensive hamburger!"

"Exactly. Expensive hamburger joints have sprung up everywhere. I doubt if we'll get a real take on where he'd been from some half-digested chopped cow."

"Barely digested cow," Doc Priss corrected. "Our John Doe here had a meal not more than an hour and a half or two hours before he was killed."

Doc Priss went on. She was thorough and clear. In the end, however, not many of the details were helpful.

The man had been in his mid to late thirties. He hadn't been a drinker, nor had he abused drugs. He had most probably attended a local gym—if not, he had a home gym or played an active sport such as soccer or football.

Bryan didn't believe the weight of the victim's brain was going to help them at all. If only they could narrow down a restaurant where he'd had his last meal, they might trace his steps the hours before and up to his death.

And if they were able to find his identity through fingerprints, that would be an amazing step in the right direction.

Bryan waited patiently for Doc Priss to finish.

Once outside with Manning and Vining, he put forward his theory.

"I believe the dead man killed Cara Barton," he said.

"You mean he was killed by the man who killed Cara Barton," Vining corrected.

"No, I mean, I believe this guy was a hired killer, and he killed Cara Barton."

"Why would you think that?" Manning asked, frowning.

"The person in the Blood-bone costume at the convention was about our John Doe's height and weight, or so I would judge by the video I've seen and what I've heard. The dead man was in really good shape. I watched the videos. The killer could move and wield a sword well. He was obviously someone who was very fit. I think he somehow failed in what he was supposed to do to, or he then refused to cooperate or went against whoever hired him to do the killing."

"That's pretty vague," Vining said.

"It's a theory. Nothing but a theory." Bryan thought about telling them he also believed a man dressed as Blood-bone had killed the man who had previously worn the costume. But Vining didn't seem at all sure Bryan's theory was in any way plausible.

He could hardly try to tell him that a ghost claimed to have seen Blood-bone kill the man they had found in Marnie's pool. He'd need proof, and the only way for that was to get out on the street and canvas as many neighbors as he could.

"So, what is your plan?" Manning asked him.

"I'm going to see if I can find anyone who saw anything," Bryan said. That was the truth.

"We'll head back to the station," Vining said, watching Bryan closely. "I hear we're going to get official help from the FBI—and it's something you already know all about," he added.

"A joint task force is going to be formed," Manning said, watching him, too. She looked as if she would have said more—or flatly asked him why it would seem he had been involved with the federal government coming in on their investigation, especially when it didn't appear anyone was crossing state lines or that a serial killer was at work.

There was no reason not to tell them everything—everything

that he could tell them. "The director for a special unit was good friends with my folks. I have worked with a few members of their team. They all knew I was coming out here."

"You must have some pull, then. It's expensive, sending agents all over the country."

Bryan thought Vining was a good guy, a policeman through and through, wanting the best outcome. Now the detective was really curious about him.

"Friendship can go a long way," Bryan said.

"I guess so. Anyway, we'll call you if we've got something. And, of course, we expect the same," Vining said.

Manning stood silent, watching him. He smiled at her. "I appreciate that," he said quietly.

"One of your friends is at Marnie's place now, right?" she said.

He nodded.

She looked at Vining. "Told you he wouldn't leave her alone. Dog or no dog, alarm or no alarm." She turned to him again. "So, are you convinced the killer meant to get to Marnie, not Cara Barton?"

"Maybe Cara was the target. But since Cara died, someone has tried to break into Marnie's place. And then someone was killed in her swimming pool. I can't just see it all as coincidence."

"I can't either," Manning said.

The detectives headed off.

Standing in front of the morgue, Bryan put through a call to Jackson.

Everything at the duplex was fine. "Do we expect you soon?" Jackson asked him.

"I'm going to be in the neighborhood, but I'll be out knocking on doors. Maybe I will come by and get George. Walking a dog might be helpful."

Jackson agreed. "People are less suspicious of a dog walker than they are of a man knocking at their door."

"Let's just hope some of the neighbors are out, and they have dogs. Or, at the least, come out for their mail or something," he said. "I hope to hell someone saw Blood-bone running around."

"That won't give us a clue to the guilty party. What about the dead man? Did you get anything off the body?"

"No revelations. He ate a hamburger and fries before he died. Was in great shape. Anything happening there?"

"Miss Davante is lovely."

"Yeah," Bryan agreed. "So all is well?"

"It is."

"See you soon. I'll be multitasking. We get to find out if an actual living witness saw a Blood-bone, and George gets a nice walk around his new neighborhood."

Marnie had to admit that if you were possibly being stalked by someone intent on homicide, she was being protected by the right people.

Jackson Crow was very professional—he was also down-to-earth, approachable and didn't mind answering any of her questions. She learned the Krewe had been formed in New Orleans when a congressman's wife had been pitched over a balcony. Jackson had met his wife—Agent Angela Hawkins—on that first case. The team had grown substantially since that time.

In turn, he asked her about *Dark Harbor*, about her fellow cast mates and all those related to her work in the past—and what she wanted to do in the future.

"As I understand it, Cara Barton is the first of the dead to speak to you?" he asked.

Marnie stared at him.

"Yes," she said softly.

"I know it's scary at first, but I can't imagine a life without them now. Ironic, I suppose—maybe not. The living have always needed the dead. The dead are our pasts. They are our mutual history as human beings. I think it's unsettling for some, often downright terrifying, but..." He paused and shrugged. "They help," he said. "They see what we don't. Sometimes they want nothing but to move on. Others…others want to stay. They don't mind that they're here—such as they are."

"I see," Marnie murmured. "No, I don't really see at all."

Jackson sat in an armchair in Marnie's living room, facing the front door. He started to answer her.

But then he smiled and straightened and politely stood, looking behind her.

Marnie turned around, rising, as well.

Cara Barton was with them.

"Hello, Ms. Barton," Jackson said.

Cara clapped her hands delightedly. "He sees me, too," she said. "And, oh, he's so cute!"

"And so married," Marnie said, smiling.

Cara waved a hand in the air. "I am all about same-sex and interracial and interfaith marriages! But seriously, Marnie, dear, don't be a dunce. The dead really can't get too carried away with the living. But that's not the point at all here. Sir, who might you be?"

"Special Agent Jackson Crow, Ms. Barton, here to work on the investigation into your death."

"My murder," Cara said grimly. "Thank you. I heard about you last night from the other tall, dark and handsome. So, has he found the Blood-bone who killed the fellow in the backyard yet?"

"Blood-bone! Blood-bone isn't real," Marnie whispered.

"Right now, so it seems, Blood-bone is very real," Cara told her.

"What did you see happen here last night?" Marnie asked.

"Blood-bone shot and killed that man and stood watching until he went into the pool, until he was absolutely certain the man was dead."

CHAPTER NINE

"I'll go with you," Marnie said.

Bryan shook his head. He'd returned to the duplex and was ready to take George for a nice long walk around the neighborhood.

"It's better if you don't," Bryan told her, glancing over at Jackson.

The field director picked up his cue.

"The man in your pool was shot. We have no idea if someone was out there hoping you'd come home—"

"No, come on. We know what went on yesterday, thanks to Cara Barton. She saw a Blood-bone character was here, and whoever it was dressed up as Blood-bone, that person apparently lured the other man here so he could shoot and kill him and leave him in my pool."

"That doesn't really matter. What matters is a man was shot. A killer out there has a gun. If someone is going to jump in front of you to stop a bullet, they have to know the bullet is coming," Bryan explained.

Marnie flushed. "I don't want anyone to have to stop a bullet for me."

"Then let me take the dog," Bryan said. "Are Bridget and Angela back yet?"

Jackson shook his head. "They should be another hour. The alarm installers will arrive just about the same time."

"I'll be back in an hour," Bryan promised.

"If they do arrive, I am here," Jackson reminded him.

"Of course," he said quickly. He had never meant to imply that his friend—field director for an ever-growing unit of special agents—wasn't capable of keeping Marnie safe while an alarm system was installed.

And yet, in a way, he had done so.

Ego or something else? he asked himself.

He never would have imagined it—with his parents being who they were, growing up he'd come across tons of beautiful people, some of them talented, some of them nothing more than gorgeous egoists—but he was definitely being affected by this particular beautiful person.

And that meant he was being foolish. He was *not* the only one who could keep her safe.

Jackson was watching him, the hint of a smile on his lips.

"Cara was here again," Marnie interjected. "She was here, in fact, until just a few minutes ago. And then..."

Marnie lifted her hands into the air, indicating Cara had disappeared into thin air.

"Ah," Bryan murmured. "Well, then, George and I are off. Even here, between Universal Studios and Hollywood, I keep thinking someone would have noticed a guy walking around in a costume like that."

"One would hope," Jackson said.

Bryan had George on his leash; they headed off down the walk.

Barham and the surrounding streets were busy—with cars. It didn't appear anyone was out. Then again, he hadn't expected people to just be standing on their sidewalks.

He didn't want to get too far from Marnie's place. By pretending to allow George a tremendous interest in a palm tree, he loitered just down the block from the duplex long enough for a woman in a casual halter dress and flip-flops to come out of her house with her garbage. She looked at him. He waved,

She went back inside.

He headed halfway down the next block.

This time, George was allowed a keen interest in a cherry shrub.

A man drove his car right past Bryan into his driveway, parked and clambered out with groceries. He looked at him a long time.

He was going to be helpful, Bryan thought.

"Hope you're going to pick up after your dog!" he said.

"Yes, sir, I intend to do so," Bryan replied.

Then, oddly, the man stuttered as he kept staring at him. "S-sorry. I mean, I just… Well, if you don't pick up after your dog, not to worry. I'll come out and handle the situation."

Why the sudden fear?

Bryan gave George a gentle tug on the leash and started toward the man's yard.

"Don't hurt me!" the fellow said.

Curious and frowning, Bryan paused and studied him. The man was about forty-five. He had most of his hair, and while not any kind of a bodybuilder, he seemed in good enough shape. But his face had gone white.

"I have no intention of hurting you. Are you all right? Has someone threatened you?" Bryan asked.

The man swallowed and shook his head. "You're just…tall. And yesterday…at the TV star's place…a man was killed," he ended in a whisper. "Isn't that wild? But there was a monster walking around the neighborhood right when it happened—can you figure that? A…a tall monster. You're, uh, tall."

Bryan nodded. "I'm actually working with the cops on it. I'm not any kind of a monster. Really. But what monster did you see?"

The guy was still studying him. He'd set his groceries down. He remained uneasy. He seemed to realize it was too late to try to get out of speaking with Bryan. He was evidently wishing he'd never spoken.

Bryan stood where he was; George sat at his feet. "Sir, you don't need to be afraid of me. Or of George here. You may call the police and ask for Detective Manning or Detective Vining. One of them can tell you that I'm a PI." He pulled out his license as he spoke.

"Oh. Are you working for her, then—Marnie Davante? She's got a great reputation out here. We're kind of neighbors, I know, but I don't really know anyone here. Still, one of those rag magazines did a story on Cara Barton and talked about what an amazing friend Marnie Davante had been to her—to all of them. Imagine, she was just a kid, but she pulled that thing that if she got a raise, they all got a raise, right when the show was really, really hot. So yeah, she might have hired you because she sounds like the kind who would want the truth."

"Something like that."

"And a man was found dead in her pool." He waved a hand in the air. "Oh, the media didn't let that out. I live here. Anyone who knows this neighborhood at all knows that's Marnie Davante's house..."

His voice trailed and faded. Then he spoke again. "I'm Bob Andrews."

"Mr. Andrews, how do you do? I'm Bryan McFadden. And this is George. And yes, the dead man was found in Marnie Davante's pool. And that's why I'm out with George now. Trying to find out who saw what. And you're telling me you saw a monster?"

"You know—one of those comic creatures. A man all dressed in black. Bone-bone...bony blood..."

"Blood-bone," Bryan said.

Bob Andrews nodded grimly. "I'm usually home just about

this time. Have an uncle in assisted living. I check up on him each morning and then come back and go to work. I'm a commercial artist—work right out of my house. My easel is there, by the window. I saw him One of those Blood-bone things walking on down the street. First, I'm thinking we're not all that far from a few of the theme parks. Then I'm remembering Cara Barton was murdered by a Blood-bone. Then I'm thinking he's gone, and he hadn't appeared to have had one of those swords, anyway. I heard all the sirens last night, and I came out and saw the commotion, and I knew, of course, it was Marnie Davante's place. But... I didn't think...until just now when I thought about how tall you are..."

"Thing is, Mr. Andrews, you did see a Blood-bone. And you'd be willing to tell that to the police?"

"I don't know. I guess it could be dangerous for me. I mean, Cara Barton was murdered by someone in a costume like that. Now a man is dead—and I saw a Blood-bone just before it happened."

"It didn't occur to you to mention the Blood-bone to anyone else, even call the police and mention you'd seen someone dressed up that way?"

Bob Andrews shook his head.

"Should have. Just didn't. And...well, honestly, I'm not sure about telling anybody. I kind of like to stay under the radar."

"No one ever needs to know you saw this costumed figure, sir. Other than law enforcement."

"I...uh... Sure. Use me or my name or whatever. Just so long as it's only cops that know I said something. Or anything. I mean, right now, I'm just talking to a man walking his dog, you know?"

Bryan thanked him. "If anyone checks with you, it will be one of two detectives, Mr. Andrews. Detective Sophie Manning or Detective Grant Vining."

"All right. I mean, I want to help. I'm just not a tough guy. I don't want any trouble."

"It's all good. Thank you."

George let out a woof; he was either in agreement or ready to move on.

Walking away from Bob Andrews's house, Bryan pulled out his phone and called Grant Vining. "I've got something," he said. "Neighbor saw a guy dressed up as Blood-bone walking around the neighborhood, right around the time our victim was killed at Marnie's. I know you're going to think I'm far-fetched on this, but since we are looking at a killer who was costumed, I still can't help but think there is a possibility that whoever orchestrated the murder wasn't pleased with his hired killer. I think the person who ordered the killing dressed up as Blood-bone and came out to kill the killer. I'm working on theory, I know. And you might find it ridiculous—even if someone did see a Blood-bone. But—"

"I'm not going to argue anything with you, McFadden," Grant Vining told him, sounding weary. "Our prints gave us an ID on the dead man."

"Oh? And?"

"His name was William Capello. He had a rap sheet a mile long—under Capello, his real name, and a half a dozen other names. He was acquitted in the murder of a Vegas showgirl as few years back. The jury never believed the burden of proof had been established. He was also suspected of a number of other murders. In every case when he was suspected of murder, he was suspected of being the finger man in a murder for hire."

Bryan drew his phone from his ear and actually stared at it for a moment.

He'd been right.

But did it help him now?

A killer had killed a killer.

But had he done the deed himself?

Or hired a killer to kill a killer?

"And by the way," Vining added. "This just became a joint task force."

"Pardon?"

"Your FBI friends are in—Joint task force, with a meeting tomorrow. So if I don't see you before, I'll see you then," Vining said.

"Wait. I need you to—"

"Not to worry, McFadden. We'll get some officers in uniform out in the neighborhood. We'll see if we can find anyone who knows where our Blood-bone came from. Hell, maybe one of them even saw him shoot our victim and thought it was a show. Maybe one of them knows where Blood-bone went after."

"Thanks, Vining."

"We are good cops."

"I know that."

"Yeah. Well, here's to a... Guess there is no such thing as a happy ending when people are already dead," Vining said. "Here's to a speedy solution."

"With no more bodies."

"Amen."

George barked. It was almost as if the damned dog understood.

"I need you. We need you. Marnie, how could you have forgotten?"

Grayson Adair was on the phone, earnest—and desperate.

Marnie felt terrible. She had forgotten. Though how anyone could ask how she could have forgotten—under their current circumstances—was ridiculous, as well.

"I didn't think you were still doing another comic con after what happened to Cara—"

"Marnie," Grayson said. "It's not a comic con. I keep telling you. It's not. We wouldn't be doing a comic con. But we've had this planned forever. Cara knew about it. She said you were definitely in."

"Grayson, it is still a fan convention—"

"Horror-palooza. That's completely different," Grayson said.

"Grayson, it's a—"

"Not just a fan convention, Marnie. I can't believe you haven't been to it before. Every fabricator in LA tries to get his or her work into this convention. The creatures, the makeup, the costumes—it's all so amazing!" Grayson told her. "Look, the rest of us were praying that Vince Carlton was going to get the show revived. He might still do it. He'll be there. Marnie, come on. Yes, it's a fan convention. It's where artists strut their stuff. It's where we can, at the very least, make some survival money. I'm sure you told Cara that you would come. It was going to be our first time attending. Please, Marnie. It's this weekend coming up."

"And you didn't mention it at the funeral, or after—"

"It is after right now."

Marnie tried to remember if she had told Cara she would attend some kind of a monster show. Obviously, since *Dark Harbor* had been filled with all kinds of creatures, they were more than welcome at a horror convention of any kind.

She didn't tell Grayson, but she'd been to one of the Horror-palooza shows before. She'd loved it. Hollywood's special effects people came out in full force. It was amazing to see what shows were coming out soon, what was the new take on an old spook, and just what was being done with prosthetics and makeup.

"I don't know if the cops will let me go," she said.

"It's a free country. They can't stop you."

"Yeah? Well, Grayson, I do not want to die."

"Oh, Marnie. What happened was horrible. But I don't intend to go the rest of my life being afraid every second. To be honest, I can't afford it."

Grayson was a good-looking man and a decent actor, too.

your neighborhood. Marnie, you are hot right now. Some people think you are some kind of supernatural character, clouded with dark shadows and evil. Some think you're a pathetic creature having a run of bad luck. But I guess, to a lot of people out there, you're looking kind of cursed."

"Great," Marnie said. "Okay, I don't know what's happening with Seth Smith or the theater at the moment—"

"Go online—check out the news. He didn't say he wouldn't rent to you, but he did give a speech to some reporter about the Abernathy having a long and proud history, adding that anything for children needed to be above reproach."

"But I am above reproach. I'm not involved in any scandal—"

"Someone died in your pool."

"I didn't put him there!"

"Perception, Marnie. Perception is everything," Roberta reminded her.

Marnie sighed softly. "Either way, I'll let you know about Horror-palooza for sure by tonight, okay? Seriously, no one would expect us all to be there. Cara hasn't been gone that long."

Roberta sighed deeply. "It doesn't matter what people expect. There will be a giant memorial to her. To be honest, one of the organizers told me we are in high demand. They want some pics before another one of us is…gone."

"Great. Just great."

"I'm sorry. And please."

"Okay, I just have to check with people."

"Like tall, dark and handsome."

"Roberta, that describes a large part of this city."

Her friend laughed softly. "Love you, Marnie. Call me."

She hung up.

Marnie hurried on out.

Bridget and Angela Hawkins had returned—so had Bryan McFadden with the dog.

George really had decided he was her dog. He pulled free

from McFadden's easy hold on his leash and bounded toward Marnie. She dropped to her knees, delighted. George greeted her with vivacious licks and kisses and a wild pummeling of his tail.

"You're amazing, George," she told the dog.

Bridget sniffed and laughed. "Hey, George. I'm the one who has promised to look after you come what may."

"He loves you, too," Marnie said.

"He probably senses Marnie needs the most protection," McFadden said.

"Speaking of which…is there any news?" Marnie asked.

"There was someone in the neighborhood dressed up as Blood-bone. I confirmed it with a man who lives down the street," McFadden offered. "The man in your pool was one William Capello. He was identified today through his fingerprints. He was a known criminal suspected of committing a number of murders by hire. I sincerely believe he was the one who killed Cara."

Marnie looked at him and swallowed.

"So whoever killed the man in the pool is the conspirator or killer who hired the killer who killed Cara?" she asked quietly.

"So it seems," McFadden said.

"Anyway, the killer killed his killer," Angela finished, watching them all.

"What?" Bridget asked, completely confused.

"And we still have no idea who wanted Cara—or someone from *Dark Harbor*—dead," McFadden said.

Bridget's phone rang.

She was startled, having been intent on the explanation being given her.

She cried out and then made a face and apologized, "I'm so sorry. That's the alarm company. Their people are getting here. Two gentlemen. Steve and Jerry. I have a picture."

She showed all of them the faces on her phone. The alarm

company was into safety. Two smiling faces were on the screen along with their names and expected time of arrival.

Even their timing was top-notch.

A van drove up in front even as they spoke.

"I'll let them in," Jackson said.

"Should we get out of the way?" Bridget asked.

"Only when they do the work. You're going to have to know your system and set your codes," McFadden said. "It will take a couple of hours. And by the way," he added, glancing over at Jackson and Angela with approval, "the FBI is now part of the investigation. There'll be a joint task force on this."

"Not just any joint task force," Angela said. "You have the Krewe of Hunters. Marnie, we will get to the bottom of this, and we will find the real killer."

Marnie smiled at her. "I believe you," she said softly.

She just prayed that she lived to see it.

So much commotion.

Police. FBI. And now a nice new alarm company.

Oh, yeah. Not to mention the dog.

All that protection, and yet...

When he wanted her dead, she would be dead!

He still wasn't sure if he would do the deed. The first— Ah, it had been surreal. Had he done it right? Yes, he believed so. If he'd been seen, so what? What could anyone say? Blood-bone had killed the bad man and pushed him into a pool. And that pool? Oh, it had belonged to Marnie Davante.

How delicious.

He'd been such a coward before. He'd never imagined just how incredible it was going to feel. The rush that swept over him.

At that moment, he had been Blood-bone in truth.

He had been a god or a demon or both rolled together.

He'd held the ultimate power, the power of life or death.

He chose death.

The stunned look on the face of the man as he'd died! So shocked. And he'd been laughing, the fool. Laughing to see another Blood-bone costume.

Now he felt something of the same thrill again. He was here, so close to her house. He was watching. He could be caught.

But what if he were? There was no reason he shouldn't be there. Even if she didn't consider him to be a close friend, he was a friend. Or a good acquaintance, if there was such a thing. Oh, no. She would say friend. Marnie being Marnie.

The odd thing was, like the rest of the world, he loved her.

He really did, he realized. He loved her.

Maybe that was best. Maybe he would do it, make it personal. Because he would do it gently; he would do it with love.

That made the power all the greater. He didn't even begin to understand it—it just was.

He loved her, and he would kill her.

And it would be right. While he worked on it all between the dog and the alarm and the cops and the macho man who had pushed his way in on it all...

Go figure. He'd never imagined in a thousand years that killing could be such a rush. That he would love it so very much, as the orchestrator...as the man who went in and got his hands dirty.

It was better than anything else he'd ever done.

Bryan had gone out, taking George on another hike.

Angela and Jackson had gone next door; they were going to sleep in Bridget's guest room.

Marnie had showered and donned one of her favorite nightshirts—nothing that hinted of seduction in the least.

And yet seduction was on her mind.

She didn't understand herself; Bryan had certainly angered her. Then, he'd been incredible in many ways.

She didn't remember ever feeling so on fire. So desperate to touch...and be touched.

Needy.

No, don't say I need him, please!

It wasn't neediness, she assured herself. Because no one had evoked such a feeling in her before. Ever. Not even when she had more or less believed she was happily dating. All the dozens of men she'd met, great, talented, beautiful people, and still...

It was him.

So much for the wariness and irritation she'd felt at first.

She was fascinated by the way he spoke, moved, looked. By his eyes, the striking length of his fingers, his height, breadth, scent.

She heard the key in the lock. The buzz of the new alarm. Bryan stepped inside with George and hit the keypad for the alarm. At first, she thought he hadn't seen her there, standing just at the arch to the kitchen.

But it seemed he knew she was there.

He turned. Smiling. "You okay?"

She nodded, stooping to pet George, who had trotted over to her.

"I'm fine. Thank you. Your friends are over with Bridget. They're very nice. I'm grateful they're here. For their help. The police on the case are certainly fine people, too. Sophie went above and beyond. And Detective Vining seems as dedicated." She straightened, looking at him. "Um, are you all right? You can have the guest room, of course, no need to sleep on a couch. I hope you do get some sleep. The room has a brand-new alarm. It should work, right?"

His smile deepened. His arms were crossed lightly over his chest. He was still in one of his suits, looking ridiculously good. Not *ridiculously*. Wrong word. Perfectly good. Wonderfully good.

"You are talking a lot. Do you think you've managed to say what you're really trying to say?"

She hesitated.

Then she shrugged and murmured, "Um...do you want to sleep with me?"

"Sleep?"

"I thought… There's no obligation. You're here to look after me. Because your mother told you had to—"

"Ouch!" he exclaimed.

He was still across the room from her and still smiling.

And then he wasn't.

He was in front of her, taking her into his arms, and the amusement was still in his eyes along with something else, something like the fire that seemed to burn in her own limbs.

"Only thing…" he murmured, his mouth close to hers.

"Yes?" she whispered.

"Obligations. I don't just walk away. You have to be protected, yes, and God knows what the future will bring, but…"

"But?"

"I'll be here come morning. You all right with that? This can't just be a thank-you-for-guarding-me sex thing, huh?"

She stared at him, feeling as if there really weren't enough air around her, as if strange little invisible fireworks were going off all around them.

She nodded.

"George, guard!" he told the dog.

He swept her off the floor and into his arms. There were no stairs, but it seemed incredibly romantic, the way he strode with her held to him to her room, the way that his eyes seemed to delve so deeply into hers. It was better than anything she'd ever fantasized.

When she lay on the bed, he slid his hands beneath the hem of the cotton T-shirt to draw it over her head.

"I should have gone with silk," she murmured.

"You could have gone with burlap," he told her.

She rose up on the bed, trying to help him undress. His jacket wound up in a corner, shirt and pants somewhere, socks and briefs somewhere else. There was a moment that might have been awkward, but somehow it wasn't, then he was finally naked and she knelt on the bed in nothing but a pair of hip-hugger panties.

She was surprised to laugh and say softly, "At least the panties are silk."

"Lovely," he told her. His eyes meeting hers, he pressed her gently down to the bed. His fingers curled over her palms as they stretched above her head, and he lowered his face to hers.

There was no apology when they kissed.

Everything about his mouth was sensual. The play of his tongue upon her lips and in her mouth. She rose to meet the kiss, relishing the feel of their flesh coming together.

Then he moved his kiss.

Down over her breasts. Her belly.

He whispered softly, "I do love silk."

Moments later she felt she had left sanity behind. She was rising into fields of exquisite ecstasy she had never come close to imagining. She writhed until she was in his arms, until he was thrust inside her and undulated all the more when they rolled and moved together wildly.

She was aware of rising to a climax, aware the fireworks seemed to be breaking everywhere again. Then intensely aware of the flesh-and-blood man next to her and reality.

And of not being one bit sorry.

He lay beside her, holding her.

He rose up on an elbow.

"I will be here," he said softly.

"Not just a Hollywood stud, huh? Arm candy?" she teased.

He winced. "Ouch again. They lie—you do have a mean streak!"

"But I don't really. I can kind of prove it, if you like."

"Oh?"

He eased back slightly.

She began to kiss him.

And tease and brush and caress him...

It was possible to forget everything, except for being with him.

Everything but him, the feel of him, being touched by him, being with him.

Much later, when they lay together, he said softly, "Hmm. Arm candy. Maybe not such a bad gig after all."

They both laughed.

When she woke, she realized he had been up, that he had showered and shaved and dressed again.

But he had not left.

And he would not, she knew. Not until this was over.

Not unless they both decided *they* were over.

CHAPTER TEN

"You're kidding me? Really? You think I should do it?"

Marnie stared at him incredulously. Bryan smiled.

"We're still nowhere," he told her. "Once the FBI came in on it, Jackson—through Adam Harrison—saw to it that every single person interviewed when it happened was interviewed again. Including every person who had been wearing a Bloodbone costume. They've done research on the major players. Their best analysts believe it has to be someone involved with one of the cast members or the show itself. Or a person close to you—someone the show or your individual lives might effect."

"I'm confused. Why would this person be at this monster show?"

"Same reason they'd be at a comic con," Bryan told her.

They were sitting on the couch in her living room. George was on the floor at Marnie's feet. Even curled up, the big dog took up a lot of space.

Bryan felt fairly relaxed. For one, Jackson and Angela were still on guard, just in the other section of the duplex.

The alarm was activated. Both back doors, both front doors

and every window on either side of the property had been covered. Both women knew how to activate and deactivate it.

Everyone was safe.

He felt good.

Marnie was good.

No, Marnie was amazing, but that was something else entirely.

It was early, and the morning was beautiful. They were talking about the Horror-palooza that was next up on the horizon. Marnie seemed amazed he thought it was a good idea that they all went and did the show.

"You want to draw someone out?"

"Yes."

"And you're not worried?"

"I'm always worried, but we can be in control of the situation."

"You—you've handled lots of situations like this?"

He smiled. "No, I have to say—this is unique."

She leaned on an elbow, watching him, truly curious. "I have to admit. I don't really get this. You're good friends with Jackson. You admire him—you're all about his group of people, his Krewe of Hunters. Why aren't you just a part of it?"

"I've been invited to join."

"Why are you hesitating? I mean, you kind of obviously know your way around self-defense and guns and—ghosts."

"Two things, really."

"And they are?"

"Bruce and Brodie."

"Your brothers? You don't strike me as the type who follows anyone else."

He scratched George's ears thoughtfully. "It's not a matter of following anyone. It's about being in it together. Life was probably a bit strange for us from the get-go. Our parents were so well-known and adored. They knew everyone, from politicians to other famous actors and actresses, multimillionaires. Heads of state—even kings and queens. And they were just good parents, really nice people. Anyway, as you're learning, it really got weird when they died." He grinned. "I wonder what would have happened if we had just kept pretending we didn't see them. I swear, it is difficult sometimes, knowing Mom will torment you until she gets what she wants. Though, thankfully, like I said, they were really good people. She asks good favors. Okay, she tells us a whole lot more than she asks us."

"I'm confused. If your brothers are the same as you, with the same…"

"We never really had a chance to talk about our plans after our service, especially with regards to the FBI. My parents knew Adam Harrison. He's a great guy—always. Before the Krewe, he did a tremendous amount of good. He didn't just give money. He gave kids a chance at art and music and drama—and history and sports and life. He formed his Krewe a few years back." He quickly filled Marnie in on Adam and Josh's story, and the formation of the special unit. "Jackson called me one day soon after I'd gotten out of the military, and I did a job with him. I've worked with him several times since. But Bruce and Brodie and I had talked about forming a PI agency. Might be pretty cool to work with my brothers, using our skill, huh? Although, as you're learning, the dead do not perform on command. They help the best they can. That doesn't mean they have all the answers. Anyway, I might join the Krewe. But I owe it to my brothers for us all to have a talk first."

"I see," Marnie told him. "It's pretty great—that you could work with your brothers."

"Yeah, we're lucky. We have a lot in common." He laughed softly. "Much to my mom's dismay, that includes the fact we definitely don't want to be actors."

"And what is wrong with actors?"

"Not a thing. My father was a very fine man and a very fine actor."

That caused her to smile.

He leaned closer to her. She didn't pull away. She was angled toward him on the sofa, the side of her head rested on her hand as she looked at him.

"I'd have liked your dad."

"Yeah, you would have."

"And your mom."

"Well, there's always the possibility you'll meet them somewhere along the line."

"Is she—here?" Marnie asked.

What a bizarre new way to "meet the parents."

He smiled. "No, but if you knew my mother…she just might find a way to get herself out to Los Angeles."

"I don't understand. She's a ghost, right?"

"Yes, and as unique a character in life as she was in death. Very talented, even as a ghost. I'll try to explain. Not that I—or anyone—can really understand everything. It seems ghosts move around a great deal like the living. Except they can appear and disappear. Young ghosts—meaning newly dead, no matter what their age at their demise—don't stay in a solid form very well sometimes. Most have to learn, gain strength, when it comes to appearing to those who can see them—to create sound, and sometimes, to do things like knock on a door, push the buttons on a coffee machine, a cell phone, flicker lights, et cetera. You know, I wish it were easy. I think that humans naturally have a fear of the unknown, which includes a fear of ghosts. But if you think about it, it's not so bad. It means there is something, an energy that does last forever, and the concept of each person's unique essence—a soul—is real."

"But…only some people stay behind?" she whispered.

"Only some."

She was quiet. At her feet, George whined.

"You think George can see Cara?"

"Possibly."

"Why?" Marnie murmured. "The thought plagues me constantly, goes in circles in my mind—and still there is no answer!"

"Why are you seeing Cara?"

"Why did someone want her—or me or someone in the cast of *Dark Harbor*—dead?"

"You still can't think of anything? Any slight somewhere along the line? Someone hurt or snubbed?"

She laughed softly. "Someone is hurt or snubbed in this city just about every minute of the day. But no. I can't come up with any reasons that to me would stand up as motive for murder. Cara could be tough to get along with on the set sometimes, but that usually had to do with the writers or the director of an episode. Roberta Alan is a doll, very easy to deal with. Jeremy and Grayson had their moments of stress, but again, they were easy to work with."

"What about Cara's life since?"

Marnie hesitated. "I think she was okay. I mean, Cara had loved it when we were on top. When *Dark Harbor* was one of the most popular shows on television. She was recognized everywhere. But the public is fickle. New stars were shining, so to say. But we were making money through residuals, and she was getting a guest starring role here or there and doing an occasional commercial."

"What about her personal life?"

"She was married three times. All three husbands were actors older than her, and two have passed away. One has been working in Atlanta on one of the important series out there, for years now. It's too bad he couldn't make it to her funeral."

"What about you? Enemies?"

"Sadly, one might say I'm the doormat—the girl next door. Seriously? I can't begin to imagine I could have made any enemies."

"But weren't you the most powerful member of the family? And didn't you become the most popular among fans?"

"Maybe. Who can say?"

"Marnie, humility is one thing. But if anyone resented you being popular, who would it have been?"

She sighed softly. "Cara."

"Well, Cara is obviously *not* trying to kill you. What about Jeremy or Roberta? Or Grayson?"

Marnie shook her head. "No way." She shrugged. "They need me. Anything tied to *Dark Harbor* needs Madam Scarlet. Of course, there aren't five of us anymore. No one knows how these things will go now. And I'm not at all sure if doing Horror-palooza is a good thing."

"I'll be with you. Jackson and Angela will be there."

"I think I like Angela," she murmured.

"Tough as nails and a crack shot," he assured her, amused.

She smiled. "I guess her appearance is one of her strengths. No one would expect such a slim and attractive woman to be so kick-ass."

"Sophie seems pretty kick-ass, too."

"So she does," Marnie agreed. "Do you think they give classes in being kick-ass?" she asked.

"They definitely have them in self-defense. Taking some of those might be a very good idea. Single women living alone should have some training and protection."

"Beyond George?" she asked, half-teasing and halfway serious.

"Beyond George," he said.

"There's no instant kick-ass, right?"

"No, but maybe we'll start at a shooting range. There's little that's more kick-ass than a bullet."

Marnie was amazed that she was actually feeling good. It wasn't that she had accepted the fact Cara was dead—or that her dead friend was visiting her.

It was Bryan. She didn't really know or understand how that could be—she hadn't known him long enough to really know him, and yet she felt she did. They'd spent only one night together, but that night had been amazing. She had always been careful and hesitant in relationships, and she had straight-up asked him to sleep with her.

He was staying with her. There was no time limit. He would be with her until this was all over. And then...

He was an East Coast man and she was West Coast, which didn't matter to her so much except for the plans in place for her theater, something she had dreamed about for years now.

After she and Bryan had talked, Jackson, Angela and Bridget had come to her side of the duplex and they had discussed Horror-palooza, one of Bridget's absolute favorite events to attend. Her cousin was happy to go but still a bit scared.

Then Marnie's phone rang. This time it was Jeremy Highsmith.

"Marnie?" Jeremy spoke her name almost hesitantly, as if he might be afraid that he had the wrong number.

"Hey, Jeremy. How are you?" She felt a flash of fear for him—she figured she might when she talked to any of her surviving cast mates in the future.

"I'm fine, fine. I didn't mean to scare you," he said. "Are you all right?"

"Yes, thank you. What's up? I've agreed to come to the horror convention. I'm bringing an entourage, including a PI and the FBI."

She didn't know if she was saying all that as a way to make Jeremy feel better or as a warning, just in case he knew the wrong people.

"Excellent. But that's not why I called," Jeremy told her.

"Oh?"

"I have another proposal for you."

"Aha. And what would that be?"

"Well, you know Vince Carlton? He contacted me again yesterday."

Marnie could feel Jeremy's miserable hesitation through her cell phone.

"He called me because Cara is gone. I guess everyone considered her the key in our family—when we were and weren't in character."

"I guess so," Marnie agreed softly.

"Anyway, he was gung ho about getting it all together again. Not replacing Cara. He said she could never be replaced. But he'd be growing the cast. In fact, he promised an episode dedicated to Cara that truly honored her."

"Jeremy, you know I don't really want to work in television anymore," she reminded him. "I believe I'm going to be able to start my theater—"

"Oh, I don't think so."

"What?"

"I guess you haven't seen Seth Smith's latest words to the press on the Abernathy."

"What has he said?"

"Oh, he's just gone on and on about how the Abernathy is truly a great old dame. She's never been tainted by any scandal. That they'd never allow her to be part of anything that isn't entirely legitimate and aboveboard—or involved with anyone who isn't legitimate or aboveboard."

Marnie felt the hardness in her tone. "I am totally legitimate and aboveboard!" she snapped.

"I know that. Anyone who really knows you knows that. But sadly, perception is part of every world—not just Tinseltown. I'm sorry, Marnie, and I could be wrong, but I don't think you're going to have an easy time—not at this moment—getting the Abernathy. Maybe in a while… Besides, Carlton was talking about reviving the series, but maybe they'll just do a couple of tie-up specials. You know, perhaps mourning Cara's character and setting the family back on a good path. Specials would be perfect. You could commit to just a few months, and then you'd be free again. It can't hurt to earn a little extra to sock away until your thing gets going."

"I'm not sure just what it is you want," Marnie said, feeling a little deflated. What he was saying was true. Making some more money didn't hurt, and Seth Smith was a snob. He and Wexler Realty might just sit on the Abernathy, rather than rent it, until they were happy. They controlled huge investments.

They could do it.

"Just meet with Vince Carlton? He's invited us all. Same studio address. They used our old standing sets for a TV movie about werewolves last month."

"I have to check out my availability," Marnie said drily.

"This afternoon? He'll be out at the studios this afternoon."

"Okay, as I said—let me check my availability."

Her availability? Sit here—except for Horror-palooza! Wait until someone else dies, wait until someone figures out what the hell is going on.

"You have to check with your guard dogs, eh?"

"Pretty much. And I have an actual guard dog now, Jeremy. He's great. But yeah, I have a very fine PI working for me right now, and he has some really fine FBI agents with him. Hang on."

She'd wandered into the kitchen earlier; she muted the phone and headed back out to her living room.

Angela was on the computer. Jackson and Bryan were reading over her shoulder.

Bridget was sitting on the sofa. She had gotten George to come up and sit next to her. He was a big dog; he didn't look really comfortable.

He looked at Marnie, tilted his head and raised an eyebrow— as if she might save him.

She called him. He bounded off the sofa to her. She stooped to scratch his ears as she told the others, "Jeremy Highsmith is still on the phone. He wants me to come out to the studio this afternoon."

Bryan, Angela and Jackson had looked up when she'd entered.

"Excellent," Bryan said.

"Yes, very good. I think it is time we get to know the rest of the *Dark Harbor* family," Jackson said.

"The surviving cast members," Angela murmured.

"And this producer who loves the show so much," Bryan added.

Through his parents, Bryan had been on set enough to have a pretty decent concept of how it all worked.

The massive studio building with huge double doors was still impressive, he thought as they pulled up in the seven-seater SUV Jackson had rented.

Dark Harbor had been filmed in a giant space owned by one of the cable networks. Every once in a while, an episode might be filmed on location. The studio was big enough that they didn't need the space for other shows, and it was more useful to them to keep the *Dark Harbor* mansion and other sets as permanent shooting spaces.

The standing set had received many changes since the original show had been canceled, but much of that had been cosmetic—set dressing and decorating. The bones of the old sets were the same.

Arriving in the studio, Bryan was impressed with the quick reconstruction that the producer, Vince Carlton, had managed.

He peered around the plywood flats to see that the family living room had been set up with the original Victorian reproduction sofas, love seats, wingback chairs, hutches, fireplace and more. Carlton had clearly pulled some strings to impress the *Dark Harbor* family.

They'd been greeted on arrival by the other cast members and Vince Carlton. He knew Marnie already, and he and Bridget had met at some kind of award ceremony somewhere along the line, *according to Bridget*. He was extremely courteous to Bryan, recalling that they had met at the funeral, and to Jackson and Angela, as well.

The group stood just inside the studio building, half-immersed in the fantasy world of the show, but with the doors open to the lot behind them.

"FBI, huh? I suppose you can never be too careful," he said.

"We really need to find a killer," Jackson said politely.

"Of course. We've had security all over this place, so no one unauthorized can get close," Carlton said. He was medium to tall in height, lean and wiry. Bryan figured him to be somewhere in his midforties, a decent-looking man, and—being a working producer—probably fairly popular and quick to accrue friends: real ones, along with those just desperate for stardom.

"So, I'm open to a lot of things. Bridget, glad you're here. I'd love to get you in my writers' room. As you can see, we've got the basics and the groundwork for what we need. I've even received a few treatments and spec scripts. We're still in negotiation as to whether we'd reboot the series or perhaps pick it up for a few special shows." He paused, looking at Marnie, and then continued, "Obviously, we would honor Cara Barton. We would not replace her with another actress. We will have new characters."

As he spoke, another car pulled up.

"Ah, yes, and here is one of those characters," Carlton said with pleasure. He sighed softly. "Nothing like when timing works—and on the fly like this!"

The car was a limo with a driver.

The driver hopped out and opened the back door. The passenger was Malcolm Dangerfield. He looked at the group and grinned. "Hail, hail. The gang is all here. Marnie, Roberta, Jeremy, Grayson, hi! Mr. McFadden, we met at the funeral. I'm sorry, I don't think we've met. Will you two be on the show?" He was addressing Jackson and Angela.

"No, we're investigating," Jackson said, taking Malcolm Dangerfield's hand, which went a little limp.

"Angela Hawkins and Jackson Crow are FBI," Bryan explained to him. "They're here working on the Cara Barton case."

"FBI," Dangerfield said. "Oh, my God, yes, of course. Because first there's poor Cara—and then that was your pool that man was found in, right, Marnie?"

He looked over at her with very wide eyes.

Such a pretty boy.

Bryan lowered his head, drily amused with himself. He didn't have anything against Malcolm Dangerfield. The man had checked out okay. He wasn't known for tantrums or being difficult to work with. He didn't seem to have any scandalous relationships in his past or bad habits to hide.

He just really was...pretty. And it was obvious that Malcolm was here to be Marnie's love interest on the show.

"Yes," she said, and she sounded strong. "It was my pool. And whatever is going on, my friends here will stop it. And catch the killer or killers responsible."

"Bravo," Carlton said. "Excellent. For now, let's look forward. Let me talk to you all about the various possibilities of what might happen if everyone is willing." He proceeded to walk into the center of the studio.

"You all remember your living room!" he said dramatically.

As he spoke, a technician somewhere started up the fire in the "living room" hearth.

It was a nice effect.

"Concept one for the show. In a segment that honors Cara Barton, Mrs. Zeta has passed away. But with her passing, Marnie suddenly acquires the ability to speak with the dead. Along with that, she also has tremendous strength—not just physically, but with the power of her mind. There is a touching scene where the family is at the graveyard, in tears. It's there that Marnie sees her mother. By the family tomb, we discover Archibald Dixon—you remember him? The vampire with a bloodlust who disappeared in a cloud of smoke from season four, episode six, 'Blood!' He's back. Marnie is in mourning when she discovers he has been killing again, and he comes after her in the graveyard. Because of her mother's warning, she is able to turn and see him in time! With her newfound strength and the help of the man who has been falling in love with her—werewolf Oliver Douglas, Malcolm here—she defeats the vampire at last!"

"Exciting. What does it have for the rest of us?" Roberta asked drily.

"Oh, well, you are acquiring the same abilities as Scarlet. She doesn't want to believe in herself. Roberta, your character, Sonia, has to convince her it is all real, and she does have strength and power. Jeremy, your character is devastated by the loss of the love of his life, and you're lost when it comes to protecting your family because you're in so much pain. And, Grayson, as Nathan Zeta, you have to deal with the fact the women in your life tend to inherit more strength than the men. Some of the writing really is great. There is so much in this that follows the paranormal trend that is always lurking out there, and then the emotions we all have to deal with."

"So, it'll be the 'Marnie' show," Roberta murmured.

"Look, Scarlet Zeta was always the sweetheart of the show," Carlton said. "But please know you're all incredibly important to me—especially now...now that we'll have to go without Cara Barton. Rest assured, all the details will go to your agents so that you can discuss the various options and possibilities." He stopped for a moment, looking at Roberta. "I hope you realize what a tremendous opportunity this is for all of you. I've come this far, aware I would not be taking you from any other major commitments at the moment."

"Ah, Roberta!" Jeremy said. "Life isn't fair, and acting sure as hell isn't fair."

"What would you do with the show if you had the rest of the family but didn't have Scarlet Zeta?" Marnie asked. "There could be a long-lost sister who appears at the funeral. There's a plotline for you."

"There is no show without Scarlet Zeta. We've done market research. It could be a massive hit, but only with Scarlet."

"Marnie, we need you," Roberta said, the sound of her voice a little desperate.

"And Malcolm," Carlton said.

"I am…high on every chart out there," Malcolm said flatly.

"Ah, to be young again!" Grayson said and shrugged. "I'm just an old hack myself, Mr. Carlton. Ready and willing to do what's offered. You have me."

"I never said I wasn't ready and willing," Roberta said. She brightened. "Maybe Marnie could be a fool and not see what's right in front of her. Maybe, in his torment, Scarlet's lover turns to her sister, needing a kind touch."

She grinned and looked at Bridget. "If you were writing on the show, you could write that magnificently, right?"

Carlton didn't react to Roberta's comment. "Scarlet turns to her sister for help. She doesn't understand her new power or her feelings for her lover. Trust me, we want a lot of family issues involved, as they were before. People loved the show because they loved all the characters and the way the family in the show—paranormal though they might be—interacted. The Zeta family had all the usual situations—falling in love, getting hurt, hurting others…the kids on the show grew up on the show, and people loved it."

"It will still be an ensemble cast," Malcolm said.

Bryan had been observing silently. He meant to do nothing but protect Marnie—to make sure everyone knew she had people looking out for her.

This was Marnie's work. But he'd grown up with Maeve and Hamish McFadden, and had an inkling of how the business worked, and so he had to ask, "Malcolm, you are at the top of your game. Are you sure this is something you want to do?"

Carlton cleared his throat, annoyed.

"Ah, clearly he's being offered a great deal of money," Roberta said sagely.

"Listen, if this show comes back, I do believe it will be a massive hit again. Marnie was actually voted one of the sexiest up-and-coming stars about a year before the show folded, but we need to attach a really big name to it to make it a guaranteed success. Putting Malcolm Dangerfield into a cult show brings together two huge fan bases," Carlton said.

"Aha," Jeremy Highsmith murmured. "Hey, the boy is looking like son-in-law material to me!" he added.

"Look, you all know this isn't the way things usually work. I call your agents, they get the offers, you take them or pass. That would be the usual. Negotiation would take place before you all ever looked at each other again. The agents would be in play, not you in a group, here like this. I'm offering you this first look because—as a series again, or even as a series of specials—this could be good for everyone involved. Today is a courtesy. And yes, I'd love to see this happen. But I have a lot of irons in the fire."

"We're certainly pleased to be here!" Jeremy said. "Very pleased."

His words seemed to break some of the rising tension. Everyone laughed.

"You have to see this," Carlton told them. "Follow me!"

He lifted his hand. The unknown tech—wherever he was—raised more lights, revealing scaffolds that were obviously there to allow cameramen to obtain different angles. But the scaffolding surrounded other sets, making it hard to determine where they were.

"Right through the living room, ladies and gentlemen. You're going to love this…"

A hallway that supposedly led to the back of the house, and was always just off camera, was generously wide and led to another door. Carlton waited until the whole group was gathered at a door.

Then he threw it open.

"Enter the graveyard!" he said dramatically.

The "graveyard" was a stunning piece of design work. The floor was moss-covered underfoot. The horizon, painted in detail onto stretched canvas walls, faded away into mist in the dim light. Angled stones appeared to have been in the "ground" from the time of the revolution and were littered everywhere. There were mausoleums interspersed throughout—one larger than the rest with the name "Zeta" carved into what appeared to be stone, though was certainly not. Everything had the gray tinge of an old cemetery around it. Gargoyles graced the Zeta tomb, and angels and cherubs rose above many graves.

"Fantastic!" Roberta said. "I love this set. Does my character—"

"Get to have all kinds of cool fun in the graveyard? You bet!" Carlton told her.

"I have to see the movie this set was designed for," Jeremy muttered.

"Incredible, right? This was what got me thinking about *Dark Harbor*. Imagine filming here. I do think now is the perfect time for a revamp. You've all seen my intention. I'll be in touch with your agents. Now that maybe I have your interest. Of course, it's all about the bottom line—we'll see where we go from here. Lastly, there's lunch for us all in the office. If you will?"

It took a moment to pull everyone away. They were taken with the amazing atmosphere of the fabricated cemetery.

One by one, the others began to turn. Bryan saw Marnie

wasn't moving. He stood near her, setting his hands on her shoulders, ready to comfort—or protect—as needed.

"Marnie?"

He murmured her name softly, and then he saw why she had lingered.

The ghost of Cara Barton was leaned against the tomb that bore the chiseled name "Zeta."

She was smiling.

"I love it," she said aloud. "Marnie, please, even if it's just a special, one show—you have to do it. Please. Let them honor me. It would mean so much."

"Cara, we're still looking for your killer—a killer who might be after Marnie," Bryan said. He didn't know how Marnie would feel; here was Cara, in the ghostly "flesh," just as the producer had intended she be as her character.

Marnie had gotten strong.

"Cara, it's possible. Let's just see where we go from here. Finding your killer is far more important than appeasing your ego."

"Great line," Bridget said, coming up to the two of them. "If they don't use it, I'm going to steal it."

The ghost of Cara Barton threw up her hands and disappeared behind the tomb.

"Are you all coming?" Vince Carlton called.

Marnie looked at him and smiled.

"Yep, on our way!" she said.

Marnie was becoming very strong, indeed. And Bryan was glad.

He had the wary feeling that no matter how he or anyone tried, she was going to need that strength.

CHAPTER ELEVEN

She just didn't want to work on a television series.

As she sat at lunch, Marnie felt bad about that. She knew it was a dream for many young women in Hollywood.

Bryan was on her left; he never went far from her.

Jeremy Highsmith was on her right, and she had always liked him. She thought that he had to be in his late fifties now. If not fantastic shooting stardom, he'd enjoyed steady work as an actor throughout his life.

That was a goal many people didn't recognize. In the eyes of many, Hollywood meant being a star. But half her friends weren't household names—they were, however, working actors. They made a living at their craft, and that, in Marnie's mind, was success.

"What are you thinking?" Jeremy whispered to her. He was still a good-looking man with his straight posture, silver hair and handsome features.

"I'm thinking that I wished I really wanted to do a series."

"And you don't. What about the idea of doing some specials? Vince Carlton does have a good idea there. To be honest, I don't like the series idea myself. And truthfully? I think the time is past. I don't think we'll be a success—even with Malcolm, who will be offered a fantastic sum of money and use up most of the budget."

"That's what happens when you're that hot," Marnie said.

"Of course." He sighed and lifted the glass of tea he'd been drinking. "Here's to Cara. Now, you know, Cara definitely wanted a series. She wanted her life on a nice schedule. I don't really blame her for that, but... I think we could make a few good specials. One to honor her. She was a good TV wife. And a friend." He shrugged. "Although we had artistic differences now and then. Upon occasion, I could have killed her." He stared at Marnie, as if stunned by what had come out of his mouth. "Figure of speech, Marnie. I didn't kill her. I mean, she was a friend. We were aging B stars together. Okay, so she thought of herself as an A star, but... I am a pragmatic man. None of that matters. I didn't kill her, Marnie. Really."

She smiled. "I know it was a figure of speech. I don't believe you killed her."

He leaned forward a little, looking past her to Bryan McFadden. "Did you know his folks?" he asked.

"No."

"I met them. They were generous people. Maeve had a heart the size of Texas."

"I've seen them in movies, of course."

He nodded. "The wonders of the internet and modern TV. We can all see things over and over again. We can even rewatch ourselves—in *Dark Harbor*." He paused. "You do understand you're the one they want. If you say no to all this, it's over."

The way he was looking at her made Marnie wonder if he really cared, if he was hoping it would all fall apart.

"I think they want Malcolm. I hate to consider myself a has-been in my late twenties, but we were huge when the series was huge. While it's nice that we have a bit of a cult following, Malcolm is the man of the moment."

He shrugged. "Malcolm will come out smelling like roses if we do or don't do the show. He's got more offers than he knows what to do with."

"True."

He sighed. "Grayson is still a fine-looking young man. I'm sure he'll land something good soon enough. And Roberta. She is a beauty."

"Yes, yes, she is," Marnie agreed.

Marnie realized then that Bryan McFadden had been listening in, though it seemed he'd been talking to Roberta, on his other side, all the while.

Across the table, Vince Carlton rose. He raised his glass of iced tea.

"A toast to you all. In remembrance of Cara Barton."

"Hear, hear! To Cara," Jeremy said, standing and raising his glass high.

They all stood.

"To Cara," echoed around the room.

Nice. She'd be happy about a toast, Marnie thought.

Then Marnie realized that Cara was casually seated in one of the empty chairs at the large conference table.

The ghost of Cara rose and walked around behind Marnie. She felt a strange brush on her nape and knew Cara had come behind her, and she was affectionately placing her hands on Marnie's shoulders.

"Lovely," she said. And then she sighed deeply. "If only I were here."

"You are here," Marnie said softly.

"What was that?" Jeremy asked.

"Nothing, sorry, just thinking about Cara," Marnie said.

Cara laughed delightedly.

"I mean, in the flesh, of course," she said. "Oh, Marnie. I want the best for all of you. But this is so hard. I wanted this show so badly."

Marnie wanted to speak to her; she wanted to reassure her. But how could she do that?

Cara was dead.

"You have to be very, very careful," Cara said.

"Yes," Bryan said very softly. He didn't turn. He looked at Marnie and smiled gravely.

"To the new show!" Malcolm said. "And," he added, "our way to do a real tribute to Cara Barton."

Roberta Alan couldn't believe that—especially with his parents—Bryan had no desire to act.

"I think it's a passion for some people and not others," he told her. He wanted to draw her out. He couldn't help but believe, no matter how improbable, Cara had been killed by someone here, someone close to it all. At the very least he could start ruling people out.

Yet it made no sense. They all seemed to really want the show—except for Marnie.

And now he knew Jeremy Highsmith wanted it only on certain terms.

He tried to imagine each of them finding out how to hire a killer. Then deciding the killer had to be killed. He tried to imagine each of them dressed up in a Blood-bone costume, luring the hired killer to Marnie's backyard—and shooting to kill.

Roberta was a lovely young woman. She was as thin as a whippet; she was a runner, she had told him. It had nothing to do with the Hollywood demands of perfection.

"Frankly, I haven't been doing that much lately. I have been looking forward to this show starting up again. Not that everything is terrible. I don't mean that at all. In a way, after a show like *Dark Harbor*, we're seen forever as that one character, and casting directors hesitate when looking at us, even if we were popular. Because new shows want to create new characters. Think of the amount of actors you've seen in series who seem to disappear right after. But I did just shoot a great commercial for a fast-food chain. It will air right around Halloween. See—that's what I mean. Although it won't say I'm Sonia Zeta from *Dark Harbor*, a lot of the audience will know me as that—cool and freaky around Halloween."

"I'll bet it's a great commercial."

Roberta laughed, smiling at him, placing a hand on the top of his. "You are so polite. So wonderful… Marnie is lucky. You know, I was truly a fan of both your parents. There's an old war movie your dad was in—"

"High Time for Heroes," Bryan said. "World War II movie. He played a soldier stuck behind enemy lines. It's one of my favorites. And one of his. He was in the military when he was young and served in Southeast Asia. The role meant a lot to him."

"He was so wonderful in it. And I've heard he was a nice guy, too. I guess that's why they raised you to be okay."

"Well, thank you, Miss Alan," he said.

She was flirting with him.

Whether she was yesterday's news or not, she was still a stunning woman. The only thing wrong with Roberta was the fact that she seemed constantly on edge. Yes, a whippet—nervous over any little noise.

"You're quite welcome. So," she said, peeking around him at Marnie, "I guess you all have become very good friends."

Marnie heard. She glanced quickly at Bryan and then looked at Roberta. "Yes," she said, much to Bryan's surprise. She spoke with a smile, sharing a confidence with her friend. "I'm sleeping with him."

Roberta laughed softly. "Bravo!"

For a moment it was as if Bryan wasn't between them—wasn't there at all.

"Does he have brothers?" Roberta asked.

Marnie told her, "Two of them! Bruce and Brodie."

"You've got to bring them out here," Roberta said, speaking to Bryan again.

"He can try," Marnie assured her.

Malcom—to Roberta's other side—said something and she turned to answer him.

Bryan looked at Marnie, smiling curiously. "I can't believe you just said that."

"I wasn't even technically correct," she said. "I've slept with you. I can't say that I've been sleeping with you, but… I was hoping it would continue."

"You are forever a surprise," he told her. "And beautifully honest."

"Oh, see! At least something good has come of this," Cara's ghost announced.

Bryan had forgotten she was behind them.

"Your parents would be delighted," Cara said.

"Dear Lord, will this lunch ever end?" he muttered.

But he was finding the lunch interesting. It gave him a chance to observe them all interacting with each other.

None of them seemed likely suspects and yet… Now Bridget was deep in conversation with Vince Carlton. She had a good job, but if Bryan understood it correctly, she worked for the production company that did sci-fi series, but she wasn't entirely locked-in—as long as she wasn't on another project at the time, she could take a contract to work on the new *Dark Harbor* scripts.

Bridget appeared happy. Whether *Dark Harbor* ever arose again or not, she'd made a good contact.

"Hey, did you have the salmon mousse?" Roberta asked. "It's wonderful!"

"Not a salmon kind of guy," he said.

"Really? More a meat-and-potatoes man?"

"Actually, I love a lot of seafood. Just not salmon," he told her.

"Sushi?"

"You bet."

Malcolm Dangerfield stood. "Guys, this has been great. I do hope we get to be a family. But duty calls. I have an appointment in an hour. Gotta head out."

That was the cue. Everyone stood.

"I just have to see that incredible graveyard one more time," Grayson said, looking hopefully at Vince Carlton. "I'm imagining what might be—if that's okay?"

"Certainly," Vince Carlton said. "We're just a few feet away. No harm in a walk-through that way."

Malcolm begged off, and he headed out to his waiting limo.

The rest of them trailed after Vince again.

Cara Barton came along with them, hanging close to Bryan— so close that he felt a ghostly arm entwined with his.

"There's something I can show you, I think. Hang on," Vince said.

He took off, leaving them at the entrance to the cemetery set.

Bryan was certain Vince went to speak to one of the technicians working in the studio.

The waiting group was right at the edge of the set.

Look one way, the world was real-life, with the cameras and lights and rigging and false walls.

Look the other, and it was pure fantasy, eerie and almost real.

In that direction, they stared at the headstones, the mausoleums, weeping angels and cherubs and gargoyles and more.

"Now," he heard Vince Carlton cry.

A fog rolled up in the cemetery. Slowly, creeping up from the ground, creating a gray mist all around the gravestones.

"Fabulous, right?" Vince said. "Oh, can you imagine the ghost of our matriarch, just standing there, watching sadly there… hoping to make contact with her children?"

"Yes, I can just imagine," Cara's ghost said softly. "Who will play me?"

Interesting question.

Marnie had heard her. She voiced it aloud.

"Who will play Cara's part?"

"Oh, here's what is so really wonderful!" Vince answered. "Cara!"

There was a stunned silence.

"The wonders of modern technology," he said. "I've gone through footage of old shows. I've found places where I can pull bits and pieces to really have Cara out here—on film, I mean. And then we have a stunt double for certain scenes. You've seen it done in other shows with wonderful actors we've lost—*Star Wars*, for one!"

"She would love it," Jeremy Highsmith said.

"I believe she would," Roberta added.

There was a natural moment of silence.

A real tribute to Cara.

"I do love it! One way or the other...make it happen, make it happen!" Cara's ghost announced to those who could hear.

Bryan glanced at Marnie.

She had heard.

She was smiling—but she did not respond.

The ghost of Cara Barton disappeared while they were still on the cemetery set. As they left, Marnie carefully looked, but no matter how she searched around tombs and stones—through the eerie rise of fog—she couldn't see Cara anymore.

Eventually, they all headed out, ushered along by Vince Carlton. They said their goodbyes. Jackson, Angela and Bridget moved on ahead of Marnie and Bryan. She was able to turn to him at last.

"Is it me?" she whispered. "I don't see Cara. But she was here...we were acknowledging her, right? This is a test for one's sanity, to say the least."

"We did see her," Bryan assured her, a grin twitching on his lips. "She is quite a personality. She's becoming a stronger apparition. Sometimes it's difficult for the dead to maintain visibility, even to those who see them. After years, I don't know how it all happens. Jackson and Angela work with a large number of people equally gifted—or cursed, as some believe—and no one really has the answers. Sometimes the dead linger for years. There's an old guy near my cabin in Virginia who died in the American Revolution. He guards a certain part of forest there. Seems happy enough. Then I know of others who eventually move on. That ray of light thing you hear about, leading to the afterlife, seems to be a real thing. A pathway, when people are ready to move on. Anyway, let's move on. We can talk more once we're out of here."

"Yes, of course," Marnie murmured.

Carlton was still standing at the giant doors at the entrance to the studios.

"Maybe Cara is doing some investigating on her own," Bryan said, speaking softly in her ear and waving goodbye to Carlton.

"That would be nice," Marnie said.

They had almost reached the car. They could hear Bridget telling Angela and Jackson about some of the scripts she had worked on.

"Science fiction is really an interesting field, and I love it. There have been all kinds of studies done and people love it as a real escape—of course, a lot is really scientifically sound. You have books that deal with space flight, planets, black holes, all of which exist. So, who is to say a massive colony of giant insects doesn't live on a distant planet in a galaxy far away? And yet, while it can be exciting and scary, a viewer doesn't believe they will be attacked by a giant praying mantis in the shower."

"But *Dark Harbor* was never sci-fi, right?" Jackson asked.

"No," Angela answered, rather than Bridget. She smiled at Marnie. "I admit, I watched the show. I thought you—and the entire cast—were very good." They were all looking at Angela, and she shrugged. "Hey, my life was weird. Made me like weird on TV. Half of America, so it seemed, was watching *Dark Harbor*, as well."

"Thank you," Marnie said. "It was a fun show to film, and I was a very lucky young person to have been working on it."

"And I'm lucky because I'm Marnie's cousin, and her connections got me out here and meeting people and finally working in a field I love!" Bridget said.

"So, today was good for you, right?" Bryan asked her.

"Excellent! I mean, I love what I do, but my contract stipulates I can work on other projects. I have a great manager," Bridget said. "And Vince Carlton is an amazing man. He has a vision for several things as far as *Dark Harbor* goes, but he has more ideas on what could really go like hotcakes, too. He was great. Wonderful. We chatted and laughed a lot—he loved *Return of the Turtle Beast*. And he pointed out that every film like that makes it or doesn't because of the characters, the emotion—and the humor. He said I have a wonderful sense of humor!"

"Excellent," Marnie told her. She was happy Bridget was so very pleased with the day.

She was happy, she realized, to be with Bryan. Crazy—as crazy as seeing ghosts. She couldn't imagine him *not* being in her life now, and he had barely entered it. Just the same, she refused to believe her children's theater at the Abernathy might really be a dying dream, while she knew Bryan McFadden would head back East. One way or the other, his future led back to the Virginia area.

She didn't want to think about that. And she didn't want to psychoanalyze herself. She sincerely mourned Cara and hoped it wasn't wrong to be so pleased to feel what she was feeling again—or had really never felt before.

"So, Marnie," Bridget said. She was in the back seat, behind Jackson, who was driving, and next to Marnie, who was in the middle. "You basically announced to everyone that you and

Bryan are sleeping together. It's going to be in the gossip rags in a few days, you know."

Marnie winced and flushed furiously. It had been one thing to make the announcement to Roberta when it seemed appropriate.

Here, in the car, with Bryan's friends—*FBI agents*—it seemed far more awkward. She caught a glimpse of Jackson's eyes in the rearview mirror; he was amused. Angela—next to her husband in the front passenger seat—turned slightly, smiling, as well.

"Um...thanks, Bridget," Marnie murmured. "Helping out just in case...everyone didn't know?"

"You said it to Roberta Alan! What are you expecting? Anyway, I'm thrilled for you." She looked over Marnie to Bryan. "I told you about the last jerk, right? Marnie was so disillusioned. And you know what? That ass thought he was somehow entitled. I mean, I hated being in a restaurant with him. I was always afraid someone in the kitchen would spit in my food just because of association."

"Again, thanks, Bridget."

"I'm your cousin. I get to speak my mind."

Bryan was laughing, Marnie realized. He caught her right hand and squeezed it.

"It's my personal belief everyone should have to work in a restaurant and wait tables," Angela said. "Learn how people can behave—and then learn patience for others."

"This is Hollywood. Everyone has been a waiter or a waitress," Bridget said.

"Not everyone," Marnie said.

"Oh, come on. When is the last time you ate out and the waiter or waitress wasn't a budding thespian?" Bridget asked.

"Last week," Marnie said. "My waiter was a budding screenwriter!"

"There you go," Bridget returned.

Everyone in the car was laughing. If it weren't for a little thing like murder hanging over all of them, life would be unbelievably good.

They reached the duplex. Marnie was impressed by the way that wherever they were—and without words—the FBI agents and Bryan managed to surround her and Bridget, even getting out of the car and walking up the steps to the duplex.

Bridget had work to do. Angela accompanied her to the other side of the duplex, assuring Bridget she had her own computer in her bag and could connect and work with their main offices back in Virginia just fine.

"I'll go out with George for a minute or two," Jackson said. He nodded at Bryan. Again, Marnie realized there was a silent communication between them.

Bryan really should join that Krewe of Hunters group! she thought.

George barked excitedly.

"We're going!" Jackson assured him.

"Excuse me a minute. I need to call the detectives on Cara's case," Bryan said. "I need to check in with Detective Vining and find out if he and Manning have made any progress. Jackson wants to plan a meeting with the local police tonight and naturally, we need them to assemble everyone they can."

"Of course," Marnie said.

It was just midafternoon. There were things that she needed to do, too. Two calls were important for her.

She didn't want to make either call.

The first was to her parents.

The second to her agent, Cybil Sherman.

"I'll be in my room," she said softly.

She left Bryan to make his call in the living room. She talked to her mom and dad. She convinced them that, as always, the papers exaggerated everything, and she and Bridget were just fine. They actually had FBI agents and a PI staying with them.

She thought that would make her folks feel better.

It didn't.

They wanted to know just how bad the situation was if federal agents had to stay with her.

She managed to make it sound as if Bryan and Angela and Jackson were there because of their family connection to Cara, and it was all just a precaution. Finally, she convinced them to stay in Australia.

Her second call was to Cybil.

Cybil immediately chastised her, saying she'd called her a thousand times. She hadn't, exactly, but Marnie had missed calls from her.

She was pretty sure her agent had wearied of her; there were bigger fish to fry if Marnie didn't want to work.

But, like the others, she had done guest star roles and commercials now and then. Cybil still sent her scripts. With the possibility of the return of *Dark Harbor*—even without Cara—Marnie was hot again.

"My dear girl, do you begin to understand the opportunities open to you now?" Cybil said. "And I heard you attended a meeting at Vince Carlton's studios today! Without me! Marnie, what are you doing?"

"No one had an agent there today, not even Malcolm Dangerfield," Marnie told her. "Cybil, forgive me, but now is not the time for...for pushing things."

"Sure! Keep on doing those silly conventions, my girl. I mean, think about it. Have you ever seen Brad Pitt or Julia Roberts or...or Meryl Streep or any such other A-list personality at a comic con?"

"Yes, actually, I have seen many extremely talented people at cons," Marnie said. She decided she wasn't going to mention the fact she'd agreed to Horror-palooza.

She heard Cybil's deep sigh over the phone. "Marnie, you can't imagine the interest people have in you lately. There are offers."

"And I can't tell you just how nice that is," Marnie said.

For a moment, she wondered just what the hell was the matter with her. She knew so many people—amazingly talented people who worked hard, who did all the right things, who could sing, dance, act, and who were all around hardworking—who never got a break.

Her passion lay elsewhere now.

"Marnie, girl, think of it this way," Cybil said as if reading her mind. "Make some big bucks, and then you can buy any damned theater you want—and let me slip away to a lovely retirement."

Marnie laughed. "I'm a little overwhelmed at the moment. Let's talk Monday, okay?"

Cybil agreed, and she and Marnie rang off.

Not so hard after all.

She walked back out to the living room. Bryan was just pocketing his phone.

"Everything okay?" he asked.

She nodded. "My parents. I'm trying to get them to stay down in Australia. They've dreamed of this trip forever, and they're finally on it and I don't want them coming back. Oh, God, you can't imagine what it's like if they're on a worried streak!"

He smiled. "Oh, hell, yeah, I can. And I'm hoping my parents are staying in Virginia!" he said. He sighed, smiled and shook his head. "You may well meet them, anyway, before this is all over."

"And you may meet mine. I also spoke with Cybil Sherman."

"Your agent."

"You know her?"

"I know of her. She has a very good reputation."

"She's a great person and a super agent. Anyway... I'll talk to her again on Monday."

He looked at her curiously. "I imagine there are offers flowing in for you now. For more than just a revamp of *Dark Harbor.*"

She waved a hand in the air and changed the subject. "Anything with the detectives?"

He nodded grimly. "They had officers out knocking on doors.

A number of people saw someone in a Blood-bone costume around the neighborhood. Cara was right."

"So where do we go from here?" she asked.

"Task force meeting later. We'll go over everything we have again."

She hesitated and then said quietly, "It wasn't in any way serious, but when I was talking to Jeremy today, he mentioned offhand, the way we all do—he said he wanted to kill Cara sometimes. I don't believe for a minute, a single second, he meant it in any way. For real, I mean. We all get angry and say that we could just kill someone."

"It's okay. I know," he said.

"Do you suspect it could be Jeremy?"

"Honestly? I can't pinpoint any of the cast as a likely suspect."

"But—"

"I said I can't pinpoint any of them. That doesn't mean any one of them is off my list. Except for Marnie, and I was with her when the man was killed in her pool."

"Clever killer, dressing up as a Blood-bone just as the hired killer was dressed."

"Yes. Because it is Hollywood. And anything goes."

"Sounds like a dead end."

"This won't be a dead end," he promised. "I won't let it be," he added softly.

"Lord, no! I'd never wish a haunting on anyone!"

He smiled and walked to her, taking her into his arms. "Miss Davante, you are continually surprising me. Actually, your casual announcement today stunned me."

She felt a blush cover her cheeks again. "I'm sorry. I really had no right. I don't know what caused me to say that... To do that."

"I like to think it might have been because you really do want to keep sleeping with me. I tend to be a monogamous kind of guy, as you might have figured, so..."

Marnie laughed. "Okay, okay, I just wanted Roberta to keep her grubby little hands off you."

"Fine by me—it was just… Wow. Shocking but nice."

Marnie leaned in. They heard the door opening.

Jackson was returning with George.

Any "sleeping" of any kind would have to wait.

They were home again. All of them.

Bridget and Marnie.

And the damned dog.

Bryan McFadden and his friends: FBI special agents. Oh, yeah, they were special all right.

So making a move on the house was out.

It was still fun to watch. Maybe it was the edge of danger. He almost wanted someone to realize he was down the street. That he was in his car—a rental car, changed frequently—and he was slunk low in the seat, able to observe without being observed. He had every right to be there, of course. All he had to do was hop out and say he was on his way to visit Marnie. Maybe he would just do so one day.

He smiled.

Not today.

Soon enough, they'd all be scrambling. They'd be in shock. They'd be in mourning again. And they'd be so confused. They wouldn't understand at all what had happened.

He did so love drama.

Soon enough.

He just wished he could get into the house. Watch how they reacted. That would be just great.

He imagined all the hell that would soon break loose.

He could hardly wait.

Anticipation, he was learning, was absolutely delicious!

CHAPTER TWELVE

Bryan became more impressed with the Krewe of Hunters—perhaps Jackson Crow and Adam Harrison specifically—as he attended the task force meeting late that afternoon.

It seemed at least a hundred police officers had been summoned to the station. He met another half-dozen detectives who had been instrumental in questioning witnesses.

Grant Vining spoke for the police, going through what they knew, didn't know and suspected. He warned the officers to be on the lookout for a Blood-bone who might just be walking down the street or hanging out.

There was no proof that Cara's killer had been hired and then in turn killed. But considering the circumstances and the identity of the body from the pool, it was a probability. Otherwise there was a copycat.

"But I don't believe so, and neither do our FBI partners on this investigation." He looked over at Jackson.

The field director walked to the center of the room, taking the floor. "We all believe these killings are directly related. We also believe Marnie Davante's home was targeted for the second killing. It was a warning to her, or just a way to torment her. We're keeping close tabs on everyone involved, as you know."

A few of the officers spoke, naming the sources who had seen the Blood-bone in Marnie's neighborhood, but they were unable to find anyone who knew anything other than "He walked off down the street." No clues as to where the killer might have gone.

Another officer reported no weapon had been found. They still searched the neighborhood, but it was most likely the killer had kept his gun or he had discarded it elsewhere.

No sword—as in the weapon that had killed Cara Barton— had been found. There were no further clues to help anyone.

"The point is we must be vigilant," Jackson said. He shrugged. "The rest of the people involved with *Dark Harbor* are still trying to function in the world. They are actors."

"They'll be doing signings at Horror-palooza tomorrow," Bryan offered from his chair.

"We've been in touch with the convention organizers, who have arranged extra security. People will be on guard. We've spoken to the comic publisher who does Blood-bone. There are no approved licensed uses of the costume tomorrow—or for any of the days of the show. Stop anyone in a Blood-bone costume."

Assent went around the room.

An officer cleared his throat. "Sir, if someone did just want Cara Barton dead with some kind of agenda in mind...well, we're going to be hard put to find out more. It is just possible that the deaths are not related."

"I almost guarantee you this is all related," Jackson said. He was quiet for a minute. "What frightens me is we believe that this is just getting started."

"Why?"

Vining decided to take the question.

"It may have started with a specific motive. A killer was hired, possibly to accomplish something in particular. But now, we believe he—or she—has killed of their own accord. And when you've hired a hit but then commit murder yourself…killing gets easier. Beyond the agenda, maybe."

Again, there was silence in the room.

"So we watch out for Blood-bone. Anything else?" another officer asked.

"High security at the *Dark Harbor* booth at Horror-palooza," Jackson said. "A watchful eye over the homes of the surviving actors. We are looking after Marnie Davante—she might have been the original target."

"Because she was a holdout on the *Dark Harbor* update?" a different man asked. His fellows looked at him. "What? I read the covers of the magazines at the checkout counter at the grocery store!" he added quickly.

"We need eyes on Jeremy Highsmith, Roberta Alan and Grayson Adair. I will leave that to Detective Vining and your managing sergeants and lieutenants," Jackson said.

"What about Marnie Davante?" someone asked. "She's the one we'd all like to watch!"

Smiles went around— No, laughter.

"We have that covered," Jackson said simply.

There were a few more random questions. Then another officer asked Jackson, "Sir, we've been taught we need three murders and a similar MO for a serial killer. Why is the FBI in on this situation?"

"We take all the help we can get," Vining said flatly.

Jackson added, "This is a very particular, high-profile situation. We're hoping we don't have a serial killer and we can end this. For now, we're trying to stop the situation from escalating.

"The LAPD is an excellent force. We're simply added resources and manpower," Jackson said. "We thank you for your cooperation."

"Thank you all!" Vining said.

It ended. The officers broke off into groups and started to filter out.

One man approached Bryan.

"You're not a cop or a fed, right? You're the PI on the case?"

"That's right."

The young officer nodded and then offered his hand. "Jenkins. I don't know if this is anything or not, but one of the men I spoke to—a fellow just off Barham—said that he thought the Blood-bone was a woman."

"Really?" Bryan said, not sure if he was surprised or not.

"I have the contact information for you to follow up. He was vague with me. A woman or, in his words, 'an old dude.' Anyway, I thought you might want to question him further."

He produced a piece of paper. It had a name, Ben Madrigal, an address and a phone number.

"I will talk with him. Thanks very much."

"Of course. I told Vining. He said you would want to do the interview yourself."

Bryan glanced over at Vining. He was giving officers instructions regarding the upcoming Horror-palooza. But Vining saw him look, and he inclined his head with a smile.

Thank you, Bryan mouthed.

A minute later, Vining came over to him. "I'll want a report on the follow-up, of course."

"Of course," Bryan agreed. "Jackson and I will head there now."

"What about Marnie? Er, Miss Davante?" Vining asked.

"Special Agent Hawkins is at the duplex," Bryan said.

Jackson was near. "Angela may look like an angel, but trust me. She's hell on wheels."

"I guess you would know," Vining acknowledged. "You work with her."

"Yes, I do. And besides that, I married her," Jackson said. He smiled. "If anyone is smart, they wouldn't mess with her. Trust me. I know I don't."

"We'll go speak with this witness right now," Bryan told Vining.

"I'll go with them," Sophie Manning had heard them talking; she had walked over.

"I'll be setting some schedules with the police. Oh, and on the rest of the *Dark Harbor* cast. We had patrol cars watch their homes." Vining pulled out his phone. "Jeremy Highsmith was back in his house by about 3:00 p.m. Roberta Adair—3:30 p.m. with a large bag of groceries. Grayson Adair, 3:25 p.m. None of them have left their homes."

"Thanks!" Bryan said.

"Shall we?" Jackson asked.

"I'll drive," Sophie said.

"I can drive," Jackson said.

"It's my neck of the woods. I know where I'm going!" Sophie said.

The two of them were heading out.

Bryan looked at Vining, who was grinning.

"Don't worry," Bryan said. "I don't give a damn who drives. It will probably be me—they'll still be arguing."

The Adventures of Huckleberry Finn, Aladdin, Alice in Wonderland...

Marnie was reading pros and cons on the production of various beloved plays for children's theater when her phone rang.

Bridget was with her, discussing the merits of each and the possibility of her scripting a new play for children Marnie might use as her introductory piece.

Assuming her theater ever got off the ground.

Angela was at her computer, doing whatever she did at her computer.

The alarm was on.

George was sleeping at Marnie's feet.

They'd all been so engrossed in their various tasks that they jumped at the sound of the phone.

"Man, I have that ringer loud," Marnie said, answering the call.

"Marnie, hey, it's David Neal."

"Hi, David. How are you?" Marnie asked.

"Fine, fine. I was just in your neighborhood and wondered if I might stop by. I have something for you."

"Oh?" Marnie asked.

Angela and Bridget were looking at her.

It was sad to her that any and every phone call had become suspect.

She covered the phone with her hand. "David Neal," she said. "He has something for me."

"What is it?" Angela asked skeptically.

"I've got a play for you," David said, as if he had heard the question—or, most probably, just responding to her "Oh?"

It seemed coincidental. Then again, David might just want to be a good assistant, anticipating what she might be needing next.

"A play?"

"It's a great play for children. It has an old wizard, a witch, a beautiful fairy and then roles for children. I mean, you're not just planning on doing plays for children—you're using them in your cast as well, right?"

"Both," Marnie said.

"The playwright passed away in 1878. The play is public domain, and it's truly wonderful. I saw it once when I was a kid in Nebraska. I couldn't find it for ages—I couldn't remember the title. And then I did. About a month ago, I ordered it from a theater shop in Chicago, and I received it this morning. I'd love for you to read it."

His enthusiasm was contagious. "It sounds great. We were just discussing the play list. I'd love to read it, David."

"Okay. I'll be right by—if that's convenient for you?"

"Yes, that will be fine. Thank you."

"He's bringing a play over?" Angela asked.

Marnie nodded. "You're okay with that, right?"

"I am—since I'm here. He's coming alone, right? And I have a Glock."

"And we have George!" Bridget said.

"Yes, and we have George," Angela said. She grinned. "The alarm won't mean much since we intend to let him in. I'll just let Jackson and Bryan know what's going on."

Ben Madrigal was quick to agree to see them when Bryan called. He was more than willing to help in any way.

When they reached his house—an impressive Colonial sitting on a nice-size lot—he was waiting for them on a rocker on his porch.

"Beautiful house," Sophie Manning said as they came up the walk.

He rose, beaming. "Thank you! Magic money. I produced music videos for years. I'm retired now. Thankfully, music videos took off like pure gold—as long as you picked the right bands. I had a knack for picking them. Didn't always like them myself, but I knew what other people might like, and I usually knew why, as well."

"Good for you, sir," Sophie said.

The man looked like a contented retiree. He was grandfatherly with snow-white hair in a small tidy Afro, a pleasant face and faded golden-brown eyes that were striking against his dark skin. He shook hands with all of them as they introduced themselves.

"The officer who interviewed you said you saw someone wearing a Blood-bone costume in the neighborhood, and you believed it was a woman. We're trying to find out if you would elaborate on that—or perhaps tell us anything else that might have occurred to you," Bryan said.

"Sure. Come in?" he offered.

"Thank you," Sophie said.

The three of them followed him into his house. They entered a hallway, and then a living room with period antebellum furniture, and a wall full of golden records and awards. Sophie chatted with him; he offered them drinks and they all declined.

And then they sat down and he talked.

"Here's the thing. I was just sitting there on my rocker on the porch, and then I saw the Blood-bone character. Coming toward me, right from Barham. Arms swinging, just as nonchalant as could be. A car would pass and someone would call out, and Blood-bone would raise an arm, click a finger as if he had a gun and wave on. No one gave him any heed. No more so than when you see a mascot in front of a nugget place...a cow telling you to eat more chicken...or, you know, any kind of a come-on."

"Exactly. But did you see where the Blood-bone was coming from?" Bryan asked.

"Down from Barham," Madrigal said.

"And he headed...?" Jackson asked.

"Up just around the next corner," Madrigal said.

"And you think it was a woman?" Bryan pressed quietly.

"Well, it could have been a woman. The movement, you know. When I was speaking with the young officer, I did suggest that. If not a woman, I think it was someone—and this is going to sound strange—either older, or just the opposite. Someone who has done stunts. If you watch any of the Blood-bone movies, you'll see that the Blood-bones are pros, actors who specialize in creatures, in movement."

"What do you mean?" Jackson said.

Bryan turned to him to explain to the best of his ability. "'Suit' actors almost never appear as themselves. They are giant animals, robots or whatever kind of being or creature. Actors who specialize in characters often take on acting jobs as themselves, meaning that they take on roles like anyone else, roles in which their natural faces and bodies are shown. But they are also especially talented in the art of wearing and moving in makeup and prosthetics. Take an actor such as Doug Jones—he is a fine actor with no special makeup or effects. But he was also Billy Bones in *Hocus Pocus*, Abe Sapien in the *Hellboy* movies, a number of creatures in *Pan's Labyrinth*, and I couldn't begin to tell you just how many other films he was in as himself or as a character."

"Doug Jones is a phenomenal actor," Sophie said enthusiastically. "He makes everything real. In my mind, there's such a difference, having an actor...or some obvious special effect."

"You still need effects," Bryan said.

"Of course. But in my mind, a lot of the old work was so much better than way too much digital manipulation," Sophie said. She frowned as her words left her mouth and said, "That didn't come out right. I was referring to CGI—computer-generated images. I happen to love a lot of the older work. Rick Baker— Oh, I remember when I was young and my brother let me watch his DVD of *An American Werewolf in London*! The work when David Naughton turned into a werewolf was phenomenal!"

Sophie definitely had Ben Madrigal's attention; it was a good situation. If they should need the man's help again, they would get it.

"Doug Jones is amazing. You also have men like Andy Serkis and Brian Steele. And, going back, few compare with the true master—Lon Chaney Jr!" Ben Madrigal said.

Bryan smiled; he hadn't had this kind of talk about the movies in a long time.

Not since his parents had died.

But though the conversation was nice, Bryan wasn't sure that they'd learned anything.

It could have been a woman.

Roberta Alan.

It could have been an older man.

Jeremy Highsmith.

It could have been any actor, one with specific training or natural talent...

"Excuse me," he said. "I just need to make a quick call." He headed to the hallway at the entrance to the home and dialed Angela's number.

"I was about to call you. We're expecting David Neal here at any minute," Angela told him. "I'm fine, but I wanted you to know."

"Why is he coming? I thought he'd already been interviewed."

"He is bringing a play—an old play, specially ordered—to Marnie."

"When you can, I would appreciate it if you could look into the professional backgrounds of Malcolm Dangerfield, Roberta Alan, Grayson Adair—and David Neal. Find out if any of them have done any creature or 'suit' work in the past."

"All right. Will do."

"We're nearly done here. See you soon."

He said goodbye and went in.

They were talking about the height of the person. "Ah, here's the thing. I should have paid more attention, but then... I've lived in LA my whole life. I've seen every manner of everything walk by. I'm pretty sure the Blood-bone didn't give a damn if he was or wasn't seen. Although... Wow, after that poor actress was murdered at the comic con, maybe I should have paid attention. It's just that...the character is loved. Hated. People love to hate Blood-bone. Hope I made sense with that one."

"You did. Not to worry. There's a Horror-palooza that starts tomorrow, and they're banning all official Blood-bone costumes and turning away con-goers who show up as Blood-bone," Sophie said. "But come Halloween, I can just about guarantee you there will be a lot of Blood-bones out there."

"The show must go on," Ben said. "And money talks. We all know that. Still, after what has happened, after everything on the news… I should have paid a lot more attention. I should have noticed height. I did notice movement, but… I couldn't tell you if the Blood-bone was five-six or six feet even or even taller. I just couldn't say."

Sophie said sincerely, "Thank you so very much for your help."

"Indeed. Young lady, you call on me anytime, you understand? And, of course, you, Special Agent Crow, and you, too, Mr. McFadden." He smiled at Bryan suddenly. "I knew your dad—great man. Looked like a linebacker, most gentle, courteous guy you'd ever want to meet. Kind of quiet but so very kind to everyone around."

"If you knew my mother, you'd know he didn't get many words in edgewise," Bryan said, smiling. "But thank you. Yeah, I think my dad was a great guy. But forgive me. He did a music video? If so, I didn't know anything about it."

"No, before I did music videos, I was a PA—production assistant," he added.

"I think I knew that," Jackson said.

"Anyway, I worked on a flick called *A Strange and Deadly Darkness*. Crime film, a bit on the noir side. Your dad was great."

"I remember. It was a movie based on a Poe story about a chimp having been trained to kill. The private investigator in the film was my dad, and he worked in a dark and seedy office in NYC. Some of the killings were in Central Park."

"Re-created right here in Hollywood," Madrigal said.

They thanked him again and headed out.

As Bryan had suspected, he'd taken the keys and done the driving while Jackson and Sophie had discussed the merits of each of them driving.

He drove back to the station to drop Sophie off to report to Vining, and he and Jackson headed back to Marnie's duplex.

★ ★ ★

"This is wonderful! I love it!" Marnie said.

The Miraculous World of the Wizard Zim.

Marnie was an incredibly fast reader, but even at that, she had barely scanned the play. Yet she could tell it was wonderful. Scanning alone showed her that. The play was a treasure that had slipped through the cracks of time.

"I think we talked about it already. I'd like to have an ensemble cast of adults—and yes, work with kids. One of the shows I have wanted to do is *Peter and the Starcatcher.* I had a friend in the cast that played here locally. I fell in love with it. It's based on the novel by Dave Barry and Ridley Pearson, and I love their work so much in novels… And the novel was then used to create a great play. With this one, though—public domain. That's a nice way to start when we really have to watch a bottom line."

David Neal grinned. "Are you happy I brought it to you?"

"Very."

"We could make quite a team," he said.

She could imagine opening her theater, using that play. She could talk some film friends into helping out so she'd have a spectacular opening.

It struck her that her life—at the moment—seemed to be on hold.

Cara was dead.

Another man was dead.

And while it really hadn't been long at all since Cara had been murdered so viciously in the convention center, it seemed as if time had become bogged down with the fear and the hope and the waiting. Today, talking to David, planning the play, made it almost seem as if the world was back to normal.

"Truly. This is wonderful! I think it's an opener. I love it," Marnie told David.

He still looked a little uncomfortable. He shot a glance over at Angela, who was working at her computer again.

On his arrival, Angela had frisked him. He'd had nothing on him but his wallet and a bottle of aspirin.

"Sorry," Angela had said simply. "There was a dead man in Marnie's pool. We have to take precautions. You understand."

"Of course," David had said.

The reassurance clearly hadn't really helped. He stared at Angela again. She was busy, but Marnie was certain she was listening in on them.

George was at Marnie's feet. If anyone were to threaten her in any way, George could probably rip them to shreds. She'd been told that the command to defend her was "Protect!"

Bridget had appeared long enough to say hello, then went to work in the guest room. Unlike Angela, Bridget liked to work in quiet, unless she was in a session with other writers and they were throwing ideas or lines around.

Angela looked up suddenly and said, "Excuse me. I have to make a phone call. I'll just be on the porch with the door open, so if you need me, a whisper will bring me back in."

When Angela had stepped out, David looked at Marnie and said, "She's very serious, isn't she?"

"Good at her job," Marnie said, still marveling at the wonderful play. "Would you like some tea or something? Soda? I'm sorry, I don't have anything stronger in the house."

"Uh, no problem," he said. "Tea would be great."

Marnie headed to the kitchen to brew a pot of tea. When she returned, David was where she'd left him on the sofa and still looked a little shell-shocked. She sat down with a tray laden with a teapot, sugar, milk, lemon—should he choose—and cups. He reached forward to help himself and his fingers brushed hers. He let them linger.

"We'll make a great team, won't we? I hope?"

It was just a brush, but the touch coupled with his words... She froze for a split second. He flushed and quickly withdrew.

She'd been uncomfortable. But the moment was over.

"Um, possibly," she murmured. Then she excused herself. "Just a second. I'll be right back. I'm going to check if Bridget would like a cup of tea. If Angela comes in, will you ask her for me? Thanks."

Marnie hurried down the hall to knock at the guest room door. She took a quick look back.

David was just pouring his tea.

Entirely normally.

She had definitely read something into his touch and words that wasn't really there. Hadn't she?

Bryan saw it was Angela on his line.

"You've got something."

"I do. I started checking out résumés and educations. You're on your way here now, right?"

"We should be there momentarily. We just dropped Sophie off."

"I have a few interesting pieces of information for you. Grayson Adair—his first job out here in LA was with a company called Bunny Studios. This isn't really being a specialist, but it's interesting. Bunny Studios provided just that—Easter Bunnies and more. Leprechauns for St. Pat's Day, Santas, elves, Mrs. Clauses at Christmas. They could provide just about anything for any season. Grayson worked with them for about two years, and then he got a recurring role on a soap opera, some TV movie roles and then *Dark Harbor*."

"Definitely interesting. Anyone else?"

"Yes. Jeremy Highsmith. He spent his first ten years in the business being what he referred to as a 'fluffy' at a number of the theme parks."

"So he's been all kind of comic characters," Bryan said. Jackson was looking at him. "Angela, I'm going to put the phone on speaker so that Jackson can hear, too. Hang on and just let me repeat quickly."

He did; Jackson listened and nodded.

"Okay, Angela, when you're ready. What's the rest?"

"Well, that's it for the cast. I can't find anywhere that Roberta Alan ever played any kind of a creature character, but—sorry, hang on," she said. She must have had her phone on speaker, too, because they heard her talking to someone else.

"You're leaving?"

The next voice wasn't clear. It belonged to David Neal.

"Yep, I have to take off—appointment later this afternoon. I just saw the time. Marnie went in with her cousin. Can you tell her that I'll be in touch and that I had to leave?"

"Sure. Take care," Angela said. "How odd. Hang on again. I'm going in the house. Marnie? Bridget? No—no, everything is fine. Just checking on you."

"Angela, they're fine, right?" Bryan said.

"Yes, David Neal just left."

"We heard," Jackson said.

"I searched him and all, but I was just outside, so…"

"We'll be there in one minute," Bryan said.

They were turning the corner to Marnie's street. Bryan drove up in front of the duplex, turned off the engine and hopped out of the car. He wasn't sure why he was worried. Nothing had happened.

He hurried up the walk. "He's gone already?" he asked Angela.

"He was in a blue Chevy Malibu. Drove off about sixty seconds ago," Angela said. She was frowning. "Bryan, I wouldn't let anything happen to Marnie."

Marnie came to the door; she had evidently heard what Angela had said. "I'm fine. And Bridget is fine. George sat at my feet like a lion. Nothing happened. I was perfectly safe, really— and David brought me a play that I really, really love!"

Bryan let out a soft breath of relief; he wasn't sure why he had panicked so much in the last few minutes.

"Anyway," Jackson said, joining them and casually slipping an arm around Angela's shoulders. "We have some FBI friends from back home arriving for the show tomorrow. Sean Cameron is coming with his wife, Madison Darvil."

"I know that name," Marnie said. "I think I've worked with Madison. Yes. She did some work with us for a werewolf story line on *Dark Harbor* years ago. She was great. Immensely talented and great to work with. Oh!" She paused, clapping her hand over her mouth and then removing it and explaining, "I remember! Sad case—a beautiful young starlet killed. And Madison worked for Archer's Wizardry and Effects. And Eddie Archer also owned the Black Box, and his son was accused of murder. But in the end..."

Jackson continued as she hesitated, remembering, "The Krewe stepped in. The guilty party was caught. Yes, that Madison. And Sean, of course, was out here working with her."

"She's brilliant. Did she become a part of the Krewe?" Marnie asked, puzzled. "I don't mean that as a bad thing, it's just that you can't imagine how fine she was as an artist."

"We seem to attract a lot of people with different talents," Jackson said. "At the moment, she's working on one of Adam Harrison's projects—a historic theater in Northern Virginia— right outside DC. Since you're doing Horror-palooza and we are concerned that something might happen again, it seemed prudent to add to our numbers. Sean is an exceptional agent, and Madison knows the industry and special effects and all kinds of things that might be helpful."

"Great," Marnie said. "I hope Madison remembers me."

"I can't imagine that she'd work with you and forget," Angela murmured, looking at Bryan. Apparently, Marnie had no idea at all she was really unforgettable.

"Angela, we were in the middle of a conversation before," Bryan said. "Let's go in?"

"But call George," Marnie said. "He's trotted off to the fence.

He can jump that little fence or could if he chose to. Good thing he's kind of a wonder dog."

"George!" Bryan said.

The animal was a wonder dog. He immediately trotted back, his tail wagging.

They all went inside.

"Okay, let me reiterate," Angela said. "Marnie didn't hear what I said to you."

"Let me get Bridget, then we'll all hear," Marnie said.

They heard a hallway door open and Bridget popped out.

"I'm here!" she called.

"And we're all gathered," Marnie said.

"And starving!" Bridget announced, plopping down in an armchair. "Am I the only one around here who thinks about eating?"

"I'll order pizzas. A vegetarian, a cheese and a meat? That covers everyone?" Jackson asked. He was aware that Angela needed to talk. Jackson Crow had a talent for taking control of what was necessary at any given time, and for giving the lead to any of his people when necessary, as well.

"Sounds good," Bryan said. "Angela, you want to go ahead?"

She did. She explained that Bryan had asked her to look for actors who had performed fully costumed or had specialized in roles with creatures—or had even had some training in the art. She told them what she'd found out.

"The neighbor we spoke to who saw Blood-bone said it seemed like someone who knew what they were doing in that kind of costume," Bryan explained.

"So, Roberta doesn't have that kind of experience, but Jeremy and Grayson do?"

"Correct," Angela said. "And I looked into Golden Boy—Malcolm Dangerfield," Angela said.

"And?" Bryan asked.

"Yes—and no. As a boy, he had a stint on a local TV show

as a robot. But that was over twenty-five years ago," Angela told them.

"Was that what we missed, what you were going to tell us?" Jackson asked.

"No," Angela said. "Right before David Neal left," she continued, looking at Marnie, "I had been about to tell Bryan about someone else who had that kind of start. Someone close—too close for comfort at the moment."

"Who?" Marnie asked, picking up her teacup.

"David Neal," Angela said. "In Chicago, he worked for one of the beer companies. He wore a draft horse costume almost every day for two years. He worked with kids in a little park there, and he even did a few commercials in costume."

"David was a performer?" Marnie said thoughtfully.

The cup was almost to her lips.

Bryan didn't know why. He didn't know what drove him, what logic he could possibly be using.

Maybe there was none.

No reason.

But...

David Neal had just been in the house. And Angela had found information on him that suggested he might well have played a damned good Blood-bone.

He had been standing there, right in front of Marnie, when the first Blood-bone character had killed Cara Barton.

"No!" Bryan shouted.

He leaped across the room, knocking the teacup from Marnie's hand.

Tea went flying everywhere.

CHAPTER THIRTEEN

Full darkness had fallen sometime ago.

He wanted to leave. He wanted to drive back and watch the house. Marnie's house. He wanted to imagine her in it—and those other people gone.

Although…he couldn't wait to see their reactions to his last little piece of "live" theater.

Foolish, of course. No one would know what had happened—what he had done—until tomorrow. Unless something truly unusual was to happen. And while he longed to watch, he knew they were watching, too. Who exactly were they watching? How closely were they watching? He didn't know, but he wasn't taking any chances.

No, he didn't dare.

There was nothing to do that night but dream, plan, envision, wonder…

Drama…on the stage…on film.

And in real life.

The important thing, of course, was that he could act. Far better than they might imagine.

His phone rang. He realized, as he answered it, he was awful hopeful it would be her calling—Marnie. That she would just need to hear his voice. Now, that was fanciful.

It wasn't Marnie.

"I'm nervous," came the voice.

"Because you're a coward," he said. "Talking isn't good. We don't know what's going on. Maybe someone's listening."

"What?" The question was stunned. And then the idiot on the other line realized that maybe their phones were somehow being tapped.

"Oh, well, just so you know, I'm unhappy, scared, and I'm starting to think…"

"Don't think. It's dangerous," he said. "And don't call like this!"

He hung up.

He realized he was thinking about murder again. About a time and a way.

It was delicious. Ever more so when it came to an annoying partner who seemed to be getting very cold feet. The idiot was scared? Well, that fear was scaring the hell out of him, as well.

Just one more who had to go. And Lord! The power truly was intoxicating!

"What in God's name?" Marnie gasped, jumping up and staring at Bryan as if he'd lost his mind.

"Bryan, what's the matter with you?" she asked. Her tea hadn't been that hot anymore; she wasn't scalded anywhere, but she was wearing a lot of it and little droplets covered the sofa and the floor.

"Got it!" Bridget said.

"Wait!" Bryan said.

Bryan had walked across the room and was studying the remains of the cup. "Here!" he muttered, carefully picking up a piece.

"What are you doing?" Marnie demanded.

He looked at her, olive eyes flashing with impatience. "He's a suspect, Marnie. He played creatures—he could wear that costume well. He was staring at you, right at you, when Cara was killed. And he was here when Angela found out about him, and then he was suddenly gone."

"Yes, but… Angela frisked him! He had no gun, no knife—"

"He had an aspirin bottle," Angela said.

"I made the tea!" Marnie said.

"And you were with that cup and the tea every second he was here?" Bryan demanded.

"Yes!" Marnie said.

"No," Bridget argued softly. She looked over at Marnie. "No, you weren't with the tea every second. You came to my door and then into the room. In fact, you said David Neal was making you feel a little uneasy."

"He was making you feel uneasy?" Bryan snapped. "Why?"

"I… Nothing deadly. He was just…"

"Touchy-feely?" Bridget offered.

Marnie shook her head. "Not even that. I don't know."

"But you weren't with the tea every second, right?"

She sighed. "No, I wasn't with the tea every second." She frowned. "You think David Neal might have poisoned my tea?"

"We can't take chances right now, Marnie," Jackson explained. "We can't take chances. We'll have what we've recovered analyzed. It's probably just tea."

Marnie sank back into a chair. She let out a soft sigh. "This is…ridiculous. I can't be afraid of everyone and everything!"

"Right now, yes, you can be," Bryan said flatly.

Jackson's phone rang. Loudly. Everyone jumped.

"Sorry!" he murmured. He looked at the caller ID before answering.

"What is it?" Angela asked.

They were all waiting for something.

Something dire, Marnie realized.

"Jackson?" Angela said. He looked at his wife and grimaced.

"Pizza," he said.

Marnie had gone into her bedroom early.

It had been a long day.

Bryan felt the emptiness of the living room with the others gone. Then George whined, setting a wet nose on Bryan's hand.

"Okay, boy, we'll go out for a last romp, huh?"

He took the dog outside. While they were strolling around the block, he suddenly had a thought and called Angela. "The car," he said. "David Neal's car."

"Yeah. Blue Chevy Malibu," she said. "You have something?"

"I don't know. I'm going to call on Ben Madrigal again, see if he saw a blue Malibu the dead-man-in-the-pool day. When Blood-bone was just cruising the neighborhood."

"We need the contents of the tea analyzed. I can take Bridget with me and drop it off first thing in the morning."

"Not necessary. I'm going to call Sophie. She'll get it tonight."

"Call me again if you need to," Angela said. "Or if you have any other ideas."

He called Sophie Manning next.

She promised she'd be right there.

Bryan then dialed Ben Madrigal, hoping it wasn't too late, that the man might be a night owl.

Madrigal answered his phone.

"I've kind of got a bit of a thinking question for you," Bryan said pleasantly. "Because, we all see cars everywhere every day. Do you remember by chance if, on the day you saw Blood-bone, you also saw a blue Chevy Malibu?"

"Well, I've definitely seen a sporty blue car parked in the neighborhood," Ben Madrigal answered him. "It's parked here frequently. I thought it belonged to someone living in a house—apartment, or duplex, studio or whatever—in the neighborhood. Come to think of it, though, it moves. It's on different blocks all the time. But yes, I've seen what I believe is a blue Chevy Malibu."

"And on the day you saw the Blood-bone...did you see the Malibu?"

Madrigal was quiet. "I want to say yes. But... I just don't

know. I really just don't know. Like I said, I know I've seen it. And like you said…days mix up, you know?"

"Of course. Yes, they do."

"I wish I could be of more help."

"You've been a tremendous help. Thank you."

He hung up. Sophie Manning was on her way, but he called Grant Vining to tell him what he'd learned, and then he called Jackson.

By the time he finished his calls, he and George had made it back to the house, and Sophie was there. He gave her everything he had collected; she took it in an evidence bag.

"How long do you think?" he asked her.

"We'll have an answer soon—by tomorrow morning. I have friends who work in the crime scene lab on the graveyard shift. They'll help me out."

"Thank you, Sophie. Seriously."

"Hey. Thank you for being out here."

She patted George and then left. Bryan locked the door and set the alarm.

Then he stared at Marnie's door.

She had been angry. He figured she was resentful of how overprotective he was being, and she was thinking she was crazy to be involved with him.

He should just stay out.

He couldn't.

It was silly, maybe… They'd spent just a night together. But she'd announced they were a duo; she had seemed to really care.

He couldn't stay away.

"George, go to sleep, please," he told the dog.

And he watched in wonder as the dog curled up to do as told.

He tapped lightly at Marnie's door. It immediately sprang open.

It appeared she had fallen asleep at one point, but then had been waiting for him. Her wealth of rich dark hair was in a wild array around her head, her eyes were exquisitely blue green and slightly hazy, and warmth seemed to glow from the length of her. She was clad again in a long cotton T-shirt—the right attire, definitely, for a time when you weren't sure who filled your house, and he approved of the way it softly draped over her curves.

"Hey," he said.

"Hey," she returned and smiled, and something changed in her eyes. A light appeared in them that was wickedly delicious. She threw her arms around him and drew him to her for a kiss.

One that included the full pressure of her body against his, her hands running down his back, her tongue delving and playing and doing things that made him pay attention.

He eased her forward, closing the door behind him. He returned her kiss, tongue every bit as wicked and erotic. The pressure of her body was hot, the feel of her kiss wet. He couldn't break that kiss, even as he tried to strip down.

Marnie was the one to break away.

She did so to move her lips and teeth and tongue across his body, down...

He was very glad that the action for Marnie wouldn't begin the next day until after ten.

They made love. And then again. And then...again. She created a desire in him that burned, hot and constant.

And was like nothing in the world when it was appeased.

Late in the night, she slept in his arms. Curled partially atop him, beside part of him.

He couldn't help but marvel. And pray that it would be forever.

First, of course, he had to make sure Marnie would be forever...forever, as in a full lifetime.

Horror-palooza was spectacular. Artists showed their creations and wares in large and small booths, in large and small quantities.

Creatures abounded—incredible creatures, created by the best in the business.

Zombies posed before a Cadillac. A family of vampires relaxed upon a Victorian couch. Aliens were here and there. Monsters created by toxic waste raged and growled in shocking tableaux. There were versions of old monsters—the Frankenstein monster, Dracula, the Wolfman, the Mummy and more. There were makeup artists offering spectacular face painting to conference goers—for a fee, of course—and also showing off with their own models, creating amazing creature effects. They were also selling their cosmetics—naturally, hoping for some big sales with the studios who would be working with makeup and prosthetics.

There were costumes, statuettes, prints, paintings.

So much art!

In Marnie's mind, the life-size creatures were the most amazing, and the tableaux that had been created to showcase them.

She'd always been in awe of *fabricators*, artists who couldn't really be defined in one area.

Like Madison Darvil.

Madison had arrived with her husband, Special Agent Sean Cameron, just before they'd left the house. Marnie and she hadn't been inseparable friends back in the day or anything of the like, but Madison had been one those people she had instantly liked, admired and with whom she'd really enjoyed working. She didn't just create costumes or makeup effects, she worked with just about everything and could create just about anything— from a life-size puppy selling insurance to a helpful robotic alien to a chilling, decaying vampire.

They'd hugged; Madison had been delighted to see her. And then she'd learned that Special Agent Sean Cameron had once studied under Eddie Archer, one of the finest fabricators to be found anywhere, as well.

In her living room, Marnie felt a little shaky as they all greeted one another.

She was lucky.

She'd come to realize she was protected and possibly alive because of Bryan McFadden; he'd brought in an elite unit consisting of Jackson and Angela, and now Madison Darvil and Sean Cameron.

While everyone hugged—and before Bridget arrived at that half of the duplex—Cara Barton made an appearance. She was delighted she'd managed to get Marnie so much help.

She was thrilled that an entire room of people could see her. She was so excited and dramatic she didn't really last—or remain visible—long.

When Cara disappeared, Marnie said drily, "I'm haunted by a bit of a diva."

Bryan sniffed, and she realized she did want to meet more dead people—she wanted to meet his parents.

Madison Darvil laughed softly. "Tell me about it."

Sean spoke up. "Madison and Bogie were just like this." He lifted his hand, showing his entwined fingers.

"Bogie? You mean Humphrey Bogart?" Marnie asked.

"In the almost flesh," Sean said sincerely, and everyone smiled.

When Bridget knocked on the door, they all went out to the cars and made their way to the conference center. Even the outside was decorated with huge and fantastic creatures—giant tyrannosaurs formed an archway over the main entry doors.

Bryan had spoken with the conference managers, and he led the way through side doors. Marnie greeted the conference workers who helped them, and autographed a few of the show programs as a thank-you, before their assigned assistant walked her through some of the exhibits to the place where the *Dark Harbor* cast would meet and greet and sign.

They had a really nice place at the front of the convention center. It was so sad, she thought, that they had risen to such prominence only after Cara had been killed.

Over the past weeks, Cara's face had graced dozens of magazine covers and hundreds of newspapers and possibly thousands of websites.

A beautiful picture of Cara with Jeremy Highsmith—as Mr. and Mrs. Zeta—covered the space behind them. The *Dark Harbor* cast was on a podium, and they had three convention hall employees assigned to watch over them and handle crowd control.

"Cara would be happy with this setup," Marnie murmured to Bryan.

"Cara will probably be here," Bryan said. He was watching Sean and Madison.

The two were speaking softly together. Madison was lovely, with large blue eyes and long silky hair; Sean was a fitting companion, tall, broad shouldered but lean, with a striking face. Of course, they would both know a lot of people at the show.

And more, they would know a number of the actors at the show who specialized in creature character work.

They could be on the watch for someone—likely not Bloodbone today, but another persona—who might be carrying a weapon and have bloodshed and murder on the mind.

"You're the second one from *Dark Harbor* to arrive," Shandra, their first hostess-crowd-control-helper, told them, walking them all from the special guest entry to the booth where they would sit.

Roberta Alan was straightening pictures on the table. She saw them arrive and gave them a beaming smile.

"Marnie! Thank goodness you're here." She hugged Marnie as if it had been years since they had seen one another and not a day. She stepped back and grinned at the others and then frowned slightly as she noticed Sean and Madison.

Looking at Madison, she said, "I know you. Why do I know you?"

Madison grinned. "Werewolves. I forget what season it was. I worked with you on the werewolf story line. My name is—"

"Madison! Madison Darvil!" Roberta said.

Well, she hadn't seen Madison for years, so maybe it was natural that she hugged her to pieces. Then, she met Sean and learned that he, too, had worked with Eddie Archer at one time.

"But you're FBI now?"

"Stranger things will happen," Sean assured her.

"Ah, yes… Well, I suppose so." She grew somber and said in a husky whisper, "Nothing was stranger—ever—than watching Cara Barton be murdered. Nothing. So horrible." She shuddered.

"And yet…it was just a little over two weeks ago," Sean said politely, smiling.

It was impossible to tell if there was a jab in his words or not.

"I have to survive," Roberta said. She put an arm around Marnie. "And thanks to friends, I will."

"And our other friends, I hope," Marnie murmured. Jeremy and Grayson had yet to arrive.

"Well, I have some other, er, kinds of friends for you," Madison said, grinning. "Friends of friends. From the team at Archer, we're providing a bit of decoration."

As she spoke, convention workers pushed carts up to the booth.

Sean asked Jackson and Bryan for help.

The three of them and the convention workers pulled off the covering sheets.

Madison had managed to get them the creature fabrications and costumes that had been used in the werewolf story line.

The werewolves were magnificent. Just a little taller and bigger than a normal man, intricately created with eyes that looked alive, teeth that gleamed and forms that truly seemed ready to pounce and bounce.

They were all admiring the werewolves, Madison, Roberta and Marnie laughing and talking about the time of their use—"Cara used to call them Tom and Dick!" Marnie told them—when Grayson Adair arrived, laughing delightedly as he remembered them, as well.

"I think I finally got to beat Tom over there to pieces!" he said.

Roberta added, "Marnie used her mind play on Dick, and he turned into a Pekingese or something."

"Yorkie, it was," Grayson said, grinning at Marnie.

"Yep, a Yorkie," she agreed.

"Doors are opening to the day crowd. You may be barraged, and I'll do my best to help," Shandra told them. She was a tall girl, probably about eighteen, thrilled to be with them—and very, very perky.

Marnie tried to smile at her.

"Jeremy isn't here yet. Has anybody talked to him?" Marnie asked.

"He isn't answering his cell," Roberta said.

Marnie looked at Bryan. He walked over and slipped an arm around her. She knew he was waiting for the results of the tests on her teacup.

She couldn't believe David Neal had tried to poison her, but Bryan was protective.

It wasn't a bad thing.

"I'll find out about Jeremy," he promised her. Then he added, "Wow!"

The doors had opened. People were flooding in.

Some wore casual dress; many were in T-shirts that advertised their favorite shows, movies or characters; lots were in costumes, from cosplay to Victorian, from the beautiful and sublime to the absolutely horrific.

It seemed that most were heading to the *Dark Harbor* booth.

That was understandable. There were some pictures left that already had Cara Barton's signature on them.

They could get big bucks on the internet.

Marnie smiled.

It was time to smile. And thank people, sincerely, for their support.

★ ★ ★

Bryan stood just behind Marnie at the booth, watching.

If anyone came near her, he was ready.

Bridget and Angela were walking around the show floor; he didn't believe Bridget was a target. He didn't want her to be collateral damage. She would be good at noting any abnormalities at the show—if anything could be considered an abnormality.

Jackson, Sean and Madison were on the floor near the booth. Many old colleagues were greeting Madison, complimenting her, asking where she'd been.

She'd been aware of the dead for a long while. Bogie had actually been "her" ghost—he had spent his time haunting her, long before she had met and married Sean.

She was good at what she did and excellent at deflecting questions, simply saying she'd found theater work she just loved out East.

Bryan knew Marnie was concerned about Jeremy, and so he called Detective Vining.

Vining was at the show himself, watching the entrance. But he called the officer on duty who was watching over Jeremy. Then he called Bryan back.

"He hasn't left his house yet," Vining told him. "The officer watching him has been on duty since 6:00 a.m., and Jeremy hasn't come out."

"He's not answering his cell phone," Bryan said.

"Maybe he's sleeping. Maybe he doesn't want to talk."

"He's supposed to be at Horror-palooza. He wouldn't just not show up, not without calling to say he was ill or something had come up." Bryan was speaking softly. In front of him, at the table, Marnie, Roberta and Grayson were signing pictures and speaking reverently about Cara Barton.

Bryan looked around for her ghost.

He didn't see her.

He imagined she'd show up sooner or later.

This would just be too good for her to miss.

"McFadden, this is a touchy situation."

"Ask the officer to knock at his door, to try to get him to open up."

"All right. I'll get back to you," Vining promised.

Bryan kept looking over the floor.

There was a sudden surge of humanity in another direction, just across the hall.

It was Malcolm Dangerfield. The man, surrounded by "his people" and what looked like an army of media, was taking up his position at his own booth. It was a little surprising that he was there, being so very popular at the moment, but he had a science fiction movie coming out soon and must have been convinced it was worth his time.

Bryan's phone rang; Detective Vining was calling back. "Still waiting on the officer at Highsmith's. But I do have something interesting for you. Lab results back on the remnants of tea you asked Sophie to have analyzed."

"If there was any kind of poison," Bryan said, his muscles tightening, "you can find David Neal and arrest him immediately."

"There wasn't poison," Vining said.

"Ah," Bryan said, cursing himself. Where the hell were his instincts?

"But there was something," Vining said. "Traces of gamma hydroxybutyric acid, a date-rape drug. Looks like David Neal was trying to get a lot closer to Marnie than she may have expected. He seemed to want more than a job."

"You are going to arrest him then, right?"

"Yes. He could be facing a felony charge for lacing her tea— and we'll have to prove it somehow, which we may not be able to do, but…at the very least, while he may not be a cold-blooded murderer, he is one hell of a slimy bastard."

"You'll get him down to the station?"

"I've got Sophie on it. As soon as she can find him, she'll bring him in."

"Thanks. Let me know."

"You bet. The minute we have him."

He rang off. Once Malcolm Dangerfield had come into the room, the line at Marnie's booth had died down a bit. She looked up at him.

He set his hands protectively on her shoulders.

Marnie frowned.

"Tell you later," he said.

Vince Carlton walked up to their table. "Good to see you all— Wow! The enthusiasm over *Dark Harbor*."

"There was lots of it—until Malcolm Dangerfield walked in," Roberta said.

"See? There you go. If I put Malcolm Dangerfield together with *Dark Harbor*? Wow. We can just wait and see. But where's Jeremy Highsmith? Jeremy told me he actually loves Horror-palooza. I can't begin to imagine he would blow it all off!"

"I can't either," Marnie said, looking up at Bryan.

She was getting worried. He was worried, too. Now about two things. He still needed to hear that Detective Manning had gotten her hands on David Neal.

But did being a disgusting piece of slime make David a murderer?

They needed to prove what he had done. Had he wanted to lure Marnie into an assault, or even worse? Either option was unthinkable.

Bridget and Angela returned to the booth then.

Marnie's cousin was excited. "There's a fantastic Horror-palooza Cave back there," she said. "So cool—it has Murderers' Row, with Jack the Ripper, H. H. Holmes and more, all on a foggy, creepy Victorian street. And then it turns into a mon-ster's mansion, and all the famous ones are there—Frankenstein's monster, Dracula, the Wolfman, a few different mummies…and the swamp creature. I swear, it gave flight to the imagination!"

Bryan saw Marnie try to smile.

"Jeremy Highsmith is still not here?" Angela asked.

"Call him again?" Bryan said to Marnie.

She did. No answer. She shook her head, looking at him worriedly.

Bryan called Grant Vining back. "Detective?"

"Our officer knocked at the door, trying to get Jeremy Highsmith to answer. Nothing. We'll break in. We shouldn't legally. But I suppose we have just cause for emergency entry."

Bryan looked across the room at Jackson, certain he would have his friend's support. "The federal government will support that decision," he said.

"I'll call you right back."

He hung up again. There was a roar of applause in the convention hall, and suddenly people were surging toward the *Dark Harbor* booth again.

The Krewe unit drew in close. Bryan was behind Marnie, while Angela and Jackson flanked the table, and Sean was just to the side of Angela, watching, with Madison just to his left, next to one of the Archer studio's werewolves.

"Malcolm and Marnie!" someone cried out. "You're going to do *Dark Harbor* together?"

"Pictures together? Hey, can't you guys let us get some pictures together?" someone shouted, not at the front of the line, but near.

Vince Carlton apologized quickly and half-heartedly to Marnie, "I had a press conference a few minutes ago. I announced the possibility of a revamp, with Malcolm and Marnie playing together. News must be spreading. You know how fans can get!"

Bryan did.

Fans could get dangerous.

"I'm here with this cast today," Marnie said.

"But maybe—just maybe—you could go over and take a few pictures with Malcolm?" Carlton asked her. He frowned. "You don't…dislike Malcolm or anything, do you?" he asked softly.

"No, of course not, Malcolm is fine," she said.

"Marnie, damn it, go," Roberta whispered. "If it were me, I'd be over there in his arms already. Then again, I'm not sleeping with—"

"I'm on my way— It's okay, right?" Marnie interrupted, looking at Bryan.

"Sure. I'll walk you over," Bryan said.

"I'll flank on the right," Sean Cameron said.

Bryan nodded. With Marnie between the two of them, they made their way across the floor.

Things that would normally seem amazing bothered Bryan then. He was hypersensitive to every mannequin and mask in the place, even those he'd already walked by.

Malcolm, with members of his security team, met them in the middle. "Just a few pics! Just a few pics—in case!" Malcolm told the crowd, delighting them.

Marnie smiled.

She stepped forward, letting him slide an arm around her.

Flashes went off. People crowded, holding up their cameras and smartphones.

Bryan was about to step forward, not because he felt any jealousy, which somewhat surprised him, but because he was being made just a little bit too nervous by the amount of *things* around them that just might be people in costume and not mannequins at all.

Marnie put a stop to it all herself.

"Thank you. Thank you all so much," she said, smiling and looking all around her. "I have to head back to the 'family.' What the future will hold… Well, we'll all see, right?"

A line had formed at the table again.

Vince Carlton was still there, beaming. Marnie took her chair.

"Scarlet, Scarlet, Scarlet!" came a yell from the crowd.

She smiled and waved, but as she took her seat between Roberta and Grayson, she asked, "No Jeremy yet? I'm getting really worried."

As if she'd been heard, the question was suddenly voiced loudly from the crowd.

"So where's Jeremy Highsmith?" someone called.

Bryan's phone rang. It was Vining.

"You found him? You found Jeremy Highsmith?"

"Yeah. We did. We found him."

"Thank God. And?"

Vining was silent for a minute.

Then he spoke, and he sounded old and weary, almost as if his voice was composed of nothing but dry and brittle leaves, shaking in the wind.

"He's dead. Jeremy Highsmith is dead."

He knew—the Mr. Macho-Man PI son-of-the-famous now knew.
Yes, Jeremy Highsmith was dead.

Delicious to watch. And now, of course, he had to spread the news.

Marnie! Oh, poor Marnie. The look on her face. She was just devastated. And the cops! Confusion!

Oh, so delicious.

And so sad. Think of it. Mom and Dad, both gone from Dark Harbor.

Don't laugh out loud. Don't laugh out loud...

And watch the smile!

CHAPTER FOURTEEN

Jeremy Highsmith was dead.

Unbelievable and unacceptable. Marnie had just sat next to him at lunch yesterday.

It was understandable the *Dark Harbor* table was empty; the surviving members of the main cast of the show had left.

They were devastated.

Marnie felt as if she were actually in the show, as if what was happening just couldn't possibly be real.

As soon as the news had come in, all the members of law enforcement had gathered by the booth—except for Sophie Manning. Sophie was looking for David Neal, since he had been followed to the convention center by a diligent police officer.

He was there, somewhere.

And he was wanted for questioning.

Marnie didn't have a chance to ask just what was going on until Detective Vining had arrived at the booth, the line had been dispersed and convention security personnel—along with Jackson, Angela, Sean, Madison and Bryan—had managed to get Roberta, Grayson, Marnie and Vince Carlton out.

The detective, the FBI agents and Bryan were all making rapid-fire comments, all of them aimed at keeping people safe.

An officer was taking Grayson home; he would stand guard at his residence.

Another was taking Roberta home, and he would stand guard at her residence.

"But I don't understand—how was Jeremy killed? Or was he killed?" Roberta wailed in the parking lot.

"The medical examiner believes that he suffered a massive heart attack in his sleep, but…well, we have to very careful," Bryan said.

"Wait. The dude chose last night to die, and we're going to lose out on today?" Grayson demanded.

"Grayson!" Roberta said, shocked.

"We have limited information at this time, but yes, that's what we were told," Bryan said.

"Jeremy just died…of natural causes? Last night?" Marnie asked.

"Yes, that's what we understand."

"But—he's dead?" she asked.

Bryan looked at her sadly. "This is according to the medical examiner's preliminary report. From what he's been able to determine so far. Jeremy went to bed last night, fell asleep and never woke up."

"Today was important for us. And I'm so sorry, but Jeremy was no spring chicken," Grayson said.

They looked at him, appalled.

They were all still grouped there when Malcolm Dangerfield came rushing out, his security personnel hurrying to keep pace with him.

"I'm so sorry! I just heard!" he told them. He looked at Vince Carlton. "Wow. I'm really sorry. I mean, sorry a man is dead. Jeremy was good old fellow. And sorry for…well, for *Dark Har-*

bor. Anyway, I guess I have to get back in there… I mean, maybe I don't—"

"I would," Grayson said. "You might have been slotted for a revamp, but you weren't in the original show, and now… Well, hell. We're all going… Dying like… Popcorn! Pop! Pop! Pop!"

"I don't intend to die!" Roberta protested.

"For the moment, until the medical examiner has really had a chance for an autopsy and can report their findings, you all need to be in your homes or somewhere safe," Bryan said.

"We'll see to it," Vining added firmly.

Grayson looked back at the convention center. "Wouldn't that be safe? There are so many people in there."

"Are you forgetting Cara Barton already?" Roberta said.

"That was a comic con."

"Grayson!" Marnie said. "There are more creatures than ever running around in that convention center. No, you're not safe in there." She was stunned that he seemed so callous—and desperate.

"We're surrounded by cops and FBI. Jeremy didn't make it here, and that was the problem!" Grayson said.

Marnie just shook her head, looking at Bryan.

"Take him home," he told the officer assigned to Grayson.

"What if I don't want to go?" Grayson asked.

"Then die, Mr. Adair!" Vining snapped. "We can't help quote-unquote 'stars' who are hell-bent on getting themselves killed."

Grayson pursed his lips. "Fine. I'm going home. The magazines will interview us all over again, and I'll tell them what I think of the police!"

"Who are trying to save your life," Bryan said.

"And what I think of the FBI!" Grayson added.

"I'm just a PI. And I really don't give a damn what you say about me," Bryan told him.

With something like a growl and a hunch of his shoulders,

Grayson sighed and said, "Whatever! Living isn't so great when you can't pay the bills!"

"Grayson, what is the matter with you?" Marnie demanded. "We've just lost another friend. A very good friend."

She felt tears in her eyes. She had just been with him yesterday. And yesterday he had been just fine.

"I'm sorry!" Grayson said. "Marnie, we're supposed to be on a panel tomorrow. Our day had barely begun, and we were being barraged."

"I'm sure Jeremy would be horrified to find out just how inconvenient his dying was for you!" she exploded.

"I am sorry. Jeremy played my dad, too, you know. But…let's face it, it's not like we met every Friday for coffee or drinks. He wasn't murdered—he died, Marnie. Died of natural causes. And we have to go on. We have to speak—"

"We don't speak on a panel until tomorrow," Roberta said.

"The organizers aren't heartless," Madison said, trying to come between them all and ease the situation. "I've been gone from Hollywood awhile now, but these people are nice. They can rearrange anything. Things do happen. You will be all right. They will understand—"

"But they'll strip down our spot and give it to someone else, and… I need to do this!" Grayson whispered.

"Not today," Marnie said. "Jeremy died."

"And we should be in there, mourning with friends."

"Not me," Marnie told him. "Not right now."

Grayson walked over to her and took her shoulders, looking into her eyes. "Marnie! I'm going to go down. My family made some bad investments, and I'm broke. I'm going to lose my house. If I don't meet my obligations, I'll lose all custody when it comes to my kids. You've got to help me."

"No one would expect us to stay, Grayson," she said.

"But…tomorrow? We can be here in honor of both of them. Share their lives with other people who loved them!"

Marnie could see Bryan wanted to step between her and Grayson then. She saw he was trying very hard not to interfere.

The cast could go back in. Jeremy's death could be announced. Sad, but—as far as they knew—natural.

And it might be right to mourn and honor Jeremy and Cara together tomorrow.

As if reading her mind, Grayson said, "A service. A moment of silence—a time when a few words are said in memory of both of them."

"Tomorrow. We'll talk about it tonight. We just found out that he's dead, Grayson," Marnie said. "We had a seat for him—he was supposed to be with us."

"We'll talk tonight," Roberta echoed.

"Really?" Grayson asked.

"Yes, yes...tomorrow. Just not today," Roberta said.

He lifted his hands and smiled at the cop assigned to him, who would be driving him home. "I'm ready. You ready?"

"Yes, sir, Mr. Adair," the cop said.

"Miss Alan?" the other officer said to Roberta.

"I'm going—this is too much for me," she said.

Then she was gone, too, walking way with her assigned officer in the wake of Grayson, who was moving quickly now toward a patrol car.

"Mr. Carlton, would you like an escort home?" Detective Vining asked.

"No, thank you, not if they believe that Jeremy Highsmith's death was natural," Carlton replied. "It's an unfortunate coincidence, to be sure. But we'll be fine. I mean, I am so sorry. But... we'd only met a few times. And I do have other business today."

"Come back in with me," Malcolm said. "I have security."

Bridget walked over and hugged Marnie.

"Let's go home," she said.

"Let's," Marnie agreed.

She turned to look at Bryan, and she could somewhat read his feelings.

Bryan wanted Marnie out of there; every mannequin and person in costume seemed like an automatic enemy to him.

But he needed to stay. He wanted to find David Neal.

"Jackson and Angela will see you home," he told Marnie. "Sean and Madison will watch over Bridget."

"You're not coming?" she asked him.

He hesitated. "I'm going to stay and work with Detective Vining and Sophie—to find David Neal."

"David Neal?" she asked, perplexed.

There was more. She had a sinking feeling the day was going to get worse.

"He was trying to drug you yesterday," he said very softly.

"Drug me...to death?"

Bridget gasped. "That scuzzball!" she exclaimed. "Oh, Marnie! Not kill you—he was trying to rape you."

"What?" Marnie said. What? He'd drugged her...not trying to murder her? But if he had managed to get something in her tea...*he could have managed to kill her if he had tried!*

"I'm sorry. Really sorry," Detective Vining said. "There were traces of a drug in your tea. Someone else could have done it, but I sure as hell don't know how."

Marnie gasped. "No, no, I made the tea! Angela was on the porch. Bridget was in the guest room. So...it had to have been David. But... Jeremy is dead. And David Neal was nowhere near Jeremy yesterday. He couldn't have seen Jeremy, unless... Cops were watching Jeremy! David couldn't have gotten to him unless..."

She trailed off.

"Unless a cop was bad—or lazy as hell. That's not the case, Marnie," Detective Vining assured her. "I handpicked people on this."

"I guess I do want to go home," she said. "David is a bastard, but not a killer."

What could his plan have been? She hadn't been alone. Angela and Bridget had both been there. Or had he thought that he could make her pliable, and that when she was doing anything that he said, he might have gotten her away with him somewhere.

She shook her head. "I don't know. Maybe somehow he is a bastard and a killer. I want a drink!"

"Marnie, you don't drink," Bridget said.

"I'm going to take it up!"

"I'll be there as soon as I can," Bryan promised her. He had her by the shoulders; she felt him trying to convey what he felt, which he clearly didn't have words to express. "As soon as I can," he repeated.

She met his eyes and nodded.

"You'll be fine. Angela and Jackson will be with you."

"And Bridget—"

"Bridget will have Sean Cameron, a really crack agent, and Madison with her."

Marnie nodded.

They split up, escorted by their protection.

Marnie looked back as they started to move away. She could see Vining talking to Bryan; he was in full professional mode.

She wanted Bryan with her. Just as soon as he and Sophie found David Neal.

Bryan headed back into the building. He pulled his phone out and called Sophie Manning.

"Any luck?"

"Luck?" she repeated. "Bryan, I'm pinching every mannequin I pass. Some of them are so real—the eyes! It's amazing. I started from the far rear, one of the main delivery entrances. I've gone through the maze, the Egyptian garden, where I was sure an Egyptian pharaoh was real, and now I'm in a section called The Gardens of Transylvania. I have been searching for Neal, and I have the convention staff looking, too."

"Thanks, Sophie," he said. "I'll take the front, row by row, and we'll meet in the middle."

"Sounds like a plan."

They hung up. Bryan did exactly as he said, moving quickly—but not too quickly. He passed incredible displays and found out he had to do much the same thing as Sophie—pinch mannequins.

It was frustrating. He went by a large double booth. A character in a lizard suit was reading while his makeup was being done.

Nice to see that monsters used their makeup time to read.

One section was dedicated to very, very creepy dolls.

He'd walked the breadth of the convention. It was time to turn and take in the next row. Even with him and Sophie both looking, David Neal could turn a corner at any time, and they could miss him. But Sophie was a local cop, and she had asked for help. Hopefully that meant that convention security was really helping out, as well.

"Fantastic things!" he murmured to himself.

There was a spectacular homage to *Psycho*, Norman Bates and the Bates Motel. The house, of course, wasn't life-size, but it was big. Along with the motel part of the movie set, it covered the space of a number of booths.

Every once in a while, a high-pitched scream emitted from the house.

From there, he moved on to alien creatures.

Swamp creatures.

Giant insects from a faraway planet.

More makeup, another booth, vying for attention.

Sophie called him.

"Any luck?"

"No. I'd forgotten there are panels going on, as well."

"Yes, there are panels." She sighed. "We need more manpower to cover this place. Vining was going to check in with the ME on Jeremy Highsmith."

"Yeah, we need to know what happened there."

"Indeed," Sophie said drily. "Rather a convenient thing, a heart attack in the middle of all this. But I have to say, I don't understand. If Marnie was the intended victim all along, as we'd thought, one might understand the motive, no matter how sick. She was the holdout—the one who might not want to do a remake of *Dark Harbor*."

"But what if," Bryan said, "we only think Marnie was the intended victim? We could be wrong, especially since Cara is dead. What if Cara was killed because she wanted the show so very much—and someone out there doesn't want the show to go on?"

"I guess that's possible." Sophie inhaled on the other end of the line. "I don't know who that would be. Of the people we've been looking at, anyway. Even Malcolm seems to be happy with the prospect of being Marnie's—Scarlet's—love interest, should there be a show."

"Jeremy wanted specials, not a full series reboot."

"Still, he was on board," Sophie said.

"David Neal... He wouldn't want the show. He wants to be Marnie's stage manager."

"Not a chance in hell of that happening now."

"Nope," Bryan said. "But let's find the bastard, huh?"

"I'm calling Vining. We'll get more help out here."

Bryan thanked her and rang off.

He passed Louisiana swamp monsters, Bigfoot, more.

He paused, not sure why, by a tableau that held a real antique stagecoach and what appeared to be spirit monsters, American Indians and giant buffalo.

Nightmares on the Plain! a sign by the tableau read.

He realized that it was a scene from a horror movie due to open in a month.

Something just hadn't seemed right when he'd looked at it.

And then he realized what.

One of the giant buffalo… Its tail moved awkwardly.

He walked around. There was no man inside the giant buffalo—no one in costume.

There was, however, a man hiding *behind* the giant buffalo.

"Get your slimy ass out here, Mr. Neal!" he snapped, reaching for the man, catching his shirt at his nape and dragging him out.

Neal didn't like Bryan—that much was obvious.

He was also obviously afraid of him.

But he was going to bluster.

"You can't do anything to me—or with me. You're not a cop. You're not FBI. You're just a private investigator, and this isn't even your state. You have no right to touch me. In fact, keep it up! I'll see that you're arrested for assault!"

"You're going in," Bryan said.

"Because of you? What, he-man? You going to throw me over your shoulder and drag me to a car? And why? I didn't do a damn thing to you. I didn't do a damn thing to anyone. You have no rights at all over me. I will sue you, you asshole. You can't take me in!"

In a way, the man was right.

But it didn't matter.

Because Sophie Manning was jogging up right behind him. She had a pair of cuffs out.

"He can't arrest you. But I can. And did I hear you use the word *asshole*? Rude, sir, very rude. Can't arrest you for rudeness," she announced. "Mr. Neal, you are under arrest for assault."

Angela made tea. Bridget tried to talk, to tell Marnie that whatever decisions she chose to make regarding Grayson and Jeremy and the horror convention were fine.

"People mourn and react to pain and loss in so many ways. I didn't know Jeremy the way you did, of course, but over the years, I was able to talk to him many times. He was a very cool dude who didn't believe any one religion or creed could be the only one, that there were many ways to a greater power. I mean, I think he would like a moment of silence and memory for him, maybe a few words, at a massive convention," Bridget assured her. "Then again, if you think it's in bad taste or wrong…"

"I don't know what I think," Marnie said. "Except I have a pounding headache. I guess I'm not going to take up drinking—I'm going to go with a giant bottle of aspirin!"

"Marnie—" Jackson caught her attention "—I'm going to head down to the morgue and meet up with the ME and Vining and, eventually, Bryan. Angela is staying here."

"Not to worry. I have complete confidence in Angela," Marnie assured him.

"And your patrol cop is still outside," Jackson said.

"All the better," Marnie said.

"I made tea," Angela said. "It will go straight from my hands to yours," she added.

"Oh, that slimy, slimy bastard. He ruined tea," Bridget muttered. Angela served tea. Marnie used it to wash down an aspirin. She really did have an absolutely splitting headache.

Shortly, Jackson left, and Madison and Sean accompanied Bridget to her side of the duplex, since she wanted to shower and change.

"I guess I will try lying down," Marnie told Angela. "I'll bring George in with me."

"I'll be in the living room if you need me," Angela assured her.

Marnie headed into her room and lay down. George looked at her with big brown eyes.

She patted the bed. "Come on up!"

He wagged his tail, whined and jumped up on the bed.

"This will not be all the time. You're a guard dog, you know. This is special. Just for today," Marnie told him.

He harrumphed.

Marnie curled up beside him, setting a hand on his back. She closed her eyes.

She could still feel the pounding in her head. It was fading, though, just a little.

Besides the pounding, she wasn't sure what she felt. Sorrow, of course. She had really cared for Jeremy; he had been kind of a father figure. They'd been good friends on set.

Maybe it was all too much. She felt cold, too, as if she should have more emotion, but she was really a distant observer, and all of this could not be happening to her.

A sweet foggy darkness seemed to be settling around her, a result of the double dose of aspirin, she thought.

She drifted off.

It was nice.

George, warm and furry, was at her side, and sleep, right now, was the most pleasing balm in the world.

David Neal rose.

"This is the most ridiculous thing in the world. I didn't assault anyone. I don't know what you're talking about. You people are about as sick as they get. I'm nonviolent. Nonviolent, don't you understand?"

"So you didn't dress up as Blood-bone?" Sophie Manning asked.

They had David Neal in an interrogation room. He looked nervous.

But at the suggestion that he'd been Blood-bone, he looked horrified.

"I didn't kill anyone. I'm not a killer. I was there—oh, God, I was there! That day. I watched Cara Barton become mincemeat. It was horrible. You're accusing me of... Oh, God!"

"You drugged Marnie Davante's tea," Bryan accused. He was seated next to Sophie.

Neal was right across the table.

"Attempted rape," Bryan said.

"Oh, you are full of it!" Neal said, but he looked nervous. He turned to Sophie. "If anyone is drugging Marnie to get her into bed, it's him. Oh, yeah—son of movie stars. Big macho watchdog. What's he even doing here? All he wants is Marnie, and he's making things up. Come on, Detective Manning, you are a cop."

"Yes. The cop who saw to the testing of the remnants of the tea in Marnie's cup."

Neal swallowed.

"Is that why you had Cara killed? And then killed her killer?" Sophie asked him. "I believe I understand now. You're in love with Marnie Davante."

"Half the world is in love with Marnie Davante," Neal muttered. He glared at Bryan.

"But you're obsessed," the PI said, easing forward. "You had Cara killed because that would have stopped—you hoped— a remake of the show. Then you got nervous that your hired hit man was going to give you away. And you killed him. And then, yesterday, you decided to make your move on Marnie."

"No!" Neal protested.

"We will arrest and try him for murder," Sophie told Bryan.

"Lawyer!" Neal said.

"Sure," Sophie told him with a shrug. She rose and started to leave the room.

"Wait, wait!" Neal said. "Wait... This is the honest-to-God truth, I swear. I—I did try to drug Marnie. I am in love with her. And I don't want the show having a revival—I want Marnie to open her theater. It's what *she* wants. But I swear I didn't kill anyone. I swear! I drugged Marnie's tea, but I did not kill anyone. I didn't. I didn't. I swear on my mother's life!"

★ ★ ★

Marnie might have drifted into something of a half sleep.

She could hear whispering.

She knew that—unless she was dead herself—Angela Hawkins wouldn't let anyone in, wouldn't let anyone near her.

George let out a little whine, as if warning of a danger he wasn't exactly sure of.

She opened her eyes.

Like a pair of little old chaperones, the ghosts of Cara Barton and Jeremy Highsmith were standing just inside her bedroom door.

"Poor dear. She's sleeping."

"She could sleep a lot more if she wasn't fooling around with Muscles."

"Jeremy! Shush! They're a lovely couple."

"Hmph."

"We could have been a lovely couple."

"What? You mean if you weren't always telling me that I couldn't act my way out of a paper bag?" Jeremy asked.

"I never!" Cara protested.

"Almost daily," he assured her. "You were always quite the old battle-ax."

"Oh!"

"You weren't particularly kind to me. And you could be hell on wheels on set."

"I had to be. The rest of you were positively doormats."

"You could be brutal."

"But—I loved you, Jeremy. Really, I loved you!"

"Ah, sweet thing. I guess it's too late for us, eh?"

Cara's ghost sighed. "Shall I wax poetic? Love is never too late."

Marnie blinked.

Yes, the two of them were there. Were they waiting for her to awaken?

She cleared her throat.

"Oh!" Cara gasped.

George whined, thumped his tail nervously and looked at Marnie. She stroked the dog. "It's okay, George. More or less okay. You know, you might have knocked."

"We should have knocked," Jeremy told Cara. "I told you we should have knocked."

"I really didn't want to wake Marnie if she was deeply sleeping. I mean, we don't really have much to say, do we? You just wanted her to...make a big deal over you," Cara said, impatiently waving a spectral arm in the air.

"It's only fair—you had a massive funeral."

"You're still lying in the morgue!"

"Must you remind me?"

"Okay!" Marnie said. "It's okay."

"Of course, it's okay. Bryan's not here right now. So, you see, it doesn't matter that we didn't knock."

"I could have just walked out of the shower," Marnie said.

"Oh, you dress in the bathroom," Cara said with another impatient wave of her arm.

Tears suddenly stung Marnie's eyes again.

They were both dead.

They'd had egos, they had argued, they had all been a little off now and then, but in the end, they had been really decent human beings, and she had loved them both.

"Marnie...my dear, sweet girl. Cry for us. You might be the only one," Jeremy said.

"Not true. People loved you both."

"Well, they loved me," Cara said. And she jabbed her ghostly companion in the ribs. "Lighten up, my love. Everybody thought you were the coolest. Best TV dad since *Father Knows Best*!"

"And you're very good at being a ghost," Marnie said, swinging her legs over the side of the bed so she could sit and look at them both easily. "You're visible, and you're barely..."

"Dead," Jeremy told her flatly when her voice faded.

"I'm so sorry."

"I had a hell of a life," he assured her. He paused and smiled at Cara, took her hand and kissed it. "And suddenly, we are together."

"Lovely," Marnie told him. His own death had to be touchy subject. "Jeremy, what happened? You...you looked fine yesterday during the day."

"You can't imagine the pain of a massive heart attack," Jeremy told her earnestly. "It's like being crushed with a sledgehammer."

"Had you been to the doctor?"

"Yes, I'd been to the doctor. Any old guy who doesn't have a cardiologist is an idiot, and I took medications for high cholesterol and hypertension," Jeremy said. "I was careful. No incidents—I took my meds just as directed. I did the right things. Watched out for what I ate, didn't smoke, only had a glass of red wine now and then... I looked after myself."

Marnie felt a little buzz. Her phone was in her pocket.

There was a text.

She excused herself and checked the phone. The text was from Bryan; he must have called Angela, who would have told him Marnie had a horrible headache and was lying down. Bryan wouldn't have taken the chance of waking her.

At the station; going in with David Neal. But got a call from Jackson, who is down at the morgue with Vining. Some tests in. Jeremy must have been expecting a date—blood work showed large amounts of an erectile dysfunction drug. Poor guy...must have wanted someone very badly.

Marnie looked across the room at Jeremy Highsmith.

"What?" he demanded.

"Uh—nothing."

"What is it, Marnie? Damn it, come on."

"All right, all right… Who was she, Jeremy?"

"Who was she? She who?" Jeremy asked.

"Yeah, who was she?" Cara demanded.

"There was no she!" Jeremy declared. He sighed. "She didn't tell you, did she? Cara. Cara and I had been seeing each other before…before…"

"Before I was slashed to ribbons!" Cara said. "And you think a heart attack hurts? Imagine getting chopped up by an actual sword."

"Well, then…" Marnie said.

"Look. I honestly wasn't seeing anyone. I didn't expect to see anyone. I was mourning Cara. I was feeling a bit dizzy, so I was in bed, trying to nap, for God's sake. What is going on?" Jeremy demanded.

Marnie took a deep breath. "There was a massive amount of an erectile dysfunction drug in your system, Jeremy."

"What?" Jeremy said.

"What?" Cara echoed.

Marnie repeated herself.

"But I didn't!" Jeremy said weakly.

"Oh, my dear Lord!" Cara said.

"I didn't," Jeremy said. He gasped suddenly. "Oh, my God. It was the mousse." He looked at Marnie. "Did you have the mousse? The salmon mousse? At lunch yesterday—did you have the mousse?"

"Um…no," Marnie said. She hadn't really liked the look of it. And there hadn't been much, not for the size of their group. She'd thought she'd leave it for people who enjoyed it more.

"Mousse?" Cara said.

"Oh, our killer is a bastard! I didn't die from any natural cause," Jeremy said furiously. "Our killer… He chose the damned salmon mousse. Unbelievable!"

"So…the killer was there. Yesterday," Marnie whispered.

She dialed quickly.

Her call went straight to voice mail, but Bryan called her right back.

"So, you got my message. I guess Jeremy didn't realize his heart couldn't take the drugs. I wonder who he was seeing."

"He wasn't seeing anyone. And he didn't take any erectile dysfunction drugs, Bryan."

"How do you know?"

"Because he's here. Jeremy Highsmith is right here. With Cara. They were seeing one another before Cara died, and now... He says the drugs must have been in the mousse. We had lunch with the murderer!"

CHAPTER FIFTEEN

Bryan slid his phone back into his pocket, looking at Sophie Manning.

Jeremy had been murdered, too.

"Murdered?" Sophie said skeptically. She studied him. "It's easy to think at this point that everything is suspicious. But Jeremy was old...er. I can't tell you how often—when I was a younger cop—I'd be called in for help, escorts on a hospital run, that kind of thing, because someone just had to impress their lover and overdid it, having an erection that went on and on for hours and hours, or as in this case, Bryan, bringing on a heart attack because their systems just couldn't deal with it. Why would this be any different?"

Because Jeremy Highsmith said so.

That wasn't going to work.

"I just spoke with Marnie. She was very good friends with both Jeremy and Cara and—only known to friends—they were seeing one another before Cara died."

"How was the drug given to him?"

"We suspect in food. At lunch."

"Then were you all running around like hopped-up rabbits yesterday?"

"It must have been in the mousse. I didn't have any. Not everyone there did. It had a kind of gray cast to it, and salmon isn't my favorite. Whether our fellows at the luncheon were having wild, wicked sex after drop-off, I don't know. We had cops at their doors, not in their bedrooms."

Sophie still looked skeptical.

"David Neal just admitted to drugging Marnie's drink, and you're sure he didn't have anything to do with this?"

"There's no way he could have seen Jeremy Highsmith yesterday. Unless your cops are bad," Bryan pointed out.

"You want me to just let him go?"

"I don't know. What he did was definitely unacceptable— he was obsessed with her. I think he wanted some sure way to be with her, but in the end he chickened out. And he ran. He can be charged."

"He could do it again—he should be charged. Although…" She paused, wincing. "Then we have to prove that it wasn't Bridget or Angela."

"He confessed."

"And he asked for an attorney. I don't know. I think we should at least hold him."

"An attorney will get him out of here unless you press charges."

"I can hold him for a while. I know that Vining and your friend Special Agent Crow are at the autopsy. I can stick around here and work on Neal and kill time if you want to see if there is anything else."

He thanked her. He really liked Sophie Manning.

"I'll do that," he said.

The autopsy would still be taking place. He wasn't sure that it mattered. He was pretty sure that what he knew now was the reason for Jeremy Highsmith's death.

And then there were none! He couldn't help but think.

Jeremy and Cara were gone.

That left Roberta, Grayson and Marnie in the main cast.

Malcolm Dangerfield...near them.

And Vince Carlton.

One of them, he was sure, was a killer.

"You need to come out to the living room with me," Marnie said. "We have to let Angela see you—and talk to you."

"I'd like that," Cara said.

"It isn't going to happen," Jeremy said.

"Why not?" Marnie asked.

"Because..." Jeremy began.

Then he faded away.

Cara sighed softly. "He's just beginning to get it. Poor man. He wanted to be at his autopsy. I said don't do it! Not nice, won't make you happy. Now, a funeral on the other hand... Everybody crying and saying wonderful things... He'll just have to get to the funeral."

She was fading, as well. She was gone when Marnie heard the last of her voice.

"Just tell them all of what he said..."

Marnie sighed. She'd told Bryan, but she could tell Angela herself.

George whined. And then he barked—loudly and excitedly.

Marnie tensed immediately. It was impossible not to worry.

This killer seemed capable of anything.

She leaped off the bed and opened the door; George raced out ahead of her.

"It's all right, George, it's all right!" she heard Angela say. "Friend, George. He's a friend."

Curious, Marnie hurried down the hall. She frowned.

Angela was there, hugging a man who appeared to be about

eighty, but a very good eighty. He was thin and very tall, and he still had a headful of silver-white hair.

Dignified—that would be the word she would use if one word was needed to describe him.

"Marnie, you're awake," Angela said, extracting herself.

"Miss Davante!" the man said. "A pleasure. I am a true fan!"

"Marnie," Angela explained, "I'd like you to meet Very Special Assistant Director Adam Harrison—my real boss. Jackson is our boss in the field, but we exist because of this wonderful gentleman."

Marnie walked forward, taking the hand that was extended to her.

"Mr. Harrison. Um, thank you. Thank you for being here. Thank you for these fine people, who are all helping me stay alive!"

"Now that really is a pleasure and privilege," he said. "In the field...well, my talent is finding people."

Marnie swallowed suddenly. She realized he wasn't alone. A slim boy of about Adam Harrison's height stood by him.

Boy, almost a man. Shaggy hair, nice eyes. He had to be about eighteen.

Then she realized he wasn't really here.

He was just really good at appearing to be solid.

Marnie couldn't help but stare. "My son, Josh," Adam said. "He's the only...only person who has passed on out of this earthly sphere whom I'm able to see." He glanced affectionately at Josh. "He is truly amazing—I don't think I have it, the gift or ability. But Josh...he can make me see him."

Marnie was proud of herself. She didn't even blink.

"Hello, Josh. A pleasure to meet you," she said.

"Miss Davante, my pleasure," the teenager said politely.

"Anyway, my other talent is money. Good investments. That has allowed me to help people threatened or in trouble through the years. I know how to make money. And that's why I'm here."

"Money?" Marnie said, very surprised.

He smiled at that. "I'm not much good in the way of keeping people alive—though I have learned to shoot, and I'm not so bad at it, if I do say so myself."

"I've fired blanks from a prop gun a few times. And I actually took archery—there were evil birds in an episode of *Dark Harbor*. They could only be brought down with arrows tipped in magic berry juice," Marnie said, grinning.

"Archery is a talent."

"Must have been so cool doing a lot of things you did on that show!" Josh said.

"Yeah, it was," Marnie said. She realized it had been. The show had been a positive thing in her life, and a deranged human being had tried to take it all away.

The show had been good to her, and through Josh, she could see that more clearly and appreciate it.

"I've had some training in fencing and a few classes in martial arts." She laughed. "Nothing extensive—enough to get through the different scenes before our very talented stunt workers slipped in."

"Never hurts," Adam said. "Knowledge, even when we're not sure we want to know, is seldom a bad thing."

"Adam, can I get you a cup of tea or anything?" Angela asked.

"I don't think I've ever turned down a cup of tea."

"Dad really does love tea," Josh said. "I have to admit, it's one of the things that I do miss."

"Oh! We don't have to have tea," Marnie said.

"Please—I love the very smell of it," Josh assured her.

The women headed into the kitchen. As she reached into a cabinet for tea bags, Marnie looked over at Angela.

"He seems like an incredibly nice man. He runs...everything?"

"Yeah. The trick with Adam is that when he encounters anyone who doesn't agree with him, he always has a friend above that person in the pecking order. He is nice—he's also as strong as steel inside. Don't let him fool you," she added with a whisper and a smile. "He can be as hard as proverbial nails."

"He lost his son when Josh was so young. It must have been excruciating."

"I met him later, when he first formed the Krewe. But yes, it was agony for him. However, he managed to turn his loss around. So many people have been helped."

"Me included," Marnie said.

"Well, he has something up his sleeve," Angela warned.

As they sat with their tea, Adam spoke up. "As I was saying. I realize that your case is ongoing, but I have infinite faith in the agents you have out here. You can't have better people helping you."

"I know," Marnie said.

"So, anyway... I own a theater."

He waited.

"You're lucky," Marnie said.

"I am. In many ways."

And in many, he had not been so lucky, she thought, and she wanted to kick herself for the words.

"I'm an idiot," she murmured.

She felt something on her hand. Josh was by her, grinning.

"It's okay," he said.

Adam continued, "My theater is in Washington. I have some incredible people working there, but they deal with adult theater. You would love them—three young women, like yourself, all involved with agents. Not that that is a prerequisite! What I'm saying is that if you want to leave Hollywood, and you really want a children's theater, I have one for you."

For a moment, Marnie just stared at him. Then she frowned. Hollywood had definitely made her careful.

And skeptical.

"It's a bribe," Adam said flatly.

"He's been chasing Bryan for a while," Josh explained.

"I value his military background as well as his abilities. But I don't want Bryan unless he wants to be in the Krewe. Because we are a different kind of unit, being with us isn't just a day job. It becomes a way of life. And our lives wind up twined together."

"I… I don't even know what to say," Marnie told him. "I can't speak for Bryan."

"No. They are decisions you have to make separately—and together."

She flushed slightly, glancing over at Josh. "Actually, we've never really talked about…"

"About the future? Yes, a future usually does depend on survival," Adam said sagely.

Marnie sat silently, letting it all sink in for a moment.

"I have a meeting," Adam said, rising. "I don't need an answer now. I was just throwing it out to you." He shrugged. "I heard that your children's theater is a big dream for you. I obviously can't offer you any kind of a big movie role," he said. "So…"

"He could somehow—if that is what you really wanted," Angela said, interrupting in a soft whisper.

Marnie looked at Angela and laughed. "You knew Adam was coming, and you knew why he was coming to see me?"

"I knew about half an hour ago—when Jackson called to tell me. You were sleeping."

"Yes, then I was awake and— Oh!" Marnie said, turning to Angela. "I forgot to tell you. Jeremy Highsmith swears that he didn't take any kind of pills. That—"

"He was having an affair with Cara. News travels fast in the Krewe."

"We try to keep communication going at all times," Adam said.

"Naturally," Marnie said.

"Jeremy is a weak ghost… Cara is trying to help him. I never knew that they were a duo. But…they are together now. Jeremy believes he was poisoned through the salmon mousse at lunch yesterday."

"And no one else had the mousse?" Adam asked.

"I didn't try it—you know me. I never really eat when we're working," Angela said. "Jackson doesn't like mousse, and Bryan doesn't like salmon. As to the others… I don't know."

"I'm sure they're on it," Adam said, starting to head to the front door. "You have my offer. There is no pressure. But know that if you're willing to come East, the opportunity is there. By the way, it's a gorgeous historic theater. We've been working on it a few years now. It's alive and well and thriving. All it needs is a children's program."

He smiled. "I have been a fan. A true pleasure, Miss Davante."

"Bye, Adam," Angela said.

"I'm out here until this one is wrapped up," he said.

"Excellent," Angela said.

Marnie hugged him impulsively. "Thank you. And I will let you know. Assuming that I survive."

Josh could actually open a door; he did so for his father.

When Adam was out, Josh looked back at Marnie before she closed the door, and he said, "I am really—really, really, really— a huge fan. And, Miss Davante, you will survive."

Jeremy Highsmith lay split open, his Y incision making him look like something unreal—something created just for Hor-ror-palooza.

If he were to come back as a ghost himself, Bryan thought, he would definitely never attend his own autopsy.

Thank goodness Jeremy had decided to reach out to Marnie instead of trying to visit his own body at the morgue.

The ME on call was an older woman named Dr. Helen Franks. She looked as if she were continually tired, but then the morgue had been built to accommodate approximately 300 to 350 bodies, but often held over 400.

The death of Jeremy Highsmith had been given a high priority despite the fact that by all initial appearances, it seemed as though he had simply died from a heart attack. With a possible serial killer at work, this autopsy had been moved to the top of the list.

Jackson had told Bryan that Adam Harrison was in town. He was pretty sure that Adam's presence meant that they would get anything they needed.

What was frustrating was that, even with all the help of the LAPD, they weren't getting anywhere.

Maybe they were by pure process of elimination.

David Neal had acted criminally, but there was no way that he could have gotten to Jeremy Highsmith.

That left Roberta Alan, Grayson Adair, Vince Carlton and Malcolm Dangerfield.

"Special Agent, Detective… Mr. McFadden," Dr. Franks said, addressing the three men around her and the split-open body on the gurney. "I will run more tests, but whether he was dating Miss Barton or not…this looks like an accidental death."

"Is there any way to tell how he digested the drug?" Bryan asked Dr. Franks.

"I'm having the stomach contents analyzed. He hadn't eaten for perhaps six or so hours before he died. Digestion had begun. But…we'll see," she promised them. "His heart…it wasn't particularly bad. I have a list of his medications. Cholesterol levels seemed under control, but each year of our lives, we're putting more and more pressure on our hearts."

"What about the rest of his organs?" Detective Vining asked.

"Sound. Lungs were clear. He wasn't a smoker. Good kidneys. For his age, he was in good shape." She sighed. "I know you want more from me. Mr. McFadden, I know that you're convinced he was somehow poisoned with the drugs or that he was given them by mistake, and yet, I'm afraid I can tell you— I've seen it too many times. People don't realize that more of something isn't necessarily better. I'm not meaning to be cruel, but the gentleman might have been looking forward to a really nice date, or..."

Her voice trailed. She thought he might have hired a prostitute. Bryan couldn't blame Dr. Franks for her opinion. This wasn't something that hadn't happened before to many an older man anxious to prove he could get it up when he wanted.

"He wasn't expecting a date." He couldn't tell her that he knew it because Jeremy had said so himself. "Mr. Highsmith had been seeing Cara Barton. Men that deep in mourning don't usually hire prostitutes."

"People deal with mourning in all manner of ways," the doctor said. "I'm not judging. Just stating facts."

"You're going to find that the pills were ground up and put in his food somehow," Bryan said with certainty.

There was nothing else he was going to learn from the autopsy.

He looked at Vining. "I'll go back on guard duty," he said.

Vining nodded. "We'll be here."

"I'll be in touch," Bryan promised.

He walked out of the morgue and headed to his rental car, fully intending to head back to the duplex.

But outside the morgue, he hesitated. He called Sophie Manning.

She didn't answer.

Worried, he called Marnie. She answered right away.

"We're fine," she said. "Actually, Adam Harrison just left."

"Yes, Jackson told me he'd come in. He's...exceptional."

"I agree. Bryan, he offered me a theater."

"A theater? Oh, yes, I should have remembered that he owns one. My mom goes on and on about it—beautiful historic place. He's giving it to you?"

"No, I'm sorry, not the whole theater. The children's division of it. It's mine if I want it."

"Wow. He's a fan of yours!"

"I think he's a fan of yours. I think he put forward the theater as incentive for you to join the Krewe."

"What did you tell him?"

He realized he was holding his breath. What if they just ran away? What if he swept Marnie up and carried her thousands of miles across the country? She'd be safe. LA—Hollywood—was this killer's beloved place, his chosen venue, and had to do with his agenda.

Bryan knew it wouldn't work. The questions would always remain. Blood would literally lie between them.

"I didn't tell him anything. He didn't ask for an answer right away."

"Ah."

"Do you have an answer yet?"

"I can't answer about your theater."

He felt her smile over the line. "About the Krewe."

"I don't know. Probably. I think."

"Then…maybe. Probably. I think."

A surge of warmth swept through him. He was pretty sure that it was happiness. Was it possible? They hadn't known each other long enough.

"Are you coming home?" she asked him.

Home. It was thousands of miles away.

And yet it wasn't. It was becoming anywhere…any place he could hold her in his arms.

They even had a dog.

"Soon. I have to stop by the police station. Any more Cara or Jeremy sightings?"

"No. All is quiet."

"I will see you soon."

Before he'd even hung up, Sophie was on the line, returning his call.

"I need to look at some of the video footage of Cara's murder again," he said. "Can you help me?"

"I was about to head out," Sophie said. "But for you…"

"I don't mean to ruin your life."

"At the moment, this place is my life. Well, it's more of a life—than my life. Never mind. Ignore me. I'll be here."

"Marnie, are you good with a conference call?"

Grayson Adair wasn't going to let it rest.

"Grayson—"

"I have Roberta, Malcom Dangerfield and Vince Carlton on hold. Conference call?" he asked.

She was already outnumbered, she knew.

"No matter what we say—"

"You'll have to talk to the cops, the agents and Bryan McFadden," Grayson said.

"Right."

She heard a click as she was connected with the others.

"Okay, so…we've spoken with the organizers. Everyone is devastated. Everyone loved Jeremy—those of us who knew him loved him as a friend. Those fans who didn't know him, well, they still loved him. Marnie, he died of natural causes! Heart attack!"

She was glad there seemed to be no news out about the true cause of his death or the reason he had the heart attack.

"He's still dead," she said.

"But you knew him. He'd love it. And Cara would love it."

"Would love what?"

"The entire convention stopping at noon tomorrow. I have a congregational pastor friend. He's happy to say a few words that would be inclusive to many religions. He won't even offend the atheists. We go back—we make money and we survive—and we honor them both, as well. You can give a eulogy if you want… or someone else can talk. We can allow the fans to mourn, and even if a fan isn't a best friend, it's still important. People need to have those they love and put on pedestals. And what if, by some chance, they can look down from heaven... Cara and Jeremy both would love it."

"I'm happy to be a part of anything you want to do," Malcolm Dangerfield said.

"He's not being crude, really," Roberta said.

Vince Carlton cleared his throat. "Marnie, it will be truly tasteful. At noon, they'll announce a moment's silence for the beloved stars of *Dark Harbor* so recently lost. And the pastor will speak. And anyone else who wishes to speak may do so—well, by anyone, I mean any one of us."

"I don't know," Marnie said. "I don't think it would be in the very best of taste."

"That's because you have other options. You were smart enough to sock money away," Grayson said. "And good for you. All hail Princess Marnie, who was just talented and smart—right from the very beginning. Marnie, I am honestly sorry. But I have to live. Please. Jeremy would not mind."

"Too bad we can't ask him," she said.

Then again, maybe she could ask him.

"He died of a heart thing, Marnie," Roberta said. "I'm going to miss him, too. And I guess we're really dead in the water when it comes to a new show—"

"Maybe not," Vince said. "I've got the financing all lined up. I've called in a lot of favors for this. I'm committed to making it happen. We could do the kids—on their own. Grown-up, suddenly both parents gone, and they are on their own. All that stands between innocents and the hidden monsters that plague the world."

Hidden monsters.

Hidden human monsters.

"I will let you all know."

"Tonight, Marnie, please?" Grayson begged.

"I'll do my best," she promised.

She'd been on the phone in her room. When she hung up, Cara and Jeremy both began to appear before her.

"I'd love it," Jeremy said.

"I would, too," Cara said, clapping her hands together and looking heavenward as she spoke. "Stopping everything at Horror-palooza to honor us. I think it's a fitting tribute. Marnie, you could speak. And you could tell everyone that we were a couple in real life!"

"And you could tell them all that I wasn't taking drugs. I wasn't trying to get it up. I wasn't after sex." He paused and looked at Cara. "The love of my life had just died."

"Let me talk to Bryan when he comes in. You two, come out to the living room. Now! While you're visible. Talk to Angela. She's really good at…"

Dead people.

She couldn't say that!

"She's far more experienced with situations like this than I am," Marnie said.

"Love to meet her," Jeremy said.

Marnie hopped up and opened the door. She hurried into the hallway, calling to Angela, who was in the living room, still on the sofa, working with her computer.

She rose quickly.

"Angela, Jeremy is here. He's going to tell you about his feelings, about everything that happened yesterday."

"We're going to find the truth," Angela assured him. "Jeremy, you could tell me…"

No, he couldn't.

Jeremy had made it out of Marnie's room and down the hall. And then he had faded away.

"Almost," Cara said simply.

And then, as if racing off to join him, she disappeared, as well.

★ ★ ★

Sophie set Bryan up at one of the station computers with three different cell phone videos of the murder of Cara Barton.

He'd already seen them. Over and over again.

But this time, he watched faces.

Roberta Alan sat on the other side of Cara Barton. She didn't rise when Blood-bone came to the table; she was looking up as Cara and Marnie improvised...

Then she looked horrified—but not until Cara's blood spilled on her.

David Neal stood in front of the table. He didn't seem to have any reaction at all.

He just stared.

Next go-around, Bryan watched Grayson Adair.

The minute the sword struck at Cara, he leaped out of his chair and backed away.

Bryan switched views on the computer, finding the video that showed Malcolm Dangerfield.

Dangerfield had stood, naturally, when he'd seen the commotion going on. His expression seemed to change from curiosity to shock.

Of course, they were all actors...playing roles?

Sophie popped her head in the doorway. "Any luck?"

He looked up at her. "Who is the actual best actor in the group?" he asked her.

"Pardon?"

"*Dark Harbor*—and let's throw in Malcolm Dangerfield. And even our boy in lockup, David Neal. Vince Carlton."

"Carlton is a producer."

"Hey, we're all actors at times."

"Well, in my mind, Marnie is the best. There's emoting—and there's emotion. Malcolm is the hottest and in a number of pretty amazing shows...but he's Malcolm. Beautiful and a personality. Um... Grayson was always fine in his role. I don't think I've seen him do much else. Sometimes it's hard to tell with someone like Vince Carlton. There's acting—and there's lying. Part of all the games, I believe. David Neal is a wild card—and still here. Though, I'm not sure we're going to get away with keeping him. He's called for an attorney. He's working on getting out. Who did I miss? Roberta. Lovely woman. Hard, though. The kind of hard that might succeed, but…but I don't see her becoming someone we consider the best actress that's out today or anything like that."

Bryan nodded, watching the gruesome murder one more time.

"Did I help any?" Sophie asked.

"I don't like David Neal," he said. "But…there's just no way he had access to Jeremy Highsmith's lunch."

"Stunt double," Sophie said. "Oh, wait, I don't think that stage managers get stunt doubles. Well, Jeremy Highsmith wasn't exactly poisoned, but the drugs he was given were like poison—to him. So, I'd say someone who knew him, knew his age, general health… Poisoning is a woman's thing traditionally. Though we can't go by tradition anymore."

Bryan rose, still staring at the computer, thoughtful. "Thanks, Sophie." He put through a call to Marnie.

She described the call she had received from Grayson—the conference call.

"What do you think?" he asked her.

"What do I think?" she repeated. "I think I'm angry, really angry. I don't know what is going on, who it is who wants what. But two of my friends are dead. A hired killer was vicious—Cara was killed so brutally. Then the hired killer was shot. And now Jeremy… This killer is a chameleon, always changing. Almost as if he—or she—is always taking on new roles. Bryan, we have to catch him, stop this—because if not, nothing will ever be safe. I'm angry. I want to do it. I want to go to Horrorpalooza, and I want to believe that somewhere, somehow, the killer is going to show his hand. I want to have a grand show where Cara and Jeremy are honored. They want it…or so their ghosts say. Ghosts. Crazy. It's all crazy. Crazy to do it. But you'll be with me, right?"

"I'll be with you," he vowed.

He looked at Sophie. "We're on for tomorrow," he said.

"I'll talk to Vining. We'll have a massive police presence to back up your team."

Five minutes later, Bryan was out of the police station door, headed to the duplex.

There was a patrol car in front of the house. The officer waved to him.

All the lights were low inside, but when he reached the door, Jackson was there to open it, George at his side.

"Midnight, and all is well," Jackson said drily.

"Marnie?"

"In bed."

Bryan gave George a good pat on the head and then headed down the hall. He quietly opened the door.

The room was dim, only the television granting it light.

Marnie was awake, seated on the bed, wrapped in a throw blanket. She was watching footage of Jeremy Highsmith's life.

"I just had no idea they were having an affair," she said. "They were both friends of mine, and I didn't even notice."

"They didn't want to be noticed." He walked over in front of the television, afraid that she would grow morose. He tried to turn the television off smoothly. He had such a great line to give her.

I do want to be noticed!

But it was a new TV, a smart TV, and he couldn't find a button anywhere.

Marnie laughed; she had the remote control. The television went off. In the pitch dark he heard her rise and come to him.

Under the throw she was naked. She walked into his arms.

He inhaled the sweet scents of her soap and shampoo and something that was clean and erotic and all Marnie. She came up onto her toes, kissing his lips with a haunting tease.

He caught her by the shoulder. "Careful... I could be falling in love."

"What do you call it when you've already crashed hard?" she whispered.

He hiked her up, and they fell onto the bed together.

His lips found hers, and then they traveled down her naked length.

He murmured against her flesh.

"Yes... I've already crashed," she whispered. He smiled, rising against her, and they both struggled with his clothing. Then he held her tight against him, feeling her warm skin against his body.

Yes, he'd crashed, too.

There was no going back.

CHAPTER SIXTEEN

There was no way to watch. No way to simply stare at a house and imagine…

The cops were on them all like a swarm of locusts.

But that didn't matter. He wouldn't let it matter. Because, all in all—as he had often imagined, as well—the cops were all idiots. Cops! That included the FBI agents—and that PI. They were all the same. They thought they knew people. They thought that they had forensics on their side and that they'd figure it all out.

Sometimes…

You just didn't get any evidence.

He smiled.

Hell, the Zodiac Killer was still out there.

He wondered to himself if—when it was all over—he'd want to keep going. Strange how this had started with one obsession and escalated into another.

He had discovered that he loved killing. The way it made him feel… better than alcohol, better than any drug. Better than sex. But kind of like sex or the best sex in the world combined with alcohol and the most amazing drugs.

Still, there was an agenda.

And tomorrow…

He sighed softly. He'd originally planned for the set… Yes, what a fitting place for beautiful Marnie to die—right over a tombstone.

But that wasn't going to work.

There was another place that would be just fine.

Oh! The anticipation was too much!

Tomorrow it would all be over.

It might have been said that the stage was set.

They were back at Horror-palooza. Malcolm still had his own booth across the room, but when the time was right, he'd be joining the cast at the *Dark Harbor* table.

Bryan didn't think that it would be possible to have more protection. Security officers lined the convention hall; police presence was doubled.

The FBI had plainclothes people walking the floor.

Angela and Jackson were positioned on either side of the *Dark Harbor* table. He was behind Marnie.

Sean and Madison were out on the floor near the *Dark Harbor* table, watching people, watching for anything strange. Bridget was staying close to them but wandering off now and then.

Madison followed Bridget. She would be safe. Madison hadn't gone through the academy, but she was with Sean—and she had learned to be savvy when she'd nearly died herself, during the murders at the Black Box Theater.

The morning brought more people than anyone might have ever imagined.

They had barely begun the day, however, when Sophie Manning came back to where Bryan was standing, looking grim.

"He's out," she said.

"What?"

"David Neal is out. I don't know what the hell happened exactly, but once he lawyered up, we had no proof. His confession, according to his attorney, was coerced. By a nonpolice officer."

"Me."

"I've warned the convention staff. His picture has been given to security at every entrance."

Bryan swore.

Sophie apologized again.

"We will catch him, if he so much as steps a toe in here," she vowed.

Bryan gritted his teeth and prayed that she was right. But while he'd considered the man a scumbag, he didn't think that he'd committed the murders.

Nothing to do but get through the day.

The organizers had been true to their word—the purpose was to honor Cara Barton and Jeremy Highsmith, and those in power were doing so. Giant screens throughout the lofty convention center showed scenes from *Dark Harbor*. Jeremy searching the dark woods and the cemetery for his children. Cara being the mom, demanding that they finish dinner before heading out to slay a vampire clan.

Fans thronged the cast.

Grayson Adair, on Marnie's left, turned to Bryan, beaming. *Thank you*, he mouthed.

Bryan nodded. He'd like the man if he hadn't been such an ass just the day before.

Right at noon there was an announcement over the PA system. Bryan, up on the dais where the *Dark Harbor* table had been set, could see over the crowd that Malcolm Dangerfield was speaking. He asked that there be a moment of silence for Cara Barton, whose killer was still at large, and for Jeremy Highsmith, who they had just lost.

Someone came running toward the *Dark Harbor* table.

Bryan almost tackled the person—he hadn't expected the running.

It was just one of the show people bringing Marnie a microphone.

She took it and stood, asking the crowd to remember Cara and Jeremy for their contributions to entertainment. She went on to tell everyone that in their later years, the two had discovered that they were in love with one another. They were, at least, together.

The crowd wildly applauded.

Marnie thanked them all.

It was then that Bryan saw Cara Barton's ghost. She wasn't alone. She was with Jeremy. It was the first time he'd seen Jeremy, but watching him with Cara, he knew that what Jeremy and Cara had told Marnie had been the truth. In the end, they'd been in love.

The two were delighted with the tribute.

Cara blew kisses to Marnie.

She and Jeremy both turned to the crowd and bowed low, again and again, as if they could be seen by the horde of people at the show.

And then the applause died.

And people moved on.

Right after noon, Roberta yawned and complained that she was hungry.

"But I'm afraid to eat," she said. Their line hadn't diminished once throughout the day.

"That's fine. We'll get you lunch, stop the line and bring it here!" the young man who was one of their convention reps said.

"I'm not eating anything from here," Grayson murmured.

"We're covered," Bryan told him. "The cops will bring you food." He raised a hand and caught Jackson's attention. The FBI field director nodded and found one of the uniforms on the floor.

Lunch had been prearranged.

"Can't wait!" Roberta said.

She drew a protein bar from her bag and proceeded to munch on it.

Their food came; the line was duly stopped for thirty minutes. Marnie looked back at Bryan.

"Aren't you tired of standing?" she whispered.

He smiled. "Nope," he said. It was a lie, of course. He could stand all day—didn't mean he wasn't getting one hell of a crick in his neck.

Finally, the closing of the day was announced. People lingered in the *Dark Harbor* line. They had been waiting patiently, and they weren't leaving.

They had almost reached the last person when Roberta Alan suddenly stood, letting out a fierce cry of pain. She toppled over onto the table.

Bryan immediately sprang into action, drawing Marnie from her chair and shielding her with his own body. Jackson was at Roberta's side, shouting for 9-1-1.

"No!" Marnie cried, trying to reach Roberta. Bryan held her tight.

"Jackson has this. The cops have it. Help is coming."

"How, Bryan? How?"

"I don't know."

"Poisoned! She was poisoned. Oh, my God! The cops poisoned her!" Grayson cried.

Those who had been in line were now panicking, running out.

They became a mob—terrified of the police.

Grayson Adair was screaming and gasping that he had to get out.

"I'll get him!" Angela said.

"Don't touch me!" Grayson shouted. "The cops are dirty—the cops are dirty! Oh, God, I might be poisoned, too!"

Chaos was reigning.

There was a plan for an escape, if necessary. Bryan already knew where he was going.

"Come on," he told Marnie.

"Bridget!" she said. "Where's Bridget?"

The question was quickly answered. "There's an exit to the far left. We can get out that way!" Bridget cried, rushing over to Marnie.

"We go this way!" he commanded.

He led them both behind their table and to the back of the convention center, racing along the wall to the exit.

The door—and a host of police—was just about a hundred feet away.

What the hell had happened? The police had brought the food. He just couldn't believe that they were involved in any way—logic didn't allow for it; the things that had happened didn't fit.

They were almost to the exit.

And then…he saw him.

Blood-bone.

And then there was another one. And another… Three, four Blood-bones. More…

He caught hold of Marnie and stopped her, thrusting her behind him. "Go! Get the hell out, go!" he said.

Drawing his gun, he headed toward the Blood-bones, shouting, "Drop it! Drop your swords right now!"

To his amazement, the Blood-bones did so.

"Whoa," one of them called out.

Bryan strode to him, ripping off the mask.

To his surprise, he saw a young man. A kid. No more than eighteen. He knew damned well that he'd never seen him before.

He went from Blood-bone to Blood-bone, ripping off masks.

"I'm not here to hurt anyone!" the first kid said. "I swear."

"None of us are!" another shouted.

"It's a show—it's just a show!" the third Blood-bone said.

"This costume was banned." Bryan's voice sounded like a roar in his own ears.

"Yeah, yeah, I know, but I have college next fall," the first kid said. "Some dude—a talent scout—called and offered us five hundred bucks apiece to wear Blood-bone outfits for an hour and just stand here. I swear, I—"

Bryan turned away from the kid.

Marnie was gone.

Marnie was chasing Bridget.

The moment the Blood-bone troop had appeared, Bridget had cried, "Oh, my God," her voice filled with absolute panic. "We have to get out of here," she'd said urgently to Marnie. "We can hide in the cave!"

"No!" Marnie had shouted.

Too late. Her cousin had already disappeared behind the doors—guarded by a pair of skeletons and adorned with a plaque reading Surrender All Hope, Ye Who Enter Here!

She might be giving up all hope, but Marnie had no choice but to follow Bridget.

"Bridget, you idiot, please," she cried. "This isn't a good place to be!"

And it sure as hell wasn't.

The convention staff seemed to have gone. The fabrications and mannequins and tableaux remained.

Which path had Bridget taken?

Marnie started down one walkway.

She found herself in Victorian London. Gas lamps had been fashioned—they were just battery-operated candles in period reproduction pieces, she knew. Still, they had their effect.

She went under a sign that read Mitre Square.

She tried to remember. Yes, one of Jack the Ripper's victims had been found there.

Catherine someone. Like most other people, she had read about Jack the Ripper, but right now facts were eluding her.

She turned a corner and jumped. Two people— No, two

mannequins in clothing from the period were leaned against a brick wall, huddled together.

They were absolutely excellent.

Madison Darvil might have created something like them, something like this scene...

"Bridget?" she called softly.

Something moved near her.

Marnie wanted to shout her cousin's name.

She didn't dare. She kept inching forward. She came around another corner. Carefully.

She drew back, her scream catching in her throat.

Jack the Ripper stood before her, a knife raised high in his hand. He was in a Victorian frock coat, a medical bag in his other hand, a top hat on his head.

He whirled around to greet her.

Bryan swore, looking down the path they'd taken. They were gone, just gone.

Bridget and Marnie. The two of them. Suddenly he had a flash of insight.

Two of them. There had been two killers. One, of course, was alpha, planning it all out. But that would allow for details like David Neal spiking Marnie's tea while his coconspirator had been the one to see to it that Jeremy Highsmith had been "poisoned" with an erectile dysfunction drug.

His phone rang, and he answered it urgently.

It was Jackson. "I'm at the hospital ER with Roberta."

Bryan kept moving. He came to the entrance to the Horror-palooza Cave exhibit.

"Marnie's missing... Blood-bones were paid to appear and throw us off. I'm following, heading into a horror cave. Get everyone searching."

"Will do. But you need to know, Roberta is freaking out. She says she's going to die. She says that she was just supposed to be sick. She's spilling her guts. Bryan, she was the woman who was in on it. Roberta Alan. But she was just acting with the man who had a plan. She was supposed to get sick from a bar she had in her own purse. A bar that we wouldn't suspect because she was carrying it herself. She's in a panic now, thinking that she was used, that she is supposed to die. And she was working with—"

"I know who she was working with—she was supposed to die, most probably. She just didn't die fast enough."

"David Neal is at his house."

"It isn't David Neal," Bryan said.

There was a whirring sound.

Jack the Ripper turned to stare at Marnie.

He had maddened, bloodthirsty eyes in a narrow, cruel face.

His arm rose.

And fell.

And the whirring sound came again.

Jack the Ripper was just an animatronic dummy.

A breath of relief escaped Marnie. She reached for her phone. Her pocket was empty; it was back at the table.

Swearing silently to herself, she stood dead still and listened. Nothing. And then...

A soft sobbing sound.

"Bridget?" she called cautiously.

"Marnie?"

"Where are you?"

"I don't know. I think... I think it's Chicago. It's really dark. Some of the lights are gone. Where are you? I'm moving. I'm moving... I can't get back to the exit!"

A killer could be listening.

"Don't talk!" she commanded. "I'll find you!"

She couldn't talk anymore herself. She could lead the killer right to herself.

She kept walking. The streets changed. It was very dark, but there were still gas lamps, and they were creating small shells of light that fell upon old brick buildings and there, ahead...

A sign announcing the Chicago Exhibition.

She had entered the realm of H. H. Holmes, the man who had slaughtered dozens more people than Jack the Ripper. He'd kept a "murder hotel," killing, among others, those who had traveled across the country, from far and wide, to visit the fair. He'd offered them lodgings, and then he'd killed them—husbands, wives and children. He'd incinerated their bodies down in the furnace.

She stumbled upon a tableau of one of his torture rooms.

A madman stood over a table. A beautiful damsel in distress lay on it, her mouth open in a silent scream. He held a wicked-looking bone saw over her head.

There was a whir...

The mannequin turned to look at Marnie. This time she was prepared.

It was just a mannequin.

She could hear sobbing. Bridget. Of course, she was terrified.

Marnie wanted to talk to her, to assure her that everything was going to be okay.

She passed another display.

A woman in a rich costume, blood streaming down her face, her eyes alive with pleasure as she seemed to consume it.

Madame Bathory. She had supposedly bathed in the blood of young virgins to maintain her youth and beauty, but...in this exhibit, she was drinking blood, too.

Marnie moved quickly.

She came to the French Revolution. There was a giant guillotine. On the ground before it there was a basket, overflowing with severed heads.

A body remained on the machine itself. An executioner stood by the mechanism for the blade. He had his hands on the next victim.

Guards from the French Revolution stood nearby, rifles with bayonets raised, ready to stop anyone in the crowd who might think that the executions were just becoming too gruesome.

"Bridget!" Marnie shouted.

The executioner turned. He was not a mannequin or animatronic of any kind.

He was real, decked out in appropriate style, wearing a hood, as seen in so many images from the era.

"Let her go!" Marnie shouted.

He turned and looked at her.

"Oh, Marnie. Not on your life. What a saying. Yes, it is your life. Time to end it. Oh, this is truly delightful. I have really pulled it off."

Marnie didn't think that she was especially courageous. She was just desperate.

She moved in a flash, lunging closer and ripping one of the rifles and bayonets from a French soldier and hurtling it at the executioner.

He screamed, letting Bridget loose as he was struck in the shoulder.

It wasn't a real blade; it wasn't very sharp. It was enough.

Bridget broke free.

"Run, run!" Marnie shouted.

Bridget turned to flee, and Marnie spun around to do the same. But she slammed into another French soldier and reversed, blindly seeking to make her way out and to safety.

She felt something touch her arm.

A hand.

A real hand.

She looked up.

She was in the arms of the executioner.

He wasn't alone in the maze of the Horror-palooza Cave.

Jeremy Highsmith and Cara Barton were with him, running—

or floating or whatever it was that they were doing—here and there, down different pathways.

Creatures loomed before him.

Real—as in created to look like human beings.

Not real—as in giant gorilla-type things and swamp lizard men.

He could hear a commotion; things falling.

And then Bridget came flying at him, screaming.

He caught her with his left hand; his Glock was in his right. "Bridget—"

"French Revolution! Oh, Bryan, she saved me and he got her. My fault, my fault—I thought we could hide in here and now..."

"Get out—I'll get Marnie."

He pushed her aside.

He hurried toward the French Revolution, barely breathing, tension making knots of his muscles, fear making his feet seem heavy.

"Marnie!" he screamed her name.

Talk.

She'd always heard that you should talk to a killer.

"I don't understand," Marnie said. "Okay, okay, you want to kill me. Dramatically. You love all the drama. But I sure as hell don't get it. You're on top of the world. And you've been so smart about it—hiring people to wear Blood-bone costumes. But now...the convention center is crowded with cops."

"Yes, but guess who else is here? David Neal. I saw to it. I finagled finances and sent in one damned good attorney. So... well, he is just so obviously a sleazebag!"

"But—you have everything. What do I have to do with anything? Why?" Marnie demanded.

He'd managed to drag her up to the platform. She struggled, but he was bigger and stronger than her.

Bit by bit, he was getting her to the guillotine.

It couldn't have a real blade—could it?

"Malcolm, why?" she asked again.

"Oh, Marnie. Believe it or not, my last box office was pathetic. My latest is going straight to video. I'm on a downhill slide. That's why Vince Carlton dared to ask me about a revamp of *Dark Harbor*. Actually, you see, you *were* the first intended victim." He paused before declaring dramatically, "You just can't get any good help these days!" He shrugged. "So...when they really suck, you just have to get rid of them."

"But without me, there wouldn't be *Dark Harbor*."

"Precisely. And without *Dark Harbor*, there would be something called *Angel-born*. *Angel-born*—that would be me. Dirk Slade. Macho name, huh? Vince Carlton had it as a backup plan. But he was pretty sure that he could get you to do the show. He really wanted you, even after Cara Barton was killed. I so enjoyed that. I intended to make her go, too, one way or the other, but... Hey. Life is what happens when you're busy making plans, right? I just wanted a show. A good show. My own show. Okay... I started and then got a little carried away."

"But Roberta—"

"Is an idiot. She believed that I would really have her as my continuing love interest in *Angel-born*—once we managed to dash all hopes of a *Dark Harbor* revamp."

"You're out of your mind."

"I've thought about it," Malcolm said, pausing as he tried to drag her over the guillotine bed. "I might be. But in the right way. Controlled, brilliant. I know the back way out. They'll arrest David Neal again. I love it. Oh, and Roberta will be dead. She thinks she's just getting something to cause vomiting... Ah, well! Leading ladies. A dime a dozen, right?"

She tried clawing at him, kicking him. She was strong—and she wanted to live.

But he was stronger. Hell, he spent half his life in a gym.

Despite all her struggles, he was managing to get her over the bed of the guillotine.

"I know these people," he told her. "Darkest Satan Studios. The guillotine is real, Marnie. They have to have the blades because, you know, they chop off not-real heads with them!"

"You will be caught."

"Marnie!"

She heard Cara Barton calling out to her.

"Marnie, hang on! Bryan is almost here!"

"Oh, thank God," Marnie said. She stopped struggling and stared at Malcolm.

"Thank God, what?"

"You're going to be shot any second." She could only pray that it would happen before she was dragged another inch, before he could cause the blade to fall.

"You were a star. You—you have everything!"

"Ah, Marnie, don't you understand? I was a star. A really bright shooting star. And that's just it. Marnie, I have to be a star. I have to stay on top. I can't be a comic con has-been!"

He jumped suddenly as if he felt something on his arm.

Cara's ghost was there. Tugging away at him—to the best of her ghostly ability.

"What the hell?"

"It's Cara," Marnie murmured.

"Cara is dead!"

"That's right. She's a ghost, Malcolm. She's there!"

He stopped, jerking at his own arm. Frowning, looking around.

He tried to drag her back on the guillotine.

"Stop it!" Cara screamed.

Malcolm heard her. He whirled around—but he didn't lose his grip on Marnie.

Bryan burst through the throng of French soldiers.

"Let her go!" he roared. "I will shoot."

"Hey, it's just the movies!" Malcolm said, thrusting Marnie violently onto the bed and grabbing the rope for the guillotine.

Bryan didn't wait.

He shot.

Malcolm Dangerfield fell.

Marnie rolled off the platform just in time.

The guillotine blade whisked through air and thudded into the wood bed.

It was well past midnight before they were home.

There was endless paperwork.

There was a trip to the hospital; she had to be checked out.

She learned that Roberta's stomach had been pumped out in time; she was going to live.

Marnie wasn't sure how she felt. She was a good person; she should be glad that no one was dead.

She'd heard people say that "they would die for a role" or that they would "kill for a role."

She had just never imagined that it could be for real.

Everyone had gathered at the hospital.

Vince Carlton was horrified. He told Marnie that he still loved *Dark Harbor* and would always want to work with her. "But right now," he told her, "I'm going to do a kid's movie. I'm going to film in New Zealand. Far, far away."

She wished him well.

Grayson came in to see her. "I'm sorry for being so selfish," he told her. "I loved them all—even Roberta. And I'm grateful to be alive. I hope to God I've learned."

She wished him the best, too.

Sophie came with Detective Vining.

Marnie thanked them.

She couldn't wait to leave.

She couldn't wait until Bryan had finished with his endless rounds of paperwork.

He finally came to the hospital for her. And they went home.

There, with George to greet her lovingly and Bridget and the whole group of Krewe agents, she thanked them all, thanked them for saving her life.

"Can't tell you how grateful we are that you're okay," Adam Harrison told her. He announced that he'd gotten the Krewe rooms at a local hotel.

Bridget went with them. She was still shaken and wanted to be near protection.

Finally, Marnie took a deep breath in the quiet of her own home.

She turned to Bryan.

"You'll stay for Jeremy's funeral, won't you?" she said.

"Trust me, you don't know the half of how legal works. I won't be able to leave for a few weeks," Bryan said. And then he asked, "You're...coming with me?"

"I've been offered a children's theater."

He smiled.

"Yeah, I'm going to start a new job, too. I'll have to be at the academy awhile, you know."

"Of course!"

He smoothed back her hair. "You probably need some rest."

She smiled.

"No. I probably need some you," she told him.

He was happy to oblige.

EPILOGUE

The man in seat 19A looked decidedly uncomfortable. As if he kept getting brushed by something in the 777's air-conditioning system.

But then, Bryan thought, he was sitting next to the ghost of Cara Barton. She was leaned against the ghost of Jeremy Highsmith, who was holding her hand and resting against the window of the plane, a look of bliss on his face.

Cara had hoped for empty chairs in first class. There were none. Bryan, with the aisle seat a few rows ahead, could look back down the aisle and see the two of them.

Marnie could not—not from her place by the window.

"I'm thinking we should have given up our seats for them," she murmured, coming in close to him.

"Wouldn't have worked," Bryan said. "The airline would have just given them to someone else with enough points to upgrade. Besides, this flight serves a great lunch. It would have been totally wasted on the two of them."

"True."

She smiled.

He marveled at that smile.

She really seemed fine with going to Virginia with him. Leaving Hollywood behind.

Of course, a lot of what happened had to hurt. It always hurt to understand that someone you had called a friend, cared for and worked with, could be willing to kill.

He hoped that she truly was in love with the offer that Adam had given her. He was sure that she would adore the group of women opening Adam's theater—they were wonderful.

He truly hoped that she was in love with him.

"What are you thinking?" he asked her softly.

"I was thinking about Bridget—driving to Virginia with Madison and Sean. And George."

"You didn't want him in cargo. And Bridget was due a vacation. And Madison was happy to spend a few more days in Hollywood, seeing old friends and learning new things."

"Yes, I agree. So, anyway… I'm a little nervous. About meeting your parents," she said.

He laughed. "And your folks are coming to see you and meet me in less than a week. And," he added, "they're alive."

She grinned at that. "I wonder which is going to be more nerve-racking. The living—or the dead."

She was casual now; she had accepted her strange abilities.

"Of course," she said. "This is madness. Completely. We've known each other just a few weeks altogether now. And yet…"

"Yet I know I want to spend my life with you," he told her. He pulled away slightly. "I don't think you appreciate yourself enough, Marnie. I'm afraid that…maybe you'll want the limelight again."

She was thoughtful. "I was lucky. I had a big break when I was very young. I enjoyed *Dark Harbor*. I never imagined… I will go back out and do that one show. But after that… Bryan, I knew what I wanted before I met you. I didn't know that I wanted you, but I wanted my theater. I think that living in Northern Virginia is going to be fine. I think this theater is going to be wonderful. I'm ready…really, truly, ready. And you… Are you ready for the Krewe?"

"You'll meet my parents, and you'll meet Bruce and Brodie, both of whom are disturbed that they weren't around to come out and help. They both know Adam and Jackson. I have a feeling that the Krewe of Hunters will wind up using three brothers."

It was a long flight. There was time to talk. Bryan told her about the cabin they'd had all their lives, and he talked about the things he loved in Northern Virginia and DC.

"The Smithsonian," she said, her voice happy. "The monuments. So many museums. Ford's Theatre! I have been to the area, you know. I will love it. Except…do you hunt?" she asked worriedly.

He shook his head. "Fish now and then," he told her. "I do love camping with a great camera for whatever wonders one comes across."

"We can do that!"

When the plane landed, an airline's escort was there to make sure that Marnie made it easily from the plane and down to the baggage claim area. Having some star power still had its perks.

Bruce and Brodie were waiting by the baggage carousels as prearranged. The brothers were waving, curious to meet Marnie.

They weren't alone.

Maeve and Hamish were with them, waving madly.

"Your brothers," Marnie said and laughed. "I would have recognized them anywhere." Then she whispered, "I didn't know your parents were going to be here!"

The McFadden boys did all look alike. Bryan was six-four, Bruce a little under and Brodie just a hair taller. Each had a headful of dark hair.

Bryan's eyes were the color of their dad's—green. Bruce and Brodie had blue eyes. The color was their mom's.

He'd nearly forgotten that Cara Barton and Jeremy Highsmith were with them—right behind them in the cart—a little awkward since the airport escort had put Marnie's travel bag in the back seat of the little cart, too.

Bryan was barely out of the cart before he was nearly knocked over by his mother.

Then he was hugged by his father.

The airport escort was looking at him as if he were certainly worrisome—as if he might have balance problems. Bryan gave his mom a fierce look.

"My dear boy! You're all right. And you saved Marnie. And you didn't just save Marnie, you brought her with you. There's hope. Oh, Hamish, there's hope. We might have grandchildren after all."

"And they just might be actors," the ghost of Hamish McFadden said drily. "I'm proud of you, son," he added.

Then the ghosts all greeted each other.

"Cara!" Maeve said delightedly.

"Maeve, you wonderful soul. You sent him out to us."

He didn't get to see the ghosts kiss and hug; he was then greeted by quick hugs from both his brothers, and he introduced Marnie. They were gathering a crowd and Bruce said, "Let's get you all out of here."

"I'll run to the car. I'll be right outside. It's an Escalade—it will fit us all."

Marnie seemed delighted with his family.

Bruce drove to the house in Alexandria. Inside, they talked about Adam and the theater and the Krewe of Hunters, and then Bruce and Brodie rose simultaneously.

"We're going to get out of here," he said.

"But they just came home," Maeve protested. "Oh, you boys run along—"

"Maeve," Hamish said firmly. "We're all going. Come on, we have a lot to catch up on. We have guests ourselves. Cara and Jeremy are here."

"I'm not sure we're staying," Jeremy said.

"We keep fading. I mean, I was never really good, but now…" Cara murmured.

"You were the best, my love," Jeremy told her.

"We keep seeing a light."

"We want to go together," Jeremy explained. "But hey, maybe we have tonight."

"Yes, maybe you will have tonight," Brodie said. "Come on, have it at my place."

"Sunrise?" Jeremy asked Cara.

"Oh, yes, sunrise," Cara agreed. "With beautiful and perfect natural lighting. So… I guess that's goodbye."

They both turned to Marnie. It was obvious she felt their hugs.

"Love you," Marnie said.

"And you…you're the best. Oh, and I must make a dramatic exit before—before I cry," Cara said. With that, she whirled out for a very dramatic exit—going right through the closed door.

"The best," Jeremy told Marnie. He looked at Bryan. "And you, young man. Thank you."

Bryan nodded.

"Don't lose her," Jeremy said.

"I will not," Bryan swore.

Then he was gone, too, his exit almost as dramatic—except that he seemed to slam into the door.

Brodie opened it for him.

"Outta here!" Bruce said. "We'll talk tomorrow."

At last, Bryan and Marnie were alone.

He looked at her, suddenly awkward.

"So…you've met the parents."

"They're incredible."

"And my brothers."

"Completely impressive," she said.

Marnie walked to him. Slipped her arms around his neck.

"But never so impressive as you!" And she kissed him.

The house was a historic Colonial. He swept her up into his arms.

Her kiss was hot, sloppy, deliciously wet. A promise.

Her eyes met his as he headed for the stairs. "Very dramatic," she told him.

"Buckle your seat belts," he said.

"It's going to be a bumpy ride!" she said.

"Yes, it is," he vowed.

They were both smiling, very much in love, as he carried her up the stairs.

It was the first night of their new lives.

★ ★ ★ ★ ★

Keep reading for an exclusive preview of the next
KREWE OF HUNTERS *book*
from New York Times *bestselling author*
Heather Graham,
PALE AS DEATH.

*Bruce McFadden will help Detective Sophie Manning investigate
a disturbing murder with overtones of an infamous unsolved case
from the dark depths of Hollywood's past.*

Available July 31, 2018, from MIRA Books.

1

Monday morning

"I thought it was a dummy—I mean, a mannequin. You know, the ones they use in store windows. I mean… Oh, my God! There's no blood… There's red around…around the…the places where she's all chopped up! But still, I mean, this is Hollywood! I thought that someone was making a movie, and then the dog started barking, and I didn't see any movie trailers or signs or… Oh, God! She was real. She was once… She still is…like flesh and blood and bone…just… Oh, God!"

Detective Sophie Manning could tell that the woman had thought the corpse was a mannequin, or at the very least, something unreal.

But the dead girl was real. It was only the brutality of her death that made her appear as if she were not, as if she were some creation of the most brilliant and lurid mind working in a Hollywood special-effects studio.

Stripped naked. Sliced in half. Slashed. Chunks of flesh… gone.

Intestines…under the buttocks.

The woman who had discovered the body—body pieces—of the unknown woman on South Norton Avenue wavered suddenly, as if she were about to pass out and collapse.

The witness was a heavyset woman who was nearly six feet tall; Sophie prided herself on having achieved a full five feet four inches. Thankfully, she spent half her life in the gym. Sizewise, she just met police requirements. She didn't have a Napoleon complex—she was simply aware of her size, aware she had to keep up with the "big boys" and was dedicated to her job and determined to be her best.

The woman began to keel over.

Sophie quickly caught her—bracing herself—and steadied her.

"I'm so sorry!" the woman apologized.

The woman was Claudia Cooper, and she lived around the block. The dog was a teacup Yorkie and Sophie had to hand it to the little creature—he was small but knew a dead body from a mannequin. The Yorkie's name was Tsum-Tsum. A crime scene tech was checking Tsum-Tsum's paws for blood.

"It's all right. I understand completely," Sophie assured her.

"You must see things like this all the time."

"Not quite like this," Sophie assured her. "You're human. So am I. And this is truly horrible and cruel and tragic. Let's have you sit. Do you mind? There's a patrol car right over there."

As she tried to help the woman, Sophie glanced across the bit of sidewalk and grass. Her partner, Grant Vining, was hunkered down by the body with the medical examiner.

Vining was one of the finest detectives in LA—or anywhere, she thought. She was lucky to be his partner. Captain Lorne Chagall, the supervising officer for their team—an elite unit as it was, handling the most vicious and sometimes *strangest* cases in Tinseltown—had announced Grant Vining as lead detective, with her assisting, from the moment the call had come in. They'd been specifically handed the case because of their recent involvement in the Blood-bone killings; Sophie figured since they'd handled the high-profile case without any major gaffes, and this new one was sure to draw media attention. The discovery of the corpse had been a little more than two hours ago, and somehow the media was all over it already.

Naturally. The way the body had been found was gruesome, to say the least.

Similarities to the old unsolved murder of Elizabeth Short—aka the Black Dahlia—were obviously intentional. The woman found dead this morning was discovered on South Norton Avenue near the place that had once been a vacant lot, where the Black Dahlia had been found. Just like Elizabeth Short, she had been killed elsewhere; she was all but drained of blood. She'd been severed in half.

Another eerie detail had been included.

The victim's face had been slashed on both sides from the corners of her mouth to the ears—creating a monstrous, Joker-like grin on the dead woman's face.

Naturally, the Black Dahlia was a case Sophie had studied. Her dad had been a cop; she'd always known that she was going to be a cop, too. Cold cases had been bedtime reading.

Even if she hadn't been, the horrible murder of Elizabeth Short was still being pondered and mused by the best of them—law enforcement and armchair sleuths. While there had been confessions galore, most easily dismissed—and even relatives claiming that it had been a relative—no one had ever proved who Elizabeth Short's killer might be.

"Are you all right now? Do you think that you can give your statement to the officer?" Sophie asked Claudia Cooper.

The woman nodded vigorously. "You must catch him—whoever did this!"

"Ma'am, I promise you, we—and every officer in LA—will be doing our best to capture this killer."

No way out of it—this was going to be sensational. Most

likely, the killer assumed that he—or she—would get away with the murder. Just like the killer back in the 1940s.

Times were different now, she thought grimly. Forensic science had come a long way, for one.

The Yorkie whined suddenly, as if aware of the terrible situation. Afraid. He hadn't minded at all that his paws were under serious scrutiny. He seemed worried about his mistress.

Yes, the city would live in fear. Women would be on extra high alert, wondering what they could possibly do to avoid the same horrible fate.

Sophie led Claudia Cooper and her tiny Yorkie over to one of the patrol cars. The young officer quickly leaped to his feet to open the door to the rear for Claudia. He had his worksheet ready; he nodded gravely to Sophie. He was ready to take the full statement.

Sophie walked back over to the place where the pieces of the corpse remained in situ. Henry Atkins, police photographer, looked at her as she approached and shook his head, wincing. It was one of the worst crime scenes they'd ever seen, and they all knew it.

"Finished. For now," he told her bleakly. Henry had a basset hound look about him. Long jowls, pale blue eyes. He was in his early fifties, and she'd heard he was close to retirement.

She nodded and looked around. Police officers were canvasing the neighborhood. Crime scene techs were busy gathering anything that might be evidence. A lot of what they would find would be chewed gum, bottle caps and smashed fast-food cups, but all of it would be collected. Any tiny piece might be of tremendous help in the investigation.

She almost bumped into one tech. Lee Underwood. Young, blond, handsome and wire muscled. He looked more like a surfer dude than a crime scene investigator.

"Sorry!" he apologized.

"My fault," she told him.

"I was just getting that butt," he told her, pointing to what remained of someone's cigarette—no more than the filter. "Cigarette butt!" he added quickly, as if his intentions might be questioned, even at such a scene. "I don't think that any of this garbage will belong to the killer," he said glumly. "This guy..." He paused, looking over at the body. "This guy went by the book—the Black Dahlia book. And, I think, some kind of forensics book. He won't have made mistakes."

"Everybody makes mistakes," Sophie said.

He shook his head. "Yeah, so we say. But we'll need good luck finding this guy's!"

He collected the butt with a gloved hand, smiled grimly and moved on.

Sophie hunkered down between Vining and Dr. Thompson.

It was a difficult place to be.

The corpse was simply so brutally displayed.

Sophie couldn't begin to imagine the terror the woman must have felt as the knife came toward her face. They weren't scratches that had created the Joker grin; they were deep gashes. There were so many other cuts on the body—both halves—as if chunks of flesh had been cut away. And by the woman's hairline there were clotted blotches of blood.

"Blunt-force trauma?" she asked, looking up.

Dr. Chuck Thompson—a big man with iron gray hair and a square ruddy face—nodded gravely. "I'll have to get her to autopsy, of course. She wasn't killed here—that's pretty obvious. I'd say, though, that her head took a good beating. Enough to kill. And the knife wounds... They could have done it, too. I mean, obviously, she's been bisected, but death—mercifully—came first."

Thompson was a dedicated man. He'd never married, and he was always ready to be there when others were begging out for one reason or another. He'd been in the county a long time and stayed stalwart despite the workload. He'd seen a lot, she knew.

Death could often be cruel, but this woman had been brutally tortured.

He grimaced. "She was alive when the gashes were made," Thompson said quietly.

Grant Vining looked resolute. Like Dr. Thompson, he'd been in his job for a long time. Despite the difference in their tenure, Vining always mentored instead of being impatient with her comparative lack of experience.

He also had a great capacity for listening. When other officers discovered something, he was grateful. He worked well with other cops and with law enforcement officials from other agencies.

"Whatever gets it closed," he often told Sophie.

Right now, he was pensive, and he shook his head and stated the obvious.

"Black Dahlia," he said. "Our officers are canvasing the neighborhood, but until we get something from them or from the forensics team, we're just waving our stuff in the air."

He was right; Sophie knew it. But as she listened to him, she noted that a good-sized crowd had grown around the police tape holding people away from the crime scene.

Many of those people were media. Some had notepads; some were with network or cable stations, their microphones and cameras visible.

Vining would make a statement in a minute, she knew. Or he would ask her to do so.

"Sophie," he said, just as the thought came to her. "They like a young pretty face better than they like mine. Tell them—tell them nothing."

"Gotcha," she murmured, rising. She'd rather be with the press right now than with the corpse. She couldn't help glancing again at the woman's face, at the bizarre grin slashed into it. Once, she thought, judging by her youth and the handsome angles that remained of the face, their victim had been beautiful.

Not so long ago, she would have laughed and her eyes would have sparkled. But now she lay like a broken doll torn apart by a disgruntled and sadistic child.

Did such a thought actually describe the killer?

Sophie walked toward the crime scene tape. People there began to bristle like a school of fish, eager when a morsel of krill moved by.

She kept her expression neutral.

The press surged forward—with a talent for making their way through the more casual bystanders.

That was when she first noticed one man.

He was different. It might have been in his curious and determined but unhurried manner. It was also his dress. He was wearing a suit, but it wasn't something many men would have on today—unless they were actors filming a period piece. It was a zoot suit, she thought. The slant of his hat, the suit... He appeared to be out of time and out of place. He was in his mid to late thirties, she thought, dark haired and with a lean face that was both handsome and engaging.

Argh! she thought. *A new guy. Maybe he thinks he's going to charm and persist and get some kind of scoop from the cops not available to others.*

"Hello," Sophie said, addressing the crowd. "I know that rumors and speculation are running wild right now, and I can't blame you or anyone for speculating at what you have gleaned about this terrible crime. But at this moment, we know that we have a victim who was cruelly murdered. We don't have an identity for the young woman. It will take time for an autopsy. Until then, we ask you to respect—"

"Black Dahlia!"

Sophie broke off. It was the guy in the zoot suit, with his pen raised over his pad.

"We're not giving this murder any kind of a moniker at this time," she said.

She was surprised when the rest of the people in the crowd looked around at one another—and then at her. They appeared to be confused.

"As we gain information, we'll make sure we get it to you," she said. "We depend on the people of Los Angeles to help us. We are a massive community, a united community in caring for others, and—"

"Black Dahlia!"

The man in the zoot suit had spoken again. The crowd shuffled uneasily. They weren't looking at him; they were watching Sophie, waiting.

A man in front cleared his throat. "Detective, we heard that she was...displayed. There's been talk. Is this murder reminiscent of that of Elizabeth Short, the Black Dahlia?"

"Yes, of course, you idiot," the man in the zoot suit said.

"There's no need, sir," Sophie said.

"Pardon?" the reporter closest to her said curiously. People were really staring at her now.

She looked back. Even Vining was watching; he seemed concerned that he had given her the responsibility of talking to the press.

But what the hell...?

When she turned back, it was just in time to see him—the man in the zoot suit—walk toward her, right through the crime scene tape, as if it was nonexistent.

She closed her eyes for a moment and prayed silently.

Not again!

It had happened when she was in college, when a fellow student, a wonderful young man other than his addiction, had died from an overdose. He'd come to her—after his death—and she had nearly had a heart attack herself, and then he'd talked to her and asked her for help with his family.

Not again, not again, not again!

After it all, her parents had insisted she go into therapy. The doctor had convinced her that she'd had the information his family needed, but in order to see that they received that information, she'd had to invent his ghost speaking to her so that she could see what she needed to do.

She'd nearly fallen apart. Doubting herself, her senses, in that way had been hard.

But back then, she'd been twenty. She'd been young and impressionable and easily swayed and confused and hurt.

Now…

She was an LAPD detective. Hard-won.

And she was going to solve the murder of the woman who lay so broken on the ground, come hell or high water.

So she ignored the man in the suit.

The instrument of her imagination—or a long-dead ghost.

"Please, whatever you're hearing, we ask that you respect the victim. These are the facts that I can give you. At ten this morning, a neighbor here discovered the body of a young woman."

The figment of her imagination was now standing by her side.

"Pieces of her body," he said.

She went on. "At this moment, she has not been identified. When we do know her identity—pending notification of her next of kin—we will let you all know. I can't share details with you right now as we are just beginning our investigation. Thank you for allowing the police to do their work, and thank you for your help. We'll have more information forthcoming soon. Thank you," she said with finality.

She turned around, ready to head back to Vining.

"Ah, ignore me, will you? Good call. But I can help you, I swear."

She lowered her head. She couldn't help asking, "You know who did this?"

"No, but I'm telling you, if you give me a chance—"

"You do not exist," she muttered. "You're in my head, and

you're just here because I've gone through a loss of my own, and now…this."

She took a deep breath. She wasn't going to have Grant Vining think that she needed time off. Not now!

"That was fine, Sophie, thank you," Vining said. He was looking at her, though, as if he was worried about her. "A little rocky at the start, but fine."

"We're going to get her out of here now," Chuck Thompson said. "You can meet me at the morgue. Autopsy tomorrow morning, eight o'clock sharp? The mayor… Everyone is going to want this ASAP."

"We'll meet you there," Vining said.

"Yes, we'll meet you there," Sophie said firmly.

Vining looked at her. "It's going to be a hell of a long day," he said. "You all right?"

"Just fine," she assured him, hating the way he was looking at her. "Where do you want me to start?"

Bruce McFadden happened to be at home—home as in his parents' old house in Alexandria—when the news coverage came on regarding the murder in Los Angeles.

"Oh, my God!" Marnie Davante, his brother's brand-new fiancée, cried out. Something on the TV had caught her attention.

Bruce and his elder brother, Bryan, had been deep in conversation along with their younger brother, Brodie, regarding their futures.

Bryan had made the definite decision to enter the FBI academy. He'd been invited to join what had just been given the official moniker of FBI Special Assistance Unit but was known throughout the academy and beyond as the Krewe of Hunters, because of the first case it had taken on in New Orleans, Louisiana. While the unit and the agency never acknowledged that they were also known as the Ghost-busters, those involved knew the truth.

In their recent discussions, the plan between the McFadden brothers had been to create a private investigation firm. To that end, upon their exits from the military, each had become a licensed private investigator. Bryan had become embroiled in a murder case out in Los Angeles at the request of their mother. An actress, Cara Barton, an old friend of their parents, had been killed in a sensational case.

Such things happened. Sons did things for their parents. In their case, however, it was a bit different. Maeve and Hamish McFadden were dead.

Now discussion stopped. They all stared at the news.

Bryan had risen to walk closer to the wide-screen television on the wall. "Hard to tell much from what the media has so far," he said. "But you can see, Vining and Manning caught this."

"Sophie is coming forward to talk to the press," Marnie murmured.

Bruce glanced at Brodie, who gave him a shrug and a look that silently said, "We'll have to wait and see what they're talking about."

Marnie's home had been LA until recently. She and Bryan had met because Marnie had been targeted by the man who'd killed Cara Barton—and despite the short length of their relationship, it did appear as if they had been destined for one another.

"Sophie is behaving so oddly, isn't she?" Marnie said. "Almost as if she's talking to someone else. Ah, she's in control again." Marnie sounded a bit proud—she evidently liked Sophie, who was, Bruce presumed, from her speech and position at the crime scene, a detective with the LAPD.

He realized that he and Brodie had both risen as well, drawing closer to the TV. It was a large set—they could have all seen it just fine from where they'd been. But maybe there was more to a sixth sense than just seeing the dead—those who chose to be seen. Because he realized that they all knew now that this wasn't a simple case. The body itself was shielded from view, but the questions and the murmurs told them what they needed to know.

A killer had re-created a crime. A horrible and gruesome crime from days gone past.

"There! Look!" Marnie said, moving forward to point at the set.

"I see it, I see it," Bruce told her, moving forward to point, as well. "As if a little white cloud is next to her."

"Human shaped," Bryan said.

"She reacted to it—and now she's ignoring it," Marnie noted. "Ah, she's our Sophie! She's not going to be deterred!"

"Where's Vining?" Bryan asked, frowning.

"Look, there, back with the body," Marnie said.

No matter how they might try, no photographer, videographer or cameraman of any kind was going to get a real shot of the body.

But you could see the police and forensic people working the scene.

And then the entire scene itself was gone. They were looking at an anchor in a news station.

"That's a smart TV—let's roll back," Bruce suggested.

Bryan picked up the remote control. The TV obediently went back to replay the footage they had been watching.

It was strange, what a camera could catch.

There was something there—a shift like fog or misty clouds. It moved. It joined the young woman speaking. And while most people might not have understood her reaction, everyone in that room did.

"There's a ghost there—and she knows it," Brodie said. He might be the youngest in their trio, but he was the quickest to state aloud what they were thinking—or fearing.

After their parents' deaths, when Maeve and Hamish had first begun to visit them, they'd each pretended that they didn't see them. Until finally Brodie had just shouted it out—they were there! Talking to them. Yes, dead. But their ghosts were there, and they'd all loved one another, so they needed to embrace this new reality.

Sophie, the detective, wasn't loving whatever was going on. She was hiding the fact that she was distressed and doing a damned good job of it.

Bruce observed the woman, wondering if she ever had a bad time being so attractive and garnering respect. She was small, too—maybe five-four, tops, and possibly 110 pounds. She had dark blond hair, well cut to fall around her features but not into her face. Her features were both delicate and strong—broad cheekbones, wide-set brown eyes, strong jaw.

No doubt, she would have worked hard to get where she was as a detective—first grade, he imagined, if she was part of this high-profile situation.

"She never said a word when we were out there," Marnie said softly.

"Maybe she never saw Cara. Remember, none of us can ever explain exactly why we see or hear or sometimes even just feel the dead," Bryan told her.

There was so much affection in Bryan's eyes when he looked at Marnie. Almost more intimate than if he was kissing the hell out of her, right there, in front of them all.

"I'm going to call her," Marnie said. "She was wonderful to me, Bryan. I want to make sure she's all right. I want to see if there's something I can do. A way I can help."

"I'll go back to LA," Bryan told her.

"You can't—you're starting the academy."

"It can wait."

Bruce had no idea whatsoever what suddenly compelled him. Maybe he was curious.

The Black Dahlia. A crime re-created. The ghost of someone—the victim? A victim from the past? Someone else entirely, there and haunting a detective on the case.

"I'll go," Bruce said.

Bryan, Marnie and Brodie turned to stare at him.

"What?" he said. "We're not starting up an agency now. Bryan, you're going to be in the academy, and honestly, I can be just as effective. I'll go," he offered.

Marnie looked at her fiancé, her eyes questioning and anxious.

"He's good," Bryan told her. "He is 'just as effective,'" he added drily.

"Whatever," Brodie said. He shrugged. "I'll go, too."

"You can't go—at least, not just yet. You said that you were going to look into the death of the maintenance man at Adam Harrison's theater," Marnie reminded him.

"Adam has a whole crew of agents," Brodie said.

Marnie offered him a beautiful and wry smile. "Yes, but you promised your mother."

Brodie groaned and looked at Bruce. "You're going alone," he said flatly.

Bruce smiled at his youngest brother. Many adults were plagued by their parents—which was okay. Having loving parents—at any age—was a great thing. Not many, however, were plagued *and* haunted.

"I'll be fine," Bruce said. He added with a shrug, trying to give Marnie his best reassuring look, "Whoever finishes up first can come out and help the other. Besides, you're worried about a cop. She's probably pretty tough."

"She is—she helped me out incredibly," Marnie said. "But… I didn't know she saw the dead," she added softly.

"I'll watch out for your friend, Marnie." He looked at Bryan questioningly. "If she'll let me. I'll try to get out there as quickly as possible—"

"They're just about magic at Krewe headquarters," Bryan told him. "If you can be packed in fifteen minutes, I'll bet we can have you on a plane in two hours."

"I can be ready."

It suddenly seemed as if a door opened and slammed; it didn't, but it might have. Maeve McFadden—or the ghost thereof—burst into the room, followed by the ghost of their weary but forever patient and tolerant father, Hamish. Both actors in life, they still carried their charisma and drama with them.

"Hey, Dad," Bruce said. "Oh, hey, Mom, you're here, too!"

"Don't be a wiseass, my dear boy," his mother said. "Bryan, Marnie, did you see—"

"We all saw, Mom," Bryan assured her.

"Well, then, you must—"

"We're on it, Mom," Bruce told her. He walked over and kissed the cold air where her cheek appeared. "I'm heading right away. Just as soon as I can get a flight."

"What about… Oh, Brodie! You can't go with him now—you promised you'd help me. I knew Justin Westinghouse for years and years. I know he was no spring chicken. But… I don't like it. I just don't like it. Bryan is going to be busy running or jumping or learning to shoot—"

"I think he knows how to shoot, Mom," Bruce murmured.

She waved a ghostly hand in the air. "Yes, yes, but he'll be in the academy. Anyway, what matters, Bruce, is that you must go. You must help that poor lovely young woman. Why, she helped watch over Marnie!"

"Mom, yeah, I know. I'm going," Bruce said.

He felt the soft, misty touch of her hand.

"I do love you, boys!" she said and smiled. "More than life and death," she added.

Maeve could definitely be a bit of a wiseass herself.

Copyright © 2018 by Heather Graham Pozzessere

JUN   2018